INTO THE FLAMES

Visit us at www.boldstrokesbooks.com

Praise for Mel Bossa

Split

"This amazing first novel was one of the best new romances of 2011."—*Lambda Literary*

"If you only read one romance this year, make sure this is the one. Its ambition is only exceeded by its flawless execution."
—Jerry L. Wheeler, *Out in Print*

"In this, her first novel, author Bossa gives an insightful and complex look at a young man's coming of age, as well as interesting examples of the fluidity of human sexuality and how a good friendship can evolve over the years. Very well written, and sure to resonate with most readers on some level. I give it a full five stars out of five."—Bob Lind, *Echo Magazine*

Franky Gets Real

"Blending the melodrama of the 1983 movie *The Big Chill* with the unsettling drunken confessions of a high school reunion, Bossa has crafted a textured novel that captures the drama of complex, realistic characters confronting the secrets and lies that threaten to fracture their friendship."
—Richard Labonté, *Book Marks*

"We're crazy for young author Mel Bossa. She's got a distinctive voice and a terrific story-telling gift."—TLA GAY.com

By the Author

Split

Suite Nineteen

Franky Gets Real

Into the Flames

INTO THE FLAMES

by

Mel Bossa

A Division of Bold Strokes Books

2012

ISBN 13: 978-1-60282-681-6

This Trade Paperback Original Is Published By
Bold Strokes Books, Inc.
P.O. Box 249
Valley Falls, NY 12185

First Edition: August 2012

Credits
Editors: Greg Herren and Stacia Seaman
Production Design: Stacia Seaman
Cover Design by Sheri (graphicartist2020@hotmail.com)

Acknowledgments

Thanks to everyone at Bold Strokes Books. Radclyffe, for her vision and dedication, and for turning me into a pro. Greg Herren, my editor, for "getting" me. I'd especially like to thank Dick Smart, Amos Lassen, Richard Labonté, Scott Cranin (TLA GAY), and others who took the time to read and review my work. Daniel, my two-spirited man, you are the reason I can write the words *I love you* and know what they mean.

For Ferris, my blue-eyed boy.

Chapter One

Neil marched into the blazing hall, his breaths steaming up the oxygen mask—warm, bitter with the scent of his last coffee. Between two steps, Neil tensed, aware of the absurdity of his job.

The tables had turned. The flames owned this place and he, a firefighter, was the intruder trespassing on their destruction. The inferno threw its orange tongue at him, wanting to quench itself on the moisture of Neil's carefully protected skin. But Neil pressed on, driven by some unspeakable desire barely acknowledged in times like these.

"McClure, what are you doing!"

Neil heard John's voice through the popping of wood and lightbulbs. What did the idiot want? What did he expect?

Retreat?

Neil did not stop or turn his head in John's direction. Screw him. Instead, he reached out, his gloved hands disappearing into the dense black smoke, grasping for something. A door handle? He couldn't tell, but his instincts told him that he'd come to the end of the hallway and there was a door ahead of him, perhaps leading into a bathroom. There was someone screaming in there. Couldn't John, the wannabe hero, hear it? A kid was crying out for his mom. A young boy, screaming for his life! Neil ignored John's commands to back down, and kicked in the door. He shoved his shoulder against it and stumbled forward, but before he could step through, he was brutally jerked back. "Get outta here," John cried, pushing him into the adjacent wall. "The roof's going!"

"There's a kid in there, asshole!" Neil's voice roared through the chaos and he fought against John's grip. They tumbled back into the hall, Neil struggling to make himself heard. "Stop, there's a kid in there. There's—"

"Shut up!"

There was nothing he could do. He was being pushed and shoved through heat and smoke, by this coward, this gutless—

"Move, move!" John barked, slamming his hands against Neil's massive shoulders. "There's nobody here, you crazy son of a bitch!"

They skidded dangerously down a flight of stairs, landing on the first floor—the living room, now a devastated pile of soaking black furniture—and John grabbed Neil's forearm. "Come on!" John propelled Neil forward, causing him to fall through the doorway onto the porch.

Into the cold, starless night.

A night buzzing with urban noises.

Sirens, ring tone, voices.

Neil spun around and leaped for the house again, but immediately collided into John.

"You goddamn maniac." John ripped the oxygen mask off Neil's face. "That's the last time, you hear me?"

"We're going back in there—"

"I'm done," John said, throwing his hat over the porch's wrought-iron rail. He wiped his brow with the back of his sleeve. His eyes cut like dull glass through the black smut on his face. "I can't do this with you anymore. I gotta a family, man. I can't—" John stopped and staggered down the three steps leading to the lawn and slowly turned around. "You wanna kill yourself, you do it on your own time."

"There was a kid in there," Neil heard himself mumble. He was dizzy. Disoriented.

A boy behind that door. Screaming.

Neil looked around. Firehouse 66 was hosing down the rest of the mess. Everywhere he looked, he met the guys' disapproving glances. It had been like that for six months now. They wouldn't look at him in the face, the hypocrites.

"I'm gonna sign the petition," John said, shaking his head. "Look, I don't have a choice. The guys don't trust you anymore. Captain says—"

"There was a kid in—"

"Oh, God, man, stop." John's attention drifted to the glimmering, wet street.

Midnight hour, and people still gathered around the perimeter, clad in their bathrobes and pajamas, watching the guys extinguish the last of the blaze. Taking pictures. Shooting videos with their expensive little devices.

"You think I hallucinated again." Neil stepped down and looked back at the dying fire. "You all think I'm losing my mind. I know you've been flapping your lips about—"

"Are you, Neil? Are you having some kind of mental breakdown?"

Neil scoffed. Being brave wasn't a fucking illness.

He pulled his gloves off and walked over to the truck. He climbed into the front seat and shut the door. The corner of his mouth twitched, but he bit into the flesh of his lip and controlled the annoying tremor.

"What are you doing?" John's features crumpled in confusion. "What—"

"I'm sitting here."

"You know, I don't get you. You're not even trying. You won't talk to the shrink. You won't even talk to me. I'm your friend—"

"You guys all made up your mind."

Neil stared at the dashboard. He couldn't get his heart to quiet down. Could barely swallow his own saliva. His hands were going numb. "I heard a kid in there," he said. He had. He'd heard *someone*.

In two strides, John was at the side window again. "Look around you! Do you hear a mother crying for her boy? Do you see an ambulance? We knew the place was empty before we even showed up. You knew it was empty—"

"Just sign the letter. Let 'em say I'm nuts. What the fuck do I care." Neil's throat tightened around his windpipe. If John didn't step away from the window, he'd jump out of the truck and make him shut—

"Wow, you should see your face right now. Okay, man. I'm signing that letter." John stepped back. "And you know what, Neil?" He gave him a final stare. "I'm not even gonna feel bad about it."

Who ever asked John to feel bad about anything? People needed absolution like water these days. Out of the corner of his eye, Neil watched John walk away.

Then he heard cries of congratulations and recognized the familiar grins of victory on his partners' faces, but to open the truck's door was beyond his ability.

And the notion that it had always been so—that he'd never known how to be part of anything but destruction—terrified him.

❖

Jamie jolted up and yanked the sheets off his bare legs. Heart racing, he worked at discerning the familiar objects of his bedroom. He was home. His new home. The condo on Sherbrooke Street.

He turned to stare at the digital clock on the nightstand, but could hardly make out the time. Where were his glasses? He lifted the pillow, hoping he hadn't crushed his Mont Blanc frames, and found them soon enough, under the fold of the heavy quilt, propped atop last night's read: the latest Edmund White. He quickly pushed the black designer glasses over his nose.

It was 5:43 a.m.

Tuesday. October twenty-fifth.

Against good sense, Jamie recalled his nightmare. It was a game he played: *How much stress can Jamie handle before six a.m.*

He'd been plagued by this dream for thirty-three years. A recurrent dream of snow. Of an aborted life. The life of his twin brother Mickey, three years old, ending without a noise.

First, the sound of wipers grating against a frosted windshield.

A mother screams.

Their mother.

Their mother rips at her face, tearing streaks of red into it, and her blood drips into the snow.

What's happening, Mommy?

His brother's tiny dead body sits quietly in a car seat. The scent of exhaust.

That morning of his brother's death so real now.

In the darkness of his bedroom, Jamie touched his throat and then his eyebrow—an automatic double touch, both reflex and compulsion.

He stretched his neck to the right and relaxed his fingers. Gently, he smoothed out his white T-shirt, gathering spit inside his mouth. If he could swallow it, he was on level one—no need to be terrified. If not, he would have to try to talk himself out of another trip to the ER, where he often spent the morning convincing the staff he was having a heart attack—wasting their time with his miserable, anxiety-induced antics.

He swallowed. It was tight, but still possible. He opened his mouth wide for the final check. If he could yawn, he was almost home free.

He couldn't yawn.

His brain was going to overload on oxygen.

"You're absolutely not having a panic attack," Jamie said aloud. "You had a nightmare in the REM stage brought on by an episode of sleep paralysis, which is the consequence of the red wine you drank last night." With numb fingertips, he reached out and flicked the lamp on. "You need a hot shower, a cup of chamomile, and half an Ativan." Hearing the sound of his own thin voice traveling across the barely furnished one-bedroom condo sent a wave of queasiness rolling through him.

Alone.

Jamie glanced out the large bay window, but turned his attention back to the white of his knuckles. Every time he caught a glimpse of Montreal's skyline, his heart wanted to bust right out of his chest. Somewhere in that iron jungle, a few streets away, in that old fixer-upper on Sainte-Famille street, Mallory and Marshall were sleeping in their bunk beds.

Nine years old and already damaged.

After their mother's death, the orphaned twins had been adopted by their playboy uncle, Mr. Basil Spasso, Jamie's ex-partner and asshole extraordinaire.

Yes, five years ago, boastful and full of theories, Jamie had entered the Spasso twins' young lives as a savior—the man who'd get them through the grief unscathed, only to leave the children, last April, suitcase in hand, a meek and nervous mess, the kids asking, "Why are you leaving us?"

Because it seemed Basil's wonderful adoptive nephew and niece were doomed to be the perpetual witnesses to adult stupidity.

And in this moment, in that cozy house Basil had renovated with his own hands, three lives went on without Jamie's presence. In the Sainte-Famille house, down the hall, past the kids' bedroom, Basil slept in what used to be *their* bed.

Was Basil sleeping alone?

"He doesn't love you anymore. Face it." Jamie slid out of bed and slipped his cold feet into a pair of wool-lined moccasins. "You forced him back into his walls. You ruined his faith." The words rolled off Jamie's tongue like a well-rehearsed sermon, but the urge to call Basil raced through him like an injected dose of a flawed, but oh-so-lethal drug.

Just one more call. One more try. One more question.

He would get better. He'd do it right this time. He wouldn't let his obsessive-compulsive disorder take over anymore. No, he wouldn't touch a hand sanitizer dispenser again in his life. He would eat with the restaurant's cutlery and shake people hands when they were being introduced. He wouldn't scrub his skin until it broke. He wouldn't—

"It's over," Jamie interrupted his inner monologue. "Own up to it." He stepped up to the floor mirror and paused.

His T-shirt hung loosely over his shoulders; he'd lost weight again. His dark eyes were red-rimmed and haunted.

Jamie moved closer and studied his face. There was an eyelash on his cheek. He rubbed it off.

"There is no cure for OCD," he said to the young, exhausted man in the mirror. "Not if the patient refuses to treat the origin of the anxiety."

And of course, the man in the mirror did not disagree.

❖

Neil shook the dirt off his nylon gloves and frowned.

The garden was a complete waste of time. He'd gotten no nice tomatoes this summer. No good lettuce. The cucumbers should have been embarrassed. It was too much work for what it was worth. If he wanted damn vegetables, he'd go to the market and buy some.

October. And now he'd have to cover every bush up and take all the stupid flowers in before the ground's first freeze.

"Come here, boy," he called to Hemingway, his twelve-year-old golden retriever.

The dog, lying by the back porch steps, raised an eyebrow, but resumed his nap. He'd been sleeping a lot in the last weeks. The old mutt had lost his spark.

Neil tried again. "Hey, come here."

Hemi cracked an eye open and sighed, but refused to move a muscle.

"You think I'm gonna crack? You think I care about what they think?"

Why would he? Winter was coming, and in Montreal, putting out fires in the middle of December was like standing in some kind of ice-cold hell. "I got time off with full pay," Neil said under his breath, tightening the jute around the last shrub. He cast the dog a quick glance. "You know what I told the captain when he showed me the damn petition? I told him to wipe his ass with it. The guys don't trust me? That's 'cause they don't have any instinct. They're soft at the core."

Neil looked around the narrow backyard. Fuck. Fall was his least favorite season. He got to his feet and wiped his palms down the front of his denim blue work pants. "Well, I don't give a shit," he said to the dog. For a while, Neil stood watching the wind rattle the maple tree's leaves. The poor little red kites clung to the branches, shivering. How pathetic.

Didn't the leaves understand the inevitability of nature?

Neil leaned back on his heels, assessing the afternoon's work. He stifled a yawn and his eyes watered. "What do you think?" he asked Hemi. "We'll rake the leaves after the rain. Let the wind do the work."

With effort, the dog rose and climbed up the steps. The arthritis had gotten worse in the last year. The day would come when Hemi wouldn't make it up and down the steps—and that day was coming soon. The dog paused by the glass patio door and sat back on his hind legs, head cocked slightly to the left.

For a moment, Neil could see the puppy he'd rescued from the flames so long ago, and with that memory, an oppressing heat, like that night's savage amber fire, flooded Neil's torso.

Fuck it.

He clenched his fingers tight.

Time was a train with no breaks. Everybody knew how this ride ended.

He met the dog on the porch and rubbed its golden ears back. His only companion. The only creature he'd ever known worth a dime.

Neil slid the door open and stepped inside. The house was dark, but warm. The curtains were drawn, except those in the kitchen—the light in there was watery, only good for showing dust, yeah, of which there was plenty. He'd have to clean this week. He'd make a to-do list or something. There was time now.

Neil went to the sink and poured a glass of water. He drank the tepid water, leaning his weight back on the counter. Tomorrow. Tomorrow, he'd clean out the shed and dump the junk at the Korean church. Not the Catholic one. Catholics didn't even believe in God anymore. They only went to mass when someone died or was resurrected.

Neil gulped the last of the water and set the glass down in the rust-streaked porcelain sink.

The bungalow was silent, except for Hemi's breathing.

Maybe he should get cable.

It was Tuesday, October twenty-fifth.

He cracked his knuckles.

All right then.

❖

"Wake up."

Something poked his ribs.

Through his dew-covered lashes, Dance Young spied a pair of black boots.

Cops.

He shut his eyes and relaxed his body.

"Get up please. You can't be here." The tone was somewhat friendly. The cops who had this beat were usually pretty agreeable. Dance knew most of them. He didn't recognize this voice. Probably a rookie, his first week in the red-light district.

Good luck, buddy.

"You think he's okay?" the rookie called out to someone. "He ain't moving."

Oh, this guy was easy.

"Yeah?" another voice said. Dance recognized that one. *Hicks.* Officer Brandon Hicks. "See that notebook there?" Hicks asked, a sly smile in his voice. "Touch it, see what happens."

Hicks, you unconscionable bastard.

No, not his notebook.

"This one?" the rookie said, but before the cop reached the marble composition book, Dance grabbed the man's wrist. "Don't," he snarled, sitting up.

"Ah, good morning, Billy." Hicks grinned at him. The big, moon-faced cop hadn't shaved in a few days. Dance could see white bristles shining through the black stubble. Nonchalant, Hicks sipped coffee out of a Styrofoam cup. Obviously, the cop had no regard for the world's environmental crisis. Dance stuffed his notebook back into his waist and pulled his gray sweater down over it. Billy. That's right. To Officer Hicks and the rest of the downtown boys, he was Billy. Billy the schizophrenic. Dance sniffled and wiped his nose with the back of his sleeve, catching the smell of motor oil and spaghetti sauce. He glanced down at himself. All good. No one had messed with him last night. One time, someone had pissed on him as he'd slept. But only once. He was pretty lucky that way.

From under his cap, Dance glared at the two men and looked over their shoulders at the dark sky. "It isn't seven a.m. yet," he said. "Drew lets me stay until seven." He pulled his sleeping bag over his legs, glancing around the store entrance. This was Drew's store, right?

Hicks looked over at the rookie, giving the baby-faced cop a self-assured smile. The rookie, whose name was Z. Gorski, averted his eyes. Was he embarrassed? Gorski was slim, with a muscular jaw and an intelligent stare. He stood a little off, arms folded over his bulletproof vest. "There's the Queer Film Festival starting today," Hicks went on, "and the city doesn't want any trouble with the queers. You know that. Fags like clean streets—"

"I'm not in the gay ghetto." Dance pushed the rim of his hat down over his eyes. "Drew said I can stay until seven and there's no one complaining—"

"You're on the border of the village and—"

"Technically," Gorski said softly, "the gay village only begins at Saint-Hubert—"

"What are we talking about here?" Hicks looked back at Gorski, and a flash of pink colored Gorski's smooth cheeks.

Dance watched on, amused.

Soon enough, Hicks set his sights on him again. "I've got orders. Get up, Billy-boy. Don't bust my balls this morning. I don't wanna have to put your dirty ass in my backseat."

Dance squinted, debating.

He was awake. Still had a little change left over from last night's work. He could get a taco at—

"Hey, come on," Hicks snapped, pushing the tip of his boot into Dance's thigh. "I don't have all day. Go get a spot in line at the Bunker. It's October, time for a shower." Hicks chuckled and turned his attention to Gorski. Gorski didn't smile. He stood quietly, his candid blue eyes on Dance.

"I gotta check in first," Dance said, swiping his hat off.

"Oh, not this. No, you're not checking in. The Mother Ship is out of town this morning. The aliens are getting it cleaned—"

"I need to report back." Dance's eyes shifted slowly to Gorski's face. "If they don't hear from me before the sun rises, they get nervous. Then I get nervous, and when I get nervous, I can't think straight, and when I can't think straight, I can't walk on the sidewalk, and if I can't walk on the sidewalk, I have to walk in the street and if—"

"Jesus, all right. Just call in." Hicks shook his head, stepping back. He nodded at Gorski. "What did I tell you about the street beat, huh? *Shit*, all shit." He exhaled loudly and threw back the rest of his coffee. "They don't pay me enough for this."

Gorski, whose eyes glimmered with curiosity, took a shy step forward.

Dance pulled his notebook out of his pants and pressed it against the side of his face. "Hello?" he called out. "I'm on the corner of"—he tossed his chin up at Gorski—"where am I again? Never mind, I remember." He spoke into the notebook again. "Corner of Maisonneuve and Berri. I am still experiencing a vague discomfort. A little disorientation, but otherwise, I seem to be adjusting to the prod. I shall contact you within the next day for further developments."

Hicks clapped his hands in impatience. "Okay, that's enough. They won't get nervous. Now, come on, Billy, on your feet."

Dance set the book down on his lap. "One day, you'll thank me." He pulled his cap over his brown bangs. "No one needs nervous aliens hovering about."

At this, beautiful Officer Gorski smiled.

❖

Neil flipped to his side and threw the cushion over his head.

The damn phone again. Telemarketers. Or maybe worse. Could be his mother calling.

How are you, son? Have you been taking your vitamins? Are you seeing anyone? And why not?

Hemingway barked twice and let out another one of his long, bored sighs.

"I'm not getting it," Neil said, throwing the cushion back on the armchair. He was trying to take a nap on the couch. He hadn't slept last night. Just lain there, thinking about nothing. "So you can quit bitching, Hem."

That dog was turning into an old spinster, harping on him about everything.

Ring. Ring. Ring. The phone wouldn't give up. Thirty-five dollars a month for this aggravation. Neil reached for the receiver, picked it up, and slammed it back down. "Leave me alone."

By the living room window, Hemi sighed again.

"What's wrong with you? You having a fucking nervous breakdown or something?"

The dog needed some air. Some exercise.

Maybe he did, too. He hadn't bench-pressed in two weeks. Hadn't even touched a barbell in a month.

Neil sat up and rubbed the dark whiskers covering his chin. His stomach growled. When was the last time he'd eaten anyway?

"Okay. Tell you what. I'll get cleaned up and we'll go for a damn walk. Okay? I'll pick up some food. I'll make a sandwich or something."

When Neil rose, Hemi jumped to his feet—arthritis forgotten or ignored—and circled him happily.

"Don't tell me I never do anything for you." With the dog on his heels, Neil walked to the window and peeked out at the street. Two boys had set up a hockey net and were sitting on the curb, tying their roller skates on. Otherwise, the street was dead quiet. Nothing but a row of ugly bungalows, sitting behind badly neglected lawns. Why the hell had he moved to this neighborhood?

He couldn't remember.

"Doesn't matter," Neil muttered. "The property taxes are cheap."

He pushed against the wall with his palm—light-headed again—and petted Hemi's head.

Then, he dropped the curtain.

❖

Dance sat in the Bunker's cluttered, claustrophobic office, fidgeting.

From over a pile of red folders, Emma, the safe house's main caseworker, studied him quietly. At last, she tapped her neatly trimmed fingernails against the desk and leaned in. Her large breasts spilled over the edge of the desk. She was a big girl, with a café-au-lait complexion and a head full of black curls. Forty-something. Sexy, but a real ball-breaker. "I can't let you use the facilities if you don't follow the basic guidelines," she said in her smoky voice. Dance liked to imagine she strained her voice crying out at night as she reached a wall-shattering orgasm. What was she into? Bondage?

"Dance, hon, are you listening to me?"

At the sound of his name—a name he seldom used anymore—Dance's cheeks burned and he shifted his weight on the chair. Another day. Another erection. Another unfulfilled fantasy. "Yeah, I'm listening."

"We have rules. You know them. You have to continue your therapy and check in—"

"I'm doing all that."

"I spoke to Dr. Scarborough about you yesterday and he says you haven't been to the PTS clinic in over five weeks." She licked her lips and stared at him. "He says—"

"I know, I know what he says." Damn it, he was whining again. But the woman did that to him. She always managed to chastise him and turn him into a pouting little boy. It was that generous bosom. He wanted to lay his head between her breasts and sleep. Or suckle. "You don't understand. Dr. Scarborough doesn't help me. He continually argues with me."

She laughed, revealing her beautiful teeth. "Boy, that's hard to imagine."

This was useless. He only needed a shower and a nap. Why

couldn't she turn her back for once? Why did they all insist on rules? The world wasn't built on rules. It was built on chaos and anarchy.

"Dr. Scarborough doesn't agree with my diagnosis," he said bitterly.

"That you're a paranoid schizophrenic."

"Clearly, you've sided with him on this." Dance stiffened and touched the bill of his hat.

"Don't pull your hat over your face on me now. We're just talking. Come on, let me see those liquid metal eyes."

She did *that*, too. This innocent flirting. This maternal affection. He didn't need that. He needed her legs wrapped around his waist.

"Dance, you're twenty-four years old. The Youth Protection Department can't handle your case any longer. The Bunker is open to young adults who are willing to help themselves. Do you want to help yourself?"

A curt laugh escaped him. Dance quickly recomposed his face into a more complacent expression.

Help himself?

What exactly did that mean? Practically. In everyday words. Not in social service slang.

"I see you sizing me up over there," Emma said. "You know what I liked about you when we first met?"

He frowned, turning his attention away. There was no window in this office. How could anyone accept working without a view to the world outside?

"Are you paying attention?"

Man, he only needed a shower and a nap.

"I liked your open mind. Your positive rebellion. Your talent." She pointed to his waist. "How long since you last wrote?"

"I can't write in my telephone, now can I?"

"You're gonna start with that? You're gonna feed me that bullshit?"

When Emma used foul language he almost felt honorable.

"Okay, Dance, what do you want? What is this about? What do you need?"

His throat tightened and he hid his hands under his thighs.

"Just a fucking shower," he said.

❖

Jamie hurried across the hall, heading for the Post-Traumatic Stress clinic.

The clinic was on the seventh floor of the Glasshouse Mental Institution, an impressive stone façade hospital covering over one square mile of surface; a landscape reminiscent of old Southern plantations. The Glasshouse was a completely independent community. It had its own gardens, stores, day care center, and various housing facilities. Founded by an eccentric psychiatrist in the 1900s, the hospital had begun with a small staff of liberal thinkers with a common goal: destroy the stigma of mental illness and eradicate all forms of invasive treatment.

Today, the institute was one of the most influential in its field.

Regardless of public opinion on asylums, Jamie liked being here.

He turned the last corner and stopped short, a few steps away from the PTS's door. He reached into his pocket and curled his fingers around the small bottle of hand sanitizer he carried at all times.

"No," he said under his breath. "Don't."

He glanced around at the empty hall; this floor was still undergoing renovations, and the remaining offices would be closed until March. The hallway was filled with planks and Gyproc sheets. Along the ceiling, grids had been removed, and wires hung down like copper tentacles. White dust covered the awaiting plastic-wrapped chairs. It wasn't a welcoming site, and the noise reached deafening levels when the workers got here around nine.

Not ideal for a highly jumpy clientele.

Jamie took the final steps to the waiting room door, pushed his glasses up, and glimpsed the inside. In contrast, the waiting room was organized and clean. Its color pattern—turquoise, topaz, and champagne—was calming, and the venetian blinds filtered the daylight smoothly, allowing the sun to flow in without the irritating glare.

In every corner, the artificial eddoe plants gave the room an organic feel.

Now all he needed to do to enter the lovely room was open this cursed door.

Jamie looked down at the metal handle, catching sight of the various fingerprints left on it. October. Beginning of the flu season.

He peered through the glass pane in the door and counted heads. There were nine people in there already. Some of them looked ill. Diseased, for certain.

Instinctively, Jamie fondled the reassuring form of the flask inside his pocket. The battle was on.

His chest vibrated, and for a moment he stood petrified.

What was that soft tremor against his breast?

"Oh," he sighed. His phone was ringing. It was on vibration mode. He produced it from his jacket and stared at the screen. His heart skipped a beat.

"Hi," he whispered, answering Basil.

Silence.

Then, "I can't talk long."

He hadn't heard Basil's voice in over a week. It was the busy season for Basil and his crew. The real estate market was at its peak and Basil was on the lookout for a new house to flip.

"Busy, huh?" Jamie asked in a breath.

"Well, you know. Hey, listen, I need a favor. Jared—remember my cousin from Orange County? Anyway, he's in town and he wants me to look at a house on the shore this Saturday." Basil's tone was clipped, every word measured carefully. "The kids have their swimming lessons—"

"I know. I can take them. Do you want me to take them?"

The line was quiet.

"When can I pick them up?" Jamie stepped back from the door, walking over to a pile of cardboard boxes. How had it come to this? There were so many things he needed to say. "Baz, are you there?"

"I don't know if it's a good idea. But I'm stuck. Matt can't babysit. He's got a funeral."

"Oh, who died?"

"An old friend of his. From Matt's circuit scene days. You never met the guy."

Matt, the man-eater. Eternally nineteen. Basil's best friend and faithful employee.

Lover, maybe?

Who knew?

"Look, Jamie, I'm going with my gut on this one. I hope I can trust it. The kids are really not handling this very well and—"

"They're not handling it well because we haven't discussed our separation to its full—"

"Can you spare me the psychobabble? Look, I gotta go. I'll call you back Friday night and let you know what the plan is."

"How long are you gonna shut me out?" Jamie gripped the phone tightly. "How much more do you want me to suffer?"

"Fuck, Jamie, I got enough on my plate."

"Then let me help you."

"Right," Basil scoffed. "You can't even help yourself."

Jamie refused to take that bait. Not this morning. Not when he was this weak. This vulnerable. And besides, he could never win. Basil Spasso was the king of verbal warfare.

"Shit, I'm sorry, Jamie, that last line was a little overboard," Basil said, to Jamie's surprise. "Forget it. Forget I said it."

Jamie's whole body leaned into the phone. He could almost catch the scent of Basil's neck, a mix of anise, oak moss, and Lever 2000. "Can we meet?" he asked. "Can we just—" But in the background, he heard Matt hollering, and Jamie lost his nerve. Basil's crew was probably unloading the van, trying to get the day started without a catastrophe. "Never mind, I guess now's not the time."

"Thank you," Basil sighed. "We've got problems with the LaSalle house, and the buyers in NDG dropped out at the last minute. I'll talk to you Friday." Basil hesitated for a few seconds and Jamie held on, dying another slow death.

Say it. Say you love me still.

"Don't let the crazy in." Basil cut the line.

The subtle assault left Jamie trembling with anger. "Jerk," he said between clenched teeth. Basil knew how much he detested that word. He forbade it around him. *Crazy.* A lethal word, full of stigma and misunderstanding.

Jamie pushed the handle down—who cares about the germs—and stepped inside the PTS clinic.

Nine faces stared back at him, and it was only eight a.m.

These people, some anxious, some stoic, sat in the new therapeutic chairs, eyes fixed to his. What did these men and women want from him? Absolution? Salvation?

Jamie forced a smile to his lips and turned his attention to Marie-Miel. She sat behind the reception desk, a steaming cup of coffee at her side, her fingers racing efficiently across the keyboard. The very sight of her calmed his nerves. Though her eyes never left the computer screen, Jamie knew that she was silently greeting him. Slowly. Respectfully. She was the only one in this room who knew the depths of him. The only one who was aware of the sham that he was.

"Good morning," he said, stepping up to the desk.

She handed him a pile of mail.

He stared at it. Mail was absolutely the most vile paper ever passed from hand to hand. Right after money.

"Rough morning?" Marie-Miel's tone invited a confidence.

But he didn't have the energy to explain himself. She knew the details of the disaster area that was his love life. He nodded and took the mail. The touch of it sent a shiver down his back.

"You've got a challenging morning ahead of you." She flashed her best smile. But her smart eyes held his. "You want me to send a few home? I can reschedule Mrs. Ingyen—"

"No, it's fine." He turned from the desk in the direction of his private office and then looked back at her. "But hold all my calls, please."

"All right." She picked up the phone and covered the receiver with her fingers. "I'll keep the coffee coming."

"Thank you, Marie-Miel."

She laughed. "Hey, Dr. Scarborough, I have a feeling it's gonna be one of those days."

Jamie nodded and gently shut the door to his office.

❖

Neil sat on the park bench with Hemi lying listless at his feet.

The dog would need at least a half hour of rest before they walked back home.

"Yeah, maybe I pushed you a little." Neil dug his fingers into the dog's golden fur, watching the Saint-Lawrence River ebb over the muddy shore. One thing about this neighborhood, it had nice access to the water. A great bike path. Not that he ever used it. Too many idiots riding their high-tech bicycles, looking like latex spermatozoa racing to some giant unfertilized egg.

If he needed exercise, he lifted weights in his basement, or went for a jog. At night. When the pregnant women weren't wobbling down the path, hogging all the space.

"When we get home," he said to the sleeping dog, "I'll give you a bath. With that expensive soap and everything."

When Hemi didn't react, Neil stuffed his hands into his coat pockets. "Suit yourself."

Soon, Neil felt the weight of someone staring at him.

Some kid, clad in a gray sweater and dirty blue jeans, stood by the swing set. He appeared to be deep in thought. His eyes were hidden by a baseball cap, and Neil realized the boy wasn't staring at him, but at the river.

The park was vacant. Kids were in school, and it was way too cold for toddlers—no, those little droolbags were home finger-painting while Mama watched the Food Network.

Neil looked away from the boy, but soon again, his eyes were tugged in his direction once more. The kid acknowledged his stare and pushed his hat back in greeting. At the contact of the boy's silver eyes, Neil hurriedly looked away, flushed.

He'd seen those eyes before. But where?

Neil rose and tugged on Hemi's leash. "Let's go."

Begrudgingly, Hemingway obeyed, and in quick strides, Neil guided him across the jungle gym area, away from the shore.

Away from the kid.

❖

Marie-Miel had been right. It had been *that* kind of morning.

In his office, Jamie sat in his leather chair, staring blankly at the vacant, newly upholstered divan.

In the last three hours, he'd listened to people's attempts at rationalizing their innermost fears and destructive behavior. He had sat, pen in hand, receptive and empathetic, while trying to keep his own anxiety from shredding through him. His patients trusted him. Some, in fact, trusted *only* him. Mr. Asimakopolos, for instance, swore he hadn't spoken to another human being since their last appointment. Social phobia. Jennifer was a few months away from passing the bar exam and had spent last night pulling her hair out, one strand at a time. She liked to pop the roots and chew on them. Trichotillomania. Tom, a city clerk, was on the verge of bankruptcy because he couldn't stop himself from buying teeth whitening products whenever he passed them in a store. Obsessive-compulsive behavior, coupled with a possible borderline personality.

Jackpot.

Wiped out, Jamie picked up his mug and sipped the last of his cold coffee. He had a fifteen-minute breather between two patients, and if he could close his eyes for a power nap, he'd be in good shape for the afternoon load.

There was a rasp at his door, and Marie-Miel stepped inside, shutting the door behind her. "Have you eaten yet?" She pushed a Tupperware container full of aromatic rice and vegetables his way. "My grandmother's recipe," she said, tearing white plastic utensils out of a sterilized bag.

How could he resist? Jamie took the fork from her and dove in. The first bite was tangy and spicy. The right mix of lemon and chili peppers.

Basil had been the cook in the house. When Basil was in the kitchen, everyone knew there'd be a feast to be had. Since their breakup, Jamie survived on bland necessities. Every meal straight out of a can.

"Thank you," he said, swallowing the warm treat.

"Dr. Scarborough, I don't know if this is the right time, but Emma called and she was wondering if you could—"

"What happened?" Jamie held the fork up in midair, tensing. "What did he do now?"

Dance Young. What a beautiful mess that boy was.

"I'm not sure, but she saw Dance yesterday and he didn't look well. He was very defiant. Well, she used the word 'uncompromising.'"

That was an understatement.

"I haven't seen him since August. Where is he living?"

Marie-Miel handed him a napkin. "She doesn't know. But Emma thinks he may be staying with his brother."

"I didn't know Dance had a brother. He never mentioned him before."

Dance had spoken about a sister once. She had an odd name. November, her name was. Or maybe it was December. Their parents were eccentrics. The mother, a street performer and poet. A suicide. The father, a professor of ethnology. An alcoholic with self-mutilation tendencies. That's if Dance had told the truth. Dance Young was a fantastic liar.

"She left the brother's number with me." Marie-Miel unfolded a yellow Post-it. "Maybe you should call him. She seemed really concerned, and you know Emma, she doesn't get worked up over nothing."

Jamie took the paper and glanced down at it. He frowned. "You said this was the brother?"

"Yes."

"You're sure you didn't misunderstand?"

"This is the brother. He lives near here."

Jamie read the name again, recalling Dance and his conversation. Dance had spoken of a sister. He was sure of it.

Then he read the name one more time.

September Young.

Yes, that's right.

The sister's name was September.

CHAPTER TWO

Jamie and the kids emerged from the parking lot elevator into the Ivory Tower's luxurious lobby.

Immediately, Jamie stiffened—he'd spotted a couple sitting on the lobby couch, a Great Dane sprawled lazily at their feet. The pair gave him and the children a biting look.

The Tower was not child friendly.

Clutching the grocery bags, Jamie guided Marsh and Mallory to the main set of elevators, which led to the apartment. Before the doors slid shut, he gathered his courage and cried out to the obnoxious couple. "Your dog is bigger than these children!" The door closed on their bewildered faces.

"Why'd you scream at them, Dr. J?" Mallory asked. Still damp from the pool, her auburn hair poked out from under her wool hat. She'd done great today. She'd almost dived off the board. Next week she'd do it. She would.

"I didn't really scream, did I?"

Marshall, whose eyes had yet to leave his Nintendo DS game, nodded. "Yeah, you screamed."

God, he was so much like his uncle. Marsh was Basil's spitting image. Blond, blue-eyed, and magnetic. It almost hurt to look at him.

"They made me feel really inadequate, I guess," Jamie said, fastening his eyes to the panel.

They reached their floor and stepped out into the narrow hall.

"What are we having for lunch?"

He hadn't prepared a meal in months. He visited the children once a week since the separation, but this was the first time Basil had permitted him to take them to his new home. "Sandwiches, I guess. And I can make that cream of asparagus you guys like."

Jamie fiddled with his keys. His nerves were raw. Damn you, Basil. He felt like a babysitter. A stranger. What right did Basil have to make up the rules?

Mallory slipped the house keys out of his free hand and unlocked the door. Bright and precocious, the girl was always looking for a shortcut to adulthood, and whenever Jamie spent time with her, he worked very subtly at slowing her escape.

But when he got discouraged, he had to remind himself of the progress the Spasso twins had made since he'd first met them five years ago, at the PTS clinic. Basil had brought them in for counseling, desperate for help. And Basil had trusted his sister's orphaned children with Jamie.

Yes, back then, Basil had believed in him.

"Dr. J?"

Jamie glanced down at Mallory. Her eyes were piercing. Woman's eyes. Beautiful. Deadly smart.

"Well," he said with false cheer. "Are we gonna stand out here in the hall all day? Or do you two want to hear about the surprise I have planned for you?"

For them. For him. Who knew why he did what anymore.

At last, Marsh turned his attention away from his portable game and frowned. He stepped inside, cautiously, as if stepping inside a snake pit.

Jamie set the bags by the door and helped Mallory pull her pea coat off. She was dressed in the latest fashion. Basil's little Italian princess. "So, what do you think?" he asked, his heart beating furiously.

This was it. They were officially a broken family.

"About what?" Marshall stood by the foyer, his coat and hat on.

"It's very nice," Mallory said, her eyes assessing.

Marshall slipped his hat off. He'd gotten a haircut. The soft curls were gone. Dear God, whoever had cut his hair had used a clipper. "What happened there?" Jamie asked, stepping closer to Marsh.

Marshall shrank back, running his fingers through the short blond spikes on his head. "What's the surprise?" he asked, dodging the touch and question.

"First, let's eat." Jamie turned from the boy, his breath getting shorter and shorter with every passing moment. Marshall had made his decision. It was clear. Basil was the good guy in this, and he was now condemned to be the coward who'd abandoned them.

And this, after all the work they'd done together. After all the nights he'd sat by Marshall's bed, keeping terror at bay, holding the boy's icy hands through anxiety attacks. Every conversational milestone. Every hug an unexpected gift. Together, he and Marsh had conquered armies of monsters and weaved a special bond.

Only to have it destroyed because of Basil's impatience. Because of his stubbornness. Because of his lack of faith.

"Are you having an episode?" Mallory watched him dutifully, carrying a grocery bag on her hip. "Dad said, if you have an episode, I have to call him. I just have to. Are you?"

How dare he! What was Basil telling them? Who the hell did he think he was? Mr. Perfect. Mr. I've got it all under control. Mr. I'm King of the Universe.

"You're very red."

"I'm fine, Mallory," Jamie snapped, grabbing the bag from her. "Don't condescend to me. And come help me with these sandwiches."

She bit her lower lip, seemed to process the sudden confrontation, and followed him silently.

Jamie pushed on the swinging kitchen doors and called back to Marsh. "Take your coat off and get in here."

This was his house. Not Basil's.

And he loved those kids.

Period.

❖

Neil knotted the last plastic bag shut and swung it over his shoulder.

Dead leaves project: done.

Not much left on the checklist. And it was still goddamn October.

He remembered why he hated October so much.

Halloween.

The very thought of snotty-faced kids ringing his doorbell

incessantly made him want to tear this plastic bag and dump all the wet leaves into their parents' yards. Every year, he shut all the lights off, but still, they came.

Probably did it on purpose. No one in the neighborhood really liked him. Fine by him.

Neil dropped the bag by the others and walked back to the porch. He stole a look at his watch.

It was eleven a.m.

Yeah, so what? Not like he had a plane to catch.

"So, boy, you wanna take a stroll by the river or something?"

Hemi stirred in his sleep.

"Don't be lazy, now. Come on, maybe you'll catch a squirrel."

And maybe we'll see that kid again.

The dog's left ear twitched, but he remained asleep.

Neil sat on the first step and watched the street. It was a warm day for October. Yes, folks, brought to you by global warming.

Minutes passed, and dazed, he tried to recall his thoughts.

He had drifted off again, somewhere between two lives, none of them his.

He heard a car, and when he recognized it, he jumped to his feet and whistled for Hemi. "Get inside," he grumbled. "I knew she'd fucking show up." He swung the door open and yanked Hemi into the entrance. He shut the door and glanced around. All the lights were off. Curtains were closed.

He pulled off his boots and threw them in the corner. "I'm not answering the door. I'm not answering that goddamned door." He paced, and then stopped.

She had reached the front door. He could almost see her there, standing close to the pane, spying.

The bell rang, and then, five decisive knocks.

"Fuck," he breathed, recoiling.

"Neil?" Christina called out. "Are you in there?"

This woman was, by far, the most aggravating, relentless dyke he'd ever known.

Hell, she was the only dyke he'd ever known. Cute and crazy. A lethal mix of femininity and balls-to-wall personality. Christina the paramedic. Christina the bully.

"McClure, I know you're in there. Open the door or I'll fake a domestic scene." Christina knocked more forcefully this time. She was petite, but her strength was uncanny. He'd seen her lift drunken truck drivers right off the sidewalk and onto a stretcher.

He cringed. "I'm jerking off," he yelled. "I'm serious, Chris. I'm about to unload here."

"Honestly, Neil, let me in. This is embarrassing."

Neil stared at the door and shot Hemi a glance. "You know she's not gonna go away."

The dog sat stiff, tail wagging. For some reason, the old beast loved Christina.

Neil popped the front door open and walked away. He headed straight for the kitchen followed by a cool draft of air...and Chris.

And, of course, the dog.

Christina slipped her red scarf off her delicate white neck and sighed. She'd done something to her hair. It was darker. Or lighter. "So, they finally canned your ass, huh?"

Christina the sensitive soul.

He took the brown bag from her gloved hand and peeked inside. "I fucking hate cinnamon buns."

She grinned. "I know. They're for me."

"Look, I know why you're here, Chris, so let's skip the jolly banter."

They had met on the job: a grease fire, tons of damage, five homeless families. Back then, she'd been a rookie, fresh-faced and nervous, and he'd argued with her about some procedure she refused to follow.

Now, four years later, she was still in his life. Like a mouse in the wall you get used to because you can't bring yourself to hurt it. Her and the girlfriend. *Judd.*

Judd the butch.

"I'm not here to give you a sermon, so you can relax," Christina said, her black eyes burning his face. "I just came by to—"

"To say I love you?" He leaned back on the sink, arms crossed, tongue firmly planted in cheek.

"It's Hemi's routine check-up, remember? And I know how nervous you get."

Damn it. How could he have forgotten? It was every three months, on the twenty-eighth.

"I was getting ready for it," he said. "Then you showed up."

"Liar."

"I don't need you to drive me."

She turned her eyes to Hemi. "What do you think? You think your big ol' bad-ass daddy's gonna have a dizzy spell like last time? You think Dr. Smith's gonna have to call me and ask me to come and—"

"All right, move your buns."

"Which ones?"

Christina the stand-up comic.

❖

Jamie watched Mallory wolf down her ham sandwich.

One thing about the little princess, she had the table manners of an ogre. "Have a sip of juice." He pushed her glass up.

"So, what's the surprise anyway?" Marsh asked for the tenth time in the last forty minutes.

"I'm getting a cat. *We're* getting a cat."

Mallory's eyes widened. She smiled, purple mustache and all. "A kitten?"

"Yes, that's right." Jamie glanced down at his plate. Many times over this week, he had imagined this scene. It would be great. They would all rejoice and begin to discuss a name for the new pet.

He saw that he hadn't even touched his lentil salad. And he realized he didn't want a cat anymore. Had he ever?

The hair. The litter box. The clawing of the furniture.

"Dad's allergic to cats," Marshall said, his features knotting into a fist of suspicion.

Oh yes, that's right.

Now Jamie remembered why he wanted that cat. They would call him Revenge. Or Vendetta. "I know, but he isn't going to be around the cat," he said, anger fading into melancholy. "You'll throw your clothes in the wash when you get home." His heartbeat had picked up the pace. His mouth was drying up. He couldn't stop his thoughts from forming their usual compulsive pattern. He could see it happening; guilt to nervousness, to cleanliness. He forbade himself to look over at the counter. The germs could wait. He couldn't allow the anxiety to surface. Couldn't let Basil win.

"When are we getting him?" Mallory's enthusiasm was winding down. Perhaps she, too, could see the farce this afternoon was. On Saturdays, it would have been swimming lessons, followed by Tony's Pizza Parlor. They'd pick up the best double cheese pie in the southwest part of the island, get slap-happy from the food, and spend the afternoon watching movies.

But instead, here they were, in this sterile condo, sitting at this spotless kitchen island, eating mediocre sandwiches, talking about everything and anything but the truth.

Enough.

"I still love your dad," Jamie said, his blood pumping hot and fast, warming his cold hands. "All right? I want you two to know that. I love him. I'm angry with him, but I love him." He met their stare, and finally, he caught a glimmer of hope in their eyes. "I don't know how it came to this, but I...I want our family back, and I'm going to fight for it."

"Why don't you just move back in?" Mallory asked. "You could just come back and he wouldn't have a choice—"

"Don't be a dumbass, Mallory."

"Marshall, don't call your sister a dumbass." How could he sound so flat? Void of authority. Helpless. "Listen," Jamie said more confidently. "We're going to be okay. We're going to go visit the animal shelter and find our cat, and then we'll come home and make chocolate chip cookies."

"Then what?" Marsh asked.

"Then we'll talk."

"Your phone's moving on the counter."

The caller ID showed S. Young.

"I have to get this, guys. Just a few minutes. Go see what's on the Family Channel."

"You got the Family Channel?" Mallory and Marsh jumped out of their chairs and shot out of the kitchen, the doors swinging behind them.

"Hello." Jamie stood, a sudden tension rising up his spine.

"Dr. Scarborough?" The voice was nasal, between two definite octaves.

"Yes, speaking."

Hesitation. The line was quiet.

"Is this September Young?" Jamie asked, wanting to get to the point.

"How did—"

"Emma from—"

"Oh, I see."

That voice. Was this a man or a woman? The inflection was soft on the vowels, feminine. Yet there was a depth to the voice. A boyish ring to it.

Jamie waited for a moment, allowing a certain comfort to seep in. He sensed a strong resistance, though he couldn't explain how he knew. He could feel it on the line. Apprehension. Maybe anger.

"Dance showed up at my apartment yesterday afternoon," September said at length. "He upset me. I think someone should intervene."

The words were polished and edited.

"He upset you. How?"

"That's very personal, Doctor." September coughed. It was a smoker's cough. "Anyway, he mentioned that you don't want to authorize his stay at the Unity transition home, and I urge you to reconsider."

"Dance isn't a schizophrenic. He's a compulsive liar."

"He hears voices. He says his notebook is a telephone. He—"

"He pretends to hear voices," Jamie said. "That's very different."

"Oh, what does it matter?" September's voice broke on the last word. "Just help him. I can't handle him when he's like this. I can't—"

"Do you fear for his life?"

"Absolutely."

"I don't think Dance is suicidal, but—"

"You don't understand, Dr. Scarborough. I fear for his life because if you don't get my brother out of my damn house, I'm going to end his life for him."

❖

Neil stood in the corner of the veterinarian's examination room, his fists clenched.

Christina blew her nose, her black eyeliner running with the tears.

"Oh God, Neil, oh God." She hid her face inside her hands. "I'm sorry, oh, Neil, I'm so sorry."

Neil stared back at the closed door and then at the empty table where, only minutes ago, Hemingway had been stretched out, passive and unknowing.

Unknowing. Trusting him to care for him. To sustain his life.

"He's going to suffer," Christina said, reaching out for his arm. "He'll die sick and mad."

"Oh, fuck, Chris, please don't touch me." Neil backed up into the wall, bumping his head against the window.

"Easy, don't freak out. Keep it together." Christina's tone was cooler now, her eyes already dry. It was the job. It did that to you. The nerves had a memory, and after being tested for years, they somehow remembered the way back to calm, whether the heart and mind could accept it. "These are your options," she said, crumpling the tissue. "You have to face them. You have to make a choice. He lives another month, in God knows what kind of shape, while you pump him full of drugs, or he goes quick and painless—"

"I heard the fucking doctor!" Neil roared, his eyes bulging out of his sockets. Goddamn her, could she just shut up? For once. Just once. He knew the options. Knew them well. He needed to think. That's all. He had to connect with something inside. Pull something out of this heart full of emotional pus. He could hear that voice yelling for him to do it.

Get rid of the damn dog. Stick a needle in him. End his life.

Because without Hemi, he was free.

Slowly, a mighty sensation—ruling and seductive—seeped into Neil's limbs.

Free to seal the garage door, sit in the car and let the engine run.

"Neil? Talk to me. Is this too much for you to handle?"

"What?" His vision was blurred.

"You're crying. Come here."

He retreated back yet a little more.

Christina studied him. She was in hero mode again. "You're cracking, and it's okay. Hemi is everything and everyone to you—"

"Call the doctor back in." His head had cleared up. All muddled thoughts, wiped out. This was the liberation he'd been looking for. This was the fucking way out. "I'm ready to talk to her."

"Now? But she said that we could take all—"

"Okay, never mind, I'll get her."

"Wait!" Christina blocked his way. "I don't think you're in the right state of mind to make a decision. I think maybe we should leave Hemi here for the night and—"

"Why are you here? Huh? What's your angle?" He saw color leak into her face, but knew she wasn't embarrassed. Hell no, she was pissed. And he wanted to hurt her. Couldn't stop himself. "You hang around me like a bitch in heat—"

His cheek stung and his head was thrown to the side.

She'd slapped him so hard, he tasted blood on his lip.

"You fucking bastard," she said, calmly, rubbing her palm. Her eyes blazed. "You're giving up." She tried to slip her purse over her shoulder, but dropped it. With a swift gesture, she swept it up and slammed it against the table. "Well, we'll see about that. Oh, yes, we will." Shaken, she was rummaging through her purse. "You're gonna kill yourself. I know the warning signs, yes I do."

She was rambling.

But she was also right.

Damn these women. What was it with them anyway? They hated his guts but wanted him to stick around this dump of a planet? How much sense did that make?

"I didn't mean what I said," he said, faking an apology. "Put down the phone. Who you calling?"

"My friend." She shot him a paralyzing look. "He's a shrink."

"Hang up right now." Neil clamped his jaw and stepped closer to her. "Chris, hang up."

She flipped the phone shut. She was pale. Beat up.

So?

She'd asked for this. He'd never wanted her friendship. Never asked for anything. He'd spent the last decade alone, and that was of his own volition. Human beings were a dangerous species. Slick and treacherous. The irony of his existence didn't escape him. He risked his life for people he'd never even help cross the street if it came down to it.

"Neil," Christina whispered without meeting his eye. "I wanna save you, okay? I realized that just now. Judd's been telling me for four years, but I never bought it." She nodded appreciatively, obviously having some kind of epiphany. Good for her. "Judd was right," she said, half to herself. "It's part of who I am. It's what I do. You understand that, don't you? For Christ sakes, you're a firefighter. You know what's it like to wanna get the last one out."

"Is this a private therapy session, or can I say something?"

Her features lightened. "How did you become such an asshole anyway?"

"Practice."

"Are you okay?"

It didn't matter anymore. For the last months, his soul had felt like a nuclear warhead, and now it had been engaged. Without Hemi, there was nothing to live for.

Hemi's last gift to him: sanction.

And no, he wasn't a firefighter. He was only a goddamned mental case on a forced sick leave. They would never take him back. He was forty-two years old, jobless, childless, and godless.

Yeah, everyone knew how this train ride ended, but he was going to get there on his own terms.

"I'm sorry I insulted you," he offered Chris, his eyes roaming over the bare examination table.

It was over.

He would go home without Hemi. He had half a bag of Hemi's food left. He'd take it over to the pet store. Some welfare family could use it. He'd take the leather leash, too. It wasn't cheap. Still good.

"Neil? You never apologize. You're making me nervous." Christina fondled her phone. "I think that if you saw him. If you saw Dr. Scar—"

There was a short knock on the door, and the vet, a stocky woman in her sixties with jet black hair and too much lipstick, entered. Her perfume trailed after her, musky and loud. Eau de Desperation. She was Dr. Smith's replacement. She had the bedside manners of a bear after a winter of hibernation. Leave it to Dr. Smith to take a vacation in October. Neil liked Dr. Smith. Hemi liked him, too. The man was thorough, quiet, and possibly allergic to small talk.

Hemi would never see him again.

"I'm sorry to interrupt," Dr. Mama Bear said, "but I have a limited staff today and I must know if we are keeping Hemingway overnight or—"

"Do what you gotta do." Neil heard his words, and recognized his voice, but he felt unhinged, like a door resting against the wall, never to open nor close again. "Put him down. He's had a good run."

"Neil," Christina cried. "You don't have to decide just now. If it's about money, I can pay for the—"

"Mr. McClure, we can send him home with you for a few days and you may—"

"And I may what?" A trickle of cold sweat was making its way down his back. His head was pregnant with a pulsing blob that used to be his mind. "Huh? Do what, exactly?" He flew to the counter and grabbed the loose sheets of paper. The consent form. The executioner's orders. Lethal injection for the crime of being a stupid cancer-infested dog. Neil's mouth tasted like bile. He picked up a blue ball pen lying nearby and brought the tip to the paper. He signed his name on the line.

"Are you gonna do it?" he said, holding the form out to whoever was brave enough to take it.

For a moment, Dr. Mama Bear was flushed. She stared down at the form and then nodded. "Yes," she breathed, slipping the paper out of his sweaty fingers. "I'm on duty tonight."

Neil jerked his chin up and sniffled. "All right then." He moved to the door, but Christina took hold of his sleeve. "Don't you wanna say good-bye?" she said, a sort of terror moving behind her eyes.

"I'm going home, Christina." He pulled free of her grip and opened the door. He stepped out into the narrow hall and glanced around—to his left, he caught sight of Hemi's profile. The dog lay by the reception desk, watching a nurse in pink slacks. The girl was eating a plum while searching for a medical record in one of the numerous file cabinets.

Hemi was quiet, ears relaxed.

Neil took a step forward and turned around. Christina stood in the examination room's doorway, a look of sheer panic on her face. Her eyes darted back and forth from the dog to him. "Neil—"

"I'm gonna pay these guys and take a cab." He walked to the reception, past the dog, one step at a time.

One breath at a time. Get out of here. Pay and get out of here.

At the reception counter, Neil focused on slipping the card out of his wallet. Then he focused on the voice that came from the mouth moving across from him. The mouth would tell him the numbers, and that would be the price. He would sign the bill and that would be that.

"Are you all right?" the voice said.

Neil glanced up. The mouth was attached to a face. It looked worried.

"How much did you say?" he asked the face.

"You just paid me." The face smiled, but its expression was confused. "Here's your card back."

"Neil?" Christina was calling his name.

Behind the counter, Hemi barked.

Neil found the door which led to the air. He needed a gulp. He needed to feel it in his hair. He turned to see Christina rushing out after him, but he was already running.

Hemi, you fucking old mutt.

Dance tiptoed across the dimly lit living room, eyes steady on his brother's face.

Ten a.m. Nap time again.

He stepped over a crack in the floor and glanced back at her: September hadn't stirred. Probably a consequence of the Ambien pills she popped like candy.

How could anyone sleep so much? Denial. That's what it was. Just another one of September's ways of keeping reality out. Or maybe it was all the vomiting. He'd heard her early this morning, gagging in the washroom. She let the tap run in an useless effort to drown out the awful noise, but Dance was on to her. "Stomach problems," September usually said.

The problem wasn't with her stomach. It was lodged somewhere in his brother's brilliant, dysfunctional brain.

Dance paused, taking in the details of the miserable one-bedroom apartment. Couldn't she have done better than this? September had always had such impeccable taste. How could she live this way? The neighborhood was as depressing as an abandoned refugee camp. The only pleasant area was the waterfront—Dance liked to hang out there to feed the ducks.

Groggy and light-headed from another sleepless night, he studied September now, standing by the door, his notebook safely in hand. September lay on her back, mouth slightly open, her arms crossed over her new breast implants. Curled up at her side was the new stray she'd adopted; a gigantic orange cat she'd named Tiny. In the corner of the cramped, moldy, and overly furnished living room, the television beamed silently. It was Maury. Obviously, the host had been reading paternity results. Some clueless man kept shaking his head while a woman wept and spat at him.

Boy, September sure liked her drama.

Dance spotted his army boots under the straw chair in the entrance and took another quiet step forward.

"Where are you going?"

The sound of his brother's voice always unnerved Dance. It wasn't the hormones, nor the new pitch. It was September's way of sounding accusatory, even when she was asking for someone to pass the salt. Dance flinched. "I'm going out to meet Elliot."

Above the seat, September's cutting steel-gray eyes appeared. "The hustler?"

"Masseuse. He's a masseuse." Dance slipped a boot on. "And he's totally legit."

"You act deranged after you've spent time with him." September sat up and tousled her hair. It had gotten very long since they'd seen each other last. The silky dark hair reached his brother's middle back now. She was still a looker, though the undiagnosed anorexia had eaten all the meat off her small frame. The disease had been left untreated for over ten years, yet September's beauty remained almost untouched. Unlike his sister, Dance preferred to hide his seraphic features under heavy bangs and baseball caps. Very early on, he'd learned that beauty was a double-edged sword, and on the streets, it could be lethal. But September lived by her sword. Surgery after surgery. Her body was the epicenter of her life—a dangerous landscape built on the collision of two tectonic plates: food and gender.

"Sit down, I wanna talk to you," she said, flipping her hand up.

Dance leaned back to the front door. "Oh man, Seth. I'm late."

"Don't call me that."

Dance winced. Once again, the name had slipped out. But regardless of his opinion, this was not the time to get into *that* conversation. He was an unwanted guest here. "I forgot. I'm sorry," he said, bending to his other boot. Unsure, he fiddled with the boot's laces. "Look, if it's any consolation to you, I might be able to crash at Elliot's place for—"

"No, Dance. No way." With effort, September eased herself out of the couch. Her tank top clung to her protruding shoulder blades. The white cotton was damp with sweat. She rose, setting the cat down with a gentleness she'd never shown a fellow human being. When she looked back at him, Dance's heart jumped. There was a terrible glare in his brother's eyes.

"You don't want me here," Dance said. He'd overstayed his welcome many times in the past, and September had never been pleased or accommodating about it, but this time, things were different. There was something in the way she looked at him; it was raw and uncontrollable hate. "I said I'd pay my share of the rent—"

"How? How you gonna do that, huh?" September's eyes narrowed and she folded her skinny arms around herself. "You don't have a job, remember?" She smirked. She never revealed her teeth. They were damaged by the stomach acids. Yet, thin as her smile was, it was vicious.

She was in it to hurt.

And Dance would allow it a little. That was their unspoken promise. A fair trade.

"But maybe the aliens could hire you. You could be their PR guy."

"I gave you forty dollars. That's all I have for now."

September needed a fight. She needed it bad. All day, cooped up in this litter box. All day, remembering what she'd lost.

"And you think that's enough? Look around you! I barely have enough cash to feed the cats! You show up here with your stories and your fucking good intentions—"

"My stories?" Oh, this was grand. The nerve of her. In a haste, Dance pulled on the other boot and threw his coat on. "You don't know my stories. You don't listen—"

"Because you're completely nuts," she yelled, the thin blue veins of her neck throbbing. "Or maybe you're just a liar like the shrink says. I don't even know and I don't care."

"You need to chill out or you'll go into cardiac arrest."

"That's right, make fun of me." September's features tightened into an expression of resolute acceptance. She scooped up the cat and stroked its head. "My brother's going to tell me that I'm a freak," she said to the cat, caressing it. Her voice was strained and her tone mocking. "Next my brother will tell me that I'm transforming this body because I hate myself. He doesn't believe in cytogenetics. Why would he? He's—"

"I haven't said those things in a long time."

September glanced up. The tempest in her gray eyes had given place to a phony serenity. She held the cat to her chest, her smooth, slightly pointed chin nestled into the cat's amber fur.

Dance held her cool stare. The surgeries had changed his brother's body, but they could never reach the depths of him. No, Seth's energy was the same: unpredictable, volatile, and self-sufficient.

But September was a windmill who refused to acknowledge the existence of air currents.

"Did you ever think that maybe you need me?" Dance asked, not expecting an answer.

"You can't stay with Elliot. He's unstable. And a user." September coughed and set the cat down. She reached for her pack of Benson & Hedges cigarettes. "But I can't help you this time." She looked around, lighting her cigarette. "I really can't." She spoke absentmindedly. Her eyes clouding over, she blew the rest of the smoke through her new, beautifully shaped nose. "I just can't."

"So you'd rather have me on the streets."

"Yes, Dance. We're not doing this anymore."

"This? You mean being brothers who care—"

"I'm not your brother anymore. I'm not him." September leaned back on the couch's arm and flicked the warm ashes into her palm. "I can't be around you right now. Do you understand? I can't think when you're here. Living with you is like"—she swept her bangs back, the cigarette still burning between her tapered fingers, and closed her eyes—"well, it's like living with him."

"Him?"

September nodded, turning her eyes to the window. "Yeah," she said, "him."

Dance pushed his notebook into his pants, defeated.

And for the thousandth time in his pointless, ransacked life, he wished he wasn't September's identical twin.

❖

Jamie pulled up in front of the house—the very house he'd called home for four years—and spotted Matt's shiny blue Durango in the driveway. "Yeah, that's great," he said under his breath. "Very nice, Basil."

Didn't Matt have a funeral to be at? The boy couldn't keep away from Basil, not even for one lousy evening.

Hands gripped tightly around the steering wheel, Jamie drove his Audi up the driveway, stopping an inch from the Durango's bumper. He flicked his eyes to the rearview mirror—the kids were still sound asleep, exhausted from the emotional day. Or maybe the kitten had worn them out. They had yet to name the black-and-white furball, but Jamie had refrained from offering ideas. Instead, he'd spent the latter part of the afternoon trying to keep his anxiety from ruining the already botched reunion. He'd sat and watched on, swallowing the resentment down with a nice bourbon on the rocks. All afternoon, Mallory had watched him dutifully, recording his every change of facial expression, and Marsh had been steadily brilliant at ignoring him.

In the driveway, Jamie sat in the car, chewing on his thumbnail, spying on the house. It was a three-story town house, typical of the Milton Park district, Victorian, built in the late 1800s—yes, but of course Basil would have known the *exact* date. Basil knew everything about that house. He had gutted it from basement to roof, restoring it with maniacal dedication and genius. Room by room, the house had been revived. For them. For their family.

In the main window, the drapes were open, and soon enough, Jamie caught sight of Basil's silhouette moving across the living room. Moments later, the front door swung open and Basil appeared.

"Oh sweet Jesus, give me strength," Jamie said, his heart pounding. "Give me the strength to keep from begging."

Dressed in his old blue jeans and a snug plaid shirt, Basil sauntered down the five stone steps, and slowed his pace. The street was masked in darkness, but Jamie still could make out Basil's tense expression.

Basil tapped his window, and Jamie realized he hadn't even rolled it down. Earnestly, he pushed the dial and cracked a smile. "Hi," he said softly, meeting Basil's sea blue stare. "They're both out cold."

Basil leaned in—just barely—and nodded. "Thanks for taking them."

Jamie unclasped his seat belt, which was digging into his shoulder, and moved to open the door, but Basil stopped him. "I got it," Basil said, opening the back door. "I'll wake them. They're too big to be carried in—"

"I'll help you. I mean, I wanna say good-bye anyway and—"

"Jamie, no." Basil stirred Mallory and Marsh. "Come on, guys, you're home."

What was this? This was absolutely childish and not at all what they had agreed on. They'd promised to handle things with maturity and never engage in these territorial tug-of-wars. Jamie stepped out and went around to Marshall's side.

Marsh was awake, but before Jamie could say anything the boy had jumped onto the pavement, heading straight to the house. "Dad, can I go downstairs and practice with Matt?" he called back.

"Hey, don't I get a hug or something?" Jamie asked, reaching out to Marsh, but Marshall shrank back two steps and waved. "Thanks for the cat," the boy mumbled, running up the stairs.

"Dad got him a new set of drums," Mallory said, touching Jamie's sleeve. "So he likes to play them a lot." She was sleepy-eyed, but obviously aware of his despair.

Was he losing Marshall?

He had no rights to these children. Legal or otherwise. He had come into their lives never imagining a day when he'd be pushed out of their existence, and trusting in Basil's love, he'd never protected himself. He let all of his walls down.

And here he was, stomach torn open, guts hanging out.

Basil coughed into his fist. "Look, I—"

"You know what it was like for me today? Do you?"

"Mallory, go inside. Say good-bye to Dr. J and go inside."

"Do you have any idea what you're putting me through here?" Jamie circled the car and stepped up to Basil. "You're destroying me," he whispered. "And on what grounds? What have I done to deserve—"

"Mal, go inside, I said." Basil's voice was contained, but Jamie knew that tone. He'd struck a nerve.

"You'll give Sylvester his treats?" Mallory asked, nearing Jamie. "Like the man said at—"

"Is that what you called him?" Jamie's throat stung. Oh please, God, not the tears. He stroked Mallory's cheek and pulled her into his arms. She did not resist. "I'll give him so many treats," he said, inhaling the scent of her apricot shampoo, "that he'll be the fattest pussycat—"

"No, that's not good for him." She peeled herself away. Gently, with grace. "Just one a day."

"Who are we talking about here?" Basil asked, faking a grin.

"We got a cat, but Dad, it's all right, we'll throw our clothes in the wash and—"

"Okay, that's nice." Basil's face hardened. "Go inside, babe. It's cold. Come on, say good night."

For a moment, they stared each other down, with Mallory, quiet and contemplative, standing between them. At last, Mallory swung her backpack over her shoulder and headed for the house. "I love you, Dr. J," she cried. Her tone was both desperate and furious. She did not wait for his reply. She slammed the door behind her.

Jamie didn't miss a beat; he tossed his hands up. "Happy?" he snapped.

"Why'd you get a cat?"

"Why'd you ask Mallory to watch me and call you if—"

"Why'd you get a fucking cat, Jamie? Huh? I'm allergic, and you know it. Not demented allergic like some of your patients who pretend to be anything but normal just so they can sit in your goddamn office for—"

"Why'd you ask Mallory to watch me?"

"Why'd you get a cat!"

"Answer my question, Basil."

Basil brought his knuckles to his mouth, eyeing him fiercely. "I'm not gonna lose my temper over this," he said, shaking his head. "You want a cat, then by all means, go ahead and get a cat."

"I already did," Jamie retorted. "Baz," he quickly added, hoping to steer this conversation back on track, "I'm just trying to—"

"I'm tired, okay? I can't deal with you right now." Basil turned away, then spun around to face him again. "I asked Mallory to watch *over* you. Not to watch *you*."

Jamie stood stiff, mouth open.

Oops.

Basil ran a swift hand over his face and shrugged. "I gotta go back inside."

"I'm doing better. I really am—"

"Look at your hand," Basil whispered, motioning to Jamie's hip.

Oh God. He hadn't noticed. He hadn't even noticed.

"You've been fondling that bottle of magic soap for the last minute."

"But I didn't take it out. I didn't—"

"I don't have it in me anymore. We've been over this time and time again. Go home, okay? Just go home, please."

"Are you sleeping with Matt?"

Basil lolled his head. "Fuck you," he said calmly, before turning away. He flew up the stairs and stepped over the threshold, then disappeared into the house, shutting the door behind him.

"Oh, baby," Jamie said, staring at the closed door. "You could never answer a straight question."

No matter, because he'd gotten his answer anyway.

CHAPTER THREE

A t his bedroom window, Neil squinted, shading his eyes.
Where did all this damn snow come from?

He peeked out, hidden from view, cursing the white mess. The neighbor's kids were scooping the snow with sand buckets, dumping it into a broken recycling bin. A stupid game it was.

Kids were out, so it had to be Saturday.

The sun was high, and Neil felt its warm rays on his face and shoulders. He had a spontaneous need to run out into the street and bathe in the sun's light, but he was too hungover. It would be a miracle if he made it to the bathroom without falling flat on his face. He rubbed his new beard and scratched his stomach.

Well, well.

He'd chickened out again, it seemed. Another broken promise to himself.

Neil stepped away from the window and padded over to the bed. He jerked the blankets off and fell onto the mattress, temples burning. He needed an aspirin. Something to eat. Maybe a tomato omelet would settle his stomach.

He remembered the night. Parts of it, at least. He cracked an eye open and looked around the bedroom. How much longer could he hang on like this? It was December. He'd sworn to himself that it would be done by the end of November.

It was the boozing. He'd get drunk and sentimental. He'd sit in his armchair and get soft, and then play around with the idea of living. Of finding a reason.

Yeah, but he was sober now.

Neil slowly flipped to his back and studied the ceiling fan. A spiderweb stretched from one of its panels to the left corner of the room, but the spider was nowhere to be seen.

Even it was busy. Out doing something. Maybe meeting up with its mate. Did spiders have mates?

"What the fuck's wrong with you?" Neil grumbled. His voice carried across the room, traveling through the empty house.

And then where?

Where did everything go?

❖

"The thing is, Dr. Scarborough, Ted shuts down as soon as I mention Cody's name, and I don't think that it's fair. To me, to us..."

Jamie glanced over at the clock on the cherry oak table. There were two minutes and forty-one seconds left to Mrs. Hennessy's session. He widened his eyes, trying to concentrate. He crossed his legs, and then uncrossed them. "And why do you think Ted retreats back into himself when you broach that subject with—"

"Are you kidding me?" Mrs. Hennessy yanked another tissue from the box. "Because he's a coward!" With her pudgy little fingers, she wiped her reddened nose and grimaced. "We have to tiptoe around the past and meanwhile, he's on the computer all night, doing God knows what. Well, I know what he does, but he denies it. How can he take me for such an idiot? I know how to check a computer's browsing history, we have three sons for..."

Jamie's eyes drifted to the bookcase; two shelves were overloaded, while one remained half-empty. He'd have to remedy that. Besides, he didn't need all these books. Some of them were quite outdated and could be stored. Had he ordered the new edition of—

"Dr. Scarborough?"

Jamie darted his eyes back to his patient's face. "Yes, go on."

"So what do you think he wants from me? What am I supposed to do, live the rest of my life with a man who can't stand the sight of me?"

Ted, Mrs. Hennessy's husband, was most possibly suffering from depression and struggling with an addiction to pornography. Now, Mrs.

Hennessy was emotionally dependent, with a passive-aggressive nature, and an addictive personality, her drug of choice being deep-fried foods and Laura Secord ice cream.

But of course, they were miles away from discussing it.

Jamie pushed his glasses up and leaned in. "I think you did very well today," he said quietly.

She sniffled. "I'm trying to understand myself. I know that I push him. I know that."

"Do you want some water?"

"Doctor, can I ask you something? I mean, I come here every week, and I tell you my most embarrassing secrets, but I don't even know a single thing about you."

The clock beeped twice and they both turned to look at it. "You can ask me next week," Jamie said. "I promise to answer your questions, if that's what you want."

"Are you married?" Mrs. Hennessy eased her voluptuous figure out of the divan. She gathered her Louis Vuitton purse and sunglasses. "I'm really dying to know." She laughed, but her eyes were still wet and swollen.

The million-dollar question.

"I'm recently separated," he said at length.

"I thought so. You seem gloomy lately." She blushed slightly. "I don't mean to pry."

"Yes, you do. It's a natural reaction at this stage."

"Because I've been coming here for so long."

"That's right."

"Most people do this?"

"Yes." Jamie stepped to the door and rested his hand on the handle. "Have a good week, and I'll see you again next Wednesday."

"You're very good at that."

"What do you mean?"

Mrs. Hennessy's eyes were on his face, green, slightly slanted. Jamie acknowledged her classic beauty. She had sculpted, sensuous lips and a mane of thick, glamorous chestnut hair. He'd never noticed any of these charming attributes before. He'd never truly looked at her.

"You excel at keeping people at a safe distance," she answered.

Her words pricked an open wound inside him and he felt a shadow move over his features.

Mrs. Hennessy stiffened and touched her chest. "I'm sorry, I didn't mean to—"

"It's all right. It's a fair assessment." He opened the door and held it for her. "I'm working on that."

"You should know that a few of us have come up with a nickname for you," she said discreetly.

He glanced around the waiting room, but could meet no one's eyes.

"I see. And what is it?" He tried to keep his tone disinterested.

"Well," she whispered into his ear, enjoying the temporary shift of power in their relationship. "We like to call you *Dr. Heartbreak*."

❖

Dance slipped an apple out of his bag.

Elliot, his best friend and partner in crime, shut the door and locked it. Quick Fix, the massage parlor Elliot had been working at for the last three months—a record for the vagabond—was officially closed for the night. The last customer, a lawyer who drooled if his ears were pinched, had just left. Elliot liked to discuss his clients' quirks and pet peeves. He was a great storyteller. Unreliable and flaky, but a true wordsmith.

"So, what are you gonna do, man?" Elliot asked him, turning the coffee machine off.

Dance nibbled on the Empire apple, today's only meal, watching some pigeons gawk outside the window. Didn't these birds ever migrate? How could they stay here, in this dirty city, when there was a whole Southern, golden world to discover?

"September doesn't want me around," Dance said, swallowing the apple's sour juices along with the truth.

They were at the massage parlor's reception desk, trying to get pumped up for a night of clubbing. Elliot pulled a desk drawer open and produced a bottle of Jameson whiskey from it. He choked on the brown liquor, and then offered it to Dance. "She's your brother, that's not right."

Dance tossed the apple core into the small bin and took a long, miserable breath. The massage parlor smelled of rosewood and vanilla tonight. Sometimes it smelled like spicy peppermint. Elliot was in charge of the aromatherapy. The girls said he had the best nose. It was probably true. Even last summer, when Dance and he had been living in a car together, Elliot had always smelled nice. He cleaned his hair in public restrooms with stolen shampoo samples he stuffed in his pockets when he was shopping for rubbers.

Dance licked his index and thumb and extinguished the last candle on the windowsill. "It's the fire. She's not gonna get over it." He turned back and looked into Elliot's face. Though Elliot pierced and tattooed his skin relentlessly, he still looked like a cherub with midnight black hair. Maybe Elliot was the same as he. Maybe he was just trying to get the child out of his face. "That fire took everything from my brother," Dance said.

"She's had a rough time, but that's no excuse to take it out on you."

Dance blinked, slipping the bottle of whiskey out of Elliot's fingers. "Then what is?"

"I don't understand."

Dance drank from the bottle, letting the alcohol sit on his tongue, swallowing it bit by bit. The burn was fantastic. The night was still young. And what could he do, if not run into it head-on, into the black. Into the city's womb.

"What's going on, Dance?" Elliot flicked his tongue in and out of his lip ring. It was a habit. He had some sort of oral fixation. Rumor was, his blow jobs left guys blank-minded, stumbling around stoned with pleasure for days.

Sometimes Dance tried to convince himself that he was bisexual just to give Elliot's lips a try, but no matter how horny he was, the idea simply wouldn't take.

"Look," Elliot said, "I'm sorry about leaving you between a rock and a hard place, but Ludovic's got abandonment issues, and whenever I mention your name, he throws a shit fit."

Ludovic was Elliot's new father figure. A Frenchman. Divorced. High-strung and whiny. But the man had gotten Elliot off the streets and amphetamines, so maybe Ludovic wasn't such a prick after all.

"I'll be all right," Dance whispered, setting the bottle down on the reception desk. "Let's get outta here, okay?"

The wind rattled the door, causing the welcome bell to jingle, and Elliot jumped. "Whoa." He chuckled nervously. "Do you feel that, man?"

Dance felt many things, none of which Elliot could ever understand. And that's why he enjoyed his company.

"I know you'll be cool, Dance." Elliot went around the desk and squeezed his shoulder. "Just be careful, that's all. This act you've been putting on is a dangerous game, you know?"

No, what was dangerous was reality.

"So, where are we going?" Dance zipped up his sweater, feeling for the reassuring form of his notebook under his T-shirt.

"Can I see?" Elliot moved closer, reaching for the book.

"No." Dance was surprised at the violence in his voice. "It's not finished," he explained, more softly.

For a moment, Elliot's amber stare lingered on his face, inquisitive and intimate, but soon enough, the light in his eyes dimmed.

Pain was contagious, both boys knew it...best not get too close to it.

"Let's go to the village," Elliot said, getting excited. "I need some contact and you sure as hell aren't the man who's gonna give it to me." He winked and unlocked the door. "Right?"

Dance cracked a smile.

Yes, contact. He too needed it tonight. So deeply. So hard. But neither Elliot nor anyone else could provide what he craved. And with that notion, Emma's words resounded inside Dance's mind.

What do you want, Dance?

"So?" Elliot asked, frowning. "Coming?"

❖

Jamie carefully placed his full coffee thermos atop the car's roof and dug into his pocket for the keys. He'd forgotten his gloves. *And scarf.*

The wind lifted off the icy riverbank like a specter and whipped snow into his eyeglasses, fogging the lens.

December, and already Montreal was turning into Neptune.

Anxious and tired, Jamie scoured his surroundings. The Glasshouse staff parking lot was dark. When was Malik going to fix the back lights anyway? This was a mental institution, was it not? Every night, the medical staff scurried to their cars, glancing back over their shoulders, wondering if tonight was the night the patient they'd pissed off without knowing it would come looming around a black corner, syringe full of Clorox in hand.

"Paranoia," Jamie muttered, finding his keys. "And a touch of prejudice." He hurriedly seated himself behind the wheel, shutting the wind out. "Ah, my fingers," he whined, shaking the blood back into them. He threw his cell phone on the passenger seat, turned the engine on, and shifted gears.

There was a thump above his head.

"What the—"

The thermos rolled over the windshield, onto the hood.

Jamie jumped out of the car and shut the door behind him. He picked up the silver container—pleasantly hot against his numb skin—and pulled on the door handle. The door wouldn't open.

Of course it wouldn't.

"Oh. Oh, come on. Oh, no." Jamie tried again, jerking the handle. He peered inside the car, staring at the keys in the ignition, and then his eyes moved to the cell phone lying useless on the seat. "Why?" he asked of no one and everyone. What a day. What a draining, never-ending day. And now this. Last month he'd taken the car to the dealership and had them reprogram the automatic lock. It would be safer. Parked or not, the car doors would lock.

He checked around the lot. No, he wasn't going to snap. No way. And he wasn't going to call Basil either. What was he, a damsel in distress? He was a man. A psychiatrist, for heaven's sake.

Jamie twisted the cap off his hot drink and swilled a third of it down. The coffee warmed his chest and gave him a jolt. "All right," he said to the wind. "All right then."

In long strides, his shallow breaths coming faster and faster, Jamie made his way through the immense parking lot to the emergency room sliding doors.

Inside, he was greeted by strikingly hot air and complete chaos. It had been months since his last stop to the ER, and now he remembered why he worked at the other end of the building. In here, he wasn't Dr. James Scarborough. No, in here, he was the lunatic with the imagined congestive heart failures.

"James," Antone called out. "Yo, my man, you all right?" Antone crossed the crowded waiting room. He was a head taller than everyone here. Undisputed king of the Glasshouse basketball court, Antone handled his patients as he did the ball: efficiently, with great care—never taking his dark espresso eyes off them. The male nurse had the two most sought-out traits in the ER. Compassion and physical strength.

Jamie smiled and waved. He could feel puddles of sweat gather under his armpits. He hadn't eaten since breakfast, and in an effort to convince himself that he was truly tackling his panic disorder, he'd skipped the afternoon's Ativan.

The panic attack was inching closer. A great white with glassy black eyes, circling him patiently.

"You okay?" Antone asked, nearing him. "It's gonna be tough getting you an EKG tonight—"

"No, it's…I don't need anything. Well, I need a—"

"You're sweating a lot." Antone touched his arm. "It's kind of hectic in here, isn't it?" Gently, but firmly, Antone pulled him away from the main waiting room, into a smaller room. "Hey, why don't you sit over here and—"

"I'm fine," Jamie repeated, trying to believe it, but he sat, obedient. He glanced around. Two nurses were drawing blood from a man's arm. One held him down while the other fiddled with the needle. It was a long, sharp needle. When it pricked the man's throbbing vein, Jamie's vision doubled and he leaned back on the seat of his chair. "Oh, that's horrible," he sighed, closing his eyes. Even in med school, he'd gotten weak knees at the sound of the word *intravenous*.

Now all he needed to do was faint, and his reputation for being the most melodramatic patient would be secured.

Antone pressed his thumb against his wrist. "Okay, put your head between your knees and breathe."

"I just need to call—"

"Watch it!" Antone yelled at the nurses, lunging for the man on the table. "He's puking."

Jamie caught a glimpse of the curdled liquid oozing out of the man's mouth, and disgusted, he quickly turned his head in the other direction.

He jerked his collar open and sat up straight, trying to bring his diaphragm down.

"Help me flip him." Antone and the other nurses were struggling with the man. "And gimme some gloves!"

Jamie shot out of his chair.

Can't breathe. Can't breathe.

He scuffled down the hall, passing stretchers and wheelchairs, shoved into a door, flew up two flights of stairs, then four others, stumbled into a hallway, ran around corners, and at last, tumbled into an empty washroom. Wild, he shut the door behind him, flipped the toilet seat closed, and fell back on it.

❖

Inside the washroom, Jamie flicked the light on.

"What did you do to yourself?" he asked his reflection.

Who was this phantom in the mirror?

He ran the tap, removed his glasses, set them gently on the toilet seat, and cupped his hands under the warm water. He splashed his face and smoothed his hair back. His shirt was drenched with sweat. His mouth tasted like metal. With his elbow, he pressed on the paper dispenser and ripped a piece of brown tissue out of it. As best he could, he wiped off his face, forehead, and neck.

"That was a bad one," he said. "But you made it. You got through it."

He put on his glasses.

He leaned back on the wall behind him, staring at himself. How could he have allowed himself to get in this state? He looked like an escaped POW. How long had he been in this washroom? It seemed like hours. He glanced at his watch, but couldn't recall when he'd left the office.

Jamie touched his throat and his left eyebrow. "You're all right now."

Outside, he heard some commotion. He stared at the door, wide-eyed.

Oh no, were they looking for him?

He adjusted his shirt and jacket, his free hand hovering over the door handle.

"Jamie?" a woman called out, close, very close to the door. "Are you in there?"

He retracted from the door, frozen.

Christina. Immediately, Jamie recognized her girlish voice, though he hadn't seen her in over a year. They'd been close once. Good friends. Then she'd met her girlfriend and naturally, their friendship had dwindled to a few e-mails here and there.

What was she doing here?

There was a knock and Christina called his name again. "Jamie?"

"Just a minute," he said, staring at the handle.

"Oh, thank God! Are you okay?"

"I'm fine, just hold on." He turned to the mirror one more time, hoping the last minute had worked a miracle on his gaunt face, but no, he looked even worse. He couldn't hide in here all night, now could he?

No.

At last, he mustered the courage to open the door a sliver. "I'm sorry," he mumbled, "I had a panic attack and—"

"Look at you." Christina, dressed in full paramedic uniform, moved closer to him. "Everyone's really worried about you. Your car—"

"Right, right." Slowly, the evening's turbulence rippled through him. "I left my keys in the ignition and my phone and—"

"Don't worry, your boyfriend's here and I think he called for someone to—"

"My boyfriend," Jamie said, heart sinking. "You called him."

"Yeah, of course. When you disappeared, Antone went looking for you and then they found your car and—"

"Right." Jamie turned from her, headed for the elevator.

It was past ten p.m. So, to come out here, Basil would have had to dress the kids and drag them out into the cold. *Here.* A mental institution's emergency room. Basil hated the Glasshouse. He hated the snow. He hated being awake after nine p.m.

"Jamie? Wait up." Christina met him and called up the elevator. "What happened tonight? Do you wanna talk about it?"

Jamie stared at the linoleum floor, conjuring up various catastrophic scenarios. Basil would be pissed beyond reason. This was it. This was the final act.

"Hey." Christina nudged him. "Say something."

"I'm sorry. I'm just really wiped out." He glanced over at her. "What are you doing here?"

"I work here. Transferred last month. I meant to come see you, but we ER people don't like to venture out into your wing." She winked. "How you been?"

He stifled an inappropriate laugh. "I'm great."

"Yeah?" She looked him up and down. "You sure look like it."

Silent, they rode the elevator down to the main floor. When the doors opened, Christina squeezed his hand. "I'm done for the night, so I'll see you later."

He nodded, his eyes searching the crowded waiting room. "Thanks for—"

"Listen, Jamie, I know now's not the time, but I have this friend—"

"Christina, I'm sorry, but I can't even think straight right now." Jamie stood by the elevator doors, his gaze bouncing off every face in the ER waiting room.

"Right. Bad timing."

"Call me Monday, or at home tomorrow, all right? We'll talk. I'll give you all the time you need."

"Thank you, Jamie." She dropped a kiss on his cheek and tossed her head in the coffee machine's direction. "Ah, there's your man. You know, I never met him before tonight, funny, huh? He's gorgeous. Lucky you." She spun around and walked away.

Jamie could not move. His feet were fused into the floor. He stared at Basil's profile, paralyzed.

He'd messed up good this time. He'd really really blown it.

Slowly, as if he'd sensed the heat of his stare, Basil turned his eyes to him.

"Oh," Jamie heard himself moan. "Keep it together."

Basil tossed his paper cup into the garbage, and leaped through the packed room, bumping into a chair on his way. His eyes were on fire. His hair was disheveled. He was wearing his Kanuck coat over his pajamas. His boots were still unlaced.

Jamie shrank back into his clothes. "I'm sorry, Baz. I'm really sorry. I didn't ask them to—"

"Oh, fuck, baby," Basil whispered, pulling him into his arms. "Oh, Jamie."

Losing all notion of where they were, Jamie leaned into Basil, ignoring the curious stares they were getting. "I'm okay, Baz. I'm okay."

Basil's chest seem to constrict, and his arms dropped. He stepped back, eyes clouding over. "Do you know what it was like driving here thinking that maybe—" But he stopped, shaking his head.

"I had a bad day and I don't know what happened, but I didn't mean to—"

"I thought you'd done it, you know. I thought you'd finally had one that had sent you off the edge and you'd done it to yourself." Basil wouldn't look at him. He gazed out into space, reliving some nightmare.

"No, what—"

"Don't you think I remember what this month is?" Basil recomposed himself, moving back. "All right, the locksmith's on his way. The kids are in bed and—"

"Because of Mickey. Because of the anniversary of my brother's death? You think I'd kill myself, Baz, huh?" Jamie's voice rose. "You really think I would do that? Who do you think I am? What about the kids—"

"Don't you yell at me after the stunt you pulled tonight."

"Look at me, I'm not yelling. I'm calm. I'm—"

"No, you're not calm, Jamie, you're sedate. That's your two modes. Hanging off the ceiling, or—"

"Or boring? That's what you were going to say."

Around them, nurses and orderlies hurried from one crisis to another. Exhausted friends paced the waiting room, cups of cooling coffee in hand.

Basil looked around, as if seeing the anarchy of the place for the first time. "You shouldn't work here," he said.

He'd said it before. Over and over.

"I love my work—"

"Yeah, I know. You keep telling me." Basil backed away, moving to the exit doors. "This is your home. Your whole fucking life."

"Baz, wait."

"No, I'm going home. My home." Basil turned his back to him and walked out.

Jamie hesitated, then leaped for the doors, exiting the warm entrance, running out into what had become a blizzard. The world was a snow globe, hostage to a furious child. "Basil," he called out, his voice muted by the wind. He pulled the bottom of his jacket over his face, shielding his skin from the hard snow, and ran to the staff parking lot, skidding dangerously on the icy patches. He spotted a company minivan parked by his car, its yellow lights cutting through the white air. He could make out the form of a man hunched over his car door, working on the lock. Good, then. That was being taken care of.

Determined to get the last word, Jamie looked around the lot. He could almost feel Basil watching him. But where was he?

Jamie walked to his car. "How long do you think it will take?" he shouted against the wind, tapping the man's heavily cloaked shoulder. The man shot him a side glance. "You're in," he yelled back, popping the door open.

Jamie thanked him and jumped into the nicely heated car. He checked the fuel gauge.

He had more than enough gas to get to where he was going.

❖

"Just a sip, please." Dance pushed the cup of chicken broth into September's limp hand. "You gotta eat something. Come on. Please."

September sat across from him, slumped over in her chair, staring at the kitchen table. Every once in a while, the wind shook the windows and the candles flickered. "No," she whispered, pushing the cup back into his hand.

An hour ago, Dance had found her sprawled out on the kitchen floor, barely conscious. He'd come to her apartment on a hunch. He'd left the club in a hurry and rode the bus using Elliot's bus pass. Yes, sometime between the tenth and eleventh Jagermeister shots, Dance had frozen up, and over the blaring club music, he'd told Elliot that he *just had to go.*

It was a twin thing.

"Where were you tonight?" September's hair clung to her sweaty forehead. "You smell like baby powder."

"I was at a bar." Dance smelled his sleeve. "And you're smelling Elliot. He throws talcum over his clothes, says it makes older men crazy."

A dry cackle was his brother's only reply. September moved in her chair and leaned back, listless again. "Hand me a cigarette, will you?"

Dance looked around for her pack and found it under an empty bag of rice biscuits. "You ate these?" he asked, handing her the cigarettes.

"No, I smoke them." September plucked a cigarette out of the pack and lit it, blowing circles of smoke into the still air.

"I meant the crackers." Dance seated himself on the chair next to hers. "I don't want you to die, Seth," he said, his voice shaking. "I know it's hard. I know—"

"Hard?" September echoed the word, flicking the ashes into the overloaded ashtray. "Do you think dying is what I'm doing?"

"Yes." Dance leaned in, his eyes dissecting his brother's beautiful, heartbreaking face.

"You're wrong, Dance. This is me being born."

"Oh, don't give me that. Don't make this out to be about transitioning. I don't care about that bullshit."

September seemed to hesitate—a comeback forming on her lips—but settled back into her chair.

"You can tell me this is about genetics," Dance said. "Chromosomes. Mother Nature fucking with your head. Getting the wrong package at the soul factory. But you know, being a transwoman is the only sane thing about you."

"You're nuts."

"And you're an anorexic with an addiction to prescription pills."

September's eyes darted up. Gray and cool. "Mom and Dad did great, didn't they?" She sucked in a deep drag of her cigarette and crushed it into the other butts.

"So you admit it," Dance said. "You admit that you have an eating disorder."

"Yes, Dance, I admit that I have an eating disorder."

"Do you want help?"

September smirked. "No, Dance, I don't want help."

"But—"

"You know what I want, brother?" September slammed her frail hand on the tabletop, toppling the cup of broth over. "I want you to stop coming around here! And I want my eighty thousand dollars back! Can you do that for me, huh?" Her voice boomed across the small kitchen, strained, yet stronger than ever. "Write me a goddamn check." She laughed, reaching for another cigarette. "Can you do that, Dance?"

Dance sat, transfixed. The chicken broth trickled over the edge of the table onto his thigh—hot, but not scalding.

"Guess not, huh," September said, exhaling a curl of smoke through her nose. "No one can give me back what I lost that night. No one. So, whatever you're doing here, this brotherly love you're selling, I don't want it. I don't need it."

"Did you ever think that maybe you lost that cash because—"

"If you say the word *faith*, I'll cut your fucking balls off."

Dance winced. "You hate me."

"I'm trying hard not to." September's gaze drifted again. There was a vacant look in her eyes. "Take off. Go south, like you always dreamed of—"

"I'll check up on you tomorrow," Dance said, getting to his feet. His knees were shaky, but he hung on. "Get some rest."

September nodded, staring at the window. "I'm sending you out into the storm, am I?"

"Yeah, you are." Dance kissed his brother's head. "But I'll be safer out there."

❖

Jamie parked the car behind Matt's Durango truck, his stomach tightening. "Oh, you little shit," he cursed between clenched teeth. What was Matt doing here!

Jamie stepped out of the car, ran up the front steps, slipped and nearly fell into the frozen shrubs to his left. He couldn't remember the drive here. Only the sensation of clutching the steering wheel, trying to see the road between the movement of the wipers.

He didn't ring the bell. He used his key. After all, he still was paying half of the mortgage, was he not? Yes, he was. Damn straight. But as he entered the quiet house, his anger, like the snow on his hair and shoulders, melted—both unable to withstand the warmth of the Spasso home.

Inside the entrance, Jamie gazed over the untidy living room, his eyes pausing on the avocado green love seat. At the sight of it, memories of Basil's naked skin, the way they'd touched each other, came taunting him. He had to force himself to look away.

"Doc? Are you okay? What are you doing here?"

Startled, Jamie spun around. "I should ask you that same question."

Matt stood in the hall that connected the kitchen to the living room, a glass of water in hand. He wore only his skimpy little Calvin Klein shorts.

"Where's Basil?" Jamie asked, his jaw tight with tension, jealousy, and a need to claw Matt's pretty face to shreds.

"He's out looking for you, Doc."

"Don't call me that." Jamie threw his wet jacket over the door handle and walked to the mini-bar. "Kids all right?" he asked, trying to keep from hurling the bottle of Canadian Club at the wall. There was a tremor in his hands, but he managed to pour himself a double. He threw it back like medicine.

"I better call him, then," Matt said, moving to the phone on the foot table. "He was really worried. They found your car and...What happened? Where were you?"

"Don't bother calling him." The liquor was working its magic, traveling through Jamie's chest and belly, smoothing all edges off. "I saw Basil at the Glasshouse, but he left me in the parking lot. Very considerate of him, of course."

Matt lolled his head, staring uneasily at the hardwood floor, his baby blue eyes shadowed by the thick black fringe of his lashes. He was probably blushing. It was too dark to see.

"Are you the only one he's fucking?" Jamie asked, coolly.

Matt was always tender and generous. Hard to despise.

But he could try, damn it. He could try. "Well?" Jamie insisted, shivering.

"What did you think would happen, Jamie? Did you think a guy like Basil would—"

"I asked you a question. Is there anybody else besides you?"

Matt sighed, folding his slender arms over his bare skin. "You should thank me. I'm keeping Baz on track."

"In that case, thank you, Matt. Thank you for keeping my side of the bed warm—"

"He's seeing a woman." Matt was serious. "Good-looking, too. Her niece goes to school with Marsh and Mal."

Jamie's head filled with hot air. "What?"

"Yeah," Matt said, sniffling nervously. "Says he's done with men. Says he's going to explore his bisexuality."

Jamie plopped down into the arm chair, deflated. "A woman." He looked over at Matt. "Now I'm never getting him back."

Matt eased his long, smooth, twenty-three-year-old body into the couch next to him, fidgeting with a pillow. "Do you want something to eat, Doc? You look like you've had a rough night."

Jamie closed his eyes, surrendering to the fatigue.

A woman.

"No," he said, turning his eyes to Matt's angelic face. "Just pour us a drink, please."

CHAPTER FOUR

Someone is calling his name.

Neil?

His father, yes, calling for him.

His father needs a blanket.

More morphine, son. Do it right for Daddy.

No, Neil doesn't want to go into the old man's musty bedroom, no.

He is building a space station, plugging the blue and red Legos into each other, and he's almost finished.

"Neil, wake up."

Confused, Neil opened his eyes and threw his arm over them. "Turn the damn light off," he groaned.

"The lights are off. It's just sunny in here."

Through his heavy lids, Neil discerned John's face. What was John the idiot doing in his bedroom?

There was the sound of feathery steps at the foot of his bed, and then Christina's face appeared above his head. "Neil, here." She offered him a mug. "Coffee."

He refused it.

"Hey, man, long time no see." John was fidgeting at the side of his bed. He picked up an empty bottle of beer and stared at it. "You growing these or something? They're everywhere."

Christina laughed, but her face was tense. "We knocked and knocked, but—"

"What do you want?" Neil pulled himself up and leaned back on his elbows. His eyes pulsed. "Oh, Jesus, get me an aspirin."

John and Christina exchanged a look, and in hurried steps, John left the room.

"What is he doing here? Get him outta here." Neil sat up, pushing the sheets off his legs.

Christina flicked her eyes to the floor. "Put some pants on."

Neil looked down at himself.

Whoa.

He glanced around for pants, but there were none, so he pulled the sheet over his naked crotch. "You can't just barge in here 'cause I don't answer my door."

"We're worried, okay?" Christina dared a glance up. "This place, Neil, it's a disaster. You can't live like this—"

"I've been busy. Haven't had the time to—"

"Busy? Doing what? Getting drunk?"

"Among other things."

John returned with the aspirin before Christina could reply. He dropped two tablets into Neil's hand and backed away. Poor sap, he didn't want to be here either. John liked to pretend he was a stand-up guy, but he was just a loser in desperate need of approval. Someone says jump, and he jumps twice. Weak and selfless, that's John.

"We wanna talk to you," Christina said, carefully seating herself on the edge of the mattress. "We're thinking of going to the animal shelter and picking you out a pup—"

"Sounds great." Neil lay back on his pillow. "Why don't you do that? Surprise me."

"I told you he'd be like this," John said between tight lips.

"What's happening to you?" Christina touched his hand. The touch sent a jolt of panic through Neil and he stiffened. Christina started wringing her hands. "They'll take you back, you know. If you get yourself together and fight for it, they'll take you back."

"I don't wanna go back," Neil said, his eyes steady on John.

John's shocked expression was ridiculous. Of course, John couldn't imagine a life without fires. He'd built his whole existence around the flames.

"So, what are you gonna do with your life?" John asked, a look of wonder on his face. "You got plans?"

Plans?

Plans were ideas people entertained in order to justify their mediocre existence. Neil held back a chuckle. This guy was something else. He almost wanted John to stay all day. This was better than television. "Yeah, I got plans," Neil said. "Are we done here?" He popped the aspirin into his mouth. He reached for a beer bottle on the nightstand and swilled the last of it, washing the pills down. Warm as piss.

"I'm gonna get going." John stuffed his hands into his pockets and retreated backward to the door. "I'll see you soon, big guy. Maybe you could swing by during the holidays. Jenny would like that."

Neil's face twitched a little, but he frowned and nodded, pushing down the unknown emotion threatening to overwhelm him. "Sure," he said.

When John shut the front door behind him, Christina rose and flashed a smile. "There was another reason for me coming." She went to the window and peeked out. She was nervous or something. Probably lying. "Um, I have a friend and he's such a klutz. He's not the manual type of guy, you know what I mean?" She didn't wait for his response. She went on with her charade. "I was thinking that since you're so good at wood finishing, well, you see—"

"What do you want, Chris? Get to the point."

She spun around. Her face was lit up. Whether it was from fear or excitement, he couldn't tell. "Would you help him refinish a piece? It's very dear to him. It's an antique buffet he inherited from his grandmother, and he's very busy—"

"Busy doing what? Being a shrink?"

Her whole head, ears, neck, everything, turned crimson. It was priceless.

She looked over at the bedroom door, then back at him, tears threatening to spill over her cheeks. He could see her throat throbbing with a restrained sob. She was hopeless and broken down. He'd gone too far.

"What does he need done?" he asked.

This girl. This damn girl. Standing there in his bedroom, with her stupid gigantic heart and her quivering lips.

She watched him, halfway between the doorway and his bed, confused. Soon enough, she composed herself and swiftly wiped her eyes with the back of her blouse sleeve. "It's…you'd have to ask him. I'll give him a call and we could come over and you guys could figure it out."

He was agreeing to see a fucking headshrinker.

Okay. Could be fun.

Neil raised a finger. "But call me first, okay? Don't come walking into my bedroom with your little shrink friend."

She smiled and took a shaky breath. "I promise." She went to the bed and leaned toward him, but he moved back. She straightened up. "You'll clean up a little? Jamie's a bit of a neat freak."

"Don't push it."

Christina turned away, heading out. "But he's also very sweet, you'll like him."

A sweet, neat freak.

No such thing.

❖

Dance shifted his weight from one leg to the other, blowing into his hands.

He banged on the door again, trying to see into the apartment. "Come on, Elliot," he pleaded under his scarf. "Come on."

It was eleven a.m. Saturday morning. Elliot had to be home. He just had to.

Dance rang the bell again, glancing around. This was a nice part of town. The high Plateau. A little too artsy-fartsy for his taste, but perfect for Elliot Nelligan, the aspiring playwright. Or was it Elliot Nelligan, the aspiring film director?

"Open the door." Dance wiggled his toes inside his boots and pulled his sweater's hood over his cap.

Last night, after he'd left September's apartment, he'd gotten the last bed at the Bunker, but when Emma stubbornly tried to coax him into attending group therapy this morning, he'd skipped out of there pronto. Since then, Dance had been walking around, checking out the store windows. Everything sugar and spice. He had nothing else to do. He had a few dollars left, but that wouldn't take him far. The holidays were coming and people got real stingy around that time of the year. Consumerism; the enemy of the panhandler. You'd ask these people for a quarter, and they'd glare at you, clutching their shopping bags full of gifts they couldn't afford to buy.

The only way he would ever squeeze a penny out of anyone this month was if he found a way to swipe credit cards with his butt crack.

Dance felt for his notebook under his shirt. Still there. He turned to look at the snow banks and banged his frozen knuckles on the door again. He was hungry—in dire need of some eggs and bread, but he obviously wasn't going to get either of those things here. He turned to leave, but stopped, feeling a warm draft of air on his back.

He spun around. "Finally," he cried.

"Sorry, I was sleeping. How long have you been out here?" Elliot stood in the doorway, half-hidden behind the door, dressed in blue and white striped pajamas.

"What are you wearing?" Dance stepped into the pleasant apartment and shut the cold out behind them.

"Ludo likes me in these."

They filed down the hall, quietly, aware of each crack on the floor.

In the kitchen, Elliot plucked open the stainless steel fridge door. "I think we're okay. Ludo took some of his sleeping pills last night. He should be asleep for at least another hour." He grabbed the egg box and various vegetables. Mushrooms. Green bell peppers.

Dance's mouth watered as he dropped two pieces of whole wheat bread into the fancy toaster. "Did you watch *Ren and Stimpy* last night?"

Elliot was fixing himself a bowl of Rice Krispies. "I missed it. Which one was it? Ludo was a fucking mess yesterday. My ass hurts." Elliot drank from the milk carton and poured the rest into his cereal. "He's got this thing, man, you should see it. It's like big like this"—he knotted his fist—"and it's got sprinkles on it."

Dance cringed, slicing the mushrooms with caution and precision. His fingers were still numb. He looked up into the kitchen window above the counter and caught sight of a young woman across the yard, smoking a cigarette on her balcony. She was in her robe, smoking and watching a bird peck the frozen ground. Her brown hair flew in and out of her eyes. She was pretty, with an angry face. A flawless combination of angst and need.

"What are you gonna do today?" Elliot asked.

"I might go to a spoken word thing on Saint-Laurent." Dance started chopping the pepper, still watching the girl. She was lonely, that's what it was. Most beautiful girls were. Especially the smokers.

"Oh yeah? You want some company?"

Dance set the knife down and stared at the cutting board.

What was he going to do with his life?

"Dance?"

"You don't have to keep doing this, you know," Dance said, staring back into Elliot's face.

Elliot's cheeks were rosy. He was a little dimpled-faced boy. And he'd survived. He'd made it out of the streets. How? And why?

"I wanna do this," Elliot said, pouting. "You know I love you like mad."

Dance looked away, studying the ceramic floor instead.

Love.

"Hey." Elliot slipped out of his seat and neared him. "Fuck me?" he asked with a grin.

"I love you too, okay?" Dance slapped Elliot's shoulder. "And I'm gonna be all right."

"I know you will. You'll find your fish."

Yes, he would.

And he had an idea how.

❖

Neil wiped his hands down the front of his jeans, glancing around the living room again.

His heart raced. And what for? Not like he had to impress this guy. Just had to convince him that he was mentally stable. All nuts and bolts in place. Then Christina would leave him alone. She'd move on to another project.

"Okay, boy," he said to Hemi, "you gotta get me through this. Nice and easy."

He'd started doing that last week. Talking to the dead dog. Over a quiet dinner of macaroni and cheese, Neil had turned his attention to the kitchen corner and asked Hemingway how he liked his new Nylabone.

Now he couldn't stop doing it.

The bell rang and Neil stared at the door. "Nice and easy," he repeated, walking up to the entrance. When he passed the mirror, he looked over at his reflection. He was clean-shaven, black shirt tucked in, socks on.

The bell rang again, and then a knock.

Christina, the patient Madonna.

Neil reached for the door handle and stopped. Damn, he was going to give himself a heart attack if he didn't calm down. He hadn't spoken to another human being—save for Chris and John—for over a month. Or maybe it was more than that. But it was like riding a bike, right?

Probably.

When Christina knocked again, Neil sucked in a short breath and opened the door.

"Hey, stranger," she said, a strained smile on her face. "You look great." She kissed his cheek. "Wow, you smell nice, too."

"Where's your friend?" Neil glimpsed the street over her shoulder.

"He'll be here in five minutes." Christina entered and slipped her coat off. She wore a pink cardigan sweater and blue jeans. Had he ever seen her in pink before? "Jamie thought it would be better if you and I had a few minutes—"

"All right. Sit down. You want a beer?"

"No, thanks."

A few minutes to do what exactly?

Shrinks.

Every single thing was an event with these guys. Something to discuss, analyze, ponder, dwell on.

Neil grabbed a Heineken out of the fridge and twisted its cap off. "I'm not liking this, Hem. I'm not liking this one bit."

"Who you talking to in there?" Christina asked from the living room.

He'd better be careful or he'd end up at the Glasshouse, spending his days drooling over crossword puzzles. "Nobody," he said, walking back to her.

"Do you wanna know a little bit about him?" Christina leaned back into the seat. She was at ease here.

"Not really, no." Neil sat in the armchair. The shrink would have to sit next to her. They could stare at him from the couch all afternoon.

"He's young and quite brilliant. His father is a child psychiatrist. Maybe you know him, Dr. Donald Scarborough? Anyway, he wrote a controversial book on sensory transfers—"

"Fascinating." Neil gulped his beer.

"Jamie's twin brother died when they were little. There was a snow storm and they were both buckled into their car seats. Their nanny was trying to get the ice off the windshield, and of course, she'd left the car running so the boys would be warm, but something malfunctioned, and unknown to her, exhaust filled the car. For some reason, Jamie got out of his seat and the car. He thinks that maybe he wanted to taste the snow." She paused. For effect, probably. "Mickey, Jamie's brother, died within minutes, and to this day, Jamie—" There was a knock at the door and she jumped to her feet, clasping her hands, staring at him intently. "You'll be nice, right?" She hurried to the door. "He's very sweet and—"

"Yeah, you said that before. Open the door, will you?"

Nice and easy.

This would be a breeze. Most shrinks were themselves complete lunatics. Pill poppers. Frazzled, looking for their mama. He'd nail this. No doubt.

"Neil, this is Dr. Scarborough, my friend."

What? This guy was a shrink? Impossible.

Maybe he played a shrink on daytime soap operas.

"Hi, nice to meet you," Scarborough said, offering his hand. "Thank you for agreeing to help me. I really love that buffet, and it's been sitting in my boyfriend's...my friend's...my *ex-friend's* garage for months now."

The doc was flustered, babbling a little.

Neil pumped his hand—soft as satin, but rough around the knuckles, and cold as the dead. "Hi," he said, and for some reason, could say nothing more.

"Let's sit down," Christina suggested with exaggerated cheer. "Jamie, do you want something to drink?"

Neil stared at the young doctor in disbelief.

Really now, a shrink?

"I'm fine. I don't need anything, thank you." Scarborough removed his coat and dropped it gently over the edge of the armchair. He sat in the damned armchair—not the couch—and poured some hand sanitizer into his cupped hand. He scrubbed his fingers, looking up at Neil.

Deer-like eyes. Haunted. Deep as the night, gentle yet impenetrable.

"Neil? Come sit down," Christina said.

Neil sat by her, trying to rein in his thoughts.

He was losing his marbles here and he needed to get every one of them back in the sachet, and fast.

"You're a firefighter, Chris tells me."

Scarborough's long nose was slightly crooked, and the doctor grew his hair long around the ears because his ears probably stuck out. Plus he wore glasses. He was definitely a geek. "I *was* a firefighter," Neil said, relaxing a bit. He wasn't going to let those ebony eyes intimidate him. "So, you wanna show me a picture of this buffet?"

Scarborough sat watching him; a prey and hunter all at once.

"Yes," Scarborough said at last, "do you have a computer? They're all in my USB key."

"It's in my bedroom." Had he just invited the doc to his bedroom? He was so out of it. This guy was hypnotizing him with his limpid voice and giant black eyes.

"Guys, oh, I just remembered," Christina said, getting to her feet, heading to the entrance. "I gotta pick up Judd at the courthouse, and—"

"What?" He shot her a deadly look. "I thought we were gonna—"

"Yeah, I know." She threw her coat on. "But you're in good hands." She bade Jamie a speedy farewell and left them, door slamming behind her.

Neil clutched his beer bottle, his eyes still fixed to the door.

What the?

He was now alone in his house with a perfect stranger. A shrink, no less.

Scarborough cleared his throat. "I apologize, I didn't intend for us to be alone. I hope this doesn't make you uncomfortable."

"It's a little weird, yeah."

"Neil, I don't like to lead people on, and I don't enjoy false premises, so I'll have to go against Chris's opinion on this and be frank with you."

"I know why you're here. I just went along with her story to shut her up."

"I thought so." At once, Scarborough rose and touched his neck, and then his eyebrow. His face was flushed pink. "Can I have a glass of water?" he asked, fiddling with his collar button.

"You all right?" Neil stood, setting his beer down on the coffee table. The doc looked like he was going to blow a fuse. "You need some air?"

"I'm sorry"—Scarborough stumbled back to the front door—"I think I should go." He opened his mouth as if to yawn and then fumbled for the handle. "I don't feel well," he whispered, opening the door.

See?

Nuts, completely nuts.

Neil stood with the doctor's coat in his hands. "Hey, wait a minute." He followed him out.

Scarborough was on the porch, leaning over the rail.

"Put your coat on," Neil said. What was happening? Had he said something wrong? Was it the smell in the house? Too hot in there, maybe.

Scarborough straightened up, but didn't face him. He stood quietly, his eyes on the empty street. "I'm very embarrassed," he said. He spun around and took his coat out of Neil's fingers. "I have a colleague who could see you, if you'd like. She's very good, the best really. She mostly treats patients suffering from major depression and—"

"Wait a minute, what's going on?" The cold air seeped into Neil's sweater, giving him goose bumps. He watched Scarborough drape his coat over his shoulders. "Doc? You have asthma or something?"

The doctor shook his head, wheezing still. "No, I—"

"Come inside for a minute. It's freezing out here."

"I'm going to speak to my colleague and—"

"Why do you wanna pass me along to your colleague?"

Scarborough's whole body was tense like a stretched bow. "I really need to go." He flew down the icy stairs, rushing to his car. "I'm sorry," he said over his shoulder. "I'll have my assistant call you."

Neil stood in the doorway, staring on, mouth agape. When the neurotic doctor had driven away, he entered the house and shut the door.

This was Christina's good friend?

No wonder the girl had issues.

❖

Jamie stood at his office sink, scrubbing his hands raw.

He'd spent the early part of the afternoon with Mr. Cochrane—probable agoraphobia coupled with a budding dissociative disorder—nodding his way through another session. All the while, he had silently cursed himself, yes, making an extensive list of every single one of his own defects and faults. He was turning thirty-seven next month, yet not only was his panic disorder worsening, it now threatened his career. He'd never come undone around a patient, either potential or actual, and that small achievement had regulated his self-esteem, keeping it barely above the self-loathing line.

But that streak was over. And he still couldn't understand why.

What had triggered that morning's anxiety attack? Why did he have to embarrass himself that way? Christina trusted him. She was genuinely concerned for Mr. McClure. And Jamie had agreed to the white lie as a means to an end, confident that after a few meetings with Neil McClure, he'd have a better perspective on the man's mental state. According to Chris, Neil McClure had been acting irrationally in the last year, putting his fellow firefighters at risk, and as a consequence of his behavior, he'd been sent home on sick leave. Then he'd been forced to have his dog put down. Those were fairly dramatic events, but if Mr. McClure accepted addressing these issues quickly, the damage would be minimal.

Hence, on his way to Mr. McClure's home, Jamie had been optimistic—in full possession of his faculties.

Ten lousy minutes into their first encounter, he'd been overcome with panic.

Nice job.

His cell phone rang and Jamie slipped it out of his pocket, staring at Matt's number blinking on the screen. "What now?" He opened his office door a wedge. "I'm going to take this personal call," he said to Marie-Miel discreetly, refraining from looking around the waiting room. "Five minutes, tops. And you can send my next appointment in, thank you." She acquiesced with a nod. He closed the door all the way and fell back into his divan. "What is it, Matt?" he answered curtly.

"Oh, I thought I'd leave a message." Matt was outside. The wind howled into the phone. "You're at work, right?"

Exhausted, Jamie rubbed his eyes under his glasses. The holidays sent his patients over the edge, thus his clinic was booked like a cheap hotel on spring break. "Is everything all right?" he asked Matt.

"Yeah, sure." Matt was out of breath. What on earth was he doing?

"Where are you?" Jamie asked.

"On the bike path, jogging."

Jamie glanced over at the window. Heavy snowflakes danced in the wind. "And Basil?"

"On the job. I'm meeting him in NDG in an hour." Matt must have slowed his pace because his voice had stopped jumping. "I was thinking…there's this really quaint little Greek restaurant by my place. And they serve the best fried calamari in town. You like seafood, right? I think you'd like it. I mean, you'd enjoy the food."

Jamie sat up, his cheeks burning up.

What?

"On Mondays, it's practically empty. Nice, you know," Matt went on, more confidently. "Hardly anyone there."

Impossible.

Matt?

Matt was pure beefcake. *Queer As Folk* material. The blond was a man with a specific type, and that type was positively *not* a skinny nervous man with eyeglasses. In the five years they'd known each other, Matt had always been uneasy around him. Every time Jamie walked into the room, Matt would cut short whatever conversation he was having with Basil, and find a reason to leave.

"Hello? Jamie?"

What kind of game was Matt playing anyway?

Only one way to find out.

"Yes, I'm here," Jamie said, pushing his glasses up his nose.

"So, do you wanna have dinner with me?" Matt asked.

Ah! He'd never trusted the little slut. Jamie nodded, smiling. "Sure. Why not?"

"Really?" Matt sounded genuinely surprised, *but* he'd taken acting classes last year, and obviously, they'd paid off. It was an Oscar-worthy performance. "Very cool," Matt said. "I could meet you at the clinic—"

"No, we'll meet there. I should be wrapped up here at seven."

If Matt wanted to play, then they'd play.

"It's on the corner of Park—"

"I know the place, Matt. You and Basil go there all the time." Jamie hung up, shaking his head. Well, well. Interesting turn of events. Matt the home breaker wanted to raise the stakes, it seemed.

There was a rasp on the door and Marie-Miel popped her face in. "I'm sorry, but they're piling up in here."

"I'm all done, send the next one in." Jamie rose, smoothing out the shallow wrinkles of his pants. "Mrs. Ford, right?"

"She canceled, remember?" Marie-Miel opened the door wider, motioning to someone. "Dr. Scarborough will see you now."

At the sight of his next patient now leaning up against the doorway, Jamie grinned. "I didn't think I'd see you until spring." he said.

"Yeah, well." Dance Young shrugged. "I got a favor to ask you."

❖

Jamie sat in his leather armchair, cross-legged, studying Dance Young's ravishing but well-hidden face.

"How long has she been this way?" he asked the boy.

They'd been discussing Dance's sister for nearly twenty minutes, but Jamie had yet to understand the urgency. September was moody, Dance explained. Perhaps depressed.

They weren't getting anywhere. The only thing the boy seemed to be interested in was the plate of falafel Marie-Miel had had the presence of mind to offer him. Dance ate with a voracious appetite, forgetting to chew.

"You mean anorexic?" Dance asked, his mouth packed with the last of the meal.

Jamie stole a look at his notes. He'd jotted nothing about an eating disorder. "You didn't use that word." He uncrossed his legs and leaned in to gather the empty plate. Dance had practically licked it clean. "Is this your diagnosis or—"

"It doesn't take a medical degree to figure my sister out."

"I see." Jamie rose and brought the plate to the sink. "And how about you? How are you doing?"

Dance burped into his fist and flashed a smile. The boy was as slick as black ice. "I'm dandy, Doctor. How you been? By the look of your hands, you're still trying to catch up to Howard Hughes."

Jamie decided to let that one go. Though Dance made an effort to come off as nonchalant, his body language told a different story. He'd never seen Dance so fidgety. The food had been a temporary distraction, but now that there was nothing to keep Dance's hands occupied, he was beginning to chew his nails.

"Not in a retaliatory mood, Doctor?" Dance leaned back into the seat, cap pulled down low over his steely eyes.

Jamie seated himself in his chair once more. He hadn't used the hand sanitizer since their session began, and he planned on staying clear from it, though subtly intrusive thoughts tickled the side of his mind, making it difficult to focus. "Have you been sleeping well?" he asked Dance, determined to steer the boy back to their on-and-off therapy. He'd been seeing Dance Young for close to two years, one of the dozen cases he took for the Bunker, pro bono, but he still knew little about Dance. The boy's file was the size of a phone book, yet all of the information Jamie had collected on the elusive liar was irrelevant. This case was a challenge, and though Jamie tried to convince himself that he was wasting his time, he relished the idea of cracking Dance's hard candy surface.

"My sister needs help," Dance said, dodging another question. "And I think you're the only one who can help her."

Flattery was also one of Dance's gifts. Jamie had fallen for it on numerous occasions, but not today. "If your sister suffers from an eating disorder, I'd be happy to refer her to—"

"Forget the eating disorder, okay?" Dance sat up straight, flustered. "You specialize in post-traumatic stress and anxiety disorders, and that's what my brother has." Dance eyed him furiously, his gaze blazing under the long bangs. "So, are you gonna hear me out here?"

"First, you should start by getting the facts straight, no? One moment you say sister, the next he's your brother. Which one is it exactly?"

Dance darted his stare to the floor, nibbling his lower lip. "September was my brother for a few years, and now he's my sister."

Jamie remembered the timbre of September's voice. "I think I understand," he whispered, relaxing back into his chair. Dance was telling the truth on this one—or some of it. "Dance, I still don't think I'm the right man for this case. I don't deal with gender disorders either."

"She doesn't have a fucking gender disorder."

"I don't mean to offend you. That's the clinical—"

"You're not listening to me," Dance snapped, sweeping his hat off. He was truly breathtaking, with finely chiseled features, almost feminine. "September's problem isn't in her shorts. It's in her head. She needs to talk to someone about how much she hates herself." His voice sank. "And me."

"Why do you think she hates you so?"

"Search me." Dance shrugged again. Typical adolescent behavior. The boy refused to grow up.

Jamie decided to try another approach. "If I agree to see her, I would be going out of my way for you." He tossed his chin up at the door. "Have you seen my waiting room? Taking on another patient, with the complexities this case seems to—"

"You want me to suck your dick."

Jamie's jaw unhinged, and for a moment, his tongue sat useless in his mouth. "There's no call for that," he said at last. "You don't need to insult me." He clung to the notepad, hoping he'd have the self-restraint not to throw it at Dance's cocky face. Wounded, he pushed his fingers into the paper, leaving imprints into it.

"How's me asking if you want me to give you head insulting?"

"Because all I've been with you is cordial and professional, and bringing this conversation down to that level is not only insulting, but completely detrimental to your emotional health."

Dance processed the words silently.

"All right," Jamie said. "Permit me to be frank." Gently, he set the notepad down on the coffee table. "We've been going through the steps of this very well-executed choreography for nearly two years, and I think it's safe to say we've reached a plateau. You either decide to commit to this—"

"I know what you want, and I'm gonna give it to you if you help my sister." Dance flipped his cap back on. "That's what I'm trying to tell you. But you don't listen."

"And what is it that I want?" Jamie smiled, though he was not at all amused.

Dance held his probing stare, his gray eyes unreadable. "You want a backstage pass to my mind."

The boy's challenging manner, his well-chosen words, all of it, sent a jolt of excitement through Jamie even as he tried to keep his face neutral.

Yes, a peep inside.

It could be fascinating.

"So, if you help my sister, if you call her tonight and make her come here to see you, and I don't give a shit how, I'll come here every week, sit in this ugly, uncomfortable, tacky vintage chair, and tell you everything you wanna know."

No. Out of the question. It was against his oath. He could not lure a patient using another as bait.

Heart racing, Jamie watched the fantastically complicated young man sitting across him.

"Come on, Dr. Scarborough, you might be my sister's only chance."

Inside his pocket, Jamie's fingers pressed the bottle of sanitizer hard up against his palm. "I want you to send me an e-mail," he said. "I'll need as much information as you can give me on September."

"I don't have a computer."

"Then go to the library." Jamie rose, his legs wobbly. A mistake. This was a mistake. "And make sure you don't leave anything out." He looked down at the boy.

Dance's eyes flickered, and he nodded. "Deal." He got to his feet and tucked his notebook deeper into the waist of his tattered jeans.

"And I want to read that as well."

Dance winked, regaining his usual caustic way. "Maybe later." He moved to the door, leaving Jamie flushed and confused.

What had he just agreed to?

"Oh, and Doctor," the boy said, plucking the door open, "I wouldn't have sucked your dick. I'm straight."

❖

Neil walked along the river, his boots rhythmically crushing the snow.

This afternoon he'd avoided the main path and chosen instead to follow the narrow trail cutting through bare bushes and shrubbery—the one flanking the frozen river, away from the speed-walkers and self-obsessed joggers. He wore his wool-lined aviator jacket and cadet cap, but they were no match for the brutal cold. The sun was setting, draining the dusty sky of all color, and Neil's thighs were beginning to burn.

Not to mention his balls.

Time to go home to Uncle Jack Daniel's.

"All right, Hem," Neil said, aware of the absolute absurdity of this walk. "Let's go."

Of course he knew the old mutt was dead. Of course he knew it.

But the dog was back. Or maybe it had never left. Actually, it was more like his spirit was back. Or maybe not. Maybe it was only a normal stage in the grieving process. Maybe it would pass.

Oh, and shit, if it never passed, what did it matter?

Not like it bothered anybody.

"Do you have a cigarette, sir?"

Neil jumped a little, lifting his eyes to the young face staring back at him. It was the kid. He'd seen him a couple of times already, hanging around the shore, feeding the ducks. This evening, the kid didn't wear his baseball cap. And Neil wished he had. This way, he wouldn't have to see that face.

Tormented. Stunning.

"Do you speak English?" The boy swayed on his feet, his hands tucked deep into his flimsy jacket pockets. *"Une cigarette?"*

"I don't smoke." Neil moved to the mound of snow at his left, heading up to the main path.

"Hey!" The kid followed. "Do you have some change. A dollar? Two?" He was winded, struggling to keep up. "I haven't eaten in—"

"Are you stupid or something?" Halfway up the mound, Neil dug his heel in the snow, spinning around to face the dumb kid. "How do you expect to make a buck in the middle of nowhere? Go downtown, find a subway station and sing a little song, dance a little dance."

The boy smiled, his eyes shrinking, assessing. "Where's your dog?"

Neil turned away, taking the final steps to the path.

But the kid was a persistent little snot. "Buy me dinner," he said, meeting up with him again. "A beer? Something. Come on, man, buy me French fries."

"What's wrong with you?" Neil stopped short, facing the kid angrily. "You know, you keep this up and I'm gonna pop you."

The kid puckered his chapped lips, his silver eyes widening. He raised a brow and nodded. "Where's your dog?"

"I killed him."

"Oh."

Goddamn it. The boy's ear was purple. He was going to start losing pieces if he didn't get out of the cold for a few hours. "I'll give you some change for the subway," Neil said.

The boy shook his head. No.

Neil stared at him, unable to cut loose. The kid's nose was dripping.

"What's your name, sir?" the boy asked.

Neil crossed his arms over his chest, resting his weight back on his heels. His name? When was the last time someone had asked his name, anyway? "McClure," he said, keeping his hand safely tucked under his armpit. "Neil McClure."

The boy sniffled. "My name's Xavier."

What kind of name was that? Nobody named their son Jack or Billy anymore.

"Sir, can I come to your house and talk to you for a little bit?"

The question almost knocked the air right out of Neil's throat. How naïve was this kid exactly? You didn't go around parks, asking strange men if they wanted to take you home and chat. Not with that face. Not with that cherry mouth.

"I just need to warm up," the boy said, taking a shy step forward. "And a cup of soup or something."

It was an act. All of it. The shiny eyes. The pouting lips. This kid was smart. He was a player. He'd done this before. And he'd do it again. Tonight? To some other guy.

And what if that guy was an animal?

A man who'd take the boy home and never let him out again?

"What do you say, Neil? Will you help me out, just for an hour?"

The boy was smooth. A real pro. But he was also thin, fragile. One twist of the arm, and that whole act would mean nothing. The kid would be toast. "I live up the street there," Neil said, walking away, the kid close behind. "You come in, you eat, you go."

"Yes sir."

"I don't want no funny business." He shot Xavier a sidelong glance. "Understand?"

Xavier nodded. "I'll be really good."

Yeah, this kid was definitely a pro.

CHAPTER FIVE

Jamie entered the restaurant, shaking the snow off his wool blazer.

He slipped his leather gloves off, glancing around. The place was empty, save for a young couple seated by the frosted window. The two youngsters were engrossed in their amorous conversation, leaning over a bottle of wine and a platter of tiropita. They held hands and played with each other's fingers. The girl turned her eyes his way and Jamie smiled politely.

Ah, straight people. The world belonged to them and always would.

"Good evening, sir." A surly man dressed in a starched white shirt accosted him. "Are we dining alone tonight, sir?" The host, who Jamie presumed was also the cook and owner, addressed him with the crisp manner of a grand hotel concierge. "This way, please."

"I'm meeting a friend," Jamie said, following him.

"Blond?"

"Yes," he said, hanging his vest on the coat stand. "Where is he?"

"He's in the washroom." The man looked uneasy. "He's been in there since he got here." He stared over Jamie's shoulder and then turned away. "I'll have Anna bring the menus."

Jamie slipped into the booth, looking back at the men's room.

What the hell was Matt doing in there anyway?

He tried to focus on the wine list.

Best not to know.

"Hello," the waitress—Anna, plump, homely—greeted him. She

placed two menus on the table and looked over at the door. "Will your friend be dining in the bathroom?" She laughed, giving him a warm, knowing smile.

"I'll go check on him," he mumbled, getting out of his chair.

The washroom's door opened and Matt stepped out, carrying a small leather pouch. He wore a simple powder blue V-neck and black slacks, but he could have been wearing a potato sack, complete with dirt and roots, and the effect of his dazzling smile would not be diminished.

"Oh, you're here," Matt said, grabbing hold of Jamie's elbows, pulling him close. He dropped a kiss on his neck, his lips grazing Jamie's earlobe, and Jamie stepped back into the table, knocking the empty candlestick down,

Matt didn't even notice. Grinning, he turned his attention to Anna, who stood watching on, seemingly amused. "I'll give you two a minute," she said with a wink.

"Can you bring us a liter of your homemade wine to start?" When she left them, Matt seated himself across from Jamie, dragging his chair up closer to the table. "How are you? You look really nice."

Nice?

Jamie looked down at himself. He was wearing his office clothes, wrinkles and renovation dust included. "Thanks," he returned, pushing his eyeglasses up. "Everything okay with you?"

"Yeah, why?"

"I don't know." Jamie smirked, composing himself. He had to remember why he was here. No matter how blue Matt's eyes were. No matter how hot his mouth had felt on his cold skin. Keep his eyes off Matt's collarbone—that was the trick. Keep them off the golden hair of his forearms. "They said you were in the bathroom for a—"

"Oh, that." Matt reached over and cupped Jamie's fingers, pulling them to his cheek. The skin on them was soft as a peach.

Jamie squirmed in his seat, unable to pull his hand away.

"I was shaving," Matt said. "I didn't have time to do so before I left the job. Didn't wanna be all prickly." He winked.

Jamie swallowed, sliding his hand out of Matt's fingers. "I see."

Matt threw his head back, laughing.

Anna set the wine bottle down on their table and flipped two glasses over. "Have you decided?"

Slightly stunned, Jamie stared down at the menu.

"We'll have the calamari," Matt told Anna, his eyes dancing on Jamie's face. "Greek salad for me and the chef salad for him. No vinaigrette for the doc, and can you please replace his baked potatoes with steamed rice. He doesn't like rosemary much."

Jamie sat, lips parted, brow furrowed in confusion.

Matt waited until Anna disappeared, and then he set his fiery blue stare on him again. "What? You don't think I paid attention in the last five years?"

Jamie sipped his water, tongue-tied.

Whatever game Matt was playing, the man was batting a thousand.

❖

Neil hadn't fixed a steak in a while. It was shamefully overcooked. Bloodless as a corpse.

He turned the gas off and poked a potato. "Hey," he called out to the boy, who was out of view. "What are you doing in there?"

"Nothing." Xavier now stood in the kitchen's doorway, bottle of Jack Daniel's in hand. "Can I have—"

"Put that back." Neil slid the piece of charred meat onto a plate and dropped a few potatoes beside it. "Wash your hands and sit down."

"I'm eighteen."

"And I'm fucking serious."

Xavier shrugged and left the bottle on the counter by the sink. "Fine." He pulled up a chair and sat, obedient. "My hands are clean. I just washed them."

Neil set the plate in front of him and stepped back, retreating to his comfort zone, which was at least three meters away from this child. He picked up the bottle of Jack and poured himself a triple. What kind of forty-two-year-old man invited a runaway into his home? Talking to Hem was one thing, but this was authentic insanity.

The kind they put your ass in jail for.

But Xavier swore he was eighteen. Cross his heart and hope to die. He wasn't just some homeless youth; he was a med student dropout. A genius, he explained. His parents were well-off, but they'd disowned him after they'd found out about his plans.

Xavier entertained fantastic ideas about impossible feats, such as winning his girlfriend back—a masseuse who'd left him for some rich man with bad teeth—and escaping with her to Chile, where they'd grow their own food and start some sort of literature commune. They'd call it the Holden Caulfield Organization. They'd recruit other like-minded youths and preach existentialism to the local children; all this in the name of social emancipation.

The kid didn't look like he was using, but one could never tell. Nowadays kids knew how to make drugs out of baking soda, cotton balls, and cough medicine. Neil had tossed all of his over-the-counter medication into his underwear drawer.

Just in case.

"Why aren't you married?"

Another thing, Xavier asked a lot of damn questions.

Neil swilled back a generous amount of his drink and stared down into the amber glass. "Who says I'm not married?"

Xavier looked around, smirking. "Your house."

"Yeah?" Neil sank the last of the Jack. "Maybe my wife's not big on cleaning."

"You don't have a ring." Xavier wiped his mouth. He used a napkin, to Neil's surprise. "How old are you?" the boy asked, slicing the rubbery steak.

"I'll get you a better knife." Neil plucked the utensil drawer open, fumbling through the mess.

"Are you into boys?"

Neil's fingers curled around the butcher knife.

"I like the potatoes," the kid said, strutting to the stove, his blue jeans barely clinging to his narrow hips. "But I won't finish the steak, if you don't mind." He fetched a potato out of the pot and tossed into his mouth.

"You have to go now," Neil said, releasing his grip around the knife's handle. His fingers had cramped up. "You ate and you look pretty warmed up."

"My toes are still frozen." Xavier looked down at his socks and then his eyes, like smoldering embers, burned Neil's face. "I won't ask you any more questions, I promise. But I don't have anywhere to go tonight, and—"

"You can't stay here."

Had to get this child out of his house. Get him out. Remove every inch of him from his view.

"Call your girlfriend," Neil said, averting the boy's pleading stare. "You call her and see if she can hook you up."

"She's out of town." Xavier sighed, his chest moving under his thin black T-shirt. "Can I have one of those, please?" He pointed to a box of chocolate chip cookies on the shelf. Christina had brought them two days ago, along with numerous other items Neil had no intention of eating. "And some milk, if you have it, and then I'll go."

"Okay, you know what, take the whole damn box, a carton of milk, and I'll give you fifty bucks." Neil pushed the cookies into the kid's chest and stepped away, heading for the front door. "Get your shoes on," he called back.

Someone would help this boy. It was inevitable. People were addicted to beauty. By the end of the evening, the kid would be sipping expensive liquor in someone's boudoir. Xavier had all the attributes— faked or not—that people found endearing. A classic face. Boyish charm. Helplessness mixed with some kind of obscene sensuality. He was bound to be somebody's pet.

"Can I see you again?" Xavier asked, walking up to the entrance, clutching the box of cookies to his breast. "We could watch a movie or something."

"Listen to me." Neil tried to keep his tone calm. "You don't know me, you realize that, don't you? You know nothing about me. And here you are, wide open. What the fuck are you looking for? A beating?" His voice quivered, but he couldn't stop the words from gunning out of his mouth. "You wanna get yourself raped or something?"

The kid shrank back, his long fingers gripping the box, and Neil realized that he was towering over the boy, menacing. He became aware of their height difference: Xavier was no more than five-seven and must have weighed under a hundred and thirty pounds. Neil's fist was larger than this kid's face.

"Well, if I stay here tonight, I won't be messed with." Xavier's lips formed a nervous smile. "Right?" He backed away, his expression changing subtly. "I really need to use your computer, if that's okay. You have one, right?"

"Will this help you find a place to stay?" Neil felt himself coming around from a place he never wished to visit again.

"Maybe, yeah." Xavier tore the package open, digging for a cookie. "I don't know, but can I use it anyway?"

The boy was lying.

"It's in the bedroom," Neil said. Twice now this week, he'd invited a male into his bedroom. "Do your thing, but don't touch anything but the goddamn mouse and keyboard in that room, understood?"

"Thanks!" Xavier ran off.

Neil fell back into his armchair, gazing around the living room.

"I know, Hem. I know."

He dove his hand between the seat and cushion in search of the remote, but instead his fingers landed on cold leather.

"Dr. Hyperventilation forgot his glove," Neil whispered, feeling the expensive material between his fingertips.

Okay then, maybe he'd stop by at the nuthouse and drop it off for him.

"What do you think, Hem?" Neil leaned back into the seat, resting his eyes. "Should we go see the shrink tomorrow morning?"

❖

Oh, dear.

He was a glass of wine away from being drunk.

"More bread?" Matt pushed the basket of warm bread across the table.

Jamie silently declined, unfastening the first two buttons of his shirt. His tie was gone, hanging on the back of his chair. "They really cranked the heat up in here," he said, before taking a large sip of his water.

"It's the spicy dip." Matt stuffed another forkful of his dessert, a decadent golden baklava, into his superb mouth.

Yes, superb. Every single thing on that man's face was superb.

All right, perhaps he wasn't a glass away from being drunk. He was a glass away from doing something stupid. Like leaning in and licking the sugar off Matt's lips. Or tongue. Jamie gulped more water and sat up straight. Time to go. He'd leave the car here, take a cab home, and masturbate until he lost consciousness.

This was Matt, for heaven's sake. Basil's best friend and lover.

The competition.

"I think I should—"

"Oh, Jamie, don't say it. Don't say you have to go." Matt cracked one of his weakening smiles. "It's cold outside." He sang the words quite nicely, his eyes twinkling in the candlelight.

Matt's charm was like fudge syrup: the more Matt poured it on, the less Jamie could remember what the original treat was supposed to look like. As a result of Matt's sweet one-liners, Jamie felt both intoxicated and nauseous.

They'd finished a bottle and a half of the awful house wine, and the coffee was coming. Hopefully soon. Jamie glanced down at his watch. Way past his bedtime. "I've got to work tomorrow," he said, looking around for Anna, the waitress. "And so do you. You know how Basil blows his lid if any of you show up late." Great. Why did he have to say Basil's name now? He'd managed to avoid bringing up anything remotely close to reality in the last two hours. There had been no mention of their shared lover. They'd talked about Matt's ambitions—he'd been training for an upcoming triathlon he planned on finishing, regardless of an old knee injury—and Jamie's work, the clinic, current affairs, the outing of some Montreal closeted film director, movies they'd seen, yes, they shared the same tastes, to Jamie's dismay or delight—but bang! With five letters, he'd spelled out disaster.

Basil. The one and only.

"The kids miss you," Matt said, his smile waning. "He misses you."

"Of course, that's why he's sleeping with you and dating a woman." It hurt. It hurt more than he could sustain.

"We're not sleeping together, Jamie." Matt sighed sharply, leaning back into his seat. "All right? Not like I didn't try, but the closest I got to his ass was washing his boxers along with mine on laundry day."

"Fine, okay." Jamie's lips were so tight, he nearly couldn't speak. "I don't care either way."

"I'm lying. I'm sorry." Matt stopped short, allowing Anna to set the hot coffee cups down. "Thank you," he told her. "We'll take the check, please."

"Will it be one?" Anna gathered their plates, unaware of the tension between them.

"Split it, please." Jamie stared into Matt's face, sobering up quickly.

"Jamie, I—" Matt paused, fidgeting in his seat, impatient for Anna to leave them again. As she stepped away from their table, he reached for Jamie's hand, but Jamie retracted back into his chair. "I'm sorry," Matt whispered, trying for his hand again. "It's just comfort fucks, that's all. It's mechanical, that's what it is, and you don't have to—"

"Be jealous?" Jamie rose, jerking his blazer off the coat stand. "Mechanical or not, you're sleeping with my ex-partner."

"Yeah? Well, every time he crawls into bed with me, he's not out with that Betty Crocker homemaker!"

Jamie threw his jacket on and shoved his hand inside a pocket. He'd eaten with the restaurant's cutlery. Drunk out of their stained glasses. Eaten the food prepared by whose hands?

He squeezed the sanitizer into his palm and rubbed his hands together, allowing the cleansing gel to get into all the cracks and crevices. It felt good. Very, very good. Never again. He'd never eat out again. The food was inside him now. Festering. He'd be sick. He could feel it coming.

"Stop doing that." Matt neared him. "You've scrubbed enough." He touched his wrist.

"Don't touch me," Jamie said, stepping back. Had to get out of this place. This whole restaurant was a germ factory. He could taste the bacteria in the air. "I'm going home." The air was thick with spores of all kinds.

"Come on, Jamie, relax. Let me take care of the bill and we'll go outside. We'll take a walk."

It was so bright in here. Had they turned the lights up? Someone sneezed, and Jamie's eyes darted in the sound's direction. Oh, he'd seen the specks of phlegm shoot out of the woman's nose. "I need to leave." He flew to the door and shoved it open.

Instantly, the cold air slapped his cheek, but he welcomed it. He leaned on the brick wall and bent over, wheezing. "Mechanical," he sneered, trying to slow his heart.

He felt the warm air on his cheek before he heard Matt's voice. "Here," Matt said. Out of the corner of his eye, Jamie caught sight of the wrapped mint Matt was offering him. "If you suck on something, it keeps your mind off the panic attack."

Jamie straightened up. "Is that why you're always so calm?" He was breathless, but still in control. He took the mint and unwrapped it with shaky fingers.

"I didn't want you to get so wired. I wanted you to have a good time tonight."

Jamie moved the mint around his dry mouth. "What is this?"

"This, what?"

"What you're doing. *This.* Dinner. Shaving. The touching of the hands. Smiling. Eating bread. Paying for—"

"Eating bread?"

"Oh, you know what I mean!" Jamie almost choked on the mint. "Look, my life is confusing right now. I'm confused." He touched his chest, his voice sinking. "I don't know what I'm doing. I don't know why I'm here. I don't know who I am, what—"

"Hey, easy." Matt moved closer. "Let's get out of here, okay? Let's walk to my place and warm up. We'll have a last drink and—"

"No. I can't. I really can't."

"Jamie, it'll be hands off, I promise. But look at you, you're so wired, I'm not letting you drive off like this." One more step and their chests would touch. "Come," Matt breathed into his ear. "Everything's going to be okay."

Over Matt's shoulder, Jamie watched the busy street. A child and a man—her father? stood at the intersection, hand in hand, waiting for the light to change. The girl's face was upturned, studying the seriousness of her father's face. When the light turned green, the man guided her safely across, never allowing her hand to slip out of his. The scene had the effect of a punch in the plexus.

"If you care about me, call me a cab," Jamie said.

Matt leaned back, his blue eyes scanning his face. For a weakness. A subtle invitation. "Are you sure?"

Jamie closed his eyes.

No, he wasn't sure of anything anymore.

Daddy wants his gun.
Son, get me my goddamn gun, now.
Mommy? Where's Mommy?

Mommy's out again.

Maybe they'll call all her numbers: B12, D34, and she'll bring a thousand dollars home tonight.

Neil, get me my gun or I'll put you down like the dog.

Daddy is yelling. Mad as hell. Jesus. Fuck. Shit. Whore. Bastard.

It's all right. It's okay. Stay out of sight. Don't make a sound. Stay out of sight. Daddy can't move. Daddy can't get out of his bed. It's all right, it's—

With a jolt, Neil opened his eyes.

A sharp breath burned his throat and he pressed his palm against his heart. He had to calm down or he'd puke. He leaned forward, head reeling. A drink, that's what he needed. With caution, Neil rose, wobbling a little, and walked across the dark living room, headed for the kitchen. At the sight of the dirty pan on the stove top, his stomach knotted and he glanced backward.

Damn it. He'd forgotten about the kid. What time was it?

He leaped for the living room and flicked the corner lamp on. That boy better not have ripped him off. Neil scoured the room—everything appeared to be in its place, untouched, including the kid's jacket and shoes.

Xavier was still there.

Neil walked down the hall, to the bedroom. The door was ajar, light still on. "Hey," he said, pushing the door opened. "Get off the computer and—" But he stopped mid-sentence. The boy was sprawled over the blankets, asleep in his bed. Xavier was on his side, curled up, face resting on an elbow. He slept soundlessly, breathing deeply through his nose.

"No," Neil grumbled, stepping to the bed. "He's not staying here, Hem. No way."

At the sound of his voice, the kid stirred, mumbling a little.

"I want him outta here," Neil said, wanting to shake the boy, yet unable to bring himself to touch him. He stared down at Xavier and looked back at the window, glimpsing the street through the slit in the curtains. It was still snowing. Still cold. Still goddamn December. How could he send a child out into this crap two weeks before Christmas?

He'd watch over him for a couple of days. No one would know. And if anyone asked, like Mrs. Sinclair for instance, he'd tell her the kid was his nephew visiting from Vermont.

"Three days, Hem. We'll keep him for three days and then send him on his way."

Xavier sighed and turned to his back, throwing his forearm over his cheek.

Neil watched him, unable to stop himself. The boy's T-shirt was pulled up, showing the blond fuzz on his belly. Soft. Everything on this kid was—soft.

Neil turned away from the bed, and quietly, he pulled two quilts off the closet shelf, draped one over the kid, shut off the light, and left the room.

In the living room, he stretched out on the couch, his feet hanging off the seat, and threw the blanket over his legs. He closed his eyes, tight, tighter still. Red blots danced behind his lids. His body pulsed. He jerked his zipper down, pushed his hand into his underwear and squeezed his erection until the pain, searing, barely tolerable, soothed him.

The wind shook the living room window and Neil groaned, his face pressed hard against the seat of the couch.

CHAPTER SIX

A t his desk, Jamie turned his computer on and sipped his coffee.

Tuesday morning: already exhausted, barely functional.

What would his patients think of him if they knew he was hungover on a weekday?

Good God, he would have to be in bed early tonight. No, in fact, he wished he was in bed *right now.*

Last night had been a close call. Way too close. He'd almost given in to Matt's persuasive arguments. Another one of Matt's hot whispers on his ear and he'd have been on his knees. Forget the mint.

Jamie smiled, waiting for the computer's million applications to load. Matt had come on to him. *Him.* What would Basil think of this surprising new twist? Well, he could always tell Basil that it was all simply *mechanical.*

"You're very bitter," Jamie said, typing in his password. "Be the bigger man." He shook his shoulders loose. The important thing was, he hadn't done anything regrettable last night. He was still the gentleman in this story.

"Wow." He mocked himself. "The gentleman?"

Determine to tackle the day, Jamie drained the last of his coffee and checked his personal e-mail in-box.

Viagra. Best Buy offers. Gym reminder. Mallory.

Mallory!

She'd written him an e-mail.

Jamie pushed his glasses up and leaned in closer to the screen.

Hi Dr. J! :-)

I'm sending you pictures of Cabosanluca! The beach is just neer are hotel. Thers a big pool right next to are room and dad said that we could go in the see and find fish. Did you give silvester is treets? Tell him that i'll be back right after christmas. I dont think that Marsh wants to go. I think he wants to stay at your house.

Im watching the simpsons.

I love you.

Mallory Evans Spasso

What?

Oh, no, you don't.

Jamie grappled for his phone and dialed Basil's cell number. At Christmastime? What was he supposed to do during the holidays, sit at home alone?

"Hey," Basil answered, male voices booming in the background. "How are—"

"Cabo San Lucas, Basil? Really?" Jamie jumped out of his chair. "When were you going to tell me? If you were going to tell me at all—"

"Jamie, can I call you back? We're in the middle of—"

"No!"

"Calm down." Shockingly, Basil's tone was almost tender. "Where are you?"

He had to hold on to the fury because without it, there would be only immense sadness. Regret. Loneliness. "How can you ask me to calm down?" Jamie cried, trying to stay angry. "You're taking the kids to Mexico without—"

"I was gonna call you tonight and—"

"How long will you be there?" He was so weak. Never could stand up to Basil. Deflated, Jamie leaned back on the oak desk. "Will I get to see them during the holidays?"

"Yeah. Yeah, of course." Basil was distracted. "Maybe New Year's or—"

"Baz? Are you going there alone? I mean, just you and the kids?" Please. Oh God, please.

"Jamie, listen"—there was the sound of a crash—"Leave it! Don't touch it," Basil yelled impatiently to one of his obedient crew boys, but soon the line was quiet and Basil sighed, finally giving him a moment of his attention. "I really don't wanna do this with you right now. I'd planned on calling you tonight—"

"You're going with Matt."

Jamie heard a door being shut, and then Basil cleared his throat. *Here it comes.*

"I'm going with a friend, and don't freak out."

This was pure pain. Many times, Jamie had sworn he felt hurt, but now he understood: He'd never truly known pain until this minute. This atrocious, vicious, and unfair minute. "The woman," he breathed, turning his eyes to the window. Of course. He should have known.

"Who told you? Did Matt tell you?" Basil sounded frantic. "That little shit, I'm gonna—"

"What, you thought you'd get to keep all our friends as well?" Jamie bounced off the desk, his heart pummeling his ribs. "You took the house, the kids, everything—"

"Calm down. Please calm down and listen to me."

Jamie gripped the phone, pulling it away from his ear, clutching it to his breast.

Enough.

He was going to shut down and clamp up. Why should he care? Why should he listen? Basil had lost his mind, clearly. The man was acting like a perfect imbecile.

Jamie put the phone to his ear once more. "Go ahead. I'm listening."

Basil's words traveled through the line, measured but quick—now he was the salesman duping a customer into buying broken merchandise. Her name was Laura. She was caring and down-to-earth. The kids liked her a lot. No, she didn't have children of her own—couldn't—but she had a strong maternal streak in her. Laura. Laura. Laura. A good girl, really. Pretty, but not too made-up. Simple, was the thing that she was. That's right, simple. Hassle-free. She was a travel agent and wow, the deals she could get. This was a deal. Couldn't miss it, right?

Jamie listened.

Who was this man on the phone with him? A stranger. Some

straight man falling for a middle-aged divorcée with big hooters and plane tickets.

"Well, say something," Basil whispered, finally ending the endless monologue. "You there?"

Jamie stared at the closed door of his office, rubbing his eyes under the glasses. "Does she know that you were living with another man for the last four years?"

"Jesus," Basil gasped, "Of course she does. What do you take me for?"

A delusional man trying to stick a Band-Aid on an amputated leg.

"I'm going to fight you, Basil. Do you hear me? I'm going to get a lawyer and I'm going to take you to court." The words shot out of his mouth, hot yet cool. "I'm going to ask for shared custody of Marshall and Mallory."

"Fuck you, Jamie. Fuck you for sinking this low."

"No, fuck *you*, Basil." Gently, Jamie pushed the End button and set his phone down on the desk.

What had he done?

Basil was a warrior. Had he just jumped into the ring with him?

Jamie fell back into his armchair, shaken to the core. How could they have come to this? They had been lovers. Fathers. Friends. It was all gone. The tears came, and Jamie let them. God, he still loved that man. That selfish, confused, and stubborn man.

"Dr. Scarborough?"

Jamie turned his head, catching sight of Marie-Miel's concerned expression through his blurred vision. He hadn't heard the door. "What is it?" he asked.

She stood in the doorway, fixing him seriously. "Do you want to talk about it?"

"Basil's flying south next week. With a woman. And the kids."

She coughed, her face reddening.

"I know." Jamie cracked a semblance of a smile.

"It'll pass," she said. "Don't worry, it'll pass." She repeated the words as if uttering them twice would make them true.

Jamie rose and adjusted his tie. He had a job to do. People who counted on him. He glanced down at his watch. "I've got ten minutes before my first appointment. I'll have another cup of coffee and collect my thoughts."

"There's someone here to see you, though." She glanced backward and lowered her voice. "Says you forgot something at his house."

"What?" Jamie stepped to the door, glimpsing the waiting room.

"Hi, Doc." Neil McClure stood by the reception desk. "You left this in my living room."

Jamie glanced around at the curious faces. What would people think? "You didn't have to—"

"I live two blocks away from here, remember? No big deal."

Boy, this man was gigantic. Yet Neil hadn't seemed so broad and imposing inside his own house. It was this room. Something about Neil McClure clashed and battled with the setting. It was in the way he stood—straight, almost soldier-like, his bulky limbs never at ease. Ready for combat.

Jamie hesitated, unsure of himself. He couldn't take that step forward. Couldn't meet Neil halfway. The effect of him was neutralizing. Was he turned on, or afraid? He couldn't seem to gauge his own feelings.

"Hey, Doc, do you think you could give me five minutes?" Neil moved to him.

It was the eyes. They were expressionless.

"I have quite a busy schedule this morning," Jamie said, casting Marie-Miel a glance. She'd get it. She'd know what to say.

"Mr. McClure," his fast-thinking receptionist said, "would you like to make an appointment—"

"You came my house. Chris said you wanted to help me." Neil spoke as if they were alone. "So now I come here and ask for five minutes and—"

"Come in." Jamie turned away, walking to his office.

First rule, contain.

Then assess.

"I'm sure I can manage five minutes for you," he said, not looking back. He waited until Neil entered his office and shut the door behind them. "What can I do for you?" He didn't need a scene.

Neil McClure stood rigid by the door, his large hands hanging at his side.

"Please, sit down," Jamie said, his voice not quite steady.

A few moments passed and then Neil sank his impressive body into the divan. "I've got a couple of things to get off my chest."

"That's what I'm here for." Jamie picked up his notepad.

Oh, but for this five minutes, Christina would owe him *big-time*.

❖

Dance stretched his toes, his mind still coated with dreams.

Dreams of vanilla ice cream and treks to the park—his brother, always two steps ahead, yelling back, *Hurry, the swings are empty.* They were boys back then. Almost carefree. *Almost*, but never quite. The ice cream would melt. And the afternoon would turn to dusk.

They'd have to go home.

Under the quilt—whose quilt?—Dance awoke. What day was it? What time?

Whose bed? He caught the scent of dust burning. The electric heater was cranked up. His mouth was parched. Dance opened his eyes, spying on the bedroom. The curtains were drawn, but it must have been day. He could feel the sun's white rays grazing the glass, beckoning him to rise.

Get up.

Get out.

But he would stay. This was a lot better than the Bunker. Here, there were only vague rules and he could break them all if he played his cards right. This was not like his sister's apartment either. The silence, for one thing, was soothing, not like the silence in September's home—oppressing and purposeful. No, here, the silence was simply an emptiness of sounds.

Where had the giant gone? He wasn't here. Dance knew it. Neil's energy vibrated on the lowest of frequencies and Dance had noticed how things seemed to shrink when Neil McClure was in a room. The vibes emanating from Neil were more like an invisible undertow, sucking the objects down below the surface.

Dance sat, excitement buzzing up his legs, into his belly, upward to his throat. No, he would not be like those objects that appeared to lose their shape and form around Neil McClure.

He was immune to the giant's powerful current. He would swim in the shallow end of this house. He'd seduce Poseidon and stay here for a while. He needed a refuge from reality, and Xavier, the med school dropout persona, would be his shelter.

He'd get a job. Doing what? He'd have to think about it, but this was a good place to start. This home. This place no one knew existed. September wanted him to disappear.

Poof, then.

He was gone.

Let her forget him. All of him, especially his anatomy. September couldn't see beyond this shell. She could only see their similarities, never their differences. If she had noticed who he was, she could have forgiven him his penis.

He'd be near, but out of sight.

Dance climbed out of bed and walked across the hall to the living room.

Right again.

Neil was not in the house. And the man had taken the invisible dog along with him. He'd heard Neil speaking to Hemingway. It was a little weird, yeah, but alarming? Not so much.

People, especially *sane* people, were all cracked.

And he?

Dance shrugged the thought off. No, not cracked. *Eccentric*, that's what he was. And smart, too. Smarter than the rest of them. He was here, was he not? No money in his pocket, a fridge full of food, a hot shower, and a cozy bed, all less than five strides away.

And all he needed to do was bat his eyes and play cute.

Sing a little song.

Dance a little dance.

In the kitchen, he rinsed his hands and face and then set out to prepare coffee. He found the espresso machine and after disassembling it, figured it out. Piece of cake. Within minutes, the strong scent of the infused beans lightened his mood and step. He missed this. Normality. A cup of coffee and a radio morning show. Today's weather. Traffic. He hadn't heard about the tedious minutiae of the urban world in too long. Being homeless for two years, he'd forgotten about traffic jams and winter tires. Peaceful, he sipped the bitter but oh-so-creamy coffee, listening attentively to every commercial on the radio. His ears pricked up at words such as: "premiums," "mortgage," "credit," "rebates," "deals," "interest-free."

Dance glanced over at the front door.

Where had the big guy gone? Could the man have a job? Maybe Neil was a postman. Or a baker. Something that would involve solitude and movement.

Dance stirred the sugar gathered at the bottom of the tiny cup and looked around for a phone. He found one in the living room, a portable, stuck between two couch cushions. He dialed *67, blocking the outgoing caller ID, and punched in Quick Fix's number. He sat in the big guy's chair, gazing out the living room window. The wind seemed to have died down. It looked pretty nice out there. A mild day.

"Quick Fix, please hold—"

"Elliot?" Dance jumped in his seat. "Don't put me on hold—"

"Dance, oh shit, dude, where are you? I called Emma and she said—"

"I'm good. I'm fine. Totally."

Elliot, poor naïve Elliot. Offering his ass up to mediocrity for a place to stay and a Visa card. He, on the other hand, wouldn't have to take his pants off for Neil McClure. The man was as horny as a brick. Definitely not gay. Probably missing a piece or two down there.

"Where you staying?" Elliot asked. "Hold on, I'm gonna find a more private spot. Dance? Where are you?"

"I'm not gonna tell you where I am, so stop asking."

Silence.

"I *can't* tell you," Dance said, more softly.

There was a sharp intake of air, and Elliot blew out a long, agonizing breath. "I'm itching like I'm coming off morphine. I need you. I need to see your face."

"I'm sorry," Dance whispered.

"I got two thousand dollars on my credit card." Elliot's voice weakened. Dance could see him clearly, hidden in some massage chamber, amongst rosewood scented candles, his pretty hands sore from rubbing oily shoulders and cellulite-ridden thighs. "Do you want me to leave everything?" Elliot asked. "Because I will, Dance. I will."

No. The boy was so close. A few more years of shacking up with the Ludovics of the world, and Elliot would break free. He would be the exception to the rule.

"Elliot, you're almost there."

There was a car pulling up in the driveway.

"I called because I don't want you to worry. I'm staying with someone. And I'm okay."

"Who is he?"

"A new friend."

"You don't know him, do you? You don't know who he is." Elliot sounded wounded, jealous, not worried.

Dance had seen Neil McClure around for weeks prior to their staged encounter. A squared-jaw man walking a half-dead dog. Neil lived three streets away from September. After he'd followed the stoic-looking man on three separate occasions, Dance had gathered that Neil lived alone, behind closed blinds. A recluse of some kind. Last night, Dance had snooped around in the man's bedroom, but found nothing truly revealing. Neil wasn't much into doing laundry and tidying, but his drawers were organized. He kept Tylenol and cough drops with his socks and underwear. A syringe, too. Diabetic, maybe? Neil owned a few books, mostly the white man's club stuff: McCarthy, Franzen, a copy of Thompson's *Fear and Loathing*. Some hunting magazines. He was a fabrication more than a man. A result, that's what Neil McClure was. Forty-something. White. Single. Self-obsessed. It was clear that Neil spent more time on perfecting his body than anything else. Dance had seen the weights in the closet. The weight powder on the counter.

This guy was only one thing, and that was an ex-something.

But an ex-*what*?

"Dance, please don't walk out of my life."

Outside, heavy heels crushed the frozen snow. *Honey, I'm home.*

"I gotta go," Dance said, standing.

"When I said that I loved you, I didn't mean it like that. I meant it like this, I *love* you, Dance Young."

Dance stiffened, feeling the words penetrate his pores, a battalion of promises marching up his skin.

Leave now.

Forget heterosexuality. Like rock, it's dead.

Go to Elliot, let him own you.

The lock turned.

"I'll call you. I swear." Dance cut the line, snapping the unseen wire that bound him to Elliot's clear voice. "Good morning," he greeted Neil. "I made some—"

"Who was that?" Neil swiped his hat off and unzipped his coat. His expression was both serious and pained. "Your parents?"

"No, it was nobody important." Dance turned away, flushed and winded. "I'll get you some coffee. I'd like to sit down and make you a proposition."

From the kitchen, Dance heard Neil's cavernous laugh, the sound swelling for a brief moment, huge and bellowing, then vanishing, as if the laugh itself had not come from Neil's throat, but from a place beyond the walls—and was eager to return there.

Dance poured the remaining coffee into a clean cup and stopped, staring out the window, into the desolate backyard.

What was he doing? Was this the right way?

He picked up the steaming drink and headed back to the living room to meet his new benefactor.

No, no need to panic yet.

He wasn't selling his soul, just leaving it at the pawnshop until he could afford to own it again.

❖

"Who was that?" Marie-Miel asked, standing in the doorway of his office. "I didn't think you were taking on new patients."

Jamie waved dismissively, his eyes steadfast on his notes. "I'm not, but this is for a friend."

Marie-Miel hesitated, navigating between her insatiable curiosity and her impeccable professionalism. Any other day, Jamie would have sated her interest, but not this morning.

Heart palpitations and a migraine.

Jackpot.

"I see that you're busy," Marie-Miel said. She tried to sound polite, but barely managed curt. "Anything I can do for you before I send the first one in? I told Mrs. Hennessy that you were running a little late. I bought you ten more minutes."

"Thank you, I appreciate it." He pulled his lips into a smile.

When Marie-Miel shut the door behind her, Jamie sank deeper into his chair.

Neil McClure. What a shallow, self-indulgent man. In less than ten minutes Neil had drained all of Jamie's minimal energy with his skewed perspective and victimization. His mother, Neil had explained with an air of superiority, was an illiterate seamstress whose only contribution to the world had been banana cakes and needlework. She thought a night of bingo was an adventure. Her days were divided between reading smutty romance novels and zapping the channels in search of scandal. And the father? A fireman. A stupid man who'd gotten himself burned like Sunday's bacon and spent the last of his pitiful years bedridden, spaced out on painkillers. It was a difficult upbringing and should have stirred compassion in Jamie, but instead, the more Neil McClure went on, the less empathetic Jamie became. It was in the man's choice of words, his monotone discourse, the vagueness in his eyes. And soon it had become apparent that Neil was not recounting these sad events for the purpose of healing, or even understanding his anger—which was as obvious as the man's bulging biceps—but for his own entertainment.

In fact, Neil had appeared to be slightly amused at times. As if this was a test of some sorts. As if he was measuring Jamie's capability to sit and listen to his horrific tale.

"That's what he's doing," Jamie said aloud, turning his eyes to his computer screen. "He's a megalomaniac." Yes, that was his first diagnosis, but of course, if a psychiatrist relied only on first impressions, the field of psychiatry would be nothing more than a wasteland where deeply misunderstood human beings would suffer at the hands of people who had a diploma and a prescription pad.

No, there was more to Neil than this brutally unpleasant manner. He had come to him. The glove had been an excuse. And could he help him? Could he muster the strength to plow through this hardened, neglected soil that was Neil McClure?

Well, if he'd been able to live with Basil Spasso for five years, he could crack Neil's icy surface with his hands tied behind his back.

Jamie rose and went to the sink. He turned the hot water on and ran his fingers under the jet. A quick rinse, nothing more. He wouldn't let it degenerate. He would wash between the fingers a bit, and stop. "Enough," he ordered himself, still scrubbing the swollen skin around his knuckles. "This is not about your hands being clean. This is you displacing your fears and anxieties. You're not a germophobe, you're a fucking nervous wreck." He turned the water off.

As a consequence of the pain he'd inflicted on himself, endorphins flooded his bloodstream, providing a temporary but ever-so-pleasant high. The chaos of the disorder was like nothing else. It was a ritual. And the high came from his own mind.

He was his own pusher.

Jamie scrolled down the last of his e-mails.

Two minutes before Mrs. Hennessy.

There was nothing worth a read in his in-box and so he cleared it and checked his spam mail. He bent to the screen, cheeks warming. "Dance," he muttered, reading the subject of Dance's e-mail.

Notes from a spaceship.

Jamie rose and cracked his door open, staying well out of view. Already he heard the impatient sighs and compulsive coughs. "Marie-Miel, five more minutes," he mouthed. "I promise."

Without waiting for her reply, he shut the door and jumped back into his chair.

The boy had come through. He'd written him an e-mail. At least something was going his way this morning.

Dr. Scarborough,

My sister is my brother and she's trying to kill both. If you need more information about trans people, please Google it and spare me the lengthy explanation. I am using someone's computer, so I'll be brief.

Seth (his birth name) is going nuts. She was always going, but now she's almost there. Can you do something about it? Put up a roadblock. Blow out her tires. I don't care, but don't let my sister get to where she's heading.

She's been "suffering," as you shrinks like to say, from anorexia for ten years now. Why? I don't know. Probably because some guy in high school told her she was fat. When you meet her, if you have the guts to do so, you'll see how wrong that asshole was. Our parents are fuck-ups, but you know that already. I did tell the truth about them. You can look it up, my mom's suicide is well recorded. My dad is still alive, but he pretends to be dead. I don't think that's why me and my sister are the way we are. She says genes.

I say too much imagination.

What you need to know is this.

September doesn't like to be told what to do. I'm sure you'll get that within the first thirty seconds of any exchange you might have with her. Four years ago, she was refused sex reassignment surgery by all competent psychiatrists in Canada. They would not sign any papers that would have made the surgery eligible for coverage by our good people in government here in Quebec. Why? Because she eats crackers and whipped cream, and then vomits. Every last one of those shrinks has crossed her off the list for gender therapy until she "addresses certain issues." Hey, let's be honest here, most of them are scared shitless she won't survive another surgery.

And I have to agree with them.

Being the reckless, stubborn bastard that she is, September decided to pay for the surgery herself. She started on her "project" three years ago. Two weeks before the fire, she'd raised close to eighty grand. How? She never told me. But I have an idea of what she was selling.

My brother, the whore.

I love her, you know. I wish I didn't, but I do.

Five months ago, my sister went to bed and left her cigarette burning in the ashtray. Two hours later, her apartment was torched down to the wires. She lost her cat and a duffel bag full of another life. She lost every single penny she'd saved. My sister didn't like banks. She didn't like signing forms that narrowed down the human species to two boxes: M. F.

We're twins, Dr. Scarborough. Identical. I am him. He is me. When she looks at me, she sees everything she wants to end. I don't know if you believe in the twin connection, but I'll tell you, sometimes, I can feel the hate she has for me burning in my own chest.

I can feel the fire. I can feel my whole body being sucked into the flames. And I wonder, if I lost a part of myself in the pyre, would I go back and get it?

> *Help her. Please. I'll be okay, but she needs you.*
> *Dance Young*

NB: I lied about letting you into my head. I'm sorry. But if you ever cared about me, you'll do this for me. And maybe one day, I'll let you read my notebook.

Jamie let out the breath that had been locked inside his throat.

Twins.

Like Mickey and him. Identical. Except Mickey Scarborough was gone, while September was still alive. How would it feel to witness his brother's death, over and over, slowly, day by day? Jamie cringed, tightening his fingers around his pen. He'd seen his brother's lifeless body only once, and the pain, the very insidious, unrelenting torment of that moment, was still as vivid today as it was thirty-three years ago, on that snowy morning in November. It washed over him now, that memory, the finality of it.

Jamie's gaze drifted to the window.

God, he missed him.

"Doctor?"

But who *he* was, of that, he wasn't certain anymore.

Mickey? Basil? Marshall?

Himself, perhaps. Yes, what he had set out to be. An eminent psychiatrist. A father. A faithful, dedicated partner.

"Can I send Mrs. Hennessy in? She says she has a yoga class—"

"Yes," Jamie said, his eyes fastened to the white horizon. "Send her in."

❖

This place smelled like dirty socks and wet newspaper.

God damn it, the world was shriveling up before his very eyes. Everywhere Neil looked, he saw ashen skin and stained dentures. No one was having any kids, that's what the problem was with society. There were more walkers and motorized wheelchairs parked outside this pretentious art gallery/coffee shop/bakery/Internet café/dump than there were baby buggies.

"I can't believe you saw him," Christina said, *again*. She glanced around the coffee shop, the new "in" place on the main strip. Some other bean and cream space recently opened by a young, ridiculously incompetent, and obviously very misinformed couple. Two twenty-five-year-olds who believed that this neighborhood was promising and "full of unexploited potential." They'd painted the walls over some crusty blood red, hung some reproductions of Lautrec, made their own organic fucking little pastries, and now here they stood, both of them in their Joshua Perets matching cardigans and Parasuco jeans, smiling painfully behind the refrigerated counter, trying to pretend like they didn't want to blow their tiny insignificant brains out. They had set out to be the next trendy thing on the comatose commercial artery. Right. All they'd be getting was the dejected guys who'd sip the same coffee for an hour until the unemployment office opened, and the blue-haired ladies looking for some companionship.

"Neil?" Christina tapped his cup with her spoon. IKEA cups. IKEA everything. "What did Dr. Scarborough say? Are you going to see him again?"

All right. He had to remember why he was here. Neil focused on Christina's face. Forget the rest. "Yeah, I will actually," he said, leaning back, folding his hands over his stomach. "I'm gonna start some kind of therapy. And that's why I called you here. I'm gonna need some space."

"What do you mean?"

"I mean, I'm gonna need to be left alone. For a couple of weeks, at least. I need some time to think and I don't want you showing up every other day."

The boy, Xavier, was home waiting. Neil's skin tingled all over. Get this over with. Get her out of his hair. Go home and start on the boy's education. Xavier was damaged, but he was still capable of greatness. The boy needed someone to teach him about heroism. Selflessness. Strength in a time when meekness was rewarded.

"Did Jamie suggest—"

"This is not about what the shrink thinks," he snapped. No. Stay calm. Cool. "It's about me asking you to respect the fact that I'm gonna be diving into some pretty deep, fucked-up issues and I need to be on my own, that's all."

Xavier was a mess, but that's because he was smart. Brilliant, really.

And smart kids needed guidance. They needed a mentor. Someone to show them how to be self-sufficient. Someone to harden them up.

"I'm proud of you, Neil," Christina whispered, her features glowing. Good, she was happy. "I'm shocked, though. You've made quite a U-turn. What made you change your mind about getting help?"

Neil brought the cup to his lips. Four dollars for "fair trade" coffee. Fair trade or not, it tasted like shit. He threw the rest of the tar back and cracked a quick smile. "You did, Chris," he said.

"Really?" she gasped. "You mean that?"

"So, will you give me a little time?"

"Yeah, of course, but, Neil, if you get the blues and need a place to go for Christmas, Judd and I—"

"That's nice, thanks." His thighs constricted, and sweetly, the pleasant cramp moved up into his groin. Oh, he had to get out of there and make sure the boy was still in the house, watching TV. "We're cool, then?" he asked, slipping out of the booth. "I gotta go."

"You'll call me?" Christina rose, gathering her coat and purse. "Just a quick call to let me know you're okay."

He agreed to her reasonable request and escorted her to her car. He smiled and waved her off. *I'll call you. Drive safely. I'll see you soon. Merry fucking Christmas.* When her little fuel-efficient made-in-Japan car was out of sight, Neil stood on the sidewalk, his heart beating hard but steady. Ten a.m., and around him people scurried from store to store, lugging their bags, cell phones glued to ears, hot coffee spilling over their cheap gloves—their faces flushed with panic. Last-minute gifts: perfume box set, decorative plate, bottle of Baileys Irish Cream, matching hat and scarf, the latest Michael Buble.

Neil turned his collar up and exhaled loudly, his breath steaming out in a long jet. "Okay, Hem, let's go home," he said, stepping over a pile of warm dog turds.

No time to hang out and window-shop. Hey, maybe he'd get the kid a little something later.

Later, yes.

But first, Xavier would have to deserve it.

CHAPTER SEVEN

Jamie sat in bed, recovering from another wrestling match with panic.

He slid his thumb across the phone's screen, the tip of his finger hovering over Basil's home number. It was a little past nine p.m.; Marshall and Mallory were most probably in their beds, off to dream land. And what was Baz doing? Was he sitting in the ill-lit kitchen, eating a cold supper, his head resting in his hand, going over numbers, bills—or maybe his dismantled life? Or was he cuddled up on the love seat, his arm around Laura's shoulder, drinking red wine? Pretending to like it, of course, when in truth all Basil could ever drink was blond beer and gin—straight up, hold the ice. Jamie pictured the two lovebirds, music playing softly in the background, shades pulled way down low. *Clink clink, dear. To us. But, Basil, dear, who's that man in the picture? Oh, him? That's just the man I swore to love for the rest of my life. Never mind him. Kiss me.*

"Damn you, Baz." Jamie tossed his phone on the bed and leaned back into the pillow, closing his eyes. It had been a very taxing day: first Neil McClure's visit, then Dance's letter and Mrs. Hennessy's pre-Christmas breakdown, followed by a string of intense afternoon appointments. Most of his patients were feeling the effects of the holidays and Jamie had acted more like a street pusher than a psychiatrist this afternoon. Everyone wanted more drugs. Please. No, they wouldn't make it through the holidays. They'd crack. Please, oh please, Doctor. More drugs. Up the dosage. Just for a few weeks.

At the end of the day, exhausted, his mind soaked to the brink, Jamie had stopped downstairs on the Glasshouse's first floor to pick up his own weekly jar of peace. Then, home at last, he'd popped two Ativan and poured himself a tall glass of Stella Artois. Dinner had consisted of hummus and a can of stuffed vine leaves.

The initial plan had been to get buzzed enough to sleep, but here he was, sitting up in bed, tense and bitter.

When was he going to move on?

Clearly, Basil had. And while Basil had been kissing the twins good night, Jamie had been standing under a jet of scalding water, scrubbing his skin raw, breathless, wild with anxiety, and for what? Punishment? That's right. Punishment. For Mickey's death. For unfastening his seat belt that morning. For stepping out of the car to taste the snow while his brother had stayed behind, asleep in his seat, dying a slow, quiet death.

For being here, when Mickey was not.

"I can't reach you," Basil had cried out, many times in the last year of their love affair. "You've shut me out. You don't hear me. You don't see me anymore."

Was that true? Had he shut Basil out?

Jamie jolted upward. Who?

The doorbell had rung.

No, it couldn't be. Could it?

He jumped out of bed and into the hall, stopping short in the entrance, watching the front door. Oh, God, yes. It had to be Basil come to apologize for being such a prick.

Jamie slid the lock and dead bolt, and opened the door a sliver.

Matt cocked a brow, lifting a bottle up in offering. "Were you sleeping?"

Oh no. The man-eater.

"What are you doing here?" Jamie glimpsed the hall behind Matt's shoulder, prepared to be ambushed. But Matt was alone. Of course he was alone. Why would he not be? Basil was at home, discovering Laura's clitoris with his tongue. Jamie winced at the image and opened the door wide. "Come in." He wouldn't sleep with Matt. Wouldn't. Wouldn't. Wouldn't.

"Wow, this is the new place, huh?" Matt set the bottle down—a formidable Pinot Noir—at their feet and slipped his coat off. "This place is very you. I love it."

Was this man for real? Jamie made an effort not to roll his eyes.

Then he remembered that he was in his pajamas, which consisted of white cotton pants and his YMCA T-shirt. He pushed his glasses up and tried not to blush. "Thanks, it isn't finished. I want that wall by the fireplace to be brick, and this bar is absolutely hideous, looks like a Midwestern House of Pancakes counter." Great, he was babbling. "And I'm definitely getting rid of the ceiling beams, they're too dark, they make—"

"Okay, Jamie." Matt smirked. "I get it. It's not finished." Matt laughed, stepping closer. Between his pulpy lips, his teeth shone like Chiclet gum squares. "Show me around."

The blond Adonis smelled like an apartment packed with frat boys getting ready for a night out on the town. It was indefinable, but overwhelming.

Jamie shrank back a little. "I've had a rough day, Matt. I was going to go to bed early and—"

"I know you had a bad day." Matt tossed his boots off, picked up the bottle, and went to the bar. "I overheard Basil talking to you this morning." He looked around and found what he needed. He uncorked the bottle and filled two glasses. "Mexico. I told him it's a bad idea. But he's got eyes big as loonies when he talks about little Mrs. Laura."

"I've had two sedatives, a pint of beer, and hummus. I'm not drinking wine." Jamie didn't move, standing his ground. "I need to be alone, okay?"

"You're always alone," Matt whispered, his blue eyes twinkling over the rim of the glass. "You've been neglected for way too long."

Oh please. He was *so* not always alone. As a matter of fact, he was with other people almost every minute of the day. "Anyway, what did Basil say?" Jamie asked, unable to stop himself from picking at the scab on his heart. "Did he say anything about our conversation?"

"Come here. Come sit down." Matt went around the bar and seated himself on one of the art deco stools. They were new. Fabulous, really. Black and white, with long, elegant metal legs. Basil would have hated them, but he didn't live here, now did he?

"Jamie, come on," Matt said, softly, reaching his hand out to him. "I'll play nice."

What did it matter anyway? Matt and he were both adults, in full possession of their mental faculties. Well, almost. Jamie smiled at his own pathetic justification and walked over to the stools.

He sat, facing Matt, his knees grazing the rough fabric of Matt's jeans. "I'm sitting. Now, what do you want?" He chuckled and was surprised at the sound of his spontaneous laughter.

Was he actually feeling relaxed?

"Wow," Matt said, setting his glass down. "Your smile is fucking fantastic." He bent to his ear. "It makes me weak, Jamie."

Jamie leaned his elbow on the bar top, fighting off the dizziness.

Heartache, that's what it was.

The pain of wanting another man when he'd believed it would never happen. He had set Basil above all other men. Had declared their love sacred, their tie unbreakable. Five months later, he was sitting here with an erection tearing out of his cotton pants, hot and bothered, ready to let Matt take him across the stool, forget the socks, sweet kisses, and foreplay.

Jamie looked down; Matt's hands held his. "You're really cute in your gym shirt," Matt said, but though his words were tainted with innocence, his eyes spoke of other things. Things that belonged only to them. In Matt's eyes, Jamie could see sanction. There would be no judgment. No blame tonight.

Jamie tugged on Matt's hand, giving him the signal.

Go. Now. Do it. Don't ask permission.

Matt was a hunter—he needed no further invitation, and tearing at Jamie's clothes and useless defenses, the man-eater went for the kill.

Jamie reached for the empty pillow by his head and threw it over his face.

He'd surpassed himself now.

This was possibly the stupidest move he'd ever made.

No, not true. Once, when he had been sixteen years old, while his parents had been spending another ski weekend in Tremblant, Jamie had brought his father's crème de menthe up to his bedroom and drunk half the bottle, sitting on his bed, phone in hand. After ten good gulps, he'd been drunk out of his wits. Then, hormones raging through his body like a squad team though a threatening crowd, Jamie had slipped out of his clothes and under the blanket—dialing the fatal number. That infamous evening, he had confessed his love to the straightest man in the world: his best friend Jeremy, the hockey freak. After Jamie's slurred but passionate declaration of love, Jeremy had mumbled only two words.

One of them being *never.*

Now, in bed, the winter sun burning through the white room, Jamie realized that stupidity knew no age. He tried not to remember the things Matt had done to him, and how amazingly well he'd done them, and instead blanked out his thoughts.

It worked for 3.7 seconds.

"Here's what you're going to do." Jamie tossed the pillow to the side and looked down at himself. Naked. Sticky. Still hard. "You're going to sit him down and—"

"Who you talking to?" Matt popped his head into the bedroom.

Jamie jerked the sheet over his softening morning wood and reached for his glasses. His fingers landed on a torn package of lubricated condoms. Dear God, he'd been an absolute beast last night. Some sort of incubus had possessed him, no doubt. He soon found his eyeglasses and slipped them on in a haste. He wished he hadn't.

Matt stood in the doorway, grinning. He was fresh as new linen. Not a crease on his face.

"You were the bomb last night," Matt said, nearing the bed. He was clad in last night's jeans, but had lost the shirt somewhere. On the ceiling fan, most probably. "I always knew you were naughty like that."

Naughty? Jamie cringed, pulling the sheet to his chin. "Can I get cleaned up without an audience, please?"

Matt frowned. "Bashful, are we?" He kissed his head. "You're late, by the way."

Late. Stupid. All of the above. Jamie flicked his eyes to the clock. "If I hurry, I'll make it," he said, shooting Matt a hard glance. "Can you give me some space so I can get ready?"

"I'm leaving anyway." Matt blushed, his jaw tightening. "I made coffee and cut some fruit for you," he said, obviously hurt.

Late. Stupid. And recently added: *jerk.* "Thank you," Jamie said, trying to redeem himself. "I'm just freaking out, okay? You understand that, right?"

Matt's features cleared. "Of course I do, but I wish you wouldn't freak out. I wish you would ask me to stick around and do something with you today." He poked his head under the bed and came back up with his shirt. Distractingly, he slipped it on and fastened it up, missing two buttons. "No one will know, all right? So you can relax. Big bad Baz won't know either." He turned away and glanced backward. "I'm gonna miss you, just so you know, and I'm gonna call you today, even if you don't answer me." Matt turned away and left the room.

Seconds later, Jamie heard the front door shut and, ashamed, he hid his face inside his hands.

Why couldn't Matt be a prick like the rest of the lot?

Why did he have to be so sweet?

❖

Monday morning.

Neil lugged the last roll of carpet up the narrow basement stairs. Three years ago, after he'd bought the house from that old retired navy officer—a wrinkled fart who'd tried to stiff him—he'd ripped the yellowed carpet off the floors and stacked it neatly in the unfinished cement basement.

Waste not, want not.

His mother's favorite words. She'd been a hoarder, storing and packing endlessly, recycling aluminum foil and wrapping paper. *You never know when you'll need it.* Except they never used anything in the McClure home. There were no birthdays to attend. No Christmas tree to decorate. The wrapping paper, along with the shoe boxes filled with ribbons, coupons, rinsed sandwich bags, remained stacked in his mother's closet, never to be opened. The objects were to Neil like phantoms forced to linger in limbo in their stale home, captive of his mother's closet, never to fulfill their earthly contribution.

Like his father, they would remain inanimate, stored away in his mother's room.

But Neil had escaped his mother's pallid hands. He'd made it out of that stinking, moldy house. And he'd done it by keeping his body in motion. Movement was man's only natural state. Action was what separated a man from objects.

He'd teach Xavier to move—keep his mind and body running. He'd break the boy down and start right from scratch.

Upstairs, Neil set the carpet roll by the others—five in all—and wiped his brow. Heavy fuckers, they were. He hadn't bench-pressed in too long. He'd become stagnant, like a pool of oil; that's what the problem was. His father—before the explosion had left his mind a decrepit piece of matter wasting away in a mangled body—had once tried to explain what made one firefighter survive while another didn't. It was a story about a rabbit running through the woods with a fox on its tail.

Son, when the little turd of hair stops, when it debates about its direction, that's when the fox gets him. A man in motion is a man alive.

Son, more morphine please.

Do it right for Daddy.

His father, the liar. His father, the big fucking talker.

But Xavier didn't know this. It wasn't his fault. The world had stopped moving, reduced to a shivering mass stuck between two spots, its ears trembling, its eyes wide with panic, paralyzed with fear.

"He's not gonna like it in the beginning," Neil said, lifting a carpet roll off the pile. "I know that, Hem. I know it." Neil carried the carpet to the bedroom, stopping by the open door. "But he'll get it later. He'll understand."

He entered the room, toting the large roll on his hip and looked down at the boy. Fuck, the kid's wrists were bleeding. Well, it was because he kept thrashing around like a wild animal. Neil set the carpet by the foot of the bed and frowned. "Xavier, I'm gonna try something else here." He moved to the bed and reached for the cord around the boy's wrists. "This rope is way too rough," he said. It was more like string than rope. Too thin. He hadn't been thinking clearly when he'd wrestled the boy to the bed. Adrenaline, maybe. Or the feel of something new under his hands.

Through the gag in his mouth, a sock—shit, that's all he had on hand at the time—the boy let out a guttural, bone-chilling roar, arching his back, struggling to inch away from his careful touch. What the hell was wrong with this kid anyway? "Stop jerking around like that," Neil said, trying for the boy's wrists again. "I'm gonna explain everything to you now, okay?"

Xavier stared at him from under his sweat-drenched bangs, defiant, fierce. But at least he'd stopped thrashing around and lay still now, his arms raised above his head, his wrists bound to the left bed post, his groans muted by the gag.

"I got excited and I fucked up." Neil went to the window and peeked out between the shades. Lots of snow and empty driveways. People were out shopping, probably. Or maybe they'd managed to save enough of their welfare checks to skip town for a few days. It didn't matter anyway. Aside from the mailman, no one ever came to his door. If he kept his head on right and called Christina the bleeding heart a few times, pretending he was roasting marshmallows over the furnace, listening to Crosby, she'd stay away.

And if not?

He'd cross that bridge when he got there.

"All right, listen," Neil said as softly as possible, turning from the window to look down at the boy. "I'm gonna soundproof this room. This way, I might be able to pull the sock out of your throat." He glanced around, rubbing his hands together. It was getting cold in this house. He definitely needed to put wood in the furnace. "Then I'm gonna give you a sedative because I need to go out. I won't be out long. I'm meeting with a new friend."

Xavier threw his head back, knocking it violently on the headboard.

"Jesus!" Neil cried, hurrying to the boy. "What the fuck is wrong with you?" He picked up a roll of carpet and, using his bare hands, tore a large piece out of it, which he placed over the headboard. He was sweating now. Hot, cold, was the heating company playing with his goddamn mind here? "Stay put. You wanna get brain damage?" Neil pressed the boy down, pushing his palms to the boy's chest. "Your heart is beating way too fast."

The kid turned his eyes away, tensing his neck to avert Neil's face.

Stubborn, this boy was.

"Okay, I know it's not easy, but when I come back from my appointment, I'll tell you what the game plan is." Neil backed up, gazing around the room. "I'm gonna give you the sedative intravenously. I know how to do it, so don't look so fucking panicked. It's just a little house mix of codeine and Rymadil." He shot the dog a hard glance.

"I know, but you don't need your medicine anymore, now do you? Besides, there's enough for both of you."

Xavier looked down at the dog.

Could the kid see Hem, too?

Of course he could. The boy was connected to the world in a visceral, instinctive way. Xavier was of his kind. Of *their* kind. They'd been brought together, their strings tugged in the same direction, for this, for this schooling.

"I'm gonna help you out of your shell," Neil said, stepping back to the doorway. "Then I'm gonna ignite your mind."

The boy closed his silver-gray eyes, shaking his head from side to side.

❖

He'd made it. Through traffic, snow, and black ice, he'd made it in time to work.

And so?

Jamie shrugged. What was that tiny achievement in the balance of things?

Whoop-de-do.

Vexed at himself, Jamie stepped over a pile of wood planks left out in the clinic's hallway, giving one of the workers—a handsome male specimen with a sexy potbelly—his best disapproving look. The man held his eyes, his cheeks coloring slightly under their dark stubble. Trying to look tough, Jamie moved the planks to the side, one by one, refusing the man's help twice. The planks were much heavier than they looked, but three-thousand-dollar suit or not, he'd send this guy a message. This was *his* clinic. God, these hard-hat types, they really believed they were the last Valium in the desert of Insomnia.

And, of course, they were.

As Jamie carried the last plank, he felt the worker's stare scorching his ass, but with effort he managed not to turn around to meet it. He wasn't *that* reckless. No, twenty-seven years of being queer had taught him one or two things. No matter how big the bulge got in these guys' jeans, it was often safer to flirt with a grizzly bear than return its deep stares. And besides, since he'd left his apartment, Jamie had been getting signals from every man he passed. Straight. Queer. Anything with a penis. He'd even caught a nonagenarian giving him a twinkling stare from his wheelchair. It was the sex on him. He was still on. Warm and willing. And that's the vibe he was throwing out there. *Come on, boys. Come and lick the crumbs from last night's feast right off my table.*

Jamie shook his head and smiled at his own humor. He pushed on the PTS clinic door, but not before stealing a quick glance back at the worker.

"Have a nice day," said the Marlboro Man, his eyes steady on Jamie's lips.

After a series of heart contractions, his face hot as lava, Jamie entered the clinic. Oh boy, if he wasn't careful, he'd be trading off one compulsion for another: washing his hands for anonymous blow jobs. Moderation was the key to mental health. Moderation, he inwardly chanted, glancing around the faces in the waiting room.

No! What was McClure doing here so soon again?

Jamie forced his lips into a polite smile and nodded at the giant in the aviator jacket. He spun around and went to the reception desk. "Does he have an appointment?" he asked Marie-Miel through pressed lips, pretending to be interested in the mail.

"Yes, I thought you said he was a friend of—"

"Fine. Fine." Jamie reached inside his pocket and plucked out the hand sanitizer. Absentmindedly, he dropped a good measure into his right palm and began to rub. "I thought I wasn't taking any more patients until further notice."

"And I thought I was getting two weeks off with full pay this year."

Jamie, startled by Marie-Miel's clipped tone, glanced up at her. She eyed him furiously, her black eyes shining with fatigue. What was wrong with him? He'd been too self-absorbed to notice how tired she was. Marie-Miel was a single mother of two young girls, and after she left the clinic late in the evening, she went home to her daughters, where between house chores and quality time with the girls, she desperately tried to catch up on her university online courses.

Embarrassed, Jamie reached for her hand. "I'm sorry. I didn't mean to snap at you," he said, squeezing her fingers.

She cracked a meek smile. "Does that mean I get my two weeks off?"

"Don't even dream about it." He turned from her desk, heading for his office, the sound of her laughter easing his nerves. They were in this together. Besides, he'd make it up to her after the holidays. She'd get some time off, and perhaps so would he. Dreaming of the Mediterranean coast, Jamie unlocked his door and looked back at her. "I need to make a call," he whispered. "Five minutes, tops."

Marie-Miel nodded. "At nine fourteen, I'm sending the first one in. Or else we'll never get through this day."

In the corner, Neil McClure coughed, but Jamie refrained from making eye contact. McClure was his first patient, no doubt about it. It was evident in Neil's posture. Jamie had noted the way Neil leaned in, elbows resting on his large knees, ready to be summoned.

Tough luck, the giant would have to wait five more minutes.

Jamie entered his office and shut the door behind him. He'd been meaning to make this phone call earlier, but every time he thought about it, he lost his nerve. Why was he so anxious about calling September Young? It was Dance's words. The way he'd painted his troubled sister. Moreover, his last and only conversation with the woman had ended quite harshly. The Young brothers seemed to share the same cutting, critical perspective of him—both judged him fiercely, yet both brothers expected great things from him.

He had no intention of letting the Youngs down. There was something in this case that called forward the most guarded aspects of his heart. Yes, the Young brothers were twins, and yes, they were both struggling with mental illness, but it was something else. But what? The last time he'd felt this strongly about a case, he'd fallen head over heels for the patients' adoptive father. This time around, he'd have to tread lightly. He would never let anyone get so close to his soul again.

Jamie seated himself at his desk, turned his computer on, inhaled as deeply as he could, and dialed September's number, hoping she was awake and in a better mood than she'd been the last time.

On the fourth ring, a raspy, barely audible voice answered him. "Is he dead?" the voice breathed.

Jamie stiffened in his chair, pressing the phone to his ear. "Ms. Young?"

"Is my brother dead?" The tone was flat. "Is that why you're calling me in the middle of the goddamn night?"

For a moment, Jamie was speechless, unsure of anything. He glanced at the time on the computer screen. All right, he wasn't losing his mind. "It's nine a.m., I—"

"Oh." September coughed. "What do you want?" There was the sound of a lighter flicking.

"I'm calling you because Dance asked me to." Jamie paused, waiting for a reply, and when there was none, he went on, trying to keep his voice calm, and his tone professional. "He's extremely worried about you and—"

"Okay." September blew smoke into the phone and coughed again. "When was the last time you spoke to my brother?"

"I got an e-mail from him last Friday."

"Do you have any idea where he is?"

"No." Jamie typed in his password. "I'm checking my e-mail. I might have a message from him." He scrolled down. "No, nothing. Are you concerned?"

"He usually calls me every other day." September blew more smoke into the phone. "I'm not concerned, Doctor." Her tone was mocking now. "My brother knows his way around."

"I would like to meet with you. That's the purpose of my call. Would you mind coming to my clinic this week, or the next, at your convenience—"

"Why?"

"Because I want to help your brother," Jamie lied. It wasn't really a lie. It was a half truth. "And he won't talk to me."

"And neither will I." September hung up.

Jamie blinked, his mouth hanging open.

Fine, then!

Why was he bothering with these two anyway? One was a compulsive liar, completely unreliable, and the other was rude and uncooperative. He was psychiatrist, not a martyr. To hell with both of them if they didn't want his help.

Jamie sighed, staring at the screen.

All right, maybe he'd just call her back later.

There was a tap on the door and Marie-Miel poked her face inside.

"Time's up." She smiled, apparently enjoying this very much. "I'm sending Mr. McClure in, along with a cup of coffee for you."

Jamie silently acquiesced and got to his feet. For some reason, he did not want to be sitting down when Neil McClure came in. He needed to meet him eye to eye. Last time, McClure had had the upper hand, sitting there on the divan, smug and cool.

This time, Jamie was prepared.

He'd show this giant what he was made of.

He'd get to the bottom of Neil McClure before the hour was up.

❖

The office smelled like disinfectant.

The art on the walls was nauseating. Fucking pretentious, these highbrow guys were. What were they teaching in Quebec's universities anyway? How to be superficial pricks?

Neil leaned back in the divan, watching the nervous doctor fiddle with his pen. It was obviously out of ink, but apparently having a university degree couldn't make up for good old-fashioned common sense.

"Excuse me," Scarborough said, getting out of his chair for the second time since they'd begun this charade. "I need to get this ink off my fingers."

There wasn't any ink on his pale, tapering fingers. Just lots of invisible germs. Neil had put it together pretty quickly: Scarborough was a complete mental case. He scrubbed his knuckles raw and had all kinds of nervous tics. In the last fifteen minutes, he had touched his eyebrow and throat rhythmically—like he was playing a symphony on his neck.

Ode to Insanity.

Neil smirked. "Everything okay?" He liked this. He liked this a lot. Scarborough was a delectable sight indeed. Fucking with his mind was like dipping a finger in warm butter. Getting him to blush was nothing short of exhilarating.

When he'd walked into the office, Scarborough had greeted him with a firm handshake, throwing Neil off a bit—he'd expected him to dodge his stare like he'd done last time, but instead, Scarborough had held his gaze, inviting an uncomfortable silence to slip between them. Good tactic for making a guy feel vulnerable, but the confidence hadn't lasted.

After Neil's last blunt answer, the doctor was clearly losing his cool.

"All right," Scarborough said, regaining his seat across from him. "Where were we?" He was breathless, leafing through his notes. "You were discussing your"—the doc's cheeks darkened yet a little more— "need to hurt, um, your desire to—"

"To feel a lot of pain when I come," Neil said, before licking his lips in pleasure. Scarborough had thought that he'd pay him $150.00 an hour to sit here and discuss his childhood? Wrong, asshole. For that price, he'd better be entertained. Neil cocked a brow, keeping his stare fastened to the doc's big brown eyes.

Clever eyes. Eyes full of grief.

"And are you concerned about this, Neil?"

Oh, Scarborough had found a way to compose himself. He'd called him by his first name, creating a certain intimacy about them. Good, then, the shrink wasn't an amateur.

The challenge was on.

Neil relished it. "It turns me on to talk about it. Is that wrong?"

"Not if you respect the boundaries of this exchange." Scarborough tapped his pen against his lip. "What does concern me is that I believe you do it strictly to get a reaction out of me."

Touché. The doc was good, real good. But he was better. "You always make strong statements like that after a second appointment?"

Scarborough shifted in his chair. "I didn't mean to offend you. It just seems a little out of character, that's all."

"So you're an intuitive kind of shrink. You believe in that whole vibe thing, don't you? You go with your gut on things."

"I suppose I do."

"Okay, then, I think I'm losing my mind." Neil heard himself speak the words, and his voice, like a neighbor's television playing behind a paper-thin wall, had a muted sound to it. What was he doing? How far would he take it? "Sometimes, I think I have it in me to hurt somebody." The admission electrified him—it sent thunder rolling through his limbs, and Neil's dick swelled inside his pants.

He'd go as far as the shrink's desire to heal his mind and disregard the evil could take him.

"I think about it a lot," Neil added, purposely looking down at his feet.

"And when do you have these thoughts the most?" Scarborough asked, his voice satiny. "What triggers them?"

"Look around you, Doc. What do you see?" This was better than he'd imagined. To be here, sitting across from this fragile, tenderhearted man, exposed to him, unveiled for him, was thrilling. "Where are the movers of the world? Where are all the John Galts? They're gone. And what are we left with? Vampires. Emotionally crippled people. Leeches. And we feed them from our very fucking veins, Doc!"

"You're angry."

"And you're blind."

Scarborough's dark eyes illuminated. "Do you feel like you've been treated unjustly by the world?"

"See, you change the subject." Neil leaned in, peering into the doctor's handsome face. "You wouldn't know the truth if it was sitting right across from you."

"Do you always begin relationships with confrontation?"

"Do you always deflect people's questions by asking another?"

"I'm a psychiatrist, my objective is to have you speak about yourself."

"How convenient."

"Why are you here?" Scarborough asked at length. "Do you want my help?"

"I need your help."

"What for?"

This was it.

This was the game he'd been dying to play.

"Dr. Scarborough," Neil said, every cell in his body wakening, "I think I need you to help me become what I was born to be."

❖

Last year, Elliot had insisted he read this new-age book.
What was the name of it?

Dance had only gotten halfway through the thing, but he remembered now.

It was about the power of the mind. Thoughts were signals, the author had explained, they were orders sent out to the Universe, and with them, we directed our Life's traffic.

Dance jerked his shoulders against the bedpost. Again. He'd do it again and again, no matter the pain, the awful, disgusting pain in his wrists. He'd do it until the skin was laid open to the bone and he could slip his wrists out of the bonds.

Directions. To the left here. Then right. Over the speed bump, then around dark corners. Yes, our minds were great. Our thoughts were capable of mapping out our worlds.

In a distance—though the sound came from his own throat—Dance heard himself moan against the wet gag in his mouth. He did it every other minute. Why, he wasn't sure. Where was the madman and his phantom dog?

Dance shook his shoulders again. His arms had gone numb fifteen or twenty minutes ago. He no longer had the strength to wear the rope down.

So, what had been his thoughts in the last years of his miserable life? What internal dialogue had he maintained with himself?

He'd wanted to disappear. That's right. He'd wanted to make them pay for paying so much attention to Seth and so little to him. Yes, those had been his thoughts. Vengeance. Hurt them. Make them see you exist by choosing not to.

And here he was.

Showing them.

Who would lose sleep over him? Who would go out looking for him in this cold, snow-covered city? Elliot? Maybe. But he wouldn't do it tomorrow, or the day after. Next week, maybe.

Dance looked around the bedroom. The giant's bedroom. The madman had put carpet on every wall and sealed the curtains to the window with duct tape, patching every possible sound leak with foam. Dance made an effort to move his jaw muscles. They were sore. His heart beat hard and fast as his gaze analyzed the empty room one more time. There had to be something here to help him understand.

Why was McClure doing this?

Next week would be too late. God damn it. It would be too late. He would be dead by then.

Oh, fuck, September, I'm going to be dead. Do you hear me? Do you fucking feel me in here, you bastard!

Education, Neil McClure said. A young man needed some education. That big disgusting maniac. He'd bite his nose off. Just needed to get the giant to remove the gag for one fucking second and he'd snap his face off with his teeth. All of it. No, no, not the face. He'd have to tear the man's jugular open. Go for the throat.

Dance moaned again, fighting off the need to close his eyes. What the fuck was in his veins?

The book talked about…

It talked about thoughts. Our thoughts were telegraphs. Or Morse code. Yeah, that's right.

Three dots/three dashes/three dots.

SOS.

September?

❖

Jamie flipped the page of his calendar.

Another year was coming around the bend, and what would that year bring him? The kids?

Basil?

He dropped the page and leaned back into his chair, glancing around his empty office. He'd made it through the day. Yes, but what was this mind-set he was in? Every day, slogging through the hours, counting minutes, waiting. And for what? Where had the joy gone in his life?

Jamie sighed heavily, recognizing the soothing effect of the two Ativan he'd placed on his tongue fifteen minutes ago. Two, when it should have been one. Two, because one was not enough. Addiction lurked about his existence, menacing and patient. *Come on, now, Jamie boy, one more for the road. One more to soothe the ol' nerves.* Yet, every day, he sat across from men and women whose whole existence gravitated around their daily hit. He filled out prescription after prescription, delivering the same cautious warnings to each of his patients. He prided himself on his responsible attitude. No matter how many cruise pamphlets or golf passes those snaggletoothed pharmaceutical reps flashed before his face, he'd never faltered. He'd never used his patients as guinea pigs to pocket more profit.

But it was all a fraud.

His own dependency was gaining ground, and pretty soon, his patients would notice the subtle changes in his posture, speech, and eyes. There is no bullshitting a bullshitter, as Basil liked to say.

Well, it was all Basil's fault anyway. He was the one who'd taken him up high, only to drop him into this deserted valley, alone, with no map, no compass.

"The addict's first defense," Jamie said aloud. "Blame others for his own problem." He rose and gathered his coat, gloves, and scarf. Outside his window, the sky was dark, gloomy as Poe's prose. The wind howled, sweeping snow across the Glasshouse's vast land, and in a few minutes, he'd have to walk across the black parking lot, uncover his car from under the massive amount of snow, scrape the ice off the windshield, and then drive through traffic, only to go home to a vacant condo—arid as the Draa.

At least he had Sylvester to look forward to. The kitten was very friendly and liked to follow him around like a puppy, jumping up on his lap at the first chance he'd get. The little furball loved to be petted. Probably emotionally dependent.

Good, that made two of them.

So then, this was who he'd become, a thirty-six-year-old man whose only companion was a needy kitten with an addiction to shoelaces.

Jamie stepped into the waiting room, finding it empty—Marie-Miel had signed off an hour ago—and he made certain everything was in order. He turned all the lights off. Then he caught his reflection in the large window; a haunted young man in need of a haircut was staring back at him through the white flakes. For a moment, Jamie barely recognized himself. He didn't truly look any different than he had five months ago, but it was in his expression.

Dr. Heartbreak. Yes, indeed.

Jamie turned away from the window and exited the clinic, shutting the door behind him. The workers were all gone; of course they were. These men had homes, families, lovers. Even Mr. Hot Stare had vanished, leaving only his hard hat behind. What had he expected? For the man to be waiting for him, sitting on his tool box? "I saw something in your eyes this morning," the hunk would say, "and I was thinking maybe we could"—

Across the hall, a child—Mallory?—called out to him, and Jamie spun around, cutting loose from his ridiculous daydreaming. Yes, it was Mallory, and two steps behind, emerging from the elevator, Basil and Marshall followed her steps. "Dr. J!" she yelped happily, jumping into his open arms. "Why didn't you answer your phone?"

He hugged her, unable to let her go. My God, he'd weep if he didn't let her little body go. "I must have forgotten to change it from silent to vibe mode," he said, releasing her, digging into his pocket for the cursed phone.

"Dad, Dr. J is here," Mallory announced, running back to Basil and her brother.

The Spasso men both stood, hats in hands, frozen in the middle of the cluttered hallway, wearing the same expression. Suspicion.

"We can go have pizza now," Mallory said, tugging on Basil's hand.

Pizza? Jamie blinked and pushed his glasses up his nose.

Basil ran his fingers through his hair and tried to smile. "The kids were harping on me all evening," he said, taking a step forward. "They really wanted to see you, and you know, I guess it isn't such a bad idea, I mean—"

"I had plans."

Plans? What was he saying?

His pride, his stupid stupid pride.

Basil gave Mallory a hard look. "Told you, princess, we can't just spring up on him like that."

"But I'll cancel them, of course." Jamie's heart pounded furiously, spinning his blood like a lone sock in a dryer. "It's nothing important," he mumbled, fondling his cell phone. He looked into Marshall's eyes and nodded. "Hi, you."

Marsh bit his lip and blinked. His blue gaze was lit with unspoken words.

Hello, Dr. J. I still love you but I'm so hurt, I can barely speak.
"Jamie, you don't have to—"

"Baz, it's all right." Jamie dialed into voice mail and proceeded with the lame charade. He asked his imaginary friend for a rain check and hung up.

First: addiction.

Then: speaking to nonexistent beings.

"Okay, let's go," he said, trying to keep a safe distance from Basil's warm, fine body. "I'm starving."

"You sure it's all right?" No matter what Basil wore, no matter what moves he made, his sex appeal was undeniable.

Now all Jamie needed to do was get a smile out of his ex-lover. Just a quick flash of the teeth, and he'd know that he still could do it. He winked, letting his true feelings show for a short, risky moment. "Yes," he said to Basil, seductively, "but can you give me a ride?"

Basil's gaze moved subtly over Jamie's smile. "Yeah," he whispered, his eyes flickering with lust.

"Let's go!" Mallory cried, holding the elevator doors opened for them.

CHAPTER EIGHT

I'm reading that book you gave me last year." Neil walked around the kitchen, phone lodged between cheek and shoulder. Where was that can of chicken noodle soup he'd bought that morning? His brain was turning to mush. Kept forgetting things. Damn it. "Yeah, yeah," he said hastily into the phone. "That one. *Initiation*, that's right."

Christina yapped and yapped. *Oh, Neil, it's so pretty outside. Judd built a snowman. The nephews are coming over tonight. We miss them, they're so cute. They're almost five, can you believe how time flies?* Her voice made its way through the line in waves of well-rehearsed Christmas cheer. She was pitiful in her attempt at pulling information out of him.

He'd put the can on the counter by Hem's bag of food. Then what? Probably in here. Neil fumbled through the cupboard's contents. Ah, there it was. "Chris, I gotta go. I'll call you next week, when I get back."

"So it's really been eight years since you've seen your mom last?" she asked, obviously trying to sound mildly disinterested.

Eight years, yeah. But he wasn't going to see his reclusive, hoarding mama. Not this year, nor the next. "That's right," he said. "Shrink says I should try to make amends in my life, so I figured I'd start with the old cunt."

"Oh, God, Neil, how can you call your mother that?"

Because "old cunt sack of useless shit" was a little too harsh. It was the holidays, after all. "I'm sorry," he said, finding the can of soup. "Old habits die hard, I guess."

"How do you find Dr. Scarborough? Nice, huh?"

If he laughed, she'd get defensive and they'd be on the phone for another fucking five minutes. The boy was hungry. Weak. He really thought Xavier was tougher than that. Maybe he'd overestimated the kid's resilience.

"Jamie is the best, you'll see." Christina was so proud of herself it made him sick. "If you stick with it, you'll be a changed man, I just know it, Neil."

This time, Neil couldn't muffle the laugh that darted out of his lips. "Thanks, Chris," he said, composing himself. "And you're right. The doc is exactly right for me."

Kind, neurotic, and recklessly preoccupied.

"What's that noise?"

Neil jumped at her question, glancing around the kitchen. Fuck, the boy was groaning again. He'd left the bedroom door opened. How could she hear it? Women. They all had bionic ears. "TV's on," he grumbled. "My supper is burning. I gotta go, Chris. And like I said, don't bother with my mail. I got Mrs. Sinclair to pile it up for me. See? I'm talking to my neighbors, aren't you tickled pink about it?"

She laughed. Good. Now good-bye.

"Have a good Christmas." He hung up.

To hell with banalities. His stomach was knotted like a fist full of arthritis.

"Okay, Hem boy, let's go see about Xavier's appetite."

Neil opened the can and dumped its lumpy contents into a large mug. He stuffed a spoon in there—plastic because damn, the boy was a feisty little shit—and walked across the narrow hall, past the gasoline containers, to the bedroom. He stopped in the doorway, shaking his head at the pathetic sight before him. Xavier had pissed himself.

"All right, little man, you've gone and done it now," Neil said, setting the cup down on the ground before ripping the filthy sheet off the boy's waist. This kid would make him nuts. He wasn't cooperative at all. Whiny and frail, like the rest of them? No, impossible, Xavier wasn't like those foreign students with a permanent cough, lounging around coffee shops downtown. Med students failing basic anatomy.

Engineers incapable of building a Popsicle-stick bridge. Artists whose main influence was Coca-Cola. This was our nation's youth? These cum stains with unpronounceable names who'd come here to suck up all the marrow from the bone, and degree in hand, leave the very place that had fed their bottomless hunger for five years, to go teach some snotty-faced democrats how—

Neil's thoughts dried out.

The boy was having some kind of seizure.

"Hey, calm down." He shook the kid a little, watching his pupils slip in and out of focus, drowned in that sea of silver. "Look at me. I brought you some soup." He raised the boy up. He was pretty loose—wasn't fighting him. When had he tied him up? Sunday, right. Okay, today was Tuesday. That wasn't bad at all. Barely two days. The kid would be zoned out for a few hours, but then he'd be calm, more receptive.

Ready for his first lesson.

"You can look at me like that all you want," Neil said, using the back of his sleeve to wipe the drool off the boy's chin, "but you're the one who's going to feel stupid later. Oh, yes, you will. I know about these things." He rubbed the boy's bangs away from his eyes, and the kid winced at his touch. "I'm gonna take the sock out of your mouth, but"—Neil waved his index in Xavier's face—"you better be quiet, or I'll knock you out."

The boy's eyes darted down to Neil's hand and slowly, the kid nodded.

"All right, then." Neil pinched the end of the protruding sock—gross—and pulled it out gently. "Don't you yell," he said. "Don't you make me put you down."

The kid whispered something.

"What? I can't hear a single thing you're saying."

The boy tried again. It was embarrassing. A pathetic little whimper.

"Speak up, boy." Neil heard his father and instinctively turned his head in the doorway's direction. What? Where was the old cripple?

"Water," Xavier moaned. "Water, you motherfucker."

Neil's face twitched.

No. Had to keep his temper in check. The last time he'd slapped the boy, Xavier hadn't come to for a few hours. Couldn't take that chance again. There was no teaching a cadaver. "Forget your manners?" He tried to smile.

Xavier cackled, his face turning a vibrant shade of red. He thrashed and thrashed, like some kind of demon child with cool metal eyes. *"Untie me, motherfucker!"* This time, the boy's voice boomed, bouncing off the padded walls, and Neil was shocked at its strength, but proud. There he was. There was the boy he'd glimpsed in the park that day. Defiant and strong.

"I'll get you some damn water," Neil said, stepping back to the door. "Keep your panties on."

"Untie me. I can't feel my arms." Xavier jerked his shoulders against the bedpost. "I'm serious. I can't feel my arms."

Neil hesitated, standing by the wall, peering into the boy's flushed face.

No, he was being played.

That face. Those pleading eyes. It was a show. The kid was a pro, he had to remember that fact or he'd be finished here.

"No," he said, turning away. "No way."

"Fuck you!" the boy roared.

Neil shoulders tensed and he gripped the door frame.

Yeah, okay, he'd get this kid some water, but to hell with the soup.

❖

Yeast and salted tomatoes were definitively on Jamie's top ten favorite scents. That and diner coffee, which he sipped now, seated across from Basil, the kids within earshot, playing some monstrous pinball machine.

Tony's parlor, their usual spot, was empty. The storm had kept even the most dedicated customers away, and Jamie welcomed the privacy. Donna, Tony's wife, was busy in the kitchen, and the delivery boy was out battling the elements.

Dinner over, Jamie was in a mild trance. Perhaps this moment was the cause for his quiet heartbeat—this minute so unexpected—but maybe it was the comfort food, the pill he'd popped, or the kids' voices meddling nearby. All those things, yes, but truly, it was Basil's sea blue eyes watching him from across the booth—that intelligent gaze steadily drugging him.

Jamie's eyelids were heavy. He could feel the lazy smile hanging on his lips.

"What are you on, man?" Basil tore another pack of brown sugar over his coffee. He didn't stir it. He never bothered with these things.

"Nothing new. It's just been a long day."

"As opposed to the other days. That clinic you run—"

"Baz," Jamie interjected, softly, touching Basil's thumb, "we were doing so good. Let's not trigger each other's defense mechanisms."

In response, Basil sighed, turning his eyes to the kids. He took a long swill of his coffee and remained silent.

"So," Jamie said, leaning back into the seat, aware of Basil's tense expression. What had he said? Why had Basil's face changed like that? "How's the LaSalle house—"

"Matt thinks he's in love with you." Basil fastened his eyes on him once more, his stare challenging and full of secrets. "You know how he gets. I feel bad for him."

Oh, this was a low blow. Here, with the kids so close by?

"Is that why you let the kids drag you out to the Glasshouse, Basil? Huh? To trap me here and—"

"For Christ sakes, James, relax."

James?

Another strike to the temple. Basil never called him *James*, unless he was sure to have the upper hand.

"I want you to know something," Basil said, his eyes turning to ice. "I never thought you were capable of being such a snake."

"And you should talk?" Jamie straightened up and then, aware that his voice had risen dramatically, he made an effort to contain it. "Do you want me to hate you, Basil? Because if you keep this disgusting behavior up, I'm going to—"

"He's my best fucking friend!" Basil yelled, slamming his palm against the table, rattling the cutlery and cups. "What's wrong with you? What are you thinking going behind my back and—"

"You slept with him first," Jamie cried, unable to keep his voice down. "You brought him into our house. My house, Basil!" He looked over his shoulder, catching sight of the kids' stunned faces. They had heard. Oh God, they were failing the twins more and more every day.

"Mallory, Marshall," Jamie said to the children, calling them forth, "come here, please—"

"Leave my kids out of this." Basil got out of his seat and tossed his chin up at the children. "Let's go, guys, it's a school night."

"*Your* kids?" Jamie echoed. Basil had finally said the dreaded words. Yes, he'd been waiting for Basil to say them, but though he'd been preparing for it, he hadn't anticipated the gash those words would tear into his soul. "Is that how it is?'

"Why can't we stay?" Mallory whined, staying put by the machine. "We haven't even had our desserts yet."

"I was weak," Jamie said quietly, for him more than for Basil. "I don't know what came over me. And I was lonely, Baz."

Basil seemed to retract back into his clothes.

"Can you appreciate that? Can you try to understand how confused I am? How much I've lost in so little time?"

"Daddy, can we have another loonie for the—"

"Marsh, I'm all out of change, okay? I'm not a bank machine—"

"I've got change," Jamie said, getting out of his seat, his legs wobbly, his head spinning. "Please, Basil, sit down. Let me give them some change and—"

"I can't be here a minute longer." Basil waved the offer off and gathered the grumbling kids. He fumbled through his wallet and dropped a fifty on the table. "For the pizza and a cab," he said, his eyes anywhere but on Jamie's face.

"Keep it." Jamie grabbed the cash and pushed it into Basil's chest. "Consider it an advance on the mortgage," he added bitterly before bending to Mallory's cheek. "I like when you write me," he said into her ear. "Ask your brother to drop me a line from time to time, okay?" He pulled the hand sanitizer out of his jacket and poured a few drops into his palms.

Mallory sniffled, her eyes twinkling with tears. But like him, she was too proud to cry. "When can we come to—"

"You can visit Dr. J this weekend," Basil said, pulling them to the door. "That's the arrangement, isn't it?"

"Until further notice," Jamie retorted, rubbing his fingers together, his tone cool again. He wouldn't let the kids see him break down. They were both staring at him as if they expected his head to split open any second now. Marshall, especially. Though the boy remained silent, the panicked glances he cast his father betrayed him.

"Be safe, guys," Jamie said, pushing himself over the brink of his own tolerance. He pocketed the sanitizer, passed Basil and the twins, and pushed the front door open, stepping out.

He'd stand here and wait for a cab, that's what he'd do.

Don't think. Just stand and wait for a cab.

Don't feel.

He leaned against the wall, watching three cabs roll by, but he didn't have the strength to hail any of them. He'd stand here a little longer. Snow fell on his nose and lips, and he hunched his shoulders, staring at the various steps imprinted into the white ground. Some prints were paired. Lovers, maybe. It was a lovely night now that the snow had stopped.

A lovely night to have your heart crushed to pieces and your pride trampled like a jockey under his own horse's hooves.

"I'll give you a ride."

Jamie looked up.

Basil stood near him, hands in pockets. Nearby, the kids were digging a hole in the snow bank by the parlor's entrance. "I lost my head," Basil said, shifting his weight from one leg to the other. "I didn't wanna bring the subject up tonight, okay? I want you to know that. I was gonna be nice and civilized and talk about it some other time, just you and me, but then, I don't know, you were sitting there looking so content or something, and I can't understand why, but I wanted to—"

"You wanted to hurt me."

"Why is that?" Basil shot the kids a glance and stepped closer. The smell of sawdust clung to him, and that old, wonderful familiar scent of a man's skin after a day's work. "You tell me, Jamie. You're the shrink. Why is it that every time I see your face, I get like this?"

"Like what?" Jamie asked, moving from the wall, nearing Basil.

"I don't know," Basil said at length, backing up. He called out to the kids and motioned for Jamie to follow.

Should he let this one go? Let Basil get away with a simple dismissive sentence?

Jamie hurried to catch up to them, debating his next move.

When they reached the car, Basil stopped abruptly and spun

around to face him. "Okay, this is how it is," he said confidently, but he paused, searching for an answer in the snow.

"This is how it is, what?"

Hold it together. Let the man speak.

"Baz?"

"I don't know." Basil popped the back door open and watched the kids slip into the seat. He shut their door and leaned back into it. "I'm sorry. I'm not making any sense."

Some invisible force propelled him forward, and Jamie stumbled the two steps separating him from Basil's body—his hands now two uncontrollable objects—took hold of Basil's cheeks, and before his lips could obtain permission from his brain, they were pressed to Basil's mouth with passion.

Soon, Basil pulled him into his arms, digging his fingers into the small of his back, his tongue parting Jamie's lips. "Oh," Basil groaned, kissing his mouth, neck, ear. "Jamie."

"Take me home," Jamie said, shivering all over.

"Oh shit, what are we doing here?" Basil tore away, his eyes wide with panic. "I'm sorry. I shouldn't have kissed you." He jumped into the front seat and shut the door.

Jamie pressed his face to the window, peering into the front seat; Basil sat behind the wheel, a look of confusion on his face, staring back at him through the slightly fogged glass.

But no matter how tormented Basil appeared to be, Jamie could not wipe the victorious grin off his own face.

❖

Daddy's hollering down the hall.

Come here, boy!

It's morning. Sunny outside. The retarded boy next door is peeing in his mama's garden. Mama says retarded boys grow up to be fine men if their mamas love 'em right.

Neil, ten years old, sits in his bedroom.

Why can't he be retarded?

Neil, come here.

Neil stares at the door resting against the wall. He stands and shuts it gently.

Are you in there?

Daddy's voice.

The retarded boy next door is pretty like a girl. He sits in the sun and his hair glows like honey.

Come here, son.

Neil leans up against the wall and holds his breath in. He won't go. Won't go. Won't go.

COME HERE.

Daddy's voice rips everything to shreds. Like that time Neil used his mom's special scissors.

Why'd you hurt the frog, baby? His mama cried a lot. *Why'd you hurt the frog, baby?*

The retarded boy next door is singing to himself. He's a fairy boy. He lifts his arms up high, all the way above his head, and he opens his mouth like he's drinking sunlight.

Daddy is calling him. Neil looks down at his hands. He's ten years old, but his hands are big.

You've got your uncle's hands. His mama likes to talk to him about his uncle. Uncle Andre is a war veteran. *No, no*, she says to Mrs. O'Donnell, *Andre isn't a drunk. He's got a job.*

Daddy had a job. Daddy was a fireman. Neil looks over at the picture on his nightstand. Him and his daddy at the firehouse. Daddy looks nervous. His hat is on straight, but Neil's hat is crooked. It's too big for his head because he's only three years old.

GET IN HERE, YOU LITTLE FAGGOT.

Mama says the drugs make Daddy act funny but it's gonna be all okay.

See you later, cowboy, Mama says. *I have a feeling about this morning. They're gonna call my numbers this morning.*

Daddy won't stop screaming. He only stops after lunch, when Neil puts the needle into his arm.

The retarded boy next door is looking at him through the window. He stands by the fence and looks at him.

What? What do you want?

The boy's eyes don't move. He looks and looks and then smiles.

Neil's mouth gets hard. His hands swell inside. His teeth fight each other.

Daddy wants him to clean the piss pan.

❖

"Oh my God," Jamie cried, pulling the sheet over his head, almost knocking his glasses off. "Please don't talk. Okay? Just please don't say a word."

Why? What kind of madness had taken refuge inside his skull last night?

"Can I just say—"

"No!" Jamie yanked the sheet off and sat up, his temples throbbing. Hungover again. Mixing uppers and downers, playing pharmaceutical roulette. "I need to be out of here in less than ten minutes." He looked around at the unfamiliar surroundings and rubbed his eyes under the lenses. "Where are my pants, please?"

"Hey, come here. Just for a second. Lay back down. Come on, Jamie."

Jamie glanced over his shoulder.

Matt gave him a sexy moue, and laughed, pulling him down. "I'll make some coffee, pop some bread in the toaster, and I'll even drive you to work myself. With my truck, we can make better time."

Jamie lay his head back on the pillow and turned his face to Matt. "Can you please try to use your intellectual faculties for one short minute? I really need you to hear me. Not listen to me. Hear me."

"I hear you." Matt smiled, his stare roaming all over Jamie's face, neck, nipples. "Go ahead, Doc, talk to me."

Jamie chuckled in spite of himself. "My God, you're so—"

"Adorable?"

Yes, adorable. Sweet, too. And smart. Matt liked to play up his player persona, but last night, Jamie had caught a glimpse behind the velvet curtain. Matt was terrified. Afraid of silence, empty apartments, and TV dinners. Another hostage to these dangerous times. And in the dead of the night, when Matt had opened up about his fears, Jamie had felt powerfully drawn to him.

Could he see Matt differently if he tried?

"What are you thinking about right now?" Matt asked, his smile fading. "Him?"

Jamie drew in a deep breath.

No, he hadn't been actually thinking of Basil.

"I meant what I said last night," Matt said, inching up closer to him. "I just wanna be open with you. And Baz. I thought about it a lot before I called him." He frowned. "I think I've always loved you, and I think Baz always knew it."

Dear God, this boy was so confused.

Matt had obviously mistaken envy for love. It was clear as day. In a world full of singles bars and botched relationships, the Spasso home had slowly become the model on which Matt based his own desires. Yes, Jamie and Basil, the stable, committed gay parents. Matt had no clue what those affirmations really entailed. From the outside, it was all picket fences and seven-course dinners, snowball fights with the kids and cuddling in front of a Disney movie, hot chocolate in hand.

"I was very upset last night," Jamie tried again. Had to talk some sense into the clueless man. "I thought I'd broken through Basil's guard, and then he dropped me off at the Glasshouse and just drove away—"

"And of all the people you could have called, you chose me."

Matt's smile reminded Jamie of one of his early patients, George, his name was; a delusional man with ideas of grandeur. George used to sit on the divan, nodding happily at everything he'd say. *Yes, Doctor, you're right, I will try that.* And the next week, they were always back at square one. Matt was just like George. He seemed to have a filter embedded between himself and reality. Every word was carefully screened, and those that might hurt never passed through the fine mesh.

"You could have had a panic attack, right?" Matt was getting excited. His cheeks darkened. He was lovely, really. If only he wasn't connected to him and Basil. If only he could be some stranger he'd picked up at a bar last night. "You didn't have an attack because you were with me. Have you noticed that you're calmer around me?"

Jamie laughed.

"See? You laugh a lot when we're together." Matt moved a little closer. His breath tickled Jamie's nose. The man didn't even have morning breath. "Jamie, I know you're scared and—"

"I don't like to do this, but you're forcing me to." Jamie climbed out of bed, and aware of his naked ass, found his pants hanging on the vanity mirror. He jumped into them and zipped up, looking around for his shirt. "I'm going to give you my assessment on your overall mental health." He found his shirt on the floor and slipped it on, buttoning it up. "Now, from what I've seen and heard in the last—"

"Wait a minute." Matt grinned, sitting up, brushing a blond lock out of his eyes. "You mean you're gonna give me your professional opinion?"

"Yes, that's right." Jamie pushed his glasses up his nose. The man was asking for it anyway. "From what I understand, you come from a fairly average home. Mother is a homemaker, father is a retired investment broker. Two sisters, straight. Married. You're the middle child."

"Go on," Matt said, his grin now splitting his face from ear to ear. "I'm intrigued."

"You graduated with honors. Graphic design program, right?" Matt nodded, and Jamie went on. "Then you went to work for a small marketing firm, and there you met your first lover. You fell madly in love with him, and when he got a job offer in Banff, you dropped everything and followed him."

Matt's smile still hung on his lips, though less provoking.

"In Banff, your lover became overwhelmed with his work with the hotel he'd been asked to manage, and you lounged about, aimless and tortured by his lack of attention. Then you met your second serious lover, a ski instructor, and fell madly in love with him. You left your first lover to move into the new lover's apartment, and soon after, if I recall correctly, that relationship ended abruptly."

"He met a girl and got married," Matt said, quite sourly. "So, yeah, it ended abruptly."

"Then," Jamie pursued, sensing all of Matt's defenses gearing up, "you met your third serious lover and followed him back here. You moved in with him and devoted yourself to helping him start his import/export business. Through a mutual customer, you met Basil, and you two had an instant connection, yes?"

"Baz's sister had just died in that accident, and there he was, this beautiful, passionate man, trying to make a living on sweat and pure luck, taking care of his sister's kids, and—"

"Okay, Matt, do you see a pattern here? Every single thing you've ever done, you've done for, or with the help of, another man."

"Yeah, so?" Matt blushed. "Fine, lay it on me. What's your

professional opinion? Come on, let me hear it." He crossed his arms over his chest.

"I think, regardless of how handsome you are, you suffer from very low self-esteem. I think that you have an excessive personality, which has led you to make brash decisions in the past, and I believe that you also may be secretly struggling with a touch of depression."

"Doc, you've just described the whole fucking country."

Jamie tensed.

"I mean, wow, is that how you see the world?" Matt frowned, dragging himself closer, cupping Jamie's hands into his. "You gotta try seeing people as people, you know?"

Jamie looked down at their hands. They fit quite nicely. Matt's were wide, with strong, elegant fingers, and his were fair and long.

"Has anyone ever turned the tables on you?" Matt asked, dropping a warm kiss on the corner of his mouth.

"What do you mean?"

"Have you ever been psychoanalyzed?"

Yes, he had. Many times. By his own father, the prominent child psychiatrist Dr. Donald Scarborough.

"My dad is a shrink."

"That doesn't count."

Jamie glanced up. "And why not?"

"Because, from what Baz told me, your old man is a complete sadist and should have been locked up for child abuse."

Jamie's whole body stiffened and he shrank back. What were they talking about here? What was he doing in Matt's bedroom still? It was nearing nine o'clock, and he'd be leaving Marie-Miel to fend for herself again. If she quit, he'd be neck-high in—

"Jamie?" Matt tried to make eye contact. "Hey, look at me. I'm sorry I brought up that subject. I was out of line."

"Look, Matt," Jamie said, getting to his feet, heading for the door. "I don't wanna do this anymore. Last night was my fault, mea culpa, but I've been really anxious lately, and I can't—"

"Okay. Okay. Take a breath." Matt jumped out of bed. "I get it, really." He made his way to him, naked, slick, and cool. He pressed Jamie's palm to his heart. "No more serious talk. Let's just have something to eat, some coffee, and I'll drive you straight to work. But stay, Jamie." Matt leaned his forehead to his, his lips skimming Jamie's. "Please. Stay."

Jamie closed his eyes.

He'd lost his footing, but when?

And where was solid ground?

❖

The giant pushed the plastic cup to his mouth, and Dance felt the first drop of water he'd been allowed today trickling over his chapped lips.

There were many conceptions of hell: Dante's, Milton's, Rimbaud's, Sartre's, even Blake's, but Dance forgave all of these men for their naïve interpretations.

They couldn't know.

Hell was here.

Hell was drinking water from this man's cup.

The divide was what pain was really about. The spaces between what one wants and what one has. And though he wanted desperately to spit the water in McClure's face, he drank and drank, and that was what burning alive must have felt like.

"All right, I like you like this." The giant smiled and set the cup down on the filthy floor. It was filthy because Dance had turned his hips when he'd relieved himself, aiming for the floor. An animal defecting in his own cage, out of pure spite.

"How are your arms?"

He'd said "motherfucker." He'd said "fuck you." Therefore he'd said everything he needed to say, and would say no more. With effort, Dance raised his right hand to the cup. More. The drinking had made him thirstier. McClure didn't oppose him and encouraged him to drink on his own. The madman sat on the edge of the bed, watching him with an air of satisfaction on his face. Like a man coming home to find that his puppy shat on the newspaper.

"I was asleep," McClure said, his pale eyes dissecting Dance's face. "But I heard you hollering. Please don't do that. It irks me like you have no idea."

Dance knew he hadn't hollered. He'd clung to consciousness all afternoon, trying to stay on top of the sedatives. With no fucking food in his stomach, it was close to impossible, but he had a system, which consisted of moving different limbs in a long, painful sequence of jerks and jolts, and then when his body was fairly responsive, he'd start on his mind. Song lyrics. Famous quotes. Anagrams. Recalling lovers' last names. Anything to keep his thoughts off the writhing of his stomach.

But shit no. He hadn't hollered. He was still in full control of his will. The giant was hearing things again. Moments before McClure had stumbled into the bedroom with a look of suspicion on his face, he'd been cussing at the phantom dog.

You tell me if you smell him in here, he'd yelled and yelled.

Who was *he*, exactly? If McClure had meant him, he wouldn't need an imaginary dog to sniff him out. Dance had pissed himself twice, though he couldn't understand where the water had come from, and he now lay in his own mess.

Good, then. If he was lucky, the mess in his jeans would keep the giant away from his ass.

Because this was clearly a sexual thing, Dance had figured that much out. McClure could preach until his tongue went numb, but the maniac was obviously clueless to his own sordid motivations. Yeah, he'd start with "the world is a vile place and I wanna save you from it" speech, but soon enough, he'd be sticking his cock down his throat.

Matter of time. And then what?

"Are you done?" Neil leaned in, peeking into the empty cup. "Let's get started."

Here it comes.

Dance's heart bumped under his skin. What was the madman's next move? The giant wouldn't risk oral sex, too dangerous, no. He'd go for penetration.

Okay. He'd never done that. It would probably hurt a lot. But if he could relax, if he could—

"First off, I won't tie you down for a while," McClure said. "I wanna see you like this, sitting nicely."

When the giant came in close, he'd play kitty with him. He'd cuddle him a little. Right. Right. Then he'd say that he wanted a shower. Had to have a shower. It would be so much nicer that way.

"You're gonna look at me, and I'm gonna look straight back at you."

All right. McClure wouldn't take him from behind, then. Change of plans, but that was good. Could even work to his advantage. McClure would have to lay his weight over him, but this way, he'd have access to the madman's face, ears, everything.

"And if you look down, I break your arm."

What?

"You can tell a lot by a man's stare." McClure moved in closer, his knees grazing Dance's. "Sit up a little more, you're a lot shorter than I am, and that's not fair to you."

Why wasn't he raping him already, this fucking piece of shit asshole?

Dance obeyed, painfully lifting himself up on the pillow.

"See, when you cross a man on the street, it's a little like playing chicken. Ever play chicken, Xavier?"

What was this? This was not planned. This was not what he'd been preparing for.

"So, we start."

"Wait." Dance cleared his throat, fighting back the fear. "What—"

"Shut your mouth, boy."

There it was. That change. Dance had seen it come about McClure's face, this subtle transformation that darkened Neil's cold blue eyes and covered his features like a thin sheet. At times, the giant appeared dazed, stumbling around the room, mumbling incoherent arguments, and then he would be like this. Composed. Calculative.

Grandiose.

"Again, you look at me, I look at you. You drop your eyes, I break your arm. The right one." McClure held his eyes to his. "Got it?"

September? Three dots/three dashes/three dots.

"Don't you dare look away, boy."

Dance set his exhausted eyes on the giant's stare. Fine. He'd stare at the ugly bastard if that's what the man wanted. They could sit here all night.

"Good. Really good. You've got life inside your eyes. Most people have dead fish eyes, ever notice?" The giant was content, his voice lifting. "In the park that day, you looked at me. It was a deep look. Ever read Twain?"

Dance made an effort to conceal his despair.

"Your eyes are like an abyss. I don't think there's a bottom to you, but I'll keep looking."

Dance's strength waned. He shivered, focusing his stare as best he could. The fatigue sank stones into his flesh. His body was nothing but a thin surface in which McClure's stare punctured holes. Or maybe he was the ant under the magnifying glass, burning in the name of morbid curiosity.

"Why were you in these parts?"

Dance winced at McClure's question, but he did not avert his eyes.

"This neighborhood is the pits. Why were you hanging around here? Know anybody around here?"

A sound mounted inside Dance's throat, but he repressed it, determined not to betray himself.

"You're agitated." Neil leaned in closer, his face inches away from his. "Talk to me. Don't be a pussy. Tell me, you know somebody around here?" McClure's eyes pushed into him, blue and mad like the tide. "Your parents? A cousin maybe? Who'd you write? Did you tell them where you were?"

Dance slowly leaned back, trying to steel his mind.

September. Hear me. Feel me.

We used to talk without moving our lips. Don't you remember, Seth?

"Oh, I can see it in your eyes," the giant whispered.

A jolt of panic struck him, and for a moment, Dance was disoriented. He flicked his eyes down, but quickly darted them back to McClure's face. The giant couldn't have noticed. It was barely a blink.

"I thought you'd last a little longer, but it's your first time." Neil sighed, glancing around. "Hem, get out. You don't wanna see this."

Dance felt the grip of McClure's hand on his throat before he could register the gesture, and when his head hit the board, a flash of night covered the room. He screamed, biting into the giant's shoulder, drawing blood—yes, blood!—all the while trying to reach down for the bastard's balls, but something exploded inside his forearm; a hot and crazy pain, oozing out of his veins, into his bone—this searing tar pain, too brutal for pleas, too sharp for retaliation.

Soon, the pain released him, and then he was tired, so tired, with nowhere to go but to sleep.

❖

Jamie rushed past the workers, running the obstacle course that was the Glasshouse's seventh floor, with as much grace as a sleepwalker on mescaline. After bumping into a few shoulders, skipping over various power tools, he made it to the clinic's door and shoved it open.

He was greeted by Marie-Miel's glare and a stuffy, overcrowded waiting room.

"Two weeks, full pay," he said, bending over the reception desk to grab the coffee she'd so generously prepared. "January." He touched his chest. "I swear to God."

She eyed him fiercely and slowly nodded, a smile forming on her lips. "Get in there."

"Thank you thank you thank you," Jamie chanted, backing up to his office door, trying not to notice the dozen faces staring back at him. But one of them caught his eye. Dance? No, it couldn't be Dance.

Dance wasn't a woman.

"Ms. Young?" he whispered, spilling coffee over his thumb.

The woman glanced around nervously, and rose from her chair. A black-haired boy with more ink on his skin than shirt helped her to her feet. She wore a gray coat over her thin frame, and against the ashen color, her eyes were luminous—reflecting the morning light like sequins. As she approached him, Jamie recognized the silver flame burning in her gaze. He'd seen it before. In her brother's eyes.

Righteous anger.

"Your receptionist said she'd try to squeeze me in between two appointments," September said.

There was no trace of a man in her features. No Adam's apple. No sign of another identity.

"I'm sorry." September held out her hand. She had a French manicure. It was impeccable. And fascinating. "I'm Dance Young's sibling."

Jamie wiped his hand against his jacket and shook her hand. "Yes, I gathered that." He smiled. Good God, he was acting like an imbecile. "I'm really surprised to see you here."

"This is Elliot, my brother's friend." September barely glanced over at the boy. Elliot cocked a brow and nodded in greeting. He couldn't be over nineteen years old. "I'd like to talk to you," September said, her voice raspy but steady. "If you could give me a minute of your time."

Jamie looked over at Marie-Miel. She shook her head. No way.

"Doctor," September said, calling his attention back. She coughed into her fist and glanced around the room again. "Look," she whispered. "I haven't been outside my house in two months, so if you don't ask me into your office pretty soon, I'm gonna jump out that fucking window."

❖

Jamie slipped the hand sanitizer back into his pocket and crossed his legs, glancing down at his notes.

"When was the last time you heard from your brother?" he asked.

He was sweating. Heart palpitations. Numb hands. *Hello, Mr. Panic, weren't you here just last night?*

"You do that a lot," September said. She was seated, poised, knees together, smoking a cigarette. His next patient would smell the smoke, and if that patient decided to report him, the fine would be exorbitant.

"What do you mean?" Jamie frowned, watching the young woman before him. Perhaps it wasn't panic he was feeling, but excitement.

"Rubbing that disinfectant on your hands." She blew a curl of blue smoke through her nose and dropped her cigarette in the makeshift ashtray—a glass of water.

"I struggle with a touch of OCD."

"I thought so."

Never had he blurted out the truth like that. Jamie uncrossed his legs and pushed his glasses up his nose. He shouldn't have revealed his jugular so quickly. "But it's under control," he added, regretting his defensive tone.

"I see." September pulled on her coat, closing the collar over her neck, and slowly, the fierceness in her eyes faded out. "Something's happened to my brother," she said. "That little shit's always played with fire." She stiffened, shook a thought off, and turned her attention to him once more. "Dr. Scarborough, what has Dance told you?"

"He's told me many things, most of them lies, I believe, but—"

"Did he tell you that I'm his brother?" September's voice jumped slightly. "Because I am."

Jamie made a conscious effort to let his understanding, compassion, and brotherly love shine through his features.

September's eyes narrowed as she waited for his response, but soon the resentment in them sank back into the shadows and her own features relaxed and opened to him.

He smiled, and his smile was tender. "Yes, he did mention it. And he also told me about the fire that devastated your apartment five months ago."

"Good then, so we don't have to get into that." She seemed utterly relieved.

"But I'd like to," Jamie said, crossing his legs again. His heart had quieted. This patient was by far the most interesting being he'd ever come across. Well, she wasn't his patient yet, but with careful maneuvering, she could be. "I would really consider it a privilege if you would agree to meet with me once a week."

She closed her eyes and shook her head. "No. I've seen enough shrinks to last me a lifetime. Don't take it personally, Dr. Scarborough, but I hate your kind. I hate your supreme power, your condescending attitudes. You know what you guys do?" Her whole body leaned forward, and her coat opened, revealing her thin, bruised neck. "You masturbate verbally, but never ejaculate."

Jamie laughed.

He'd never heard that before.

"Fair enough," he conceded, smiling.

She squinted, analyzing him for a moment. "This OCD you have, how bad does it get?"

"I don't think we should be discussing my—"

"Then I don't think we should be discussing my shit either." She reached for her pack of cigarettes on the center table, and with steady fingers flicked her golden lighter, lighting another cigarette. "My brother's been coming here for two years, yes?"

"That's right."

"So I have every right to know who my brother's been talking to. Who he's made himself vulnerable to."

"When he comes here, he is not in a vulnerable position, I can assure you." Jamie's tone was clipped. She'd pissed him off with her subtle affront. "I don't take advantage of my patients, if that's what you're insinuating."

"Are you gay?"

Jamie's jaw set.

"It's a reasonable question, Doctor." September took another drag of her cigarette, her eyes roaming over his face.

But Jamie realized she was not trying to provoke him. She was simply asking a question. "Yes, I am," he answered as candidly as he could.

"I thought so. Probably why my brother likes you." She glanced over at the door. "My brother and I like to pick up strays. I prefer cats, and he likes to collect gay boys. Take Elliot, for instance. He's been following my brother around for years, and Dance encourages him. It's quite cruel, I suppose. My brother is straight, as you must know."

"Yes, I'm aware, and it's irrelevant. And just so we're clear, I'm not a stray. I'm your brother's psychiatrist."

September flicked her ashes into the glass. "What did my brother tell you about our relationship?"

"He'd never mentioned you until a few weeks ago." Jamie felt remorse for purposely trying to hurt September. "I suppose he wanted to protect your privacy," he added. Why couldn't he maintain a distance with this case? Why was he so easily affected by the Young brothers? Because they were twins, yes, beautiful, slightly mad twins. "At any rate," he said, "we rarely spoke about his family life. Aside from a few confidences, Dance never allowed me into that cellar."

"Well, consider yourself lucky, then." She looked over at the door again. "I should go."

"Why did you come here, Ms. Young?"

She put her cigarette out, and her eyes, cool as autumn rain, peered into his. "The last time I saw my brother, I threw him out of my house." She swept her bangs back. "I don't regret it. My brother's cunning and brilliant, and completely deserving of my anger, but this time—" She paused, staring down at her hands.

"This time?"

She glanced up, tapping her manicured nails on her gray leather purse. "Do you believe in the twin connection, Doctor?"

"Your brother asked me the same question." Jamie leaned in, crushing his notepad against his abdomen. Should he? Should he tell her about Mickey?

"When Dance and I were boys, we would run out in the field behind our house, across the construction site, and find a cement sewer pipe to hide in. We'd sit in there and talk without moving our mouths."

"Have you ever read *Sensory Transfers*?" Jamie asked. "A book about the—"

"About the clinical studies of a child psychiatrist on his own twin sons."

"More like experiments, yes."

"I did read it. I've read everything on the subject. Every possible explanation. Understand, Doctor, there was a time when I was obsessed with the idea of being attached to my brother for the rest of my life."

"You resent him."

She shook her head, her body tensing.

"I understand why, and I would like to help you understand it as well, if you'll let me."

"I don't want anything horrible to happen to him." She coughed, obviously trying to disguise her watering eyes. "At least at the hands of karma, or another human being. I'm the one who is supposed to hurt him. That's my job."

"You asked me if I believed in the twin connection, and my answer is yes, absolutely." Jamie slipped his hand into his pocket, curling his clammy fingers around the sanitizer. "The book I mentioned, *Sensory Transfers*, do you recall its author's name, by any chance?"

She exhaled more smoke, shrugging. "I've read so many—"

"His name is Dr. Donald Scarborough."

Her eyes widened and then narrowed.

"He's my father."

"But—"

"I'm also a twin." Jamie plucked the flask out and popped the cap open. He dropped the liquid into his cupped palm and began to scrub. Mickey.

"And your brother died. I remember reading—"

"That's right. We were three years old."

September tapped her nails incessantly. Her posture was rigid. Her eyes clouded with anxiety.

"I want to help you, Ms. Young." Jamie set the notepad on the table. "And your brother."

"Do you know anything about gender disorders?"

Jamie was taken aback. "We briefly went over the subject matter during my studies, but—"

"If I agree to this, would you be qualified in diagnosing me with Gender Identity Disorder and helping me with the paperwork required for an SRS?"

"No."

"Could you contact a colleague who could, and convince him of your diagnosis?"

"Oh, September," Jamie said. "I wish I could, but that would be fraudulent and—"

"I have all the goddamn requirements."

"But you also have an eating disorder that needs to be addressed before—"

"And if I address it?" September tapped her nails. Tap. Tap. Tap.

"Then, and only then, could I consider it."

She leaned back into her seat, letting out a sharp breath.

Jamie smiled. "So?"

She tapped her nails. Tap. Tap tap. Tap.

Jamie picked up his notes and briefly leafed through them, giving her some time to mull it over.

Taptaptap. Tap. Tap. Tap. Taptaptap.

"What is that?" He glanced up, spying at September over his glasses. "That tapping. Do it again. I know that sequence."

September looked down at her hand. "I don't know. I can't remember."

Jamie went back to his notes, and then stole a look at the clock. Marie-Miel would have his head for this.

Taptaptap. Tap. Tap. Tap. Taptaptap.

"That. What you just did. Three shorts, three longs. That sequence."

September smiled, hiding her mouth behind her hand. "Wow, you're definitely highly strung."

"No, I know that signal."

"Signal?"

Jamie's heart jumped. "Yes," he said, "three shorts, three longs, three shorts."

"What? Why are you looking at me like that?"

"It's a distress signal."

"You mean like an SOS?"

"Not like," Jamie whispered. "It is."

CHAPTER NINE

S weat dripped into his mouth, and Neil savored it.
It was hard-earned sweat.

Lying on the bench press, eyes burning from the strain, Neil held the barbell at the end of his arms, holding the breath that scorched his chest.

Hold it. Steady. Steady now.

His deltoids trembled, his biceps bulged, and Neil rolled with the pain, tumbling under it—he was an empty bag now, spinning under the tow of this ocean of brutality. He let the gulf of anger fill him until it threatened to tear him at the seams, and when his elbows bent, he dropped the bar. The sound of metal crashing against metal reverberated through his chest cavity, across the cement basement, and back through his head, shaking his brain like a maraca.

Three hundred sixty-five pounds. He'd done better than that. God damn it, it was the beer, and the channel surfing. He hadn't worked his triceps in too long, and those key muscles were weak.

Neil sat up and wiped his face with his T-shirt. He'd throw all the beer down the sink, and from now on, he'd drink nothing but water and protein shakes.

Neil clenched and unclenched his fists, scanning the dusty, cold basement. There was nothing down here. Nothing but a washer and dryer, and this bench press. What a waste of space.

Maybe he should have put the boy down here.

"Nah, he'd probably hurt himself," Neil said, signaling for the dog to come closer. "I know I broke his arm, but I wrapped it up pretty good, and the swelling stopped." He grimaced, shaking his head. "Look, I said I was gonna take it easier on him next time, what more do you want me to do?"

Upstairs, Xavier called his name again. *Neil.*

Yeah, the boy called him by his first name now. What a smart little boy.

Oh Neil, please Neil, oh God Neil. Begging all the time. Bargaining.

"Shut up!" Neil yelled, jumping to his feet, and up the staircase. "Quit it! You're driving me fucking crazy with your hollering."

No, he couldn't call a goddamn ambulance. They wouldn't understand. They wouldn't get it. He wasn't finished yet, but when it was over, they'd get it. They'd really, really get it.

Neil, oh please Neil. Please. Please. Please.

Fucking cripple junkie. Lying there all day. Lying there in piss and shit. All day, calling. *Come here, boy. Come here and help your daddy.*

"Shut up," Neil cried, shoving the bedroom door open.

The boy lay on his side, holding his knees to his stomach, rocking himself. "I can't take it, I can't, please, Neil," he said, his face hidden in the pillow.

Neil sniffled, frowning.

No.

❖

The coat-check boy—a ginger-headed boy with a phony smile— took his blazer and scarf, and dropped a ticket into his palm.

"Thanks," Jamie mumbled, slipping the ticket into his pocket.

What was he doing here? Tuesday night, at a dance club? The last time he'd been in a club was over four years ago, and even then, he'd stuck out like a chicken wing in a vegan buffet.

The gingerbread boy stared at him, and Jamie winced.

Did he have something on his nose?

"Tips aren't included," the boy said with a slight, but obviously faked, lisp. He tapped the cookie jar. The container was filled with bills, though it was barely eight p.m.

"Sorry," Jamie said, turning away. "I don't have any change." His stomach tighter than most of these men's shirts, Jamie made his way through tank tops and blue jeans, and trying not to touch anyone, he crossed the empty dance floor, heading for the brightly lit bar. Matt had to be here already. They'd said eight.

Jamie scanned the premises, catching a few vaguely disinterested looks, but he couldn't spot Matt. Great. He'd have to sit here like a loser, pretending to be waiting for someone. Well, he *was* waiting for someone, but he'd have to make it very obvious. He pulled his silk pants up and seated himself on one of the stools—the one farthest from the barman. He pulled his phone out and punched in the calculator. He'd go over his budget for the month. How much was his electricity bill for November?

"Hello."

Startled, Jamie looked up.

"Drink?" the barman asked, setting a Budweiser coaster before him. He was young, sculpted, and playing gay for the boys. Straight men knew how to make a buck, couldn't deny that fact.

Jamie smiled politely. "No, thank you."

The barman winked and moved on.

Jamie went back to his calculator. Yes, that was the extent of his charm. He could barely keep a barman's attention. All his life, it had been the same. After he stepped out of the Glasshouse, when he was no longer Dr. Jamie Scarborough, he was only this. A nervous, overdressed geek who would rather fiddle with a calculator than have a conversation with another living organism.

Jamie frowned and tucked his phone back into his pocket.

Enough.

Around him, clusters of men stood around high tables, talking, laughing, hunting. Yes, hunting, their eyes moving faster than their lips, always aware of their surroundings—the new face that had just walked in. Who was he? And that one over there, sitting alone by the window?

But their eyes systematically skipped over him.

Jamie glanced down at himself and back up at a group of young men who'd bravely ventured out on the dance floor, dancing with their eyes closed, trying to get a semblance of a party going. All three boys wore designer jeans, low-cut and fashionably used, and brightly colored shirts.

And what was he wearing? Black shirt, black pants, black tie.

Dear God, he was attending his own burial.

Jamie slipped off his stool, heading for the nearest washroom. He came to a doorway opening up on a large red-tiled washroom, complete with steel-chrome sinks and dazzling floor-to-ceiling mirrors shooting light from every angle. The stalls were painted dark red, and in the corner, there was a glamorous red love seat. Two young men sat amongst its plush pillows, apparently trying to retrieve gum lodged deep inside their throats with their tongues.

Jamie quickly averted his eyes and walked to the mirror. If he concentrated on the music—Gaga again—he might be able to tune out the boys' heavy panting. He refused to be embarrassed. He was a free, liberal-minded, twenty-first-century gay man. No need to burst the blood vessels in his cheeks over this scene. He studied his reflection; in this yellow light, his complexion was no longer fair and milky, but shockingly pale, almost translucent. Perhaps he'd missed his calling. He would have made a dashing vampire.

Jamie smiled, catching the gleam in his eye. They were dark, almost black. Gypsy eyes, Basil had called them. That was a long time ago. Back when Basil was fascinated by his quirks.

Jamie removed his jacket and tie. He rolled up his sleeves up to his elbows and unfastened the two first buttons of his shirt. He ran the tap and cupped his hands under the stream.

"Oh, fuck yes, oh yes," one of the young men groaned. "Faster."

Don't look. The trick was not to look. Jamie strained his eyes trying to keep them from shooting to the left, where the boys sat. If one of them ejaculated, that would definitely not be *hygienic.*

Using his fingers, Jamie slicked his dark hair back, tucking all loose strands behind his ears. He didn't like his ears, but the mobster hairdo looked pretty good on him. As a matter of fact, he looked better than he had in a few weeks. Classy. Maybe even a little dangerous.

Well, maybe dangerous was pushing it, but the look was a step up from his usual accoutrement.

The two young men laughed, and this time Jamie couldn't stop himself from sneaking a peek. Were they mocking him? He turned his head and caught one of them zipping up.

They were done.

Jamie waited until the boys had stepped out of the washroom and checked his reflection again: He couldn't recognize his own expression.

The confidence on his face was not his, but a still picture of another man. A man who could have been, but never came to be. His brother. Mickey. Though they had only walked this earth together for three years, Jamie could recall his brother's face perfectly. They were identical twins, yes, but so very different in their manner. Mickey was rambunctious, daring, and careless at times. Mickey grinned from morning to night—at ease with the world and all its unseen turns and twists. How often Mickey had lifted his finger to Jamie's face and laughed.

Jamie has no smile.

In the mirror, it was Mickey Jamie glimpsed.

"I miss you," Jamie whispered, touching the glass. "Brother."

"Hey, there you are." Matt stumbled into the washroom, a can of Red Bull in hand. "Whoa, look at you."

Jamie stared at their reflection. "What?"

"You look different," Matt said, nearing him slowly. "You look fucking hot."

Jamie turned around. "Oh, this isn't sweat, I was wetting my—"

"No, Jamie." Matt laughed, his teeth gleaming in the neon lights. "I mean sexy. Crazy sexy, actually." He pushed Jamie's hair back and bent to his lips, burning them with a kiss. "I missed you today," he murmured.

Jamie pulled back a little, flushed, and way too turned on. "Matt, I've had a strange day and—"

"Come here."

"I was in here thinking about my dead brother because I saw a patient today, and the session stirred old—"

"Come here," Matt said, pulling him into his arms again. "That was before. This is now." Matt kissed his neck, his warm lips moving up to his earlobe, sending chills down Jamie's back. "You can't do anything for your patients right now, but, Doc, you can do a lot for me."

Jamie tried not to laugh, but it was impossible. "What do you want?"

Matt put a finger up to his own lips and winked. He held Jamie's hand and tugged him toward the stall.

"No way, Matt." Jamie shook his head. "I'm not committing any kind of sexual act in a public washroom. Who am I, George Michael?"

Matt pulled on his hand harder, refusing to let it go.

In all fairness, it *was* Tuesday night. The club wasn't busy. He hadn't seen anyone use a stall in the last fifteen minutes. They were probably fairly clean.

"Oh, come on, Jamie, live on the edge a little." Matt pushed a stall door open. "You won't touch anything but me."

"Hold on, my phone." Jamie turned away, staring at Basil's number blinking on his screen. "Be quiet," he said to Matt, casting him a threatening glare over his shoulder. "It's Baz calling."

Jamie heard Matt curse under his breath, but ignored him and exited the washroom, looking for a quiet spot. No such thing. He hunched in a corner, near a pay phone, and heart in mouth, answered Basil. Something was wrong. He could feel it. "Hey, everything okay?" he asked against the blaring music.

"Where the hell are you?"

"In a club. What's wrong, Baz?"

Basil said something, but Jamie couldn't hear anything. "Hold on," he screamed into the phone, pressing it hard against his ear. "I'm going to go outside."

Matt jumped up in front of him, halting his step. "What's going on?"

Jamie waved him off and shoved the emergency exit door open, climbing over the snow mound on the threshold, his shirt flapping in the brutal wind. "Baz?"

"What the fuck are you doing in a club on Tuesday night?" Basil's voice quivered with restrained fury. "I'm over here losing my freaking mind, trying to get Marsh through a panic attack, and you're out playing—"

"Wait a minute, I—"

"Are you with Matt?"

"What's happening with Marshall? Is he all right?"

Basil laughed. It was a vicious, bone-rattling laugh. "No, James, he isn't *all right*. He's flipping his lid. He's locked himself in the bathroom and—"

"I'm on my way." Jamie shivered, his wet hair slowly freezing against his forehead. "I'll be there in—"

"Don't bother."

"Baz, you stubborn bastard! I'm on my way." Jamie hung up and leaped back into the club, frantic. "I have to go," he announced to Matt, brushing by him. "Marsh is having a panic attack."

"I'll come with you." Matt held Jamie's jacket. "Put this on, your lips are turning blue."

"You can't come. You just can't, Matt."

"But—"

"Don't you understand?" Jamie cried, jerking the jacket out of Matt's hands. Oh boy, this man needed a reality check. "This is about me and Baz. About our family." He threw his jacket on.

And then, his mind conjuring up Marshall's intense blue eyes, Jamie rushed through the club.

What had he and Basil done to those kids?

❖

The face on the wall looked like his mother's.

Before she'd shot a hole between her eyes.

Dance stared at the carpet nailed to the wall, following its weave patterns, letting his vision focus and then blur, focus and then blur, focus and then blur.

His mother stared back at him, her face quiet, expressionless. Dead. He wasn't scared of the face in the carpet.

No, he liked looking into it.

Are you coming for me? Mom?

The giant was downstairs again. What did he do down there? What was that noise he made? Was he piling metal rods down there? Building him a cage? What was he doing? What was he doing?

His mother stared on, her face set as stone.

I won't go with you. Never. If I go, I go alone. I hate you.

Dance closed his eyes and then cracked them open. The face still stared back at him.

You left us. Seth is all fucked up because of you.

I'm all fucked up because of you.

Mother.

Selfish. You never wanted us. You wanted your philosophy books and solitude. Your downtime and naps. Your prose, your phone calls, your inner journey. Your coffee and cigarettes. Your wine and literature mags. Your afternoon walks, your morning television. Your headaches. PMS. Hangovers. Psychoanalysis. Self-discoveries.

Dance licked the tears on his mouth.

Not so much noise, boys. Keep it down, boys. Don't interrupt, boys. Don't come in here when I'm typing. Don't knock on the door when I'm in the shower. Don't ask me what's for dinner. Don't look at me like that.

Did you come for me, Mom?

Fuck you.

Dance shut his eyes.

❖

Jamie stood on the porch, waiting to be let in.

He had his house keys, but couldn't make up his mind about using them. He peeked through the frosted glass pane in the door, glimpsing a short silhouette.

The door opened—finally—and Mallory, dressed in her yellow Tweety pajamas, invited him in. Her eyes were glassy and her nose red. She'd been crying. Had Basil even noticed?

"Hey, baby," Jamie said, pulling her into his arms.

"You're cold." She shrank back, turning away from him, heading for the couch. She lay down and pulled a heavy quilt over herself. "Good night."

Jamie froze in the entrance. Was she upset with him? Was she turning on him as well? He took a few steps to her and retreated back. Clearly, she'd been pushed over her limits tonight, and the child needed her rest. "Good night," he whispered. "I love you."

She pulled the quilt higher up on her face.

Jamie hung his jacket in the entrance closet, catching sight of Basil's steel-toe boots, and his throat clenched. This had been their closet. This had been their home. He slipped his shoes off, his gaze slowly reaching up the staircase. The house was silent. Perhaps the storm had passed.

In his pocket, he felt for the reassuring form of the hand sanitizer flask.

No. Marshall needed him. And he needed him to be together. Strong.

Jamie looked over at Mallory and found that she slept already, her eyes jumping under their lids.

One down, one more to go.

He climbed up the eleven steps leading up to the second floor and, on the last, purposely cleared his throat. "Baz?" he whispered.

Nothing.

Jamie reached the landing and peered into the dark hallway; at its end, Basil sat with his back leaning up against the bathroom door, holding his knees to his chest. Was he asleep?

"Baz?" Jamie tried again.

Basil gave a startle, and for a moment, he remained transfixed, his eyes searching the end of the hall. "Jesus," he gasped. "I thought you were an apparition or something."

Jamie would have liked to smile, but his mouth was hard and his hands clammy. "Is he still in there?"

With obvious effort, Basil got to his feet—he'd had a bad day, it was evident. He'd probably been pushing himself, again, trying to tie all the loose ends before Christmas.

Christmas. Mexico. Little Miss Laura.

"It was really bad," Basil said, staring at the closed door. "But he's worn himself out, I think."

Jamie nodded, choosing not to speak until the image of Basil rolling under hotel sheets with a strange woman washed over him. When it had, he knocked on the bathroom door. "Marshall? It's me, Jamie."

Basil and he waited, ears pricked up, breath withheld.

"Marsh," Basil said, louder. "Dr. J is here. Come on, buddy, you've been asking for him all night. Well, he's here. Open the door."

Marshall had asked for him? Jamie tried again. "I've had such a terrible day, Marsh. I feel like I'm going to snap." He caught Basil's surprised, but curious expression, and went on. "I need to talk. You're the only one who really understands me."

Basil sighed, watching the door.

Jamie knocked again. "Please, my heart is beating a million miles an hour. I can't think like I usually can. My mind feels like it's playing a movie and I don't know any of the actors."

Basil smiled, shaking his head, but did not intervene.

Jamie jiggled the handle. "Marshall, I need to talk. I need you to open the door and help me calm down."

Inside his fingers, the handle turned, and then there was the sound of the lock sliding.

Basil exhaled with relief. "You still got it, Dr. Scarborough."

The door opened, but Marshall stayed behind. "Just you, Dr. J," the boy said.

Basil nodded. Yes. He would stay out of their way. Jamie watched him walk away, his stare so hot on Basil's plump ass he thought he'd burn a hole right through the man's jeans.

Focus, Jamie boy, focus. He pushed on the door a little. "Thank God," he said, entering the washroom. "I was having a total meltdown out there." He sat on the lid, looking up at Marshall, whose face was chalky.

"I broke the pole." Marshall pointed at the towels lying on the floor. He'd ripped the metal pole right out of the tiles.

"Did you hurt yourself?"

"Only a little." Marshall hid his right hand behind his back.

"Let me see." Jamie reached out, but did not touch Marshall. "Come on, now. Let me have a look."

Marshall's blue stare dropped to the floor and he shook his head. No.

"Can I put my thumb on your wrist?" Jamie grazed the boy's sleeve. "I have to make sure Mr. Ticker isn't having a party in there."

Marshall frowned. "He was jumping up and down on his bed before."

"Show me how." Jamie took hold of Marshall's left hand and Marshall allowed the touch. Pleased, Jamie brought the boy's hand to his own chest and pressed the palm against his heart. "Like this?" He tapped Marshall's hand against his chest.

Marshall stiffened. "No, like this." He bounced his hand over Jamie's heart, hard and fast.

"Mr. Ticker is definitely misbehaving in there." Jamie lolled his head.

Come on, Marsh. One look. One instant of eye contact.

"He's probably acting out, huh?"

"Probably." Marshall stared at Jamie's socks.

"Is he quiet now?"

Marshall shrugged.

Jamie's heart sank. "Hey, talk to me."

Marshall's lips moved, but he only shrugged again.

Oh, to hell with the clinical approach. Jamie pulled the boy into his arms, inhaling the scent he'd missed the most; cheap mountain breeze fabric softener and Mr. Bubble liquid soap. Marshall remained rigid, but he did not fight the hug. "I'm sorry," Jamie said, holding on tight. "I messed up."

Marshall leaned back, his eyes like two moonbeams. "It's not your fault," he said under his breath. "Dad's the one who should go live with a cat."

Jamie forced his face into a serious expression and looked the boy straight in the eye. "Do you feel sorry for me?"

Marshall's cheeks darkened.

"Is that what it is? You're playing tough guy with me, but deep inside, you feel bad for me?"

This time, the boy nodded.

Yes.

❖

Somebody was out there.

Some sneaky son of a bitch, walking around his goddamn property.

Behind the living room curtain, Neil spied on the dark street.

Show your face, motherfucker.

He'd blow his head right off.

"How come you don't tell me these things?" Neil kicked the dog. "What good are you to me, you old sack of fur?" This dog. Following him all day, all night. Whining. No sense of smell.

Neil stopped three feet short from the front door, listening. All right, then. Go time. He jumped to the entrance closet, ransacked its contents—coats, old boots, empty moving boxes—and finally, his hands landed on the cold neck of his shotgun. Maybe he'd get to use it this time. It wasn't registered. So?

"Go around the back, see." Neil glared at the dog. "And be quiet."

The boy. Damn it. What if he called out? Head swimming, Neil stepped back from the door, heading for the bedroom. That kid better not start hollering. He paused by the doorway, peeking into the dark room. "Xavier?" Nothing. The boy was either giving him the silent treatment or sleeping again. That's all he liked to do. Sleep and pout. "Hey, you awake?" Neil leaped to the bed, barrel up, and with his free hand, he shook the boy. "Are you sleeping?" He shook harder.

Xavier didn't respond. This kid was so out of it, never following the regimen. What did he need from him anyway? He'd fed him that afternoon, given him water. Painkillers, too. What else did he want? A massage?

"There's somebody at the door," Neil said, poking the kid with the shotgun's nose. "You make a noise, I'll skip through the curriculum and go right to the final exam, got it?"

Xavier didn't stir. Neil stared at him, trying to decipher the boy's expression in the dark. He was breathing.

Not dead.

There was a knock on the front door and Neil spun around, eyes wide. What the...? Better not be some fucking Jehovah's Witnesses pushing baby Jesus pamphlets into his hands, or there'd be one more chosen lamb going to meet his maker tonight.

Neil stepped away from the bed and into the hall. He gripped the shotgun, cautiously making his way to the front door. Upon it, he called out. "What? Who is it?"

"McClure, it's me."

John the idiot? Oh, this was great.

Wait. What if John actually had half a brain in that thick, Irish skull of his? What if he—

"Neil? I'm freezin' my balls out here." John laughed. "Come on, man, let me in."

Neil stood, motionless. Many times, he'd fantasized about pummeling John's face into tomato puree. This could be his shot at it. This could be the night. "What do you want?" he asked, nearing the door, toting the shotgun. "I'm busy."

There was another knock. This one more convincing.

This guy. This egg-shaped, tofu-eating yoga disciple.

Neil slid the lock and cracked the door open a wedge, keeping the gun out of view. "What are you doing here?" he asked the simpleton, sneaking a peek at the quiet street behind John's shoulder.

"You're sweating," John said. "Were you working out?"

Behind the door, Neil tightened his fingers around the barrel. "What do you want?"

"Look, Neil," John said, standing on his toes, obviously trying to see into the dark house, "Christina put me up to this. She's worried. Says you're leaving tomorrow and—"

"Yeah, so?"

He'd let John in and then he'd sit him down with a nice beer and a shot of booze. He'd watch him throw it back and stuff the barrel into John's mouth—blow a trail of lead right down his throat.

"Can I come in?" John shrugged. "How you been? The guys have been asking about you and—"

"I was doing fine before you showed up. I got someone here. Busy, you know." No, he couldn't dispose of this dimwit. Too many people went looking for dimwits nowadays. People liked to pretend they cared, when really they secretly felt relief at the thought of the world being cleansed of another useless man taking up space. "I got a date," Neil added, forcing a smile on his face. "I was gonna get some tail until you showed up."

"Oh." John drew back a little, unsure. "I didn't see a car."

"She took a cab, asshole."

John blinked and then glanced around. "I'm sorry."

See? You called a guy an asshole and he apologized. Spineless. He'd have to spell it out for him.

"John," he said, "go home. Don't ever come back here again."

"But, I—"

"You what? You fucking two-faced, goat-humping, pitiful excuse for a human being. You signed a paper that sent me home and now you come here to relieve your conscience? You ain't gonna fix this leak with a cotton ball. Now, you turn around and walk off that ledge, back into the ocean of shit you came from."

John gasped, his eyes glazing over with confusion.

"Giddy up, motherfucker." Neil shut the door.

Inside, he stood, clutching the shotgun, immensely frustrated.

Damn it, he'd come so close to doing it right, but he'd chickened out. Consequences, that's what had put the fear in his heart. The idea of spending two life sentences in the slammer. And was that worse than allowing a subhuman like John to keep breathing?

Neil sucked in a deep breath. Okay, fair enough. He'd lacked the guts to follow through, but he had to forgive himself this time. He was still learning.

"How's the boy?" Neil stared at the dog, clenching his fist around the barrel of the shotgun. "Should we wake him?"

❖

Jamie paused on the last step, heart in mouth.

Marshall was in bed, at last. The boy didn't want to go to Mexico. He didn't like Laura all that much either.

Good, that made two of them.

Jamie stepped down to the first landing and wrung his hands. What could he say to Basil without causing another round of verbal punches? He'd have to be clever about it. And soft-spoken.

"Baz?" he called out, entering the living room.

All the lights were turned off, except for the string of red and white bulbs hanging lazily on the Christmas tree. Beneath the tree, a pile of poorly wrapped gifts awaited the kids. Santa hadn't come yet, but Grandma and Grandpa Spasso had obviously been feeling extra-guilty this year. They still believed they could buy their way into Basil's good graces.

Good luck.

Basil still carried a grudge against his parents, and with good reason. They had contested their daughter's will upon discovering that Delphine had named her brother sole legal guardian of her two children.

The Spassos had taken their only son to court and fought for custody of Marshall and Mallory. After three months of torment, Quebec's judicial system had made its decision: Basil had walked out of the ordeal a single gay father.

Correction, a single *bisexual* father.

Delphine, Basil's strong-willed sister, had probably signed those notary papers years before her premature death, never imagining the tear it would cause in their family. She hadn't breathed a word to anyone about it. Without letting Basil know of her intentions, she had drawn up these precautionary papers thinking they would never be needed. No.

She would live a long life and see her children grow. She was a single mother, but never hopeless.

Then one night, she'd never come home. The paramedic said she hadn't suffered much. It had been a clean death.

If there was anything clean about a head-on collision with a tow truck.

Basil, twenty-eight years old at the time—a single man whose main activity was getting over a hangover—had gotten the call. He'd run the five blocks to his sister's apartment, shoeless, mad with grief, to find the babysitter weeping in a police officer's arms.

Then he'd caught sight of his nephew's sleepy eyes, and when the boy had cried for his mother, Basil had cursed his sister for putting the invisible gun to his head. *Why me?* That question had been the only one on his lips for months, but the answer became clear to anyone who ever spent more than a minute around Basil and the twins.

Basil was the best thing that could have happened to them, short of having their mom.

"I thought maybe you fell asleep up there." Basil stood in the hallway, his face hidden in the shadows.

"I almost did." Jamie smiled, but his chest was tight.

Was he the best for this man? For this family? Was he causing them more harm than good?

"It's pretty bad out there." Basil walked past him to the living room window. He lifted the curtain. "You didn't put your snow tires on." He shook his head, dropping the curtain. "I told you to call Cy and—"

"I know. I meant to, but—"

"But you were busy." Basil sighed, plopping down into the love seat. Their love seat. Awful and green, but perfect. "So, what did Marsh tell you?" he asked, digging a toy car from under the seat.

Jamie stood by the cluttered coffee table, fidgeting. Should he sit down? Offer to leave?

"Hello?" Basil leaned forward, his blue eyes glistening in the red light. "Well? What did he say?"

"He's apprehensive about the trip." Jamie stuck his hand into his pocket, reaching the hand sanitizer, but then, he quickly pulled his hand out. Basil would bite his head off if he caught him indulging in his compulsion. "He's rather dissociative about it, which is normal—he's struggling with his mixed perspective of the events, because in all—"

"Fuck, I hate it when you do that." Basil leaned back, resting his head on the seat. "You're gonna charge me for this, Dr. Scarborough?"

Jamie looked down at the carpet, embarrassed. He'd done it again. He'd managed to irritate Basil in record time. "I'm sorry," he whispered, shrinking back. "I don't do it on purpose."

"Just give it to me straight. Does my son hate me?"

"No, of course not," Jamie said, taking a hesitant step forward. "He's adjusting, that's all. And he's an introvert, you know his ways—"

"That's what Laura says. She's also a little bit of a shrink, but without the OCD."

Bastard.

How could Basil stoop so low?

"Jamie," Basil said, leaning forward. "Listen, I didn't mean that. I—"

"Go to hell, Basil." Jamie leaped to the entrance—his vision blurred from the adrenaline surge and bitter tears—and looked around for his boots. This man would be the end of his reason. He'd go over the edge. He'd snap.

He jerked his coat out of the closet.

"Wait." Basil touched his arm, sending a jolt through him. "I don't know why I said it," Basil whispered, his fingers still on Jamie's sleeve.

Jamie backed up to the door, his face hot with anger. "You keep saying that. You hurt me and then act like—"

"I know. I know I do that."

God, he couldn't do this anymore. This was it. He couldn't take another hit. Jamie hid his face inside his hands for a moment.

Had to catch a breath.

"Jamie, hey. I'm sorry, okay? I'm sorry I say these things."

"Okay, fine." Jamie smoothed out his shirt. It didn't matter anymore. What mattered was the kids. If he could stay in their lives, he could live out his own and try to heal. "Good night," he said, dodging Basil's stare.

"That's it?"

"Yes, that's it." Jamie turned away and found his boots. He slipped them on, trying to keep from cracking. Basil would have to stew. He'd have to figure things out on his own this time.

"Fine." Basil walked away, heading for the kitchen. "Send me your bill, Dr. Scarborough."

"Have fun in Mexico." Jamie slammed the door behind him. On the porch, he stood breathless for an instant, then picked up whatever his hands fell on and threw that across the snow-covered lawn. "Prick!" he yelled, his voice breaking. He skidded down the front steps, catching sight of the object he'd thrown clear across the front yard. It was Basil's shovel. Jamie looked down at his shaky hands and back at the shovel. His eyes moved to Basil's truck.

No. Calm down. Don't do it.

What would the kids say if they woke up to find Basil circling his smashed-up truck?

Jamie walked to his car, fumbling with his keys.

"Jamie, wait," Basil called out, sauntering down the steps. He stopped a few feet short of him, shivering. He hadn't bothered with a coat. Or boots, for that matter. "I went too far this time, right?"

There was something in Basil's eyes that threatened to undo him. There was passion in Basil's stare. And love. So much love.

"Jamie, I wish—"

"You're right, Baz. You did go too far. And I can't be your punching bag anymore." Jamie finally unlocked the car door and pulled it open. "I want to be in the kids' lives, but I'm not going to get on my knees. What good would that do for them? Already, Marshall feels pity for me." He locked his eyes to Basil's. "*Pity*, Baz."

"D'you ever think maybe he feels pity because of all the stunts you've pulled in the last five years?"

"Stunts? You mean panic attacks?"

"I'm doing it again."

"You have so much resentment toward me, I don't even know how you can stand to be in the same room as me." Jamie moved to get into the seat.

"You're wrong," Basil said, softly.

Jamie flinched.

Basil stepped closer. "I don't know how to do it."

"Do what?"

"Don't you get it?" Basil held himself, his teeth clattering.

"You should go back inside, you're cold."

"Yeah, right, back inside." Basil turned away, and then spun around again. "Do you still love me?"

Was this a question, or another draw?

"You don't." Basil's face twisted as if he'd been stabbed.

"Do *you*, Baz?"

"I asked you first."

"I'm going home."

Basil turned away. "Fine, good night then."

Clearly, Basil wasn't willing to draw his pistol.

So be it.

Jamie shut the car door and turned the engine on, watching Basil climb up the stairs.

Well, he wouldn't be dumb enough to be the first to shoot.

❖

"Open your eyes."

Dance smelled the giant's breath. Chocolate and dust. It was the protein shakes McClure drank all day. Powdered vomit. The giant made him drink the shakes, too. Gulp gulp gulp. Morning and night. *Eat your protein, boy. Build up your muscles. You're a twig, boy. A bag of bones.*

"Look at this!" McClure grabbed Dance's crotch. It hurt, but not as much as the pain in his neck, shoulders, arms. "You're filthy." The giant lifted him up on the pillows. "You're a demon boy. You're the vessel for something, and I don't know what, but I'm gonna get it out of you."

Dance nodded, keeping his eyes shut tight. But he'd glimpsed the shotgun. Oh yes, he had. Semi-automatic. Single barrel. Right there in the giant's paw. Shiny and sleek. Gray maybe. If something gray killed you, did the gray leak into your soul? Could he ride the gray metal all the way down there? There, where he was going?

"Shut the fuck up!" McClure's voice thundered across the padded room, its trail dying before it hit the carpeted walls. "You bark at me like that again and I'll shoot your leg off."

Dance wiggled his toes and moved his ankles.

Shit, that phantom dog had better be careful.

"Someone was here," McClure said, his breath on Dance's face.

Someone had come. Someone human with human eyes and human breath. Dance's heart began to pound, sending shards of pain through his chest. This house still existed. There was a street out there.

"Open your mouth."

The shotgun was pressed to his lips.

The shell would burn through his nasal cavity and reach his brain before he'd feel it. It wouldn't hurt. It wouldn't hurt.

"I want you to suck on this."

Elliot would take care of his notebook. Where was it? Had the giant seen it? Did the notebook still exist? Elliot would lie with it pressed to his chest and rock it to sleep. The pages would smell like talcum powder and blueberries. Elliot would grow old, water his garden and think of him. He'd eat his own pears and wear a hat and think of him.

"Open your mouth, you little man whore." The giant's fingers curled around his throat. How could McClure be so strong? Had the mad man swallowed the world? Had he feasted on its rocks and boulders? Dance gasped for air, but he hadn't meant to. His body wanted to survive. His mind had nothing to say about it. McClure held him to the bed, one hand wrapped around his windpipe, the other shoving the barrel between his lips, bruising his gums.

"Show me what you do."

Dance opened his eyes, gazing into the monster's contorted features.

"Oh, you like it, don't you?"

The barrel entered his mouth, slowly, inch by inch.

Dance closed his eyes.

Why can't he run as fast as Seth? His throat burns. He can't keep up.

"Seth!"

But Seth never looks back, no, he doesn't like to slow down. He says he might fly if he can get his heels off the ground. Dance runs, jumping over wood planks, skidding across a patch of gravel, his eyes on his brother's feet. Seth might do it.

He might just take off and fly away.

"Wait, Seth!"

It doesn't matter. He doesn't need Seth to show him the way. They come here every afternoon, after school. Across the construction site, to the abandoned farm. The haunted farm. Animals were slaughtered there, they say. Cows and pigs. Seth says unicorns, too.

Dance slows his pace. He bends over, catching his breath. The sun is hidden behind a cloud. Just one. A cumulus, he's learned today. Cumulus nimbus. Where are all the other clouds? He straightens up and scans the field. The wheat is high and yellow. His brother calls to him.

Dance.

But there is no sound. Seth is using his other voice. The one only he can hear. It's a pretty voice.

Where are you?

Dance tries to answer his brother inside his own head, but he's not very good at it.

Come.

Sometimes, Seth is a girl and she shows him how to make music with leaves.

Boo.

Seth steps out of the long, shimmering wheat. His mouth does not move. His silver eyes beam like mom's polished spoons.

Come on.

Follow me.

Sometimes Seth cries with no tears, but today he is smiling.

Where are you going?

Dance yells, running again.

Seth?

September?

CHAPTER TEN

❝...at dinner, and he's staring at me. I ask, 'What's wrong, hon?' and he says, 'You overcooked the testicles again.' And I look down, oh, and there it is, this giant scrotum, just sitting there, purple and wrinkled like—"

"Excuse me." Jamie coughed into his fist, his eyes watering. Dear God, he hadn't even had his breakfast yet. He crossed his legs and jotted the rest of Mrs. Hennessy's dream down.

Sexual organs. Overcooked. Possible unconscious fear of emasculating husband.

"Can I have a glass of water?" Mrs. Hennessy smiled, her expression musing. "It's very dry in here."

"Of course." Anything to end this. Jamie rose and went to the sink. For a brief moment, he fought the urge to clean his hands, but his knuckles were swollen and cracked already. He poured a glass of filtered water for his patient and applied more cream on his hands.

"So, any plans for the holidays, Doctor?"

His back was turned to her, but Jamie could easily imagine the glimmer in Mrs. Hennessy's perspicacious eyes. She was his first patient this morning, and he was glad of it. After her, everything else would be a walk in the park. The woman exhausted him, always searching his face, watching his every reaction, obviously trying to finagle personal information out of him.

"Here you are," he said, setting the tall glass on a coaster. He stole a glance at the clock.

"You seem agitated this morning." Mrs. Hennessy's lips were painted a dark shade of cherry red. She brought the glass to them and winked. "What are you writing in there?" She leaned in, offering a generous view of her cleavage. "I'd like to see."

"I'd rather not."

"And why not?" She laughed, but her eyes dimmed.

"My handwriting is embarrassing."

There was a knock on his door and Marie-Miel's red-rimmed eyes appeared in the wedge. She was clearly on her last leg. "Doctor," she whispered. It was more of a hiss. "Take her call or I'll—"

"Can you excuse me, please?" Jamie smiled uneasily and neared the door, turning his back to Mrs. Hennessy's curious stare. "I can't, Marie-Miel. I can't talk to her right now. Tell her—"

"Jamie, I swear to God, she's been calling nonstop for the last ten minutes. She's going to make me scream in front of the patients. It's *me* Antone will have to strap down. You take the call or I—"

"All right, all right." Jamie let out a sharp breath. "Put her through." He shut the door and looked down at Mrs. Hennessy. "I apologize, but I—"

"Go ahead, I understand." She watched the phone ring. "Don't mind me."

Jamie picked up the receiver, angling his body away from his nosy patient.

"Why didn't you leave a message with Marie-Miel?" he breathed into the phone, trying to keep this conversation private.

"She's an illiterate. And since when does a mother have to leave a message with her son's secretary?"

Jamie closed his eyes, rubbing them under his glasses. One sentence from his mother and he already had a headache. "How are you, Mother?"

Jane Scarborough sighed. "I may have cancer."

Jamie smiled. "Who's your oncologist?" Apparently, his mother had been playing the alchemist again, dropping her Lithium into her vodka and lime.

She coughed. "I'm not seeing an oncologist, but a woman knows her own body."

"Is this like the time you thought you had a tapeworm?"

"Ah. Just like your father. Mocking me with your corrosive contempt."

Jamie's jaw hardened. "Mother, is it Christmas already? I was saving up on my corrosive contempt for when we'd meet, but—"

"So, you are coming for dinner, then."

"I wouldn't miss it for the world." Strange how he hadn't spoken to his mother since last Easter, yet their tongues hadn't dulled. They were both sharp as razor blades. He couldn't help himself. Her snobbish, superficial, aristocratic stance on the world clashed with every one of his humanitarian fibers.

And she knew it, too.

"In that case, your father would like you to bring the shrimp mousse you made last year."

Jamie blinked, holding back a laugh. He'd never made a shrimp mousse in his life. He cast a backward glance at Mrs. Hennessy. She sat, transfixed, listening to every one of his words.

"James?" his mother asked, a tremor in her voice. "You are coming alone, yes?"

Alone.

"Yes," he said, her question digging into his wounds. "Basil and the kids will be in Mexico."

"Well, it was expected, James, you don't understand the nature of these relationships you insist on having with men."

"Mother, you always hated Basil. You met the kids once. What do you know about—"

"Oh darling, let's not quarrel. It's the holidays."

Jamie relaxed his grip around the receiver. His fingers hurt. "How is Father, by the way?"

"Oh, he's fine. He's in Connecticut, giving a conference. Have you read his new book? It's quite different from what—"

"I have a patient here. I have to go. I'll see you in two days."

"James? Are you still running that stress clinic? You know, your father would really like to pass on his clientele to—"

"Mother, I'm not going to spend the rest of my life treating middle-aged upper-class housewives with fabricated neuroses—"

"Expect him to bring the subject up."

"And tell him to expect me to bring the shrimp mousse."

She chuckled. "I love you."

Jamie shook his head, fighting a smile. "I love you, too." Gently, he set the receiver down and faced Mrs. Hennessy. "Where were we?"

"Mothers can be tough, huh?"

"Would you mind cutting this appointment short a few minutes?" Jamie picked up his notes. "I need to—"

"You need to get your game face on." She rose, nodding appreciatively. "I don't know how you do it. Most of us can't even handle our own lives, and here you are, listening to other people's problems, day in, day out. It must be genuinely difficult."

Jamie bit his lip, frowning.

"But it must be even more difficult for those who choose to love you." She gathered her purse. "I'll see you after the holidays." She winked again. "Maybe I'll have figured out my marriage by then. Who knows what the new year will bring us."

"Indeed." Jamie escorted her to the door. When she stepped out, he caught sight of his next patient.

No! Not him!

Sitting in the first chair by his door, hat in hand, face turned upward like a schoolboy waiting for his daily whipping, Neil McClure watched him.

"I'll be right with you," Jamie mumbled, stepping back into his office.

"Take your time, Doc," Neil said, grinning. "I'm in no hurry."

❖

In less than twenty-four hours, Basil and the kids would be flying high above him—the children's excited faces pressed against the window, looking down on his mediocre, dust-covered world.

And he?

He'd be sipping his father's scotch, sitting between Jane and Donald Scarborough in their overfurnished drawing room, up on the hill.

"People pay you for this shit?"

Jamie snapped out of his self-loathing thoughts and focused his stare. "What's that?"

"I don't know," McClure said, cracking his humongous knuckles.

Crack. Crack. Jamie shuddered, but Neil didn't notice; the giant furrowed his brow, still staring. "Seems kinda counterproductive, Doc. People come here to watch you sleep with your eyes open."

"I don't think I understand." Jamie pushed his glasses up his nose. Oh, but he understood all right. Twice now, this big jerk had insulted him. In an effort to contain his temper, Jamie uncrossed his legs and leaned back into his leather chair, allowing a long silence to give him repose from Neil McClure's unpleasant, self-righteous attitude.

Neil watched him for a while and then turned his attention to the window. "It smells like Javex in here."

What was the purpose of Neil's visits? What on earth was he hoping to achieve with this farce of a therapy?

"Have you been sleeping well?" Jamie asked. Now he'd give him the boring run-down. See how he'd enjoy that. "How's your appetite?"

Neil smirked. "I read about your dad on the Internet."

Jamie winced, but kept his expression clean of any emotion. This man was a peeper, that's what he was. A voyeur of human feelings. Clearly, Neil McClure got off on other people's reactions to his comments and insinuations. These meetings were nothing but an emotional peep show to him.

"Your old man wrote some pretty controversial stuff." Neil ran his tongue over his front teeth, savoring this, perhaps. "Your brother and you were his guinea pigs, huh?"

"Don't believe everything you read on the Internet." Jamie felt his cheeks warm. Great, he was blushing. "Let's get back to what we talked about last time you were here." He leafed through his notes. Why? Why was he so affected by this brute?

"I was telling you that sometimes I think I could kill somebody. And you asked me if I was pissed with the world."

"Actually, you said that you could hurt someone, and I asked you if you felt the world had treated you unfairly."

In your face, sucker.

Neil nodded, clasping his hands together. "So, you do pay attention."

"Listen, Neil." Jamie regained his cool composure. "Can I call you Neil? I don't think I'm the right man for this"—inside his pocket, his phone vibrated, and Jamie pulled it out, sneaking a peek at the caller ID—"Oh," he gasped, forgetting McClure's presence for a moment. "What now?"

"Do you need to get that, Doc?" Neil cocked brow, a smug look on his face. "Never know, could be an emergency."

"Actually, I do. Excuse me." Jamie rose, turning his back to Neil, and for the second time in the last hour, he answered his private phone. "Dr. Scarborough speaking."

September coughed dryly and blew smoke into the phone. "Can I come by later?" she asked, her voice thin with dread. "I need to talk to you."

"Any news from—"

"No, Doctor, nothing." September called out to someone. "I'm on the phone with him right now," she told this person before addressing Jamie again. "Elliot is here. I can't get him out of my hair. He's like warm bubblegum or something." She cackled. "It's been a week, Doctor."

"And Emma?" Jamie asked, sensing Neil's stare on the back of his neck. "Have you spoken to her?"

"Of course I have. And she says no news."

Could Dance really be in trouble this time? Had the boy angered the wrong cop? Or slept with the wrong wife? "When was the last time you—"

"It was the Friday before last." September inhaled a long drag of her cigarette. "He goes and feeds the ducks here sometimes. By the river." She paused, and made a sound. Was she crying? "Fuck!" she screamed, chilling Jamie's blood. "That little bastard is right here, do you understand me, Doctor? He's here, I can feel him. I can hear him. I can almost touch him."

"Please, calm down," Jamie said, softly. "I'm sure everything is fine." His own lie unnerved him. "And yes, come by if you like, I should be finished by six this evening."

"I'm eating."

Jamie glanced back at Neil and then looked away once more, understanding September's last words. "Do you mean—"

"I haven't purged since last night." September coughed again. "Anyway, I thought you'd be excited about that, you know, since you types like to brag about early breakthroughs and such."

"That's wonderful," Jamie whispered, feeling elated for a minute.

"Yeah, well, Dance is hungry." She cut the line.

Jamie stood, phone still pressed to his ear, listening to the dial tone.

Fascinating.

September was using her brother's disappearance as an excuse to save herself.

Impatient to return to his notes on the Young case, Jamie settled back in his chair, giving Neil a distracted glance. "I'm sorry, where were we?"

"I think you were about to dump my ass."

Jamie held his breath.

"Am I right?" Neil asked, cracking his knuckles again.

"I have a waiting list of patients that—"

"Hey, it's all right." Neil McClure rose, and when he stood, Jamie suddenly felt vulnerable. For the first time in his career, he had an inclination to use the panic button under his desk.

"I don't like your face anyway," Neil said, glaring down at him.

Jamie drew back in his chair, sweat flooding his armpits and hands.

"You're fucking ugly, you know that?" Neil McClure moved closer, his eyes colorless and beaming with rage. "You should do the world a favor and jump out that window." He jerked forward, and Jamie shrank back.

"Get out," Jamie managed to say.

"Look at you, you pathetic pack of nerves." Neil McClure barked a laugh, retreating to the door. "You fucking pill-popping fag."

Jamie jumped to his feet. "You know what you are?" he cried. Oh God, to hell with this man. "You're beyond help."

Neil McClure's eyes flickered and he opened the door, standing wide in its doorway.

"Marie-Miel, call Antone."

"Don't bother, Doc." Neil stepped away, backing up to the clinic's door. "I'm gone. But you'll remember me."

"Get out." Jamie's voice quivered, but he held on. He felt every pair of eyes on him. Every breath withheld in his patients' chests. And it gave him courage. "You're wrong, I won't remember you."

"Oh, yeah, you will," McClure said, holding the door open, his stare pushing into Jamie. "When you come undone, you'll remember me."

"Is that a threat?"

Neil McClure tossed his chin up and stepped out.

"What a jerk." Marie-Miel touched his shoulder. "Are you all right?"

❖

What did he know, that overeducated puppet?

Neil shoved the Glasshouse's doors open, sending them hard against the wind, and stepped out of the madhouse.

That skinny kitten, in his Holt Renfrew suit, sitting there in his two-thousand-dollar leather chair, scribbling down his self-congratulatory, insignificant little notes, barely capable of giving somebody an honest glance. A tight-lipped, condescending, left-wing, Anglo-Saxon white boy eunuch.

What was he thinking coming here anyway? This place was nothing but a taxidermy exhibit. Stuffed bodies full of hay and chemicals, watching the world with glassy eyes. Poseurs. All of them. Faking life.

Scarborough had no idea who he was dealing with. Because the Doc had forgotten what a real man looked like.

"Neil?"

He'd come back for him, maybe. Yeah, see what was under all that silk and satin. Lots of pale skin probably. He'd make Scarborough get on his knees and beg for another chance. Another shot at the game. It could have been great. They could have played it right down to the bone.

"Hey." Someone grabbed his arm.

Neil looked down at the gloved fingers on his forearm.

"Neil? What are you doing here? I thought you were with your mother."

Who the fuck was this bitch?

"Were you with Jamie?"

Neil blinked.

"Neil?"

Christina.

"Yeah, I was," Neil said, heat rising up from his collar to his ears.

This girl. She was like salt on torn flesh, this one. "What the hell are you doing here?" he asked her.

"I have a meeting here. I work here." Christina's pupils were pinpoints, her eyes shining under a pink wool hat. "You didn't go? To your mom's, I mean."

What? What was she talking about? His mom? His mom was a hundred and fifty miles away from here, stinking up her old house, probably buried under pile of collectables she bought on the Home Shopping Network.

"Are you okay?" Christina asked, releasing his arm. "John said that—"

"I'm fine. Leaving later."

The boy was at home. Hem was keeping an eye out, but the dog was as blind and deaf as God on a Sunday morning. Xavier wasn't feeling too hot. He wasn't moving much anymore. Maybe he'd have to cut back on the injections. Give him a little breather. A bath or something.

"Oh," Christina said, glancing around nervously.

Why was she so edgy? Why was everybody so goddamn jumpy these days?

"Well, I'll talk to you soon, then," she whispered, moving to the doors. "My offer still stands. If you want to come over for—"

"Yeah, okay."

She didn't mean it anymore. It was bogus. The offer was a bad check.

"Merry Christmas, Neil."

"See you," Neil said. They wouldn't meet again, he knew.

She walked away, casting him a quick glance over her shoulder.

"Hey, Chris," he called out.

"Yeah?" She paused.

She was cute. Too bad.

"Don't stand too close to John."

She squinted, and nodded, slowly turning away from him.

Neil pulled the brim of his jacket up.

All right, he'd been fair.

He'd given the girl a warning.

❖

It sat there watching him with its burnt chestnut eyes, tongue poking out.

Through swollen lids, Dance stared back at the dog, each breath stabbing his chest. "Get out of here," he whispered, his chapped lips tearing with every painful word. "Get."

The dog did not mind him. It sat on its hind legs, its tail resting on the filthy carpet.

Why did the giant even bother binding him to the bed? He had no strength left in him.

"McClure's gonna kill you, too," he said to the obstinate dog.

Soon, very soon. Today maybe.

This afternoon.

And it would be over. Twenty-four years in this body, this head, and nothing done. There was supposed to be more time. He was on his way to figuring things out.

"You're following the wrong master," Dance said. Were his own eyes closed or opened? Was he asleep? Awake? "My arm is gonna rot." He gripped the pillowcase, his worn nails digging into the soiled cotton. Bound. Helpless. Him, helpless? How could it be? How could it have come to this? There had been no signs. No warnings for him. "Do you fucking hear me!" Dance cried in a broken voice. "I'm gonna die in here!"

The dog remained still.

"Hem, come on now, boy. Be a good dog. Go get Seth. Come on, boy."

The dog vanished.

"Hemingway!" Dance yelled, bruising his vocal cords. "You fucking coward! Get back here!"

Where did he go? Where did phantom dogs go? Dance tried to wet his lips, but his tongue was dry. How many days left? How many days gone? What was a lesson worth if one didn't survive it?

"Come back here," Dance moaned, his eyes burning red. "Oh please, Hem, please."

Seth was him and he was Seth and September was Seth and he was September and she was him. And round and round it went. Through and out, and through and out. "Damn it! Hem, don't leave me like this."

And if he died, the paperman string would be cut.

"I'll fight him, Hem. Please."

Twenty-four years was a prologue.

"I'll stay alive."

It wasn't even a chapter.

"If I get out of this, I'll change everything."

The dog reappeared, his eyes shining under golden fur.

Dance tried to reach his hand out, but the movement tore a trail of hot pain through his arm, and he moaned. "Go get September, Hem. Go. Tell her I'm here. Tell her I'm with the monster who killed the unicorns behind our house."

Dance fought sleep, struggling to keep his eyes open. Thoughts, like birds flitting across his mind, batted their wings, and he clutched the pillow's edge.

Once, when they'd been fifteen, Seth had locked himself up in the bathroom and refused to come out for hours. When Seth had finally stepped out, cool and collected, impervious to Dance's anger, he'd walked straight past him to his bedroom, never acknowledging Dance's questions. Seth had shut the door behind him, and furious, Dance had stood in the hall, dumbfounded by his brother's ability to shut him out. Then Dance had entered the washroom to find that on the white ceramic tile, using their mother's lipstick, Seth had spelled out the answer for him.

Now, in the monster's bed, Dance opened his eyes, seeing the pink letters again right there before him, bold against the carpet.

Pretending to be someone you're not is like kissing a live grenade. It feels smooth with your eyes closed, but remember, brother, like it or not, you're still kissing Death.

Dance laughed, tears stinging his eyes.

"Thank you so much, Marie-Miel."

Her smile broadened. "Doctor, promise me you'll try to rest."

Jamie nodded and then dropped a kiss on each of his receptionist's cheeks. He shrank back nervously, fiddling with his gloves. "Well, I'll see you next week."

Everything was in its place. The waiting room was quiet and dark. This was it. They were officially closed for the next five days. Good God, what would he do with all that spare time?

"I really wish you had let me buy you a gift," he said, opening the door for her.

"Doctor, you know how I feel about your culture's strange way of mixing God and Santa Claus." She stepped out, tightening the purple silk scarf around her face. "I've been here for seven years, and I still can't quite understand it."

Jamie laughed, following her to the elevator. "I suppose it can appear bizarre to you, but it's just a way for us to celebrate and spend time with our loved ones."

Right.

When said loved ones weren't in Mexico.

The elevator doors slid open and September stepped out, her gray hat shielding her eyes.

Jamie's heart skipped a beat. How could their meeting slip his mind? He was obviously overworked. "Hi," he greeted September, holding the elevator doors open for Marie-Miel.

Marie-Miel's eyes were fixed to September's thin, graceful body. September's features were classic, almost from another epoch, and in her gray wool coat and slim, high-heeled boots, she reminded Jamie of a Fifth Avenue storefront mannequin.

"You were leaving," September said, her gaze, poised and tranquil—silver eyes beaming like rhinestones. "You forgot."

Marie-Miel bade them farewell and quickly entered the elevator box. She was flustered.

Jamie understood her reaction. September Young had that effect on people, and perhaps it wasn't her transsexuality that people perceived but her power.

"I had a really shitty day," he said, putting his cards on the table. He remembered Neil McClure's insults, the wicked gleam in the man's pale blue eyes, and he blinked the memory away.

September stood still by the wall, a supernatural force amongst the bland settings. "You look tired," she said, turning her eyes away. "I shouldn't have come. You must be eager to go home."

Home. That bleak condo?

"I have no one waiting for me, aside from my cat," he said, pushing his glasses up. "And he's probably tearing through my curtains as we speak. He's very passive-aggressive."

September coughed into her gloved hand, covering her smile. "I see."

Jamie looked around, unable to make a decision. Should they go into his office, or perhaps, somewhere else?

September coughed again, obviously uncomfortable.

At once, he realized she hadn't come here seeking psychiatric help, but she had come here for him. For his friendship. And as their eyes met, he understood his own feelings. He didn't want to sit across from September, a notepad on his lap. No, he wanted to get out of here. He wanted to find refuge with her.

September's shoulders stiffened. "Are we going to stand here all evening?"

Jamie called the elevator back up and turned to her, glimpsing the spark of humor in her eyes. "Would you like to come to my place and talk?"

For a moment, September's eyes narrowed with confusion. Then her natural coolness resurfaced and she smiled without showing her teeth. "Why not."

"Good, then," Jamie said, inviting her to step into the elevator. "I'd love your company."

Had he just invited a patient's brother to his apartment?

CHAPTER ELEVEN

Jamie carried the steaming cups of tea to the living room, watching out for Sylvester, the tricky kitten, and then set the cups on the glass table by the couch.

September stood by the bay window, a moonbeam grazing her profile. She was still on the phone with Elliot, and so Jamie went back to the kitchen for the sugar and milk, cat in tow.

The fridge handle slipped out of his clammy hands and he realized how anxious he was. Why did everything he do feel like sin?

The kids weren't here. Basil wasn't here. And he wasn't committing a crime of any kind. September wasn't his patient. Wasn't he allowed to make a friend?

"Yeah?" Jamie smirked. "Then why are you justifying your choices to yourself? You're beginning to mistrust your own instincts and—"

"Doctor?" September cleared her throat.

Jamie spun around, flustered. "I do that," he admitted, his face hot as the teakettle. "I chastise myself out loud. I've done so since I was boy."

"Are you having doubts about me being here? Well, you shouldn't. I don't need a shrink, and even if I did, I wouldn't come to you."

Defensively, Jamie folded his arms over himself. "Oh?"

"You couldn't handle me."

He frowned, assessing her words. Could he? He'd never met anyone like her, much less treated anyone with such a vivid, emotional intelligence.

"Since our last meeting," September said with an unusual candor, "I find myself thinking about you and wondering if maybe you're thinking about me, too."

Jamie's heart jumped. Was she making a pass at him? Impossible.

"It's been a very long time since I met anyone whose opinion I sought. Well? Are you going to say something?"

"I'm flattered."

What?

How pretentious of him. He'd meant to say a million other things, but his defense mechanisms had kicked in before he could formulate a sincere reply.

"You think I'm coming on to you, don't you?" September shook her head, smiling wanly. "Doctor, you're not my type, so you can resume your breathing. I'm simply telling you that I like you, and that I'm mystified as to the reason why."

"I like you, too." Jamie took a step forward, shortening the distance between them. "Very much. And if we're going to be friends, stop calling me Doctor."

September nodded, her jaw tightening. "Jamie," she whispered, "something's happened to my brother. I'm convinced of it now. I can't deny it any longer." She brought both hands to her mouth, overwhelmed. "Do you know how many times I wished for him to vanish?"

"This isn't your fault."

"I had this dream this morning. I can't make anything of it, but I woke up with this feeling"—she clutched her chest—"like someone had ripped a chunk of flesh right out of me."

"Elliot still hasn't heard from him?" Jamie went around the island and pulled a stool out for her. "Maybe Dance met someone," he said. "You know how blissful things can be in the beginning of a brand-new love affair. Maybe he hasn't even realized—"

"Dance always checks up on me, and he certainly always checks up on Elliot. You don't need to hear all of this." She rose, glancing around. "You've got your own problems and—"

"I thought friends listened to each other, but it's been so long since I made one, I may be mistaken."

"You really want to hear all my stupid shit?"

"Let's go to the living room and talk."

September sighed. "All right, but can I smoke in there?"

❖

The twins' birth, September swore, was immediately looked upon as a curse by everyone who knew Miriam Young—their mother—the savage poet and eternal student. All involved had expected the woman to crack under the burden of accidental motherhood. It was inevitable, they had all believed; Miriam would fall into postpartum blues as an exhausted diva would a bed of feathers, because it would be expected of her. It would be a perfectly suitable excuse for Miriam to finally indulge her dormant depression.

The boys' father, Sid Young, professor of ethnology, viewed fatherhood as a necessary endeavor, a phase all good-standing men needed to enter before the end of their prime. Tonight, September could not recall if their father had ever smiled. They seldom saw the man, but she remembered his scent and the feel of his beard on her forehead. Sid was a deeply ethical man, a man full of good intentions, a man whose life was a never-ending to-do list. His eyes were never on anything— his gaze always blurry, his attention divided and rarely on the boys. His ambitions were impressive, but his will was equally weak, and as the boys grew, their father spent more and more time in his study, typing away at another self-proclaimed masterpiece, hiding from his volatile and violent wife. Before long, Dance, who was the more sensitive of the twins, had come to this conclusion: The only thing their yellow-eyed, aging father would ever be capable of finishing was a bottle of Glenfiddich.

September remembered her brother's words. They had been nine years old, lying in their twin beds, facing the open window, the last of summer breathing its sweet air into their dark room. "Isn't it weird that our parents don't love us?" Dance had asked.

September had frowned, processing the statement with her habitual coolness. It was true. And how puzzling a truth it was—the worst kind, plain and irrefutable. Miriam and Sid Young were not parents, September had decided, or concluded. They were human beings, but not parents.

"Do you think we are who we really are?" she had asked her brother, her skin tingling again. Those days, her body wanted to rid itself of something, but all its obstinate organs, muscles, and bones held on tight, hence September now lived in a constant state of awareness, prepared to fall apart—yes, soon to be dismembered—right before her schoolmates' eyes.

One morning, her skin would simply fall off, and everything would come undone.

"You didn't feel like you truly inhabited your body," Jamie said before sipping the last of his tea. Thus far, he hadn't wanted to interrupt September's tale, but they were getting to the essence of something crucial, and he felt compelled to steer the conversation in its direction.

Poised, September sat, nestled into the couch, hugging a pillow. "You're being the shrink again," she said, her eyes shining under the corner lamp.

Jamie bit his lip. Good God, why couldn't he simply listen without offering his clinical observations?

"Jamie, it's okay. Don't look so apologetic." She threw the pillow to the side and lit another cigarette. "And you're right. Yes, that's exactly how I felt." She blew out a cloud of smoke. "But there was something else," she said, her voice hypnotic. "After Dance and I realized that our parents didn't love us, there came a sense of freedom. I can't explain it properly, but it was as if we weren't expected to fulfill any of their dreams, and so we could choose to be other people."

Jamie nodded, putting the pieces together as best he could. Partly, this could explain Dance's compulsive lying—a complex and dangerous coping mechanism.

"We played pretend a lot, and then, I don't remember when or how, but we stopped pretending and started believing."

"You mean your games became real."

September scooped up Sylvester, who immediately nestled himself in the folds of her skirts, purring. "Yes," she said. "I'd come home to find my brother in our bedroom, reading, and I'd say, 'Good afternoon,' and he'd look up from his book and greet me with a quick liner, which we used as codes, each one letting the other know what persona we were that day. We never allowed the other to slip out of character and we knew each and every last one of them perfectly. When he was Mr. Rochester, I was Jane, and when he was Jem, I was Scout." September paused, her gaze focusing on her milky hands. "But the more Dance's range expanded, the more mine dwindled, until one day, I was only capable of one performance, and that was when September was born. Crazy, huh?"

"No," Jamie whispered, setting his cup on the table. He reached for the pack of cigarettes and slipped one out. "May I?"

"Oh, look at you, Dr. Rebellious," September teased, crushing her stub into the ashtray. "I've corrupted you."

"I used to smoke." Jamie inhaled a drag and his eyes watered. He thought of Basil and smiled. "If my ex-boyfriend could see me right now, he'd have a cow."

"Tell me about him. What happened between you two?"

"It's such a long story." Jamie coughed a little, but determined, he sucked in another drag, this time inhaling profoundly, letting the nicotine and various death agents flood his bloodstream. Suddenly, he felt like a nice gin and tonic. "Do you want a drink?"

"A *long story* means you still love him."

Jamie rose, heading for the bottles. "We were together for five years. We raised his nephew and niece together." He lifted up the Beefeater. "Drink, yes?"

She joined him, but declined the drink. "You're in a lot of pain," she said, matter-of-fact.

The blunt remark moved him somehow, and Jamie flicked his eyes to his glass. "Yeah, I am. You have to understand, Basil and me, we were"—what were they? A team? Lovers? Husbands?—"a family," he finally said. "But I drove him insane with my compulsive behavior, my constant worrying, my inability to relax, to take anything easy—no, everything had to be complicated with me. I was a mess." Jamie drank his gin. "I'm still a mess."

"And this Basil of yours, he's perfect, of course." September watched him, her eyes full of intelligence, gray and steady on his face. Her sarcasm was comforting.

Now the gin moved through Jamie's chest, chasing the nervousness away. "Can I ask you something?" Bold, he filled up his glass and drank heavily from it.

September traced a red fingernail along the bar top. "You want to know why I want the reassignment surgery."

Jamie's heart jumped at her forthrightness and spot-on presumption. He threw back the rest of the gin, hoping it would give him courage. "It seems to me that maybe—"

"My brother says it's barbaric. Dance believes in the idea of Seth and I cohabiting together."

"Your brother loves you." Jamie regretted the glass of gin—he was dizzy, well on his way to being drunk. Sedatives and booze. Great, he was turning into his mother. "What I mean is," he said, trying to speak clearly, "is that you're beautiful."

"And so are you, Dr. Jamie Scarborough."

"Have you ever known the truth about anything?" Jamie asked, pushing the cigarette to his lips. He forgot to light it, and it dangled there until September brought the flame of her lighter to it. "You know," he said, "I'm going to be thirty-seven in a few weeks and I've never been so unsure about anything."

"You fall in love with people because you don't know where you start and they end."

"I'm a fraud," Jamie said, staring down at the cigarette burning between his fingers. "How can I help any of my patients? How dare I sit there and pretend to have answers?"

He'd silently pledged his life to Mallory and Marshall. He'd said, "I will never let you fall," and then he'd stepped away from the ledge and left them dangling from it. Just like his own father, Donald Scarborough, the eminent, revered, and sometimes hated *Dr.* Donald Scarborough, the man who'd given him life only to poison it day by day, until Jamie wished he had stayed in that car that November morning and died with his brother.

"What's wrong, Jamie?" September grazed his hand.

"McClure was right. My father did use my brother and me as guinea pigs." Jamie looked up, but he did not see September's face. He could only see his father's—a giant, polished face of marble, with eyes as dark as craters and the look in them—a look of disappointment, disdain, of disbelief even. "Mickey was his favorite. To my father, he was Michael, of course. Michael the Archangel, incapable of anything but greatness, and I was"—Jamie dropped his cigarette into the glass and shook his head—"I was nothing but the remnants of my brother. An aborted idea of him."

"That's fucking disgusting. So it's true. All those experiments he refers to as sensory transfers in his book, they really did happen?"

Jamie looked down at the bar top, seeing imprints on it—sweaty traces of germs and unseen bacteria lathering the glass. At once, his stomach heaved and he reached for the sanitizer inside his pocket, pulling it out. "Prior to our birth, my father was working on a theory that he believed—*still believes*—would prove the human mind capable of transmitting physical sensations to another mind, and when my mother announced that she was pregnant with twin boys, my father had found his ideal subjects." Jamie poured the liquid sanitizer into his palms, scrubbing hard. *Stop it. Your hands are clean.* But he couldn't stop. Couldn't. And the skin on his knuckles burned, but he scrubbed harder still. "My first memory of these experiments is vague, but I remember being in my crib, in the darkness"—Jamie squeezed his fingers painfully, one by one—"the night lamp had been turned off. And I stood, clutching the bars, crying out for my mother."

"Stop. Stop doing that." September snapped the flask out of his hands and held it tightly inside her palm. "You're going to make your hands bleed. Why were you left alone in the dark? Where was your brother?"

Jamie remembered hearing his brother laughing, playing perhaps, with their father, in the next room? "I don't know where he was, but that night, my father wanted to teach me how to see the light without witnessing it firsthand."

"You mean he locked you up in the dark while your brother was somewhere in a brightly lit room."

"I never could satisfy him. I cried and whined, and never followed the guidelines of the experiments."

"What the fuck, Jamie? You were a child, for chrissakes. What did your father expect?"

"Maturity and a sense of duty." Jamie rubbed his sore hands. His chest was tight, his breath short. If they didn't change the subject soon, he'd have a panic attack. "Anyway, that's the past."

"There is no such thing," September said. "No such thing." Her eyes lit up and then dimmed once more. "When Dance and I were fifteen, Miriam shot herself in Sid's study. My brother was the one to find her. When the police showed up, Dance was gone. The cops spent the afternoon interviewing Henry Miller instead."

"Oh God," Jamie gasped, forgetting his own miserable childhood for a moment. "Did she leave a note or—"

"No, just a composition book filled with blank pages."

Dance's notebook. How tragic.

Where was the silver-eyed boy tonight? Could he have done something stupid and horrible to himself?

"After my mother died, Dance and I secretly blamed each other, I think. We used to pass each other in the hallway and cast uneasy glances at one another. We wouldn't speak of Sid and Miriam. We took our make-believe game to a whole other level, I guess."

"Is that when you stopped eating?"

September silently acquiesced. "And three weeks later, Dance was gone. Physically, this time."

"And your father?"

"I lived with Sid for six years, while Dance came and went—my elusive and greatly talented brother traveled a lot, and he spent some time on the West Coast. As for me, I finished high school, and one morning I knocked on Sid's bedroom door, walked in clad in my best Hepburn dress, wearing my Lancôme rouge, and announced that I was moving in with my boyfriend. I would be going to Toronto for two years to get my certificate in tourism."

Jamie smiled. "Your father, Sid I mean, did he know that you were—"

"A woman?" September laughed, and her features tensed. "He made me, didn't he?"

"And the boyfriend? What happened to him?"

"Richard loved a certain part of me, but couldn't stand looking at the rest." She lit another cigarette. "He was straight. As were all my lovers. Look at us." She laughed, never showing her teeth. "We're incapable of moderation. One intimate disclosure is not enough, no, not for us. We always have to have more, go deeper, suffer more bitterly, and give more than is asked of us."

"You're right, and I think you've missed your calling. You should have been a shrink."

September dropped her heels and sighed. "I wanted to be a hotel manager."

"And what stopped you?" Jamie asked, instantly regretting his careless question. "I could help you," he said, spontaneously, without censoring himself. "I could use my connections to arrange your surgery, if that's what you want. I could do it."

Anger flashed across September's pale eyes. "Don't ever do that," she snapped, stepping back. "Don't give me your pity. I don't need it, and I certainly don't need a friend to compromise his career for me."

"Okay, I understand," Jamie muttered. "You're right again."

"And stop telling me I'm right. Who knows, I might be the coldest bitch on earth, and here you are, standing there with that sweet face of yours and those big brown eyes, and oh, fuck, Jamie." She leaned back on the door, quickly dabbing at her makeup. "I was fine before. I was going to live out my life, secluded from the rest of this fucking world, and then you had to go and look at me in that disinfectant-smelling office of yours and make me feel human again. You know I hate you for that."

"The same way you hate your brother."

"Yes."

"Because we won't allow you to disappear." Jamie neared her, cautiously, aware of the tension still lingering between them.

"Where is he?" September cried, banging her head back on the door out of frustration. "Where did my brother go? Here I am, doing everything the little shit wanted, and he's gone!"

"Come back to the living room. Come on." Jamie wrapped his arm around her, easily, without any doubt, and drew her to his chest. She allowed the embrace and followed him to the couches.

"It's late," Jamie said, stealing a look at his watch as he fell into the pillows, sitting next to September. "Why don't you stay here tonight? I could sleep on the couch and you could—"

"What cologne do you wear?" September leaned her head on his shoulder, obviously taxed. "Hand me a cigarette, will you?"

Jamie fetched the pack for her. "It's Clean."

September choked. "Jesus," she cried, moving her elegant hand through the smoke. "You really are a neat freak." She smoked, leaning up against his shoulder.

"Basil loves the scent. He picked it up for me. I don't think he saw the irony in it."

"Wait a minute," September cried, sitting up. "You said a name before. You said McClure."

"What?"

"That name, it rang a bell for me, and I've been trying to remember why."

"Neil McClure," Jamie said, rubbing his eyes, pushing the pest of a cat off his chest. "He's the guy who almost threw me out a window this afternoon, remember, I mentioned it earlier, on our way here."

"Big guy, right?"

"Huge. You know him?"

"I might." September flicked her cigarette into the ashtray, turning her face to him once more. "Is he a fireman?"

"You know him," Jamie whispered, his stomach knotting.

"He went back for my bag that night." She squinted, her pupils pinpoints. "The other assholes wouldn't listen to me, but he went back for the bag." She waved dismissively. "He never found it, of course. Eighty grand, gone up in smoke. My whole future, given up to the flames."

Neil McClure? That foul-mouthed brute?

"After the fire, I saw the man a few times around the neighborhood, but he never acknowledged me."

The world was at times so small it seemed to be nothing but an elevator ride between hell and heaven. "Have you seen him recently?" Jamie asked.

"No. Why? And what has he told you? Why is he seeing you anyway?" September leaned back once more, resuming her place on his shoulder. She was relaxed, smoking slowly. "Come on, Doctor, aren't your friends entitled to some juicy gossip about your patients once in a while?"

"There's nothing juicy about Neil McClure. He's as dry as a block of concrete, and I'd prefer you cross the street if you ever should come face-to-face with him again."

"Why? He seemed harmless. Lonely, I suppose. Walking that old dog around, his brim pulled way down low—"

"He lives near your place, then?"

"Yes, just a few streets down."

Jamie nudged September, forcing eye contact. "Listen to me. McClure is a hater, all right? And he's dangerous."

"It's funny we should be talking about him." September smoothed out the creases in her blouse. "Because I had a dream about that old dog of his. He was right there in my living room, staring at me with those glassy, feverish eyes. And the strangest thing is that he wore a fireman's hat. Those cheap plastic ones, the kind you get at the dollar store."

"Well, McClure had that poor dog put down a few weeks ago and went into some kind of massive breakdown."

September's gaze drifted to the window again. "My brother's

starving." She clutched her neck. "I'm losing him," she whispered. "I'm losing Dance."

Jamie reached for her hand and squeezed it.

Be quiet. Don't dish out monotone one-liners.

Don't be the shrink.

"Has my brother ever allowed you to read his notebook?" September asked, her eyes livening up. "During your sessions maybe?"

A notebook for a suicide note. Miriam Young's despair had made her cruel. "Never, but he promised I could. If I—" Jamie stopped short, assessing the consequence of his next words on September.

"If what?"

"Dance came to see me a few days before his disappearance, as you know, and he said that I could read his notebook if I promised to help you."

September's face filled with pain. "Looks like he may have to make good on that promise," she said, her eyes still searching the night. "I keep remembering his face the last time I saw him. He stood by the door, and I remember thinking how much he looked like Seth."

"You mean how much he looks like you."

September sighed, shrugging. "I suppose so, yes."

"And Seth is a wonderful, highly attractive young man."

"But he only measures six inches."

Jamie laughed, throwing his head back. "Well, six inches goes a long way, my dear." He stood. "Come now, you're exhausted and so am I." He bowed. "Ms. Young, would you do me the honor of sleeping in my ridiculously large bed and keeping me company for the night? As a friend, of course."

September nodded, graciously accepting his hand.

❖

The boy wasn't at all what he'd put forth in the park that day. For one thing, his metal cool eyes were always closed now, and his face, which Neil remembered to be fine and attractive, was nothing but a gaunt yellow-and-blue mask of flesh.

What a fucking mess.

Neil lugged the kid across the hall, feet first, trying not to damage the boy's empty head. And why was he being so careful anyway? Not like Xavier was going to be using his head for anything anymore. The kid was all out of ideas. He didn't even try to get on Neil's good side these days. He just lay there and took the needle up his arm. Hooked on dog drugs and painkillers. He'd go nowhere, this kid.

But the boy sure as hell couldn't stay here.

Neil stopped by the washroom and dropped Xavier's legs on the floor.

"Shut up!"

The fucking dog was at it again. Wagging its tail, circling the boy, happy happy happy.

"Get outta of here!" Neil yelled, his voice thundering through the quiet house. "I'm sick of you!"

Then the dog was gone.

Neil stepped over the kid, entering the clean washroom. Clean because he'd spent the morning fucking scrubbing it.

"Okay," he said. "Okay."

He'd gotten new clothes for the boy, size medium on everything, jeans, blue T-shirt, white socks—the black ones were overpriced—and a belt, not leather, but close enough, and some shoes, yeah, some shoes, too. Size seven. The boy had small feet. He had small everything. His dick was tiny. His ass had no meat on it.

"I'm gonna wash you, dress you, and then you're on your own," he said to Xavier, not looking back at him, never looking back, couldn't look back, wouldn't look back. "You can't sleep in my house anymore."

Who did this kid think he was anyway?

Neil rolled the shower curtain around the pole. Jesus. This would stink.

"All right, come on." He jerked the boy up and slapped his face. Not too hard. "Wake up and get in there."

Xavier lay listless, his head dangling like overripe fruit.

Half of the time the kid was faking it, but it was difficult to tell today. Neil lifted the long, bony arms up—the dark, swollen one, too—and when the boy didn't react, he pulled Xavier's disgusting shirt over his head. There. Halfway done. He pushed Xavier down—the kid landing heavily on his back and maybe his head—and worked on slipping his soiled pants off.

The gloves. He'd forgotten to put them on. Now look at this. Shit all over his hands.

"This is all going in the trash," Neil grumbled, stuffing the clothes into a plastic bag. "No way these stains are coming out."

The dog bent to the boy's face and licked at it. The crusty blood around the nostrils. The swollen eyes. Slurp. "Get the fuck out of here!" Neil belted out at the top of his voice. "I'll shoot you right between the eyes, I swear to God."

Xavier whined about something.

"What's that?" Neil asked, pulling Xavier up. "Get in there."

The boy blinked, his pupils sinking in and out of a silver storm. "No," he said, lolling his head.

"You stand up and get in the tub." Neil jerked Xavier to his knees, gripping his hair for leverage. "You're getting out of here today, you hear me?"

Xavier's eyes focused into a look of sheer, unabashed hatred.

"What? Why you looking at me like that for? Did you think you'd stay here forever? You and your stupid, useless piece-of-shit dog?"

Where was the old mutt anyway? Neil glanced around, holding the boy by his thin neck.

Gone again. Where did he go? Where did they all go?

"You're a liar!" Xavier roared, his throat jumping inside Neil's hand. "You're gonna kill me in there and roll me into that curtain."

"I'm not gonna kill you," Neil said, squinting, now fighting another flash migraine. "I just wanna clean you."

Xavier laughed and then closed his eyes.

"Hey, don't you fall asleep on me again." With force, he yanked the boy up to a standing position and then pushed him into the big white tub.

Xavier lay there, his good arm a sling to the broken one, and stared at him.

Neil held the boys eyes, his stomach stirring. "Why did you talk to me that day?" he asked, his chest hard, the breath gone from him.

Nobody ever looked him directly in the eye the way this kid did.

"I'm cold."

"I'll turn the water on." Neil spun the hot water dial, then the cold one, swiping his hand under the jet. "This good?" God, his fucking head. Split right down the middle, and this rock, this jagged piece of earth and clay digging into his left temple.

"I'm still cold," Xavier said, more forcibly this time. He struggled to sit up, but couldn't.

Neil dropped some soap on the boy's stomach.

Look at him, lying there, stomach taut—little mushroom dick stirring under the warm soap. Neil put the washcloth under the hot water, and when it was full and heavy, he held it still, watching the boy, whose eyes were closed.

"I'm cold," Xavier said again.

"I can't fill the tub until we get all this crap off you or you'll be sitting in your goddamn filth." Yes, had to get it all off. Neil swallowed hard, his hand hovering over Xavier's thigh. The boy shivered badly now, each tremor worse than the previous. "Don't move," Neil warned.

He lowered the washcloth to Xavier's skin, just below the pointed knee, and started rubbing.

❖

Dance lay against the edge of the tub, watching the giant get his kicks.

McClure rubbed and scrubbed, breathing heavily through the nose, a nanosecond away from coming hard into his house pants.

Pig.

Did he have the strength to wrap his legs around McClure's neck and snap it?

The giant's hand, pressed hard against the cloth, moved up and down Dance's body—Xavier's now?—soothing his sore limbs, yet nauseating him. How could he let McClure clean him? Drug him? Own him? Break him down bit by bit? What had he allowed, and when had the invasion began?

"Feels good, huh?" McClure's voice dripped, oozed even, out of his thin lips. "Like this?"

Dance blinked, his right fist clenching.

Hold tight. Don't move. It's coming. That moment.

"With your legs like that, you almost look like a girl," the giant said, "but you've got nothing to grab up there." McClure's fingers pinched his nipple.

A pang of pain traversed Dance's chest, but he kept his features relaxed. McClure, using a plastic glass, rinsed the dirty water off his chest, belly, thighs, and when the giant was satisfied, he dropped the plug in, letting the water fill the deep tub.

Dance shut his eyes tight, sinking a little.

"Why did you talk to me that day?" McClure asked again, his hand probing, touching, but Dance did not open his eyes. He listened to the water make its way up his legs, higher and higher, reaching his empty belly, and then rising still, up to his beating heart. He listened to the inflection in the giant's voice—it was different now. What did he want?

A conversation?

"You came to me, Xavier, remember?"

Yes, he had. He'd made that dumb, ruthless, and embarrassing mistake. Dance listened again. The giant had turned the water off. There was only the sound of the small waves McClure stirred with his big, fat fingers.

"Answer me, boy."

Dance tried not to smile, but his lips curled anyway and he fought back a chuckle. Why this was funny, he couldn't tell anymore. But it was. It was fucking hilarious. A broken, half-dead boy, taking a bath.

"What's so funny? Why are you smiling like that?"

Dance stared at the dirty tiles on the wall.

Good morning.

Good morning, Miss Brodie.

Seth smiles, looking around for her hairbrush.

Good morning, Mr. Lloyd. What marvelous pictures have you painted for me today?

Well, it's you, Miss Brodie, the fascist. You in every picture. You, everywhere I look.

Oh, Mr. Lloyd, tell me more.

"What's so fucking funny, Xavier?" McClure asked again.

This was pretend. Just like he and Seth played, before Mom had to go and kill herself. He wasn't Xavier, any more than he was Mr. Lloyd.

"I don't even exist," Dance said, opening his eyes to stare at his tormentor. "You don't even know whose shit you're cleaning."

"What?" The giant's eyes lost their shine and he frowned, his face twisting into an expression of perfect stupidity. "What are you talking about, boy?"

Boy.

"What?" McClure slapped the water, splashing Dance's chin and mouth. "What do you mean, I don't know you?"

Dr. Lowenstein, can I come in?

Not if you're going to yell at me again, Tom.

"Why are you smiling like that?" The giant grabbed his chin, tearing his fingernails into Dance's skin. "Look at me."

Xavier wasn't real. He wasn't here. He never was. He never was. This arm was not broken. This body was not the giant's possession. "You think I'm a boy," Dance whispered against McClure's thick fingers. "But I'm not a boy. I'm twenty-four years old."

"No. You're not." McClure's face twitched. "You're a liar, that's what you are. A little whore turning your mind tricks."

Tom and Mr. Lloyd stood in the corner of the room, nodding.

"He's right," Tom said, shaking his head, turning his eyes to one-armed Mr. Lloyd. "Always playing, this Mr. Young."

"Yes, indeed," Mr. Lloyd returned, fading back into the tiles. "Indeed."

"Wait," Dance cried out. "Take me with you."

"Where the hell am I supposed to take you?" McClure asked, leaning back from him, his stare hard and confused. "I changed my mind," McClure said, flicking his eyes to the edge of the tub, his cheeks darkening. "You're staying."

Dance sank his head under the water, immersing his mouth, nose, eyes. He wasn't Xavier. He wasn't really here anymore. How could he prove it to this beast? He didn't even have ID on him.

"Trying to drown yourself?" The giant pulled him out of the water, his fingers digging into his armpits. "You're strange, you know that? Very fucking strange." McClure watched him suspiciously. "Why did you talk to me that day? Answer me."

Seth? September?

Mom?

Mr. Lloyd?

"Answer me, why did you come to me that day, in the park?"

And Dance? Was Dance here?

"Because you looked stupid enough to believe my stories," Dance said, peering into the shadows of McClure's blue eyes. "And you did, didn't you?"

The giant stared at him, his lips parting slightly. "You're good at this," he finally said, his expression setting like stone. "There might still be hope for you. I might be able to teach you a thing or two yet."

"You can teach Xavier all you want, but I won't be here."

McClure frowned.

The giant slapped the water. "You're fucking crazy," he said, his voice shaking.

Dance held his broken arm against his chest and listened to the water draining down the pipes.

CHAPTER TWELVE

Morning, and the sun flooded into the bedroom, its pale shafts reaching through the curtains.

Jamie lay on his side, knees drawn to his chest, staring at the wall. September was in the shower—how unnerving and sweet the idea of it was—and he stared, lost in his own thoughts. Quietly, his mind lapsed into the past, taking him back to the large and immaculate kitchen of his childhood home.

He could see himself as he was then, a boy three years of age, tight-lipped and wide-eyed, sitting across from his father.

Two days after his brother's death.

His father leans in, his breath heavy with scotch. "Again, James."

His mother retreats to the corner of the kitchen and watches.

Jamie's mouth is sticky and dry. He wants to ask for water, but can't remember the name of things.

"James—"

"Please, Donald, can't you see he's—"

"Jane, leave us. Now."

His mother sets her teacup in the sink and leaves.

No Mommy.

"James, do you know what they do to catatonics?"

His belly tickles. Needs to use the potty.

"I want you to explain it to me again."

He squeezes his thighs together and squirms in the big hard chair.

"You wanted to taste the snow."

Jamie nods, tightening his groin.

"You stepped out of the car," his father says. "Was Michael awake when you severed yourself from him?"

Severed. He hasn't learned that word yet. Mrs. Lupini only likes to teach the A words.

Apple. Ant.

"Was he? Was he awake, James? Answer me. Did you smell it, James? You did, didn't you? You smelled the exhaust and exited the car."

Snow is made out of water. But it's dirty water. Mrs. Lupini showed them a glass of melted snow last week and it was brown.

"Did you feel anything? Did you feel different? James, look at me. Wipe that dumbness out of your eyes. Tell me. Did you feel it when it happened? You did, didn't you? You felt Michael die."

Jamie presses his knees together, tighter still, but too late—the warm pee trickles down, onto the big hard chair.

"Jesus Christ, James. You just soiled yourself. You really are a dirty boy."

"Are you sleeping?"

Jamie jumped and turned to face September. "No," he said, shaking off the painful, humiliating memory. He sat up, looking around for his glasses.

September offered them to him. "You should try contacts. You look really cute without these."

"Contacts hurt my eyes." Jamie watched September fidget by the bed. She was obviously uneasy. "Are you leaving so soon?" he asked, hoping she wouldn't.

Good God, December twenty-third, two days to Christmas, and nothing but loneliness ahead of him.

"I have to be honest with you, I'm completely shocked at myself." September looked rested, her face smooth and her eyes clear, yet her movements were nervous. "I can't believe I slept in your arms last night and I felt safer than I've ever felt in my whole, very complicated life." She laughed without smiling. "You have a sort of healing power, do you know that, Jamie?"

She was so wrong. He'd never healed anyone. Not even himself.

September seated herself at the edge of the bed, facing him. Her hair was damp, pulled back into a ponytail, strands of it falling into her luminous gray eyes. She was dressed in last night's clothes—a gray blouse and dark pleated skirt—and Jamie recalled the surprise he'd felt, last night, when he'd seen September in his gym pants and T-shirt. She'd been stripped of her makeup then, and had stood in the doorway, her thin arms wrapped over her breasts. At that moment, Jamie had known and understood her whole world; a permanent transition.

"Are you okay?" she asked him now, cool and collected again—the night over and done with.

"Yes."

"You're lying."

"I'm fine."

"Hey, what's going on?"

Jamie's throat clenched and he shrugged.

"Come on, get out of bed."

Jamie pushed his glasses over his nose and looked down at his hands. "Why do you trust me?" he asked.

Why did she?

Why?

"Because you're kind. Now, get dressed and drive me home."

"And you're bold. The bravest man—" Jamie stopped, flushed. "I mean woman, I've ever met."

She was. Last night, they had lain in each other's arms, calling all their invisible scars by their names. They had whispered about their own truths, at first, tentatively, and as the night had reached its thickest, their words had been rushed, their conversation hurried and unbridled, as if they'd been waiting for a moment like this forever.

And maybe they had.

"Why don't you call him today?" September asked, walking to the floor mirror. She studied her face.

What did she think of her beauty? What had been its cost?

"You mean Basil."

She turned to him, casting him a piercing look. She picked up the cat and stroked its tiny black head.

"And say what?" he asked her.

"Don't go to Mexico. I love you. You're killing me." Her eyes strayed back to her reflection and she leaned in, assessing her fresh makeup.

Jamie pushed the blanket off his legs and rolled out of bed. He was exhausted still. When would this fatigue let him be? He woke up tired every morning. Barely had the stamina to get through his days. "I know exactly what's going to happen," he said, his tone flatter than his morning hair. "I'll call, he'll put one of the kids on the phone, and then he'll come back on the line to give me a quick, detached good-bye."

"If I saw a picture of you two, I could tell you more."

Jamie chuckled a little. "Is that so, Madame Young, clairvoyant extraordinaire?"

She shot him a cold glance. "That's right, Doctor. I'm an extremely good judge of character. It's a survival mechanism, I suppose." She puckered her lips and nodded appreciatively at her reflection. "I need to go, Jamie. Really." She set the cat down gently and spun around. "I'd love to laze around here with you all day and join your pity party, but I've got to take care of a few details of my life." She leaned in and dropped a quick kiss on his hair. "Thank you."

"Are you going to eat today?"

"I might," she whispered, extending her hand to him. "Come on. I want to go home. I want to think. I want to clean my apartment. I want to see if Elliot is still there, poor kid."

What was he to do with his day? Long, excruciating minutes awaited him.

"Jamie, I know it hurts, but you need to learn how to do the little things well, so that you may do the bigger ones great."

"I promised the kids that I'd get him back."

"Show me a damn picture."

Jamie pointed to the nightstand, to a frame lying face down. It was of Basil and him, smiling up at the camera.

She turned the frame up and stared at it.

He studied her face, holding his breath. "So?"

September squinted, her eyes drinking in all the details. She set the picture down on the table. "He looks bisexual."

Jamie threw his head back and laughed.

"What? He does. It's clear as those big blue eyes of his."

"I didn't think it would be an issue, the whole bisexual thing."

"How is it an issue now? Would you have preferred Basil be seeing a man? This Matt boy you told me about? What does it matter who Basil is seeing?" September pulled him to the door and then pushed him out into the hall, in the washroom's direction. "No, what matters is that the man you love isn't seeing *you*."

Jamie, at a loss for words, rolled his eyes and locked himself in the bathroom.

"I'll feed the cat," September said, walking away from the door. There was a sly smile in her voice.

Boy, this woman was good.

❖

The car had finally warmed up and the second coffee was kicking in.

"I'm right up this street," September said, breaking the comfortable silence between them. "Turn left here."

Jamie drove, looking around at the desolate neighborhood. Suddenly, he felt ashamed, though he'd done nothing wrong. He'd simply been born into a rich family. Sent to the best schools. And later, as an adult, he'd lived in the most coveted neighborhoods in Montreal—neighborhoods where children pinned their ski passes to their Kanuck coats, took piano lessons on Saturday mornings, spent spring break in Europe, and shared more quality time with their dog walkers than their own parents.

Yes, he had been fortunate, but had he been happy?

"Wow," September said softly, "I never realized how crappy this neighborhood is. There's more plastic bags in the trees than there are branches. And look at the sidewalks. Cracked, full of dog turds." She leaned back into her seat with a sigh. "Dance was right. I should move."

"It's got a lot of potential," Jamie returned. Those were the words Basil used when he was trying to sell an old house for twice its worth. "But you could do better," he added, believing it.

"I don't have a job, and my savings account is somewhere in the folds of my couch."

Jamie laughed. "Did you ever get your certificate in—"

"No, I got boobs instead." September pointed to the three-story apartment building on their right. It was typical of this neighborhood—red brick, wrought-iron staircase, brittle windows, and crooked balconies. "This is me."

Jamie parked the car and sat there, tongue-tied.

September unfastened her seat belt. She looked tired. She had refused breakfast, barely sipped her coffee. "I'd ask you to come in, but—"

"It's all right. I understand."

"I really would, Jamie. But Elliot is there, and it's too much—"

"Can you promise me something?"

September nodded, her eyes gray gemstones.

"Eat something. And call me later."

"Thank you, Dr. Scarborough," she blurted, blushing for the first time since they'd met. She groped the door handle, then stepped out of the car without a backward glance.

Jamie watched her, this woman, this boy. When she shut the front door behind her, he shook his shoulders loose and swilled the rest of his coffee.

Now he watched the street.

Neil McClure lived three streets away from here.

Jamie chewed on his thumbnail, debating.

He put the car in drive and turned the radio on.

One last house call to make.

❖

Sirens outside.

A fire truck zoomed down the boulevard, just a few blocks from his house.

Probably heading for a crack house full of live skeletons asleep in the flames.

Good luck to them all.

Neil rubbed his face, trying to stay awake. The dog lay next to him, dozing off. The same dog who'd been dead once—he'd signed the forms. Yeah.

No?

Maybe.

The sirens grew dimmer now, and Neil closed his eyes, resting his head on the wall, sitting knees up, on guard.

In the freshly turned bed, the boy, Xavier—the lying whore—slept.

Was this kid fucking with his mind? Had he come with the dog? Were they a pair of devils, come up from hell to torment him?

Before Neil had plunged the needle deep in the bruised flesh of the boy's arm, Xavier had been rambling about September. What the fuck was so important about September? What made September any different from December or January?

It was January now, wasn't it?

No, Christmas hadn't come yet.

Neil opened his eyes, staring at the succubus in his bed.

The thing slept with its mouth open, eyes rolling under thin lids, its penis swollen beneath the sheet. Even in its sleep, it played.

"Get off me," Neil said to the other devil breathing on him. "I know what you are now. And I know what I gotta do."

The boy-devil moaned, stirring.

But he wouldn't let it get inside him. No, never. All his fucking life, these things had taunted him with their creamy skin and little asses—they'd stood by his fence, eyes blue as heaven's blood, watching him, calling his name without a sound, baiting him to come, come closer now.

Jezebel boys.

Neil pricked up his ears, tensing.

Someone was walking up to his door.

He jumped to his feet, sprang for the boy, and watched him. Was he really asleep this time? He leaned in closer, nostrils flaring.

Yeah, he was out cold.

The doorbell rang, and Neil spun around, his gaze reaching the front door.

If it was John, he'd destroy him this time. No two ways about it.

The bell rang again, and then a voice called his name.

It wasn't John's voice.

Neil smiled, recognizing the satiny inflection; pumped, he stepped out of the bedroom, shutting the door behind him.

Oh, the good doctor wanted to play another round, then.

❖

Jamie waited, glimpsing McClure's impossibly tall silhouette through the glass pane in the front door.

How could it be? Had the man grown?

And what would he say to Neil McClure anyway? What had possessed him to come here?

Jamie felt for the sanitizer inside his pocket, his breath catching in his throat. This wasn't a good idea. As a matter of fact, this was potentially the worst move he'd ever made—aside from professing his love to Jeremy, the hockey freak, and oh, sleeping with the man-eater, of course.

"You tell Neil McClure how he made you feel that day," Jamie said to himself. "And then give him a chance to apologize." He released the flask inside his pocket and stiffened, throwing his shoulders back, watching the doorknob turn.

Neil opened the door, his large shoulders taking up the whole frame, it seemed, and frowned. "Doctor, what can I do for you?"

Tell him how much he hurt your feelings. Tell him it wasn't necessary. Tell him you can help him deal with his anger.

"Yeah? What?"

"I wanted to talk to you," Jamie said, his voice jumping on every word. *Be brave. Be kind. Be the better man.* "I was hoping we could talk about what happened…I mean, what you said to me, how you acted, what you"—Good God, he was babbling like a bullied teenager—"Neil, you said some pretty nasty things to me and I think you owe me an apology." He tried to swallow, but his throat was too tight.

For the longest two seconds in Jamie's life, Neil McClure simply stared at him, his gaze even and expressionless, moving up and down, up and down.

"I think that maybe I may have set you off," Jamie added, shaken by the cold in Neil's eyes. "And I've been thinking about what happened. Maybe I went about it the wrong way and—"

"Wait a minute." Neil McClure smiled. No, it wasn't a smile. It was a mocking grimace. "You mean to tell me that you left your uptown luxury apartment building and came all the way down here to the pits to suck my ass? Man, you are so pathetic. I ask you to jump out a window and you come to my house to try and make friends?"

"No, I—" But Jamie stopped. Why was he standing there? Why wasn't he clocking this jerk? Because it was his job to stand there. Because that's what was expected from him. "I know that you're scared, Neil. I can feel it, right now. You're terrified." At those words, Neil's face changed subtly, morphing into a boyish expression, and Jamie pressed on, heart pounding. "I know what's it like to doubt everything. To wonder if you're doing the right thing. To want to ask for help, but to be too proud for it. And if you—"

"I'm gonna tell you something right now," Neil said, his face hardening once more. "You can't come near here anymore."

"Why? Why, Neil?" Jamie took a shy step closer, feeling the immense panic stirring inside the man before him. "You don't have to be ashamed or—"

"You just can't." Neil moved back, retreating into the house. "Go home. Just go home."

"What are you hiding from, Neil?" Jamie stood on his toes, trying to see into the house. "Are you alone? You shouldn't be alone during the holidays, you should—"

"I'll call you," Neil said, fumbling back another step. A slim trickle of sweat inched its way down his broad forehead, and the color was gone from his face. "Just go home. Get outta here."

The man was having an anxiety attack. Was he stable? Was he on the verge of collapsing? "I'd like to come inside. It's cold out here. And we could talk, just sit down and talk a little."

"Look, I can't." Neil's eyes widened and he looked back into the hall.

"What's that? Is someone here?" Jamie moved forward. He'd heard a voice.

"I got the TV on." Neil's features blanched a little more, and he began to shut the door. "Can you give me some time to get a handle on things here? I need to take a nap and get my head together, okay?"

Jamie hesitated.

"Oh, come on, Doc, didn't you say you were the 'go with your gut' kind of guy?" Neil peered into his eyes. "And what does your gut tell you right now?"

Was Neil McClure trying to get him out of his hair so he could blow his brains out? Jamie stared back at the calm, suddenly composed man before him.

No, perhaps not.

"Go home, Doc. Have some eggnog or something." Neil offered his large hand. "And I'm sorry. I said some things I didn't mean."

This apology was obviously difficult for McClure—the man was sweating again.

Jamie accepted Neil's hand and pumped it firmly. There was no need to push too hard. They'd meet again soon, he could feel it. "All right then," he said. "Merry Christmas." And turned to leave.

"Hey, Doc," Neil called him.

"Yes?"

"The next time you see me, I'll be fighting fires again."

"You *had* to make noise," the giant groaned, loosening the tape around his wrists. "You almost got him to come inside, too, huh?" McClure stopped, staring down at him. "But your game is weak."

Dance tried to move from under the giant's hands, but couldn't lift his head. He lay, sunken deep in the pillow, his arms free of bonds now, yet flaccid and useless. The daily injections were taking their toll on his brain. Soon he'd be incapable of understanding his own thoughts. Time was running out for Xavier.

And Dance?

"Well, you can't have that man, no. Anyway, he's got protection." The giant rambled on, busying himself with the sheets, the pillows.

What was he talking about now?

What man?

Had someone come here?

"There's two of him, you know." McClure watched the wall behind Dance's head, his eyes searching the invisible world.

"Who?" Dance managed to ask. "What are you talking about?"

"Never mind who. Mind your own business." McClure gave him a menacing look. "I know something you don't know. I think I figured your ass out."

Since the bathtub confession, Dance had been trying to convince the giant that he was, indeed, a twenty-four-year-old man; homeless, yes, but of his own volition, and not because his well-to-do parents had cut him off upon learning that he'd quit med school.

Fuck, he'd never even finished high school.

But McClure wouldn't hear him, no, he only stuck the syringe into his broken veins, calling him a boy-devil. That was the new term for him.

"Where are they?" Neil asked, a bluish vessel squirming under the translucent skin of his forehead. "What did you do with them?" He jerked Dance's T-shirt up his chest. "I saw your tits that night. Perky little knobs under your robe."

Dance turned his face from the giant, his belly exposed, his legs burning from lack of movement. Had to think of something. Had to reach the humanity inside McClure's big hairy chest. "What do you want?" he whispered, the question reminding him of Emma's words, that day in the Bunker, that wonderful Bunker he had hated so. And how he wished he were there this very minute, sitting across from Emma, answering the very question he'd resented.

What do you want?

"Freedom," he'd scream, rising from his chair, to jump up on her desk. "I want to be free of them. Tom and Lloyd, and Dr. Lowenstein, and Jem and Scout, and Jack and Dean, and Seth, and Mom, and this notebook."

The notebook. Did the giant have it?

"You were a girl that night. I remember you," McClure said, pulling Dance's T-shirt down, his face recomposed into a calm mask of white putty. "And I went back into the flames to get your stupid bag, but there was no bag. Did you wanna kill me, Xavier—or whatever your name is?"

What? The bag? What bag?

"And then you saw me on the street and you made eyes at me. But I didn't look at you, 'cause I knew you had a prick. Yes sir, I knew it was there, tucked away neatly inside your panties."

Oh, God. Seth.

"The guys at the firehouse knew it, too. They all talked about you. The he-she with the perky tits."

Dance forced a breath into his lungs, his nerves zapping under his skin.

"But I'm smarter than they are." McClure smiled a haunting smile. "I should have known you'd come back for me."

McClure was a firefighter?

Yes, a man who walked in and out of hell, that's what he was, and always had been.

"What? Why you staring at me like that?" The giant's breath—scented with bitter coffee and putrid food—brushed Dance's face. "Admit it," McClure said. "Admit that you're a she-devil."

This man had been in September's presence. This man had looked upon her face.

Dance, with strenuous effort, sat up. "I would have set myself on fire, if it meant meeting you again," he said, reaching deep inside his soul for the last bluff.

McClure's features tensed. "You're lying again."

"I didn't know how to"—Dance tried to steady his voice—"how to get close to you."

Silence.

September lived so close to here. What if the giant saw her again? What if they crossed paths on one of the rare occasions that Seth ventured out? McClure would snap. Yes, he'd snap for good, and what did that mean for Seth?

"Get away from me," the giant screamed, kicking the air. "Fucking dog!"

"I'll get rid of him, if that's what you want, and I'll—"

"Why did you bring him here? Is he your guardian?" McClure looked around, wide-eyed. "What do you want from me?"

"Tell me who was at the door."

"Make your tits grow."

"Tell me who was at the door."

"Show me how you do it."

"Tell me who was at the door!" Dance yelled, his voice cracking under the strain.

McClure's eyes twinkled. "Tit for tat, huh?"

"Tell me."

The giant stared at him, and cocked a brow. "A headshrinker. Nobody important."

"A psychiatrist?"

"Yeah, now make them grow." McClure reached for his nipples, but with his good arm Dance swatted the giant's hand away. "Why was he here?" he asked McClure, his pulse racing. "Is he yours?"

"He wants to be, but I think all he really wants is my dick up his ass."

Dance swallowed the little saliva he had left, trying hard not to let the intensity of his emotions surface.

McClure was seeing a psychiatrist. Who? Where? Why? The Glasshouse was only ten minutes from here, could it be that the firefighter was one of its outpatients? And if he was, what were they treating him for?

What kind of imbeciles would allow a man like him to come and go?

"Now show me." McClure pushed his beefy thumb into his breast.

"I can't do it just now. I'm weak. I don't have the strength." Dance wet his lips. He was thirsty, so thirsty. "Tell me his name. Your shrink."

"I told you, he isn't my shrink. Just some faggot four-eyed doctor with a bad case of the jitters."

No. It couldn't be. No. Not him. Not him.

"Tell me his name," Dance bargained, seeing Dr. Scarborough's liquid black eyes shining behind his own eyes, "and I'll show you everything you think you want to see."

"No." The giant frowned, stepping back from the bed, shaking his head. "No. You're playing with me. You're trying to get inside here." He tapped his temple, grinning. "But you don't know what's coming for you, no you don't." McClure tumbled back another step, hitting an invisible wall, glaring down at him. "And when your judgment comes, you'll regret every fire you've ever lit."

"I never lit a fire in my life!" Dance cried, unable to contain himself. Damn it, this maniac kept jumping from crazy story to the next—his mind clearly splitting at the seams, coming apart. "You wanna punish me? Then punish me, but do it for the right fucking reasons. I'm not a woman, a devil, a phantom, or even a whore. I'm not a fire starter, and I'm not even that interesting. I'm a compulsive liar, that's all I am. Now, if you wanna kill me, do it now, motherfucker."

Do it now. End it.

I deserve it.

I stand here, accused.

"Come on, Neil, finish it."

He would never know love. He would never be a father. A husband. He would never find himself staring back into the eyes of the woman who today maybe walked alone, somewhere in this city, thinking of her faith. He would never grow old, and never make peace with himself, the world…Seth.

September.

"My name is Dance Young," he said, remembering his brother's frantic call that night, the night the fire had stolen Seth's life from him. Seth screaming in the empty diner, her eyes bulging out of their sockets, barely standing, her robe hanging off her like a broken wing.

Oh God! It's all gone!

September had wanted to die then, and Dance had hated her for it. Hated, yes, because his love for his brother was too deep to reach. He couldn't stop loving him, and so he hated him as best he could.

Was that how Seth felt about him? Were they mirrors to each other, mirrors whose reflection could cut?

"I have a twin brother. He's a trans-woman. You met her that night, not me." Dance opened his eyes. "I came to you that day because I'd spotted you before, in the park, and I thought you'd be easy." He looked down at himself, seeing the dark flesh of his arm, his shallow chest. "You were my first mistake," he said, letting go. "My first and last." He glanced up, catching sight of McClure's shocked expression. "Believe me, Neil, we can walk away from this, if you want to."

McClure's brow twitched, but he remained silent.

Then, dragging his boots, the stunned giant left the room.

❖

"Looks like it's you and me, buddy," Jamie said, rubbing Sylvester's furry ears.

In the living room corner, the antique clock kept time, but time itself seemed to be following another beat. What would he do with five days off, with nowhere to go, but to bed?

Perhaps that's what he needed…rest.

Jamie leaned his head back on the couch and held back a sigh.

What was happening to him, to his good sense? He was blurring the lines more and more, breaking all of his rules, seeing patients outside his clinic, popping more pills than he should, eating out of cans. When was the last time he'd read a novel or listened to music? When was the last time he'd seen some sunshine, for that matter?

"That's it, enough." Jamie bounced off the couch and flew to the entrance where he jerked his coat out of the closet and snapped his cell phone out of his pocket. He walked back to the couch and sat down, staring at the phone.

Call him. Tell him.

Jamie squeezed his eyes shut, organizing his thoughts, trying to keep his heart from bursting right out of his chest. When red dots danced behind his lids, he opened his eyes and sat, perched at the edge of the seat, still staring at that dumb piece of plastic resting inside his palm.

The kitten jumped off his lap onto the coffee table and sat there, staring at him.

"What?" Jamie wiped his sweaty fingers against his pants. "He's not going to want to talk to me. He's going to be busy with packing."

The cat stared on.

"Fine, fine." Jamie dialed, watching the kitten's startling green eyes assess him.

Four rings, and Mallory answered. "Hello? Spasso residence."

Jamie laughed. "May I speak to the lady of the house, please?"

"Dr. J! You're not at work? Hold on, I'll get Dad, he's shaving."

"Wait, I want to talk to you—"

But the phone had obviously been dropped into something soft—probably the couch, and Jamie waited, every muscle in his body tensing.

"Hey," Basil said, "I was just about to call you."

Jamie moved forward, hardly sitting anymore, but hanging. "Did I catch you at a bad—"

"Didn't I say that I was just about to call you?"

"I'm sorry," Jamie said, silently shooing the cat off the glass table. "I'm nervous."

"Why are you nervous?" Basil's own voice was shaky. "Anything wrong?"

Wrong? The question was a slap more than an enquiry. Was anything *right*?

"Hello? You sound really tense, Jamie. What's up?"

They were going to do this? They were going to pretend?

"It's been an intense month, you have no idea, Baz." Jamie rubbed his eyes under his glasses. "Crazy, really."

"I thought you didn't use that word."

"I don't mean crazy as a derogatory term for mental illness, I mean—"

"Hey, that's what you get when you choose to run a psychiatric clinic all on your own. You get crazy."

This again. This redundant subject. They'd hashed it out so many times in the last year. What did Basil expect from him? Should he burn his medical degree and trade his three-piece suit for a work belt?

"You know," Basil said, his voice smooth and even again, "you said you'd get help two years ago, and since then your practice has tripled and—"

"I haven't had time to look into that."

"You never have time for anything, except for your patients."

Jamie sat up, stiffening. He opened his mouth to return a sharp line, but paused, evaluating Basil's words carefully. Quickly, his mind retraced the last five years.

And as he looked back, he was deeply ashamed. He couldn't remember one single weekday dinner with Basil and the twins. He could barely recall helping Basil with the kids' homework. No, he had been home late every night, later still in the last year of their relationship. Hiding. Avoiding conflict. And when he did make it home in time to tuck the kids in, he'd spent the evening reviewing his notes or nodding off with a book in his hands.

He'd been a pitiful lover, always way too highly strung to enjoy anything but an orgasm. How could he have been so blind? He'd had Basil Spasso always a touch away, and yet had allowed his panic disorder to keep him from enjoying Basil's terrific sensuality.

"Anyway," Basil said before Jamie could admit to anything, "I know you do the best you can. I guess we all do."

Jamie stood, reaching down for some courage. "You're right, I never should have put my work ahead of you and the kids, but I wanted them—*you*—to have the best, and you guys had this bond, this wonderful amazing bond. I felt like an outsider, and I wanted to—"

"How could you feel like an outsider? I did everything to make you feel like you were part of this family. I tried to include you, but your head was in another space all the time." Basil stopped, and there was the sound of a door being shut. "I couldn't keep your place because you never owned it," he whispered. "Look, Jamie, I gotta get ready, and I really don't wanna get into this with you now."

"See, you do that," Jamie said, pacing. "You start something, but when you've said your piece, you seal yourself up."

"Because I'm in fucking pain!" Basil screamed into the phone, to Jamie's shock. "I walk around like a sleepwalker. I don't even know how to get out of this nightmare anymore."

Jamie bit his inner cheek.

Don't talk. Don't say one single word. Listen. Just listen to him.

"Do you know what it was like for me? Huh, Jamie? I wanted to help you, but you never needed my help. I wanted to understand you, but you never explained anything to me." Basil's voice sank. "I wanted to touch you, but you never let me close enough, did you? I don't even know what it's like to really make love to you, do you know that? Everything was always so hurried with you, like you couldn't wait to go take a shower and wash me off your skin."

"Oh, no, Basil, no, that's not true. Never. I wanted you so much, but I just—I didn't know how to tune everything else out and—"

"It doesn't matter," Basil sighed.

"I'm sorry." He was going to cry. "I'm so sorry," he said again, for himself more than Basil.

"I fucked up, too."

"I miss you so much."

"Don't, Jamie. Please."

Jamie walked to the bay window and pulled the shades back, blinking at the afternoon winter sun. "I need to tell you how I feel before you get on that plane."

"Now you're freaking me out. Are you having some kind of premonition?" Basil coughed. "You think we're gonna crash?"

Jamie smiled through his tears. "No, so you can put the rosary beads down."

"Can I call you when I get back? I've got nothing packed and— well, do you wanna talk to the kids?"

"I'm still madly in love with you, Basil. More than I ever was."

"Now, Jamie? You're gonna do this now?"

"Basil, I—"

"Oh, I can't fucking believe your timing!" Basil left the phone and was now tossing—furniture?—around. Most of the time, Basil was cool and sensible, but when pushed, he'd fly off the handle, and in those times, no plate, shoe, chair, or wall was safe.

"Baz?" Jamie tried again, but the ruckus continued. He leaned his forehead against the window, taking in some sunshine.

This could last awhile.

But soon Basil, breathless, his voice broken from the shouting, came back on the line. "I love you, too," he whispered, still winded.

Jamie's knees buckled.

"Jamie, are you there?"

"Yes, I'm here."

"You make me nuts, you know that? But I love you. I love you more than I've ever loved anyone in my whole life."

"Don't go to Mexico."

"I can't just back out eight hours before the—"

"Or if you do go, don't enjoy it."

"That, I can do."

Silence filled the line, but Jamie didn't want to break it—breaking it meant breaking the spell they both had fallen under.

"I'll put Mallory on the phone, okay? I gotta clean up the bedroom."

What now?

"I don't know what to say," Basil said, softly.

"Tell me you love me again and then hang up."

And Basil did.

Wearing his pajama bottoms and favorite dark blue sweatshirt, a cup of chamomile and honey within reach, Jamie perused his in-box. He hadn't checked in for the last twenty-four hours, but there was no hurry. His patients didn't have this e-mail address, only his friends did, hence the in-box was miserably empty, save for a message from Christina—what could she need now?—dated yesterday.

Jamie sipped his hot drink, double-clicking on Christina's

message, hoping it would keep his mind off Basil, if only for a few, merciful minutes.

Hey Doc:-)

I hope you're having a great holiday! I love Christmas, don't you? There's something magical about this time of year—as if the whole world is ready to change!

Jamie rolled his eyes. Right.
But determined not to weaken and call Basil, he read on.

I called your clinic and the machine said that you were closed. Wow, Jamie, I'm shocked.:-) Anyway, I lost your cell phone number—boy, I really hope you check this e-mail once in a while.

I'm worried about Neil, have you seen him recently? Is he still your patient? John (he's a friend of mine and a firefighter with Neil's station) passed by Neil's house the other day and he says Neil was acting strange—says he was aggressive...very aggressive. I'm a bit confused!

Neil said he was going to visit his mother, but I think he lied.

I saw him the other day, and I have to tell you, I didn't recognize him.

He seemed so out of it.

Have you prescribed any medication?

I also found out a few things about Neil which I feel compelled to share with you, if only for professional reasons. You should know who you're treating, right? John said the only reason Neil got into firehouse 66 is that the captain was an old friend of Neil's father—used to work with him. John doesn't know the whole story, only that Neil's father was some kind of hero who was badly burned in a fire explosion in the eighties—bedridden for months, until he finally succumbed to his wounds. Rumor is Neil's mother made her son take care of his disabled father and that to the neighborhood, Neil was known as some kind of mute giant. Things get blurry around adolescence, but John says that Neil tried to get a job in the post office after graduation, but was refused—on what grounds, John doesn't know. Then later Neil tried to get into the police force and was again refused. The army didn't want him either. He was eventually hired as a security guard somewhere downtown, where he worked for over ten years. Neil told everyone he'd quit, but John heard a different story: Neil was fired from his security desk job for breaking a man's jaw and collarbone. Then Neil (according to John—I haven't verified any of this) asked his father's friend, who'd just got promoted to captain, if he'd give him a shot. Neil worked out of 66 for four years, but during those four years, he was sent home five times on sick leave for various reasons!

All of which are kept confidential, in his union file.

I just thought you should know all this.

Your friend Christina.

PS: *Merry Christmas and Happy New Year! I hope you get everything you want—you deserve it, Jamie.*

Jamie sat back in his chair, fixing the screen, not seeing the words on it, but images—images of Neil dressed in a security guard uniform, beating a man to a bloody pulp.

So, McClure had a violent past.

Why was he so surprised? Jamie turned the computer screen off and drank the rest of his tea. He hadn't picked up on Neil McClure's violent temper, though the man had threatened him—bullied him, really.

Jamie went back for his notes in his bedroom and, sitting on the bed, he leafed through them, looking for the McClure entries.

He read his own words, more and more shocked at his naïveté.

First meeting with potential patient, Neil McClure, forty-two years old, a firefighter. Possible depression. Patient has been forced to take sick leave. The patient seems guarded, yet he stares at me, my every move. Check: repressed homosexuality. Check: childhood trauma. Check: grieving of one's animal. Check: abandonment issues.

Jamie remembered that day—he'd gone to McClure's home, invited under false pretenses. Hadn't he had a panic attack on the porch? He had been intimidated by the man, but now he couldn't remember what had set his anxiety skyrocketing.

He skipped pages, in search of the next entry, and soon found it.

December 16, second meeting with patient Neil McClure. Patient uses an excuse to visit the clinic—I forgot my glove in his home. Patient's body language is relaxed as he recounts his childhood pains with ease. Check: ideas of grandeur. Check: megalomania. Check: social phobia. Patient tries to provoke me. McClure is intelligent and blunt. Patient does not look for reassurance. Patient does not ask any questions. Patient seems at times amused. Check: emotional voyeurism.

What had happened that day, prior to McClure's unannounced visit? Jamie chewed on the tip of his pen, working that morning out.

He'd spoken to Basil that very morning, yes, and Basil had dropped the Laura bomb on his lap. He'd been distracted during Neil's session—not at all present of mind.

Jamie found the last two entries and read on.

Today was the third meeting with patient Neil McClure. There is no semblance of trust. Patient is still guarded, yet more provoking. Patient exhibits signs of paranoia. #world full of vampires# I ask Neil McClure if he feels he's been treated unfairly by the world. No answer. Check possible quote from book? #I need you to help me become who I was born to be#

Fourth and possible last meeting with patient, Neil McClure. Patient knows of my personal history. McClure is angry. Why? Patient is sweating. Check: cabin fever, agoraphobia. Situation escalates. Patient insults me. #pill popping fag#
Internal homophobia?

Patient leaves abruptly. #when you come undone, you'll
remember me#

Jamie tapped his pen against his lips, watching the sun sink into the indigo horizon.

Since when had he become so lazy about his notes, his work? He hadn't followed through on any of these checks. He'd been much too preoccupied with his personal affairs to even take a second glance at his patients' files after work. These people counted on him. They paid him, for God's sake.

Did he even listen to them anymore? Or did he sit there, dazing off, listening to the clock on the cherrywood table? Had he ever really, truly tried to help any of them?

Sylvester jumped up on the bed, startling Jamie.

"Maybe Basil is right," he said, scooping the cat up in his arms. "Maybe I'm in the wrong line of work."

Why was he a psychiatrist anyway?

❖

Baby, look at me.

Dance sobbed, his face turned to the wall, staring back at his mother.

Mom? Where is he?

He's here still.

But what will he do to me? Mom? Oh God, I'm so scared.

Don't be, baby. I'm right here.

No, you're not. I'm fucking hallucinating. You're not here. You never were.

Dance, don't cry.

Dance licked the tears on his mouth, rocking himself.

Listen to me, baby. Seth is eating a hard-boiled egg.

No, Seth doesn't eat anymore.

Yes, she does. Every day. She eats, sitting at her kitchen table, and Elliot watches her.

You're lying.

I didn't mean to cut you boys up into pieces.

You shot yourself in our house.
I was weak. I was terrified.

Dance closed his eyes, listening to the empty silence. Where was the giant? Where had he gone? He'd left him here, tied to this bed, no water, no food, no fucking drugs.

Baby boy, you're going to live through this.
I'm not. I'm not.
You will, Dance, you will.
I'll rot here and where will I go?
Mom?
Mom?

"Mom!" Dance yelled, his scream bouncing off the carpeted walls. "Get me out of here!" He thrashed, lifting his body inches off the bed, trying to break free from the straps around his waist, thighs, arms. "I wanna go home! You hear me, you fucking maniac? Where are you? Where are you?"

Shaking terribly, he listened again.

The house was quiet.

❖

Here goes nothing.

Jamie held the shrimp mousse to his bosom—a seafood shield—and glanced about the street.

His childhood street.

Where he'd been grown, but never been raised. There it was, spread before him, an agglomeration of turn-of-the-nineteen-century mansions, enormous shiny SUVs, and giant, terrifying trees. Yes, they still gave him the jitters, those ancestral ogres made up of knotted bark and twisted branches. Even now, they seemed to want to pick him right off the porch and hurl him down their brown mouths.

"Keep this up, and you'll be regressing to the potty stage," Jamie scolded himself, peeking into the front window of his old house. The Christmas tree stood in the living room corner, immense, furnished with silver and gold ornaments—other colors were forbidden, deemed tacky—and aside from the flat-screen TV beaming on the wall, there was no sign of life.

But that was normal. His parents never could stand sitting in the living room. The TV was an atrocious thing they only turned on as a decoy. A message to all potential burglars: We're home.

No, Jane and Donald Scarborough did not watch television. They read.

And, of course, they also practiced the art of silence with riveting perfection. As a child, Jamie had quickly learned that silence was a form of communication in the Scarborough home. There were many subtle differences in these silences, and as a boy, he'd recognized and followed the unspoken rules of the household.

The mousse was going to freeze so Jamie rang the bell, thankful he'd had the wisdom not to wear light colors tonight. He was sweating already.

Before he could turn around, throw the mousse over his shoulder, and bolt down the west face of Mount Royal, his mother opened the door. "You're here," she said, moving forward as if to hug him, but stepping back. "You brought the mousse."

Yes, Mother. Along with thirty-seven years of repressed emotions.

"Well, don't just stand there, you'll get a cold." His mother drew back into the elegant entrance, motioning for him to follow. "When did you get this?" she asked, touching his knitted blue scarf. "Did you make it?"

His mother did that. She imagined all sorts of nonexistent hobbies for him. Sometimes it was ice sculpting, tonight it was knitting. Perhaps it was a way to comfort herself; her son wasn't lonely, no way, he surely spent all of his spare time doing marvelous things. Like making shrimp mousses.

"It was a gift," Jamie said, carefully removing his boots before placing them on the appropriate mat by the door. The scarf had been a gift from Basil's mother. Another attempt at making peace with her stubborn son.

"Oh," his mother returned. She didn't probe. She never did. Questions inevitably led to answers, and answers then led to an actual conversation.

"It smells wonderful in here."

She waved off the compliment and walked away carrying the

infamous mousse, heading for the kitchen. Of course, she hadn't cooked tonight's meal—the whole nine courses provided by a caterer.

But it would be fantastic, nonetheless. At least he'd get a decent meal out of this.

Jamie hesitated, standing in the entrance, looking around the house. Everything was exactly the way it had been when he was living there. For a moment, he almost believed he could catch himself—the boy he was—stepping down that staircase, on his way to his father's study, heart popping like dry wood inside his thin chest, hoping to sneak a certain book out of his father's wall-to-wall bookshelves.

A book that contained a certain picture.

Michelangelo's David.

In the entrance, Jamie smiled, vividly remembering the sensations that had run through his ten-year-old body as he'd looked upon that glossy page—seeing the picture that had captured every single one of his boyhood desires.

And later, much later, when he'd first seen Basil naked and standing at the foot of his bed, Jamie had known he'd finally come full circle.

"You should hang your coat."

Jamie faced his father. "Yes, sir." He slipped his coat off and fumbled with a hanger. "How are you, sir?"

"I'm sure your mother told you," his father said, stepping away to the sitting room at their right. "I've just returned from a series of conferences along the American East Coast."

That meant *I'm doing great, as opposed to you.*

"She mentioned it, yes." Jamie wiped his clammy hands down his thighs and offered his right hand to his father. "It's nice to see you, sir."

His father didn't respond. He entered the sitting room, going straight for the beautiful, handcrafted glass bottles. Perhaps his father still believed that drinking from crystal negated the damaging effects of the alcohol on his brain, manners, and life.

But if Jamie refused the drink, his father would perceive it as an insult. He accepted the glass and pretended to sip it. He hated scotch. Especially when served by his father.

"Sit down, son."

Heel, boy.

Jamie obeyed, seating himself on the edge of the Louis XIV chair, across from his father. "Merry Christmas," he said, regretting his cheerful tone. Cheerfulness was meant for the red-nosed hobos down the mountain, or so his father believed.

His father frowned and drank the contents of his glass. He set the glass down, folding his hands together over his neatly hemmed wool pants. He wore his leather house shoes—they were not referred to as slippers—and suddenly, Jamie realized how old his father looked. His hair was almost completely silver now. His face was weathered, and the lines of his once-generous mouth were tight—perhaps from lack of smiling?

"I saw Dr. Andropov the other day," his father said.

Andropov…the name rang a bell.

"She's doing very well. She just opened a clinic a few streets from here, on Summerset, I believe."

Well, good for her.

"She asked about you."

Andropov, right. Jamie remembered her—a beast of a girl. They'd shared some classes at university.

"What did you tell her?"

His father scowled again. "I told her you were ruining your health trying to run a stress clinic."

"It isn't a stress clinic—"

"Don't be tedious. You understand the reference." His father rose, the leather creaking—or maybe his bones—and went for another drink.

Jamie stole a look at his watch.

He'd survived six minutes and forty-three seconds.

"Mother tells me you're living alone again."

"Basil and I were having some problems, but—"

"As homosexuals often do."

Jamie looked down at his glass. To hell with being sober. He threw the whole two ounces down his throat and leaned back into the seat, smiling. There, that was a lot better.

"Your mother worries about you."

"I'm fine."

"Are you checking in on your medication?"

"Yes."

"How is your obsessive-compulsive disorder?"

"Better."

"You've lost weight."

"I've changed my eating habits." Jamie watched his father ease himself back in his chair.

On the shelf, the clock ticked.

"At any rate, James, you don't look good."

"Thank you, sir."

"Sarcasm is the anger of the weak." His father took a long sip of his drink, studying him. "Truth is, I don't understand how you can live the life you live."

Jamie looked down at the carpet, counting threads. Why couldn't he stand up to the old bastard?

"I've upset you," his father said.

Jamie glanced up, surprised.

"I did the best I could with you boys, James. I tried to teach you—"

"Yes," Jamie mumbled. "I know."

"Don't eat your words like that. You know how I despise it."

"What can I say? I don't agree with you."

"Is that so?" His father's dark gaze swept over his face. "You think you could have done better?"

Could he?

"You know, son, you have no children of your own. You have absolutely no idea—"

"No, that's not true," Jamie said, his cheeks burning. "I raised Marshall and Mallory from the time they were four years—"

"Did you now?"

"Yes, I did. Granted, I wasn't there as often as I should have, and I may have made some mistakes, but I never hurt them—"

"And you think I hurt you and Michael?"

Jamie's heart jumped up his throat. "You did more than hurt us," he cried, unable to contain his voice. "You traumatized me. You made me doubt everything. You put fear so deep inside me that I still carry it around today, and now you—"

"I put fear in you?" his father echoed with disdain. "No, son, the fear was always there. You were born with it. I simply tried to rid you of it. Your brother, on the other hand, was fearless. And if he were alive today, he certainly wouldn't be sitting in my house, insulting—"

"Yes, I know. I know." Jamie tried to swallow, but his throat was clamped up. No, he wouldn't give his father the satisfaction of seeing him have a panic attack. "You've been telling me all my life how much better Mickey was than me."

"Have I?" His father smiled musingly. "Or rather, have you?"

"Don't talk to me like I'm one of your patients."

"Then don't act like one."

"Do you love me?" The four-letter word—the one never spoken between them—for an instant seemed to reverberate, as if spoken louder than the others; flustered, Jamie got to his feet. "Never mind," he muttered. "I'll go see if Mother needs help unwrapping the meal or something."

"What do you need from me, James? What is it that you want to hear? The truth? Don't you think that sometimes the truth is best not said?"

Jamie listened to his father's calculated words, seeking to string them in the right order across his mind, but he still couldn't believe them.

Had his father just admitted *to not loving him*?

"Son, I wish you wouldn't look at me like that."

Jamie stared on, holding his father's gaze, but seeing only his own reflection. Then he recalled September's words, the ones she'd spoken with a healthy detachment he'd admired—yes, almost envied.

And their meaning was clear now, full of new layers.

"Father," Jamie said, his nerves cooling, a sardonic smile forming on his lips, "if you see Dr. Andropov again, tell her I never liked her mustache."

His father grimaced in horror. "What kind of medication are you on?"

Jamie laughed and, a little tipsy, made his way to the kitchen.

❖

"And the government raised the minimum wage again," his mother went on, picking at the flesh of the duck. "Now, who's going to pay for that? Us, of course. Always us."

Jamie reached for his glass, missing its stem, almost tipping it over, but managed to avoid spilling the red wine all over the lace tablecloth—oh God, he needed every ounce of that precious liquid—and brought the glass to his mouth.

Across him, seated at the end of the table, his father ate, chewing his food slowly, his dark eyes watching.

"Property taxes are constantly on the rise, and we're expected to contribute to these people's drug habits?" His mother burped behind her napkin.

"Well, yes, Mother," Jamie said, leaning heavily on his hand. "*These people* can't get their drugs over-the-counter, as *you people* can."

His father frowned, but chewed on.

"What do you mean?" his mother asked, her glazed eyes narrowing slightly.

"Oh, nothing."

"What are you implying, Jamie?"

This duck had been stuffed with so many oranges, it could have been made into a marmalade. Jamie dropped his fork, his stomach knotting.

"What's the matter?"

"Pass me the wine." He settled back into his chair with a sigh.

"You've had enough."

Jamie glanced up at his father, catching the disapproving glare he was giving him. Yes, there he was, sitting there, across the table, with his big black eyes and stone-cold face. "What?" Jamie snapped. "Why are you looking at me like that?" He reached for the wine bottle, his sleeve dragging across the salad. "I'm thirsty."

"Have some water."

"Why don't *you* have some water?" Jamie poured the rest of the wine into his glass and raised the cup, proposing a toast. "To Mickey," he said, heart pounding, head spinning.

His parents remained silent, casting uneasy glances at each other.

"Come on now," Jamie said. "Raise your glasses. This one's for Mickey." He sank the wine.

Mickey.

Look at this, brother. Look at what this family has become without you.

"I'll make some coffee," his mother said, getting out of her chair. As she passed Jamie's chair, she touched his shoulder. The touch, though delicate, weighed on him even as his mother disappeared into the kitchen.

Jamie stared at his empty glass, watching the chandelier throw streaks of light across the crystal.

Light and shadow.

"When Mickey died," he said, not looking at his father, "you never asked me how I felt. Why is that, huh? What kind of psychiatrist are you?"

Finally, he was drunk.

Mission accomplished.

His father placed his fork across his plate. "Okay, James, indulge yourself."

"Oh, is that how you see this? Me indulging myself? Because I'm speaking about my feelings, my—"

"Yes!" his father cried, and then his voice dropped. "Clearly, you want to wallow in your pain, and like all good masochists, you need an audience."

Jamie dropped his stare to the salad bowl, temporarily at a loss for words.

"Yes, son, let's look at your life, now shall we?"

"No, Father, let's look at yours," Jamie promptly returned, feeling stronger. How he wished Basil were here right now. On the rare occasions that Basil and his father had been in the same room together, Basil had been sitting on his hands the whole time. And later, when Jamie had asked him about it, Basil had said, "How else am I gonna keep from punching your old man?"

Oh, Basil, you were so right.

"My life?" his father asked, an arrogant smile creeping at the edge of his mouth. "Look around you, James. Look at this house. My career. My books."

"All right, let's look at that," Jamie said, pouring himself a double scotch from his father's bottle. Hey, maybe scotch wasn't so bad after all. "Your house? This house is a funeral parlor. Your books? Your books should be sold at the dollar store, in the personal hygiene aisle. Your career?" Jamie laughed, clinking his glass against the bottle. "Well, I have an idea. Why don't you bring me along on your next conference tour? You know, as proof of your extensive knowledge of human psychology."

"You're a disgrace."

"Am I?" Jamie finished his drink. "Or are you?"

"Your brother would never—"

"You know what Mickey would say if he were here?" Jamie closed his eyes for a moment, feeling the booze sink him down under. "He'd say, 'Fuck you, Dad.'"

His father jumped out of his chair, rattling the plates. "How dare you? You ungrateful—"

"I wish I'd died that day, instead of Michael."

No, it's the alcohol talking. Jamie could hear Basil's voice, soothing him. *No, baby, that's not true. Not true.*

"What's going on?" his mother asked, carrying a tray of cups to the table. "Donald?"

"Ask your son."

Jamie rose. "I'm sorry, Mom, but I can't be here."

"What's wrong?" His mother stood before him, stopping him. "Don't go, Jamie."

"I can't breathe in here." Jamie pulled on his tie, his collar. "I don't feel right around him."

"Him?" his father echoed.

"Yes!" Jamie screamed, facing his father. "You! You and your judgments. You suffocate me!"

"Get out—"

"Donald, no, don't throw our—"

"Shut up, Jane."

"Don't you talk to her like that," Jamie growled, his jaw tightening. Clock him. Hit him right across the jaw. "If I walk out that door, sir, you'll have no son to call your own."

"My son died a long time ago."

"Oh, Donald, how could you say something—"

"No, it's okay, Mom," Jamie said, holding his father's stare. "I asked him for the truth, and now he's given it to me." He blinked. Good, his eyes were dry. "Thank you, sir."

His father's stare flickered, but he did not say a word.

"How can you let your only son walk out of our lives?"

Jamie heard his mother's cry, but he walked out of the dining room, hurrying through the house—this house full of ghosts—and threw his coat and boots on before his mother could come running to him.

He pushed the door open and escaped, skidding down the front steps, past the terrifying trees, the SUVs, and then past his own car.

❖

Blood on his knuckles.

His blood?

Neil moved his swollen fingers, one by one, watching the blood trickle from one joint to the next. Slowly, his gaze scoured the basement, seeking an answer. Had he busted his hand on the wall?

What day was it? Where were his shoes?

You sure did it now, son. You sure went and did it to yourself.

Neil gripped the sides of his head, recoiling into the shadows. "Shut your mouth," he moaned, crouching behind the bench-press table.

His sick bastard of a father had found his hiding place.

Oh, Neil. Where are you?

Neil looked around, frantic, his breaths chasing each other.

How could he be here? How could his father know where to find him? He'd watched his father die. Seen him exhale his last miserable breath, lying there, eyes rolling from side to side, fingers clutching the filthy sheets.

Whatcha gonna do now, son? They'll come here soon. They'll come knocking on your door. The boy-devil's got a sister. A sister with a dick. She'll find you, like I did.

"No," Neil whimpered, shaking his head. "She can't have him back. He's mine."

Yours?

Neil peeked over the weights, trying to see into the dark cement basement. What was behind the staircase? Whose eyes were those?

"I'm not gonna give him up," he said to the eyes.

Yes, you will! The dog lunged for him, leaping out of the shadows— its jaw a gaping hole full of bloody gums and fangs. *You fucking will, you murderer. You did me like you did your father.*

"Get away from me," Neil yelled, throwing his arm up over his face. "Daddy asked me for the needle! He wanted me to do it!"

"Neil!" the boy-devil whined, up above. "Where are you? Please."

No. No. He wouldn't let the incubus go. He would need him later. He would need an escort to where he was going.

"Neil? Please Neil. Please," the boy raved.

What do you think they'll do to you? The dog sat now, its shiny beetle eyes twinkling in the darkness. *They'll put you in a cage and throw away the key. They'll put you in with the child molesters.*

Neil brought his knuckles to his mouth, tasting the blood on them.

Oh, Neil, you fucked up. You dropped the piss pan again. Only this time, there's no cleaning it up.

Still crouching, Neil inched his way to the corner of the basement, his eyes fixed to the shotgun's sleek barrel.

You're going to shoot that devil?

"It won't do nothing to him," Neil said, picking up the shotgun. "He'll come right back again."

He'll come back like Dad.

You murdering sack of shit. The dog smiled, touching a cigarette to his lips. *Find the bag for me and I'll blow you.* The dog brushed its long brown hair back, blowing blue smoke into the stale air. *Come on, go back into the flames for me, Neil, and I'll show you my tits.*

"You're her," Neil breathed, wiping the sweat off his brow, the taste of it mingling with his blood. "You're the girl with the rain in her eyes."

We're all here. All of us.

Neil snapped his head around, eyes scanning the dark. *Who?*

A pang of sunlight cut through the dust, and standing there, the fairy boy grinned. *Come play with me, Neil.*

"Oh, God, no," Neil said, shrinking back, the shotgun pressed against his chest. "Don't come near me."

Come, Neil. The boy trailed his small finger through the fiery dust, his golden eyes closing. *I want you to.*

Neil's fingers clenched around the barrel.

Whatcha gonna do now, son?

Come play with me. Murderer.

Neil felt the cool mouth of the shotgun against his lips.

That's right, son, push it in like that.

CHAPTER THIRTEEN

Matt wrapped a towel over Jamie's shoulders, rubbing his arms briskly. "I'll get you some clothes," he said, releasing him.

Under the towel, Jamie shivered. "Thank you."

Matt left him in the white tiled bathroom, and Jamie, still a little drunk, fell back on the toilet seat. He looked down at himself—here he was, wet and naked, his skin still reddened from the cold and a searing hot shower. "Oh, Jesus," Jamie whispered to himself, sliding off the lid, trying to get to his feet without slipping on the treacherous tiles. Yes, that would be a lovely end to this night: cracking his head open on Matt's bathtub.

Why had he called the blond stud anyway?

Jamie dried off as best he could without toppling over, then stood before the fogged mirror, the room moving around him, though he was pretty sure he was standing still.

He reached out and wiped the steam off the mirror.

"Hello, there," he said to his reflection. "Are you done now?"

Done with acting like a child. Done with blaming everyone for his self-inflicted pain.

"Here you go." Matt stood in the doorway, offering him a pile of clothes. He scratched his head. "They might be a little big, but they should do."

"Look, I don't really remember what I said when I called you and—"

"It doesn't matter." Matt smiled his disarming smile. "I couldn't hear you very well. I'm just glad you called." He entered the washroom and leaned up against the counter, facing him. "So, what happened exactly?"

"Were you at a party?" Jamie asked, ignoring the question. He managed to slip into Matt's loose cotton pants without dropping the towel.

"Yeah, but I was happy to get out of there." Matt touched his arm, sending a chill across Jamie's skin. "Is it your dad?" Matt asked him, his tone subdued.

Jamie nodded. "I'm sorry if I ruined your—"

"Didn't you hear me? I was happy to leave."

"Where were you for the last week?"

Oh, Jamie, I'm so in love with you.

Right.

So in love, I don't call for a whole week. I disappear.

Matt blushed a bit. "I was up north."

"I figured your attention was elsewhere." Jamie pulled the warm sweater over his head, rolling it down his chest. "So, who is he?"

"Nobody important," Matt said, reaching for his arm again. "Come here."

"Don't." Jamie pulled away, leaving the washroom. Where were his things? His wallet? His house keys?

"What's wrong, Jamie?"

"Nothing." Jamie found his clothes atop Matt's futon. "I'm going home. I have a headache, and I feel like throwing up."

"Stay then. I'll make you some tea and—"

"Stop it, Matt. Just stop it." Jamie threw a hand up, stepping back to the door. "Thank you for picking me up off the street and thank you for the hot shower, the clothes—"

"You're pissed because I didn't call?" Matt neared him, his blue eyes insistent. "I'm sorry, okay? It was a sort of spur-of-the-moment thing, and one thing led to another, then—"

"I don't care!" Jamie shrank back into his sweater, surprised at the power of his own voice. "What you do with your time is not my business," he added, more calmly. "We're not a couple. You don't owe me an explanation."

"I know, but—" Matt stopped, chewing on his lip.

God, this boy was so irresistible when he wasn't getting his way.

Jamie sighed, taking a small step forward. "Okay, I'm going to try something else." He took hold of Matt's hand, pulling him into the living room. "Sit down," he said before sinking his own sore body into the futon. "Look into my eyes." He faced Matt, holding his hands inside his.

"Wow, your eyes are amazing."

"Stop it. That's not the point." Jamie made an effort to remain patient. "Look deeper. What do you see?"

"What do you mean, what do I see?"

"I mean exactly that." Jamie widened his eyes, staring harder. "What do you see in my eyes?"

"You're freaking me out here. I have no idea what you want me to see in there."

"Exactly." Jamie released Matt's hands, leaning back on the edge of the seat. The room had stopped spinning. Good, maybe he was sobering up. "When Basil and I stare in each other's eyes, do you know what we see?"

Matt shrugged.

"We see our whole world. Our lives. Our future. Our past. Everything."

"Yeah? So why did you call *me* instead of him tonight?" Matt moved away, obviously a little bruised.

"Because Basil is in Mexico, and I was walking aimlessly downtown like some drunken—"

"Oh," Matt gasped, his face turning a dark shade of red.

"What do you mean, 'oh'?"

Matt looked down at his knees. "I thought you knew. And I thought you wanted me, instead of him."

"Knew what?" Now Jamie's heart beat so, it caused his voice to shake. "Knew what?"

"That Basil didn't go to Mexico."

"No! What?"

"Yeah, he called the whole thing off at the airport. He called me from his car, a few minutes before you did, and I thought that you knew—"

"He didn't go," Jamie said, jumping to his feet. "Wait, you're absolutely sure?"

"Yeah, Jamie. She went crazy, you know, the girl." Matt laughed without smiling. "Baz said the airport security had to detain her. He bolted out of there with the kids faster than—"

"He's home, then," Jamie said, his eyes fixed to the front door, though seeing nothing. For a moment, he could not move, nor think.

"So, you're gonna go?"

"What?" Jamie snapped out of his trance and looked down at Matt. "Where?"

"*Home*, Jamie."

"Oh my God." Jamie clutched his heart, a beat away from an attack. A real one, this time. No doubt. "Should I? What should I do?"

"Well," Matt said, glancing at his watch, "it's half past eleven, so technically, it isn't Christmas yet. If you hurry, you can make it before Santa does."

"Where's my phone?" Jamie looked around, panicked. "I need a cab."

"Forget the cab." Matt got to his feet. "I'll drive you."

Jamie brought his hand to his lips, holding back the tears.

"Come on now, Doc. Keep it together." Matt pushed him gently toward the door. "I'll give you a mint to suck on."

"Can you get me there before midnight?"

"Will you change into a pumpkin or something?" Matt laughed, helping him with his coat. "Yeah, Jamie, I can get you there before midnight."

"Wait," Jamie cried, causing Matt to jump back. "I have gifts! I need to get the kids' gifts out of my closet and—"

"Would you calm down? Who cares about the gifts?" Matt dropped a kiss on his lips. "You'll be their gift. And let me tell you, that's way more than enough."

Would he be their gift? Could he bring joy into their lives? Could he let go of the past and come back to his family new, sparking clean—minus the sanitizer—but most of all, come to them all a free man again?

Jamie stepped out into the cold night, following Matt to his truck, and with every step, the answer grew clearer.

He'd try, damn it.

At least he'd try.

❖

Eleven fifty-three and they both sat in Matt's truck, parked a few houses down from the Spasso home.

Matt had stopped his incessant pep talking—apparently, the man had exhausted even himself.

Jamie, his forehead pressed to the cool window, revised all possible outcomes. Would Basil be sleeping? And if so, should he creep into the house and then find refuge in Basil's bed? Would Basil welcome the surprise, or would he be upset with him for assuming—

"That's it," Matt said, breaking the silence and Jamie's rambling thoughts at once. "Get out of my truck, Doc."

"Just give me one more—"

"No, enough." Matt shifted gears, driving off in the direction of Basil's house. "You know what your problem is? You think too much. That's right. Think think think." He came to the house and pulled into the driveway, stopping short of Basil's car. "Let's go." Before Jamie could protest, Matt had jumped out of the truck, gone around, and popped his door open.

Matt grabbed hold of Jamie's collar. "Out you go."

"All the lights are off. They're sleeping."

"So?" Matt pulled him forward, leading him up the stairs, and to the door. "Stay out of view," Matt said and then knocked. "He's coming," he whispered, shoving Jamie to the side. "Stay behind me."

"What? You're shorter than I am."

"Crouch, then." Matt raised himself on his tiptoes, glimpsing the entrance through the glass pane. "There he is."

What was this? Some kind of juvenile peek-a-boo prank? Was he expected to jump out from behind Matt to deliver a singing telegram to Basil?

"What are you doing here?" Basil's voice. Tense. Full of sleep.

Jamie made himself as small as he could, tucking his arms in, listening.

"I came here to deliver a gift," Matt said, a smile in his voice. "A last-minute—"

"Matt, I told you, I don't wanna fuck around anymore. It was a mistake—" Basil stopped, and Jamie held his breath, heat moving up from his collar to his ears. "Who's that behind you?" Basil asked, his blue eyes rising above Matt's shoulder. "Jamie, is that you?"

"He's your surprise," Matt said, his tone deflated.

Clearly, the man had realized how pathetic this whole situation was.

Jamie waved. "Surprise."

There.

Now, he'd really proven how mature, sane, and normal he was.

"And Merry Christmas," he mumbled.

"Where you going?" Basil laughed. It was a relaxed, easy laughter, and for a moment, Jamie recalled the best of their times. "Hey, Matt, what kind of gift is this anyway? He's returning himself without me having a chance to unwrap him."

On the first step, Jamie paused.

"I don't know," Matt said, playing along. "I didn't keep the receipt."

"Tell your gift to get his ass back up here. I want a better look at him."

Matt grabbed Jamie's wrist, drawing him to the door once more. He turned him around and dusted the snow off his shoulders. "He's the latest version—"

"Matt, go home. But thank you." Basil winked. "And you," he said to Jamie, his smile weakening Jamie's knees. "Come inside."

"Who, me?" Jamie pushed his glasses up his nose, grinning with no conscious effort.

Basil leaned forward, his mouth skimming his, soft and familiar. "Yes, you," he murmured against Jamie's frozen lips. "But be quiet, the kids are sleeping."

Jamie followed Basil into the house.

His house.

Their house.

❖

"She ripped a tiny part of my earlobe off, I think," Basil said, out of view, his mouth obviously full of toothpaste. "I swear, Jamie, two security guys had to wrestle her off me."

Jamie leaned back into the plush pillows of the bed—their bed—fiddling with his boxer shorts. On or off, that was the question. On would be sexier. Basil liked to remove them. "What did you tell her exactly?" he asked Basil, who was still in the master bedroom's washroom. "I mean, what were your words?"

Basil popped his head in the doorway. "What do you mean? My *exact* words?"

"Yes," Jamie said, pulling the blanket up his chest. He'd lost too much weight. He looked positively skinny in this light.

"I can't remember." Basil frowned, scratching his belly. He wore nothing but his jeans, and looked better than he ever had. Or perhaps he'd always looked so sexy—Jamie had just never noticed it.

How could he have not noticed this body lying next to him, night after night?

Sculpted and lean, conditioned to perform, deliver, and excel.

"I think I said, 'I still love my husband. I can't do this.'"

Jamie swallowed hard. "You said 'husband'?"

Basil threw his toothbrush over his shoulder, the thing landing in the sink with a clink, and, swaying his narrow hips for Jamie's pleasure, he strutted to the bed. "Well, yeah, I mean, that's what you are, no?" He sat on the edge of the bed and fell back on the pillow, looking over at him. "Or could be, I guess. So, why were you wearing Matt's clothes again?"

"I got drunk at my parents' and told my father off, then ran out. Matt picked me up."

"You told your father off?"

"Yes."

"Really?"

"He doesn't love me."

Basil sighed, his finger tracing Jamie's lips. "I know. And I'm sorry, Jamie."

Jamie lay still, calm and together, watching every one of Basil's subtle but evocative expressions. Basil could never hide anything behind that face, those eyes. No, Jamie could read him like a mood ring.

"I hurt you, didn't I?" Basil asked, a shadow moving across his eyes.

"And I hurt you."

"When I asked you to leave, I didn't think you would do it."

"I know," Jamie said quietly. "And that's why I had to leave."

"I missed you. The kids missed you. This house isn't the same without you."

"Call me baby again."

Basil inched himself closer, and then reached over to turn the light off. "Baby," he whispered. "I got you now." Hesitantly, he wrapped his arm around Jamie, sealing him to his chest.

"You smell like home," Jamie said, his nose pressed into Basil's fragrant neck. "I never want to lose this."

Basil kissed his ear, moving slowly to his cheek, his mouth, and then his hand, knowing all of the well-rehearsed steps, glided down into Jamie's boxers.

"Wait," Jamie said, softly, tugging Basil's hand. "Not so fast."

"Yeah?"

"Yes." Jamie kissed Basil's lips again, this time, deeply.

Basil pulled away a little, looking down at him. In the dark, Jamie could make out the surprise on his lover's face. "You sure?"

"Move slow. Let's take our time."

"Doctor," Basil whispered, his body hard and taut against him. "That, I can do."

❖

Jamie turned to his side, finding the bed empty.

He fumbled for his glasses on the nightstand and put them on, glimpsing the time on the digital clock.

7:23 a.m. Oh, boy, way too early to be awake.

He rolled over to his back and listened—Basil was in the shower.

Exhausted, Jamie closed his eyes, drifting in and out of light sleep—his body warm, the scent of Basil on his skin, his hair.

"Daddy!" Marsh yelled, running into the bedroom, his hair tousled, his cheeks rosy. "Hurry, there's a million gifts down—" The boy stopped short, his mouth hanging open.

"Hi," Jamie said, looking around for his T-shirt. He found it under the pillow and slipped it on hastily, knocking his glasses off his nose.

Marshall stood by the door, speechless.

Jamie pushed his glasses up and smiled as calmly as he could. "I know you're shocked to see me here," he said, freeing himself from the tangled sheets. "But don't freak out or anything. Okay?"

Marshall nodded.

"Good. You can handle this." Jamie motioned for the stunned boy to sit down by him.

Marshall shook his head. No.

"Hey, buddy, you're up already." Basil stepped out of the washroom. Trailing behind him came the scent of Lever 2000 and shaving cream. "Where's your sister?" he asked, his eyes sharp and inquisitive on Jamie's face—his stare asking silently, "What do I do? What do I say?"

"Marshall says there's tons of gifts downstairs." Jamie rose out of bed, walking to Basil. "So, we should go check that out, huh?"

Basil smiled a crooked smile. "Sounds good." He looked over at Marshall, who still stood in the doorway, his crisp blue eyes full of unanswered questions. "Are you all right?" Basil asked him.

"He's fine," Jamie said, touching Marshall's shoulder. "He's relieved to see me, but not sure why I'm here or if he can trust me." He bent to the boy, cupping his chin, raising his face. "Right?"

"You said you'd come back," Marshall said, blushing.

"That's true, I did." Jamie remembered his promise to the kids. "And I did, didn't I?"

"I guess so, yeah."

"Well, that's a start."

They watched each other for a moment, unsure, yet unguarded.

"So, should we wake up Mallory?" Basil asked, his fingers skimming Jamie's hand.

"I'll do it!" Marshall gunned out of the bedroom. "She's already trying to wake up," he screamed, his voice booming in the hallway.

Basil leaned his face into Jamie's shoulder, sighing. "Thank you."

"What did they think about not going to Mexico? Were they disappointed?"

"When I told them that I wanted to spend Christmas with you, that was the end of that."

"We'll have to sit down and talk with—" But now, Jamie heard the familiar ring of his cell phone, cutting his sentence short, and he tried to ignore it. "We should be more open with the twins about—"

"Shouldn't you get that?" Basil asked, handing the annoying phone to him. "Could be your father." He looked at the caller ID. "Who's S. Young?"

Jamie's heart skipped a beat. "A patient, I mean a friend." He slipped the phone out of Basil's hand and turned away. "I have to get this, I'm sorry."

"A friend, huh? Anyone I know?"

Jamie answered the call, folding his fingers over the phone. "I'll explain everything later, love."

"Okay, but don't forget, it's Christmas morning." Basil's tone was already a little clipped. "I'll be downstairs."

Jamie gave him a quick nod and answered September. "Hi, is every—"

"You know, no matter where my brother was, no matter what hotel he was staying at, or car, for that matter, Dance always called on Christmas morning." September's voice was strangled. "And you know what he'd say? He'd say, 'Remember, Seth, Santa's got body dysmorphia disorder.' And I'd try not to laugh."

Jamie stared at the snow outside his window, feeling September's silent screams move through him. "I'm sorry. No news yet?"

September blew smoke into the phone, but remained quiet.

"I wish I could ease your mind," Jamie said, pacing. "I don't know what to say."

"He's dying today." Now September was crying. He could hear her sobs, and Jamie closed his eyes, listening to her pain. "I'm so fucking ashamed," she cried. "How could I push him out of my life? How could I—"

"We're all so flawed, that's all." Jamie opened his eyes, leaning his head against the window.

"Where are you?" September was calmer. "How was your visit with—"

"I'm home. I mean my old home. I'm with Basil."

She gasped, and then laughed. Her laughter was poignant, full of her own grief.

"September, do you want me to come by, or maybe you could come here?"

"No. My place is here. With Elliot."

"How is he?"

"I had him all wrong. As I did most people, I suppose. Elliot is a kindred spirit." There was the sound of her lighter flicking, and then she exhaled loudly. "He's a lot stronger than I am."

"And he has no possible idea where Dance could be?"

"None whatsoever. Isn't that bizarre? Him and Dance are like peas and carrots."

Jamie smiled.

"Doc, I dreamt of my mother last night."

"Yes?"

September hesitated.

"Tell me," Jamie insisted. "I'm listening."

"When we were little, Dance and I used to play in a wheat field by our house, and nearby, there was this old run-down farm. We would walk past it every day, never looking back at it, because it terrified us. People said there'd been a slaughter there. A massacre."

"True?"

"No, probably not. But we believed it, especially Dance. One day, the boy put it in his head that the reason there were no unicorns left on earth was because they'd all been murdered in that farmhouse. Or maybe I'm the one who made up the story. I can't remember now."

"And the dream?"

"My mother stood in my bedroom, the bullet hole still smoking between her eyes, and she said, 'Dance is with the man who killed the unicorns.'"

Jamie shivered, deeply rattled.

"I feel like I've been awakened, Jamie."

"I understand."

"I need my brother's grace."

"I know, I know."

"I think I'll die if I get that call."

"You won't. You won't get that call. It won't go down like that. We'll find him."

"This family has seen so much tragedy." September's voice broke again. "I don't think we can take any more."

Jamie clutched the phone.

Keep it together. Don't let her hear your worst fears.

"Baby?" Basil called out, behind him.

Jamie spun around, catching sight of Basil's concerned expression. "Coming," he mouthed over his fingers.

"You have to go," September said.

"No, it's all right, I can—"

"No, go to him. Go be with your family."

"I'll check up on you later, September."

"I know you will."

Jamie hung up and then let out a long, heavy sigh.

"Hey, are you okay?" Basil watched him from the doorway.

Dance, oh Dance. Come back. She needs you. Fuck the unicorns.

"Babe?"

"Let's unwrap gifts," Jamie said, his mind working out an invisible web. He stopped by Basil and kissed his mouth. "But then I'll have to tell you a tale."

"About?"

"About two brothers, one girl, one boy." Jamie pulled Basil into the hall. "Twins. The Young brothers."

❖

Basil lay on his stomach, lost under cables and wires. "When was the last time you spoke to the kid?" he asked, between impatient grumbles. He'd been trying to hook up the new PS3, speakers, and Wii console—headache courtesy of his parents.

Jamie looked up from his newspaper. He sat on the couch, coffee in hand, while the kids ran around playing with empty boxes. Fifteen hundred dollars' worth of gifts scattered all over the living room floor, and *this* was what the twins had found to amuse themselves with. Boxes. "Dance wrote me an e-mail not long before he vanished," he said.

Basil sat up, leafing through an instruction manual. "Sounds to me like maybe he doesn't want anyone to find him. Maybe he needs a little space, you know?"

"September doesn't feel that way, and I can't deny that something feels terribly wrong." Jamie sipped the last of his coffee—God, he'd forgotten how good Basil was at making coffee—and set the cup down on the cluttered table. "They have this connection."

"Right, the twin connection." Basil tossed the manual to the side.

"You still believe in that stuff? Even after the crock of shit your dad wrote about it?"

Jamie shrank back, his defense mechanisms kicking in. Then he relaxed, determined not to fuel this potential fire. "Sometimes," he said, "people, not only twins, have a deep, almost supernatural bond, and I think that you know what I mean, Mr. Rational."

Basil was clearly holding back a smile. "All right, whatever you say, Doc."

Jamie leaned forward in his seat, his mind beginning to race again. "Baz, are you *absolutely* sure that Matt will take care of my cat—"

"Don't worry about the cat. The cat couldn't be in better hands, and you know it." Basil cleared his throat and quickly changed the subject. "And what about this McClure guy? Since when do you treat sociopaths anyway?"

"I don't." Jamie looked around. Where had he left his sanitizer?

"I wish you'd told me about what happened with that creep. Me and the crew would have paid McClure a little visit."

Jamie rose, searching for the flask. His fingers were full of newspaper ink.

"Babe, what are you looking for?"

"Nothing." Jamie paused, trying to paint an innocent expression over his face. "More coffee?"

"Your miracle soap is on the table, in the entrance."

"I wasn't looking for it."

"Yeah, you were."

Jamie fell back into the couch, defeated.

"I know you're making progress," Basil said, crawling to him. "I see it. But I'm impatient for more, that's all."

"I love you, Baz."

Basil kissed Jamie's soiled fingers, staining his lips. "Yeah, I love you, too."

Behind the couch, the cardboard box wars had begun. The kids' excited shrills were deafening.

"They've had too much maple syrup." Basil got to his feet, pulling Jamie along. "Let's go for a walk or something. Or maybe we could take them to the park, the one by the river, near the Glasshouse. They like that one."

Sometimes, my brother goes there to feed the ducks.

"Jamie?"

"Wait, just wait." Jamie blinked, blood rushing through his ears.

"What? Talk to me."

"The park by the river. Dance hung out there a lot."

"Yeah, so?" Basil turned away, heading for the kitchen. "A lot of kids do."

"He isn't a kid," Jamie said, following Basil. "Dance Young is a bit of a hustler. I mean, he lies to get what he wants from people."

Basil gathered the empty plates off the table before sinking them into the soapy water. "Yeah? So, maybe he finally met his match."

Jamie sat, staring down at the hardwood floor.

It's funny we should be talking about him.

The dog was wearing a fireman's hat. You know, the cheap ones they sell at the dollar store.

There's something you need to know about Neil McClure, if only for professional reasons.

Sometimes, I think I could hurt somebody.

"Oh," Jamie moaned, his head spinning.

"Whoa, what's wrong with you? You're whiter than a sheet." Basil crouched down before him, grabbing hold of his hand. "Jamie?"

When you come undone, you'll remember me.

"Baz, call Matt." Jamie shook, his chest tightening like a vise. "Ask him if he can babysit."

"Now? Jamie, what the fuck's going on?"

"I just…I just have this feeling."

"What is it? I've never seen you like this. You're scaring me."

"He had to nurse his sick, badly burned father. He watched him die. He had an absent mother."

"Who?"

"Absent mother. Severe childhood trauma. Subject later shows interest in highly structured, violence-prone professions. Subject fails all psych exams. Subject entertains ideas of grandeur. Subject is antisocial, displays symptoms of paranoia—"

"Who are you talking about?"

"Finally," Jamie murmured, his hands freezing over, "subject is confronted with his childhood trauma through the loss of his dog, and unable to sustain the mental pressure, subject begins to regress. Until subject is no longer able to tell present reality from past traumatic events." Jamie lifted his eyes to Basil, reestablishing a link with his surroundings. "He met September. He must have been deeply affected by her. And then he must have come across Dance one day, in the park, and maybe—"

"You're talking about that giant who wanted to—"

"I went to his house. And he didn't want to let me in. I should have insisted. I should have—"

"All right." Basil ran a nervous hand through his curls. "I can't believe I'm doing this, but I trust you. Get up."

Jamie sat, transfixed.

Two weeks. It had been two weeks since Dance had disappeared. They would be too late.

"Jamie, get up. And get dressed."

"I fucked up, Basil, oh God, I fucked up."

"We don't know that he's there. This might be the stupidest—"

"I should call September. I should tell her what—"

"No, we don't know enough." Basil stared him deep in the eye, holding his shoulders. "But we're gonna find out."

Jamie nodded, slowing coming to his senses. "I was so wrapped up in my own problems—"

"I know, Jamie. I know." Basil flipped his phone open and punched in a number—Matt's. "I always told you, baby, you're in the wrong line of work. You're way too sensitive for this shit." Basil pressed the phone to his ear, walking away, speaking to Matt in a hushed tone.

Jamie watched the kids run around, their heads buried under cardboard boxes, and at once, all the immensity of the world—all its creases and folds—began to unravel behind his eyes, temporarily disconnecting him from the house.

This street.

And for a moment, alone and strong, he traveled, riding the seat of his soul, bending his whole being to McClure's door.

Hold on, Dance.

I'm coming.

❖

Dance opened his eyes, awakening with a jolt.

How long had he been sleeping?

Was he even awake?

Water. I need rain. Is it raining?

"I'm gonna put you down," McClure yelled, his voice shaking the very floor beneath Dance.

The giant was in the basement.

Below.

Always below.

A shot was fired.

Dance closed his eyes.

Mom?

Mommy?

He's coming for me. He's coming. He's coming.

Yes, he is.

No, I don't want to die.

"Stay back, you hound," the giant yelled.

Here he comes, Mommy.

Another shot.

Oh please God. Oh please.

"Don't touch me, stay back, dog!"

Dance shut his eyes tighter, listening.

What was the maniac doing? What was that sound?

"I'm gonna send you back to hell! All of you!"

Mom? I want to go with you. I want to go with you. Take me with you!

"I'm gonna feed you to the fire," McClure roared, somewhere inside the house.

Please, oh please.

❖

They sat at a traffic light, silent.

Jamie jerked his knee up and down, trying to contain his growing panic.

They'd left the kids with Matt. On Christmas day. What was he doing? Why wasn't he home with them?

"They're fine," Basil said, reading his thoughts. "They love Uncle Matt."

Jamie chewed on his thumbnail, his eyes jumping with tension. "Maybe we should turn back. I'm not sure about this anymore." He looked over at Basil. "I think I'm acting *crazy*."

"Stop it," Basil said, driving through the intersection, now only a few blocks from McClure's home. "You're acting saner than ever."

"Hear that?" Jamie bolted up in his seat, catching his hair in the seat belt, glancing around the quiet street. "Sirens."

"Oh shit, yeah." Basil looked up into the rearview mirror and his eyes widened. "They're coming up on us."

Jamie twisted around, catching sight of three patrol cars zooming past them, sirens blazing. "Oh Jesus," he breathed. "Oh, Basil, they're going to his house. I know it. I know." He leaned in, his chest pressed against the belt. "Drive faster."

"Calm down, sit back, I can't drive with you sitting on the fucking dashboard—"

"I'm calling nine-one-one." Jamie snapped his phone out of his pocket.

"Wait, wait." Basil gripped the wheel, turning sharply on McClure's street. "Oh fuck, you're right—"

"Let me out! Park the car!"

"Hey," Basil yelled, groping his arm, pulling him back. "What is all this?" he asked, his voice dimming, his features blanching. "Look at this." Basil pulled in behind a cruiser, fifty feet from McClure's house.

Jamie, half-hanging out the window, looked on, unable to understand what he was seeing.

Parked at various angles across the street were half a dozen patrol cars. Cops were circling McClure's house—McClure's house!—some crouching, some running, and through the sound of the fire truck's wailing sirens, Jamie heard himself cry out, "Dance!"

"Stay in the car—"

"Dance," Jamie screamed again, freeing himself from Basil's tight grip, jumping out of the car, onto the pavement—chaos buzzing around him. He heard Basil speak, but couldn't answer, no. He cut loose from Basil once more and ran to the house, colliding with something.

"Whoa, easy. Stay behind the line, please." The something was a man. A cop. He stood before him, his hand pressed firmly against Jamie's pounding heart.

"I know the guy who lives here," Jamie said, trying to see past the man's broad shoulder. "I'm his psychiatrist."

The man frowned, wiping his brow. "ID?"

"Look, he's Dr. Scarborough," Basil intervened. "He was treating this guy. What's happening?"

"Come here," the cop said, pulling Jamie forward. "I want you to talk to Lieutenant—"

"McClure's got a shotgun," someone yelled. Another cop.

Jamie hid his face inside his hands for an instant, crushing his eyeglasses against his nose. "What's going on?" he asked in vain.

"Jamie?" Christina shouted, running to him, clad in her uniform. "Oh my God! Did he call you? Did he say anything?"

"What? What's happening, Chris?" Jamie bent over, wheezing.

"Baby, let's back up a little—"

"No," Jamie cried, tearing away from Basil yet again. "I need to be here." He rubbed his face, forcing himself to calm down. "Chris, talk to me."

"I don't know anything, Jamie." Finally, the sirens were turned off and he could hear her. "A neighbor called nine-one-one. I think there were some shots fired." She looked around, shaking her head. Her eyes were red-rimmed, twinkling with tears. "Why can't they let me in, damn it!" She took a shaky breath, her gaze searching the windows of Neil McClure's house, but all the curtains were drawn close. "He's gonna do something horrible," she whispered. "I should have known it."

"Chris, is he alone in there?"

But before Christina could answer him, another shot was fired, the sound of it cracking through the chaos. Christina drew back, gripping Jamie's sleeve. "Oh, no, Neil," she cried. "Neil!"

"Everybody back up!"

"Dance is in there," Jamie said, his voice muted by the men shouting all around him.

"John!" Christina waved, jumping up and down. "Over here."

"Baby, please, get back in the—"

"No, Basil, no." Jamie moved forward, meeting John halfway. "Is he alone in there?" he asked the fireman against the madness that had become the street. Everywhere, people emerged from their houses, forming clusters around the string of useless yellow tape some cop was trying to keep from tearing. "John, is he alone?" Jamie repeated, this time screaming.

John glanced back and forth, his face a knotted fist of apprehension. "He's got the dog in there. Says he's put him down." He backed up to leave.

"But the dog's dead," Christina shouted, and then she turned to Jamie, clutching her vest. "I was there when Neil signed the papers—"

"Back the fuck up from that house. Hold your fire!"

Jamie bolted forward, Basil on his heels, pushing through the men in blue. "Don't shoot him," he cried. "Let me talk to him!"

"Are you out of your freaking mind?" Basil grabbed him, spinning him around. "What are you doing? Look at me, Jamie. Look at me."

"I want to talk to him!"

"No, no." Basil held him, binding him to his chest. "No, Jamie. No. I'm not losing you!"

"He's coming out," a man shouted. "Back up!"

Jamie sprung out of Basil's arms, his eyes fixed to McClure's front door—the door he'd knocked on only a few days ago, the door he should have stepped through.

Slowly, the door opened, and in its frame, Neil McClure stood, toting a shotgun.

"Neil!" John screamed. "Don't do it, man. Don't do it."

"Oh, God," Basil said, pulling Jamie back. "Don't say a word, please baby, please."

"Get away from here," Neil ordered, lifting the barrel. "I soaked the house with gasoline."

Silence fell on them.

Jamie saw the cops casting communicative glances at one another.

"Neil, don't," John pleaded again. He spun around to address the cops. "Put your guns away, for fuck's sakes!"

"Hold your fire," a burly cop barked, waving frantically. "He's got a butane lighter in his hand."

"Oh, no, no." Jamie struggled inside Basil's powerful, desperate hold.

"I'll torch this place!" McClure waved his shotgun around, aiming it straight at John. "Get back."

"Dance!" Jamie cried out.

McClure swayed in the doorway, still aiming the shotgun at John. "I said, get the fuck back."

"Hold your fire!"

Neil flicked the lighter, throwing an orange flame through the air, and before Jamie could understand what he'd seen, a firecracker had gone off inside his ear, the sound traveling like a sleek arrow of lead. Instantly, McClure's head snapped back and forth, his arms flailing. With one final cry, McClure tossed the lighter into the house, releasing hell behind him. The giant fell back into the entrance. "Neil!" Jamie screamed, his mouth filling with smoke, but before anyone could react, the flames had claimed his patient as their own. "No!" Jamie leaped forward. Then a flash of heat licked his face and he drew back, covering his eyes.

"They shot him!" a man cried.

Thunder bellowed above them, though there was no storm; helpless in Basil's arms, Jamie stared at the house being engulfed in flames. "Dance," he moaned, his knees bending. "Dance, no, no."

"It's over, Jamie, it's over. Stop. Stop." Basil held his head, covering his ear. "It's over."

"No! No, he's in there. He's there."

"Look," Basil said, forcing him to turn his face to the pyre that was the house. "They're going in there, okay? They're in there. There's nobody in the house to find."

Christina ran to them, her face streaked with makeup. "They killed him," she said, turning back and forth from them, to the house. "They shot Neil. They didn't need to shoot him."

"September," Jamie said, his eyes burning with tears and smoke. He coughed, still trying to cut loose from Basil. "I need to call—"

"Oh Jesus," Basil said, his grip loosening around Jamie's arm.

"My God," Chris moaned. "Who's that—"

"Dance." Jamie fell to his knees, watching John pass through the gutted doorway, carrying a body over his shoulder. "Basil," Jamie sobbed, unable to say anything else. "Basil, oh, Basil."

"Baby, I'm so sorry—"

"Chris!" a man called out.

Jamie lifted his eyes, seeing the man—a paramedic—gesturing violently.

"Get over here!" the man barked. "We've got a pulse on this one."

Jamie wiped his glasses, trying to see what the fuss around the ambulance was.

Chris tapped his shoulder, springing forward. "He's alive, Jamie," she shot back over her shoulder. "I'll take care of him."

"Where are you taking him?" Basil cried out, but then he leaped back, dragging Jamie with him, scraping Jamie's knees on the pavement. "Oh fuck! The roof's going." Basil held him down, protecting their faces with the flap of his coat, and through the smoke, Jamie watched the house crumble—its roof caving in with a terrible, almighty roar.

"September," Jamie said, closing his eyes. "I have to call September."

❖

"Sit down," Basil said into his ear.

Gently, he guided Jamie to a plastic chair in the hallway of the hospital.

Jamie, ears buzzing, obeyed.

He looked up at Basil, blinking new tears onto his cheeks. He'd been crying for an hour now—crying without a sound, the tears just dripping out of him like his head had been wrung. Nerves. Just the nerves.

"He'll be okay. Don't worry." Basil leaned back on the wall, tapping his heel. "Don't worry," he repeated, for himself, Jamie supposed.

Twelve days.

Dance had been McClure's hostage for twelve days.

"Oh," Jamie moaned, covering his mouth with his hand, his mind showing him Dance's face under the oxygen mask over and over again. "His arm, they're going to have to amputate—"

"They said maybe." Basil crouched down before him, forcing eye contact. "Maybe, Jamie. Okay? Maybe."

"Fuck," Jamie snapped, staring over Basil's shoulder at the closed door across them. "What are they doing in there?"

"These things take time. They're examining him." Basil turned to their left, and his face darkened. "That's him...I mean, her, right?"

Jamie looked over, and a jolt of pain, physical and very real, stabbed through his chest. At the end of the hall, helped by Elliot, September was making her way to them. Jamie quickly wiped his eyes under his glasses and jumped out of his chair.

He'd made the call. The call he'd thought would kill her.

Twenty minutes ago.

After he and Basil had arrived at the Saint-Luc hospital—after he'd been able to hold a phone and dial a number, to Jamie's confusion and relief, September had listened to every one of his words and merely said, "I'll be right there."

Calmly. Quietly.

Now she stood before him, cool, collected, her silver eyes dry of tears, her mouth a straight line.

"Where is he?" Elliot asked, holding September tight against his shoulder. The boy's eyes were so swollen it was difficult to tell what color they were. "I wanna see him."

"They're still in there with him." Basil gently squeezed September's arm. "I'm sorry," he whispered.

Her gray eyes darted up to Basil's face—cutting and steely. "You're Basil."

"Yeah, I—"

"You have an extraordinary boyfriend," September said, her tone flat, her voice strained. She turned her attention to Jamie before Basil could reply. "Is my brother conscious?"

"They've sedated him. He's severely dehydrated and they can't operate on his arm until—"

"Why?" September frowned angrily. "I wanna talk to them. Who ever *them* is."

"Doctor in charge is—"

"Where's Neil McClure?"

"What do you mean?"

"Where's his fucking corpse!" September cried, but Elliot whispered something into her ear and she fell silent again.

What could he say to her? What could he do? Helpless, Jamie folded his arms over his chest, trying to keep from coming undone.

"Where are all the cops?" Elliot asked.

"They come and go," Basil said. "They're gonna want to talk to you both."

"September, I should have—"

"No, Jamie, stop." September waved dismissively. "We all share the blame."

She was too calm. Too detached.

s"I'm fine." She frowned, her cool eyes set on the door.

"You can let it go, I'm here if—"

"Jamie," Basil said discreetly, pulling him away. "She said she's fine."

"But I—"

"You may go in now." A nurse stepped out and smiled. Her smile was contrite.

September didn't move. "You've examined my brother?"

"Yes, Dr. Shostakovitch is still with him and he'll explain—"

"What's the damage?" September asked, her tone as cold as her stare.

"The damage?" the nurse echoed. She glanced over at Jamie, a look of disdain and superiority on her face.

"Yes, honey doll," September said. "The damage. What did that sick motherfucker do to my brother?"

"The doctor will—"

"Did McClure rape my brother!" September screamed, a blue vein throbbing in her slender neck. She sucked in a short breath and composed herself. She stared at the nurse, her face, a still portrait.

"I'd rather Dr. Shosta—"

Elliot threw his hands up. "Just answer the lady's question!"

The nurse raised her chin, her dark brown eyes flickering. "No, he wasn't raped."

At the sound of those words, September slid out of Elliot's arms, collapsing.

Jamie sprang for her.

"September," Elliot cried, trying to keep her on her feet.

"Get her some water," Basil said to the nurse. "And a fucking Valium or something."

"It's okay," Jamie murmured into September's ear, stroking her hair, rocking her. "He didn't touch him like that. He didn't hurt him like that."

September sobbed, digging her face into his shoulder. "He didn't rape him. He didn't—"

"It's okay, please, breathe—"

"Mr. Seth Young?" a man called out behind them.

Jamie glanced up, catching sight of a cop, blond and fair, with eyes like those of a child, standing near.

"Her name is September," Jamie said to him, still holding September. "And I don't think she can talk to you right now."

"I understand," the cop said, retreating a little. "But I really need to talk to Mr. Young—Ms. Young."

September pulled back, sniffling, dabbing her makeup. She gave the young cop a thorough sweep of the eye. "I want to see my brother first, and then I'll answer your questions Officer"—she squinted, reading his shield—"Gorski."

Gorski backed up, his fine hands hanging at his side, a bloom of pink opening over his boyish face. "Yes, ma'am," he said quietly. "I'll go get myself a coffee."

"Yes, blondie, why don't you do that." September had regained her usual cool. She narrowed her eyes, watching the young cop walk away.

Then she took a step toward her brother's room.

"Do you want to be alone with him?" Jamie asked.

She paused in the doorway and looked over her shoulder at them all. "Dance and I are never really alone." She stepped into the room, shutting the door behind her.

"Thank you for everything you've done for them both," Elliot whispered, resting his head against the wall at Jamie's side. "If you ever need a good massage, just say the word."

Surprised, Jamie turned his face to the striking young man with the pierced lip and tribal tattoos. And softly, fresh tears still stinging his eyes, Jamie laughed.

And when Elliot chuckled, overwhelmed with contradictory emotions, Basil let out a nervous laugh as well.

For minutes, all three men stood lined up against the wall, laughing quietly, their eyes never leaving that door.

❖

"Everything okay?" Jamie asked, meeting Basil in the doorway.

"Yeah, everyone's fine at home." Basil sighed, looking over Jamie's shoulder at Dance. "But I should head back. Matt has to be at his parents' in an hour and—"

"That's a good idea." God, he was exhausted. He could barely stand. "I'll stick around a little more, and then I'll—"

"Take your time." Basil bent to his ear, warming it with his breath. "You impressed me today, baby," he whispered. "You held it together."

Jamie tried to smile, but was too tired for anything.

"Nice to meet you, Elliot," Basil said, waving. He kissed Jamie's forehead. "And I'll see you later. Say good-bye to September for me." Basil turned away, leaving Jamie numb by the door. "And, Doc," Basil said, without turning around, "you didn't use your magic soap one time."

True.

Where was the cursed thing anyway?

"Your man is so hundred percent." Elliot sat in the chair at Dance's bedside, holding Dance's limp hand.

Jamie joined him, pulling a chair up at his side. "Hundred percent?" he asked.

"Yeah, you know, hundred percent there. Like all there. Hundred percent everything."

"I see." Jamie nodded, watching Dance, who was sleeping deeply, his breaths fogging up the oxygen mask. Slow and even. "You're right. He totally is."

"You see this guy right here?" Elliot cleared his throat, obviously holding back the tears. "I love him." The child in Elliot's face was gone. Vanished. He frowned, nibbling the silver ring on his bottom lip. "But he doesn't love me that way." He laughed, shaking his head. "Well, shit."

"Sometimes, we use love as a form of punishment. It's a complex system of self-loathing and barriers that we—" Jamie stopped. What was he doing again? This man didn't need a therapy session, he needed to express himself, that was all. "I mean, I know how you feel. I've been there."

"Yeah?"

"Yes."

"So, how'd you keep from going nuts?"

"I became a psychiatrist," Jamie said, his own words drawing a grin out of him.

Yes, he'd done exactly that. He'd set out to heal himself through the healing of others. He'd studied mental illness, hoping to cure his own.

Had he succeeded?

"Did you ever read Dance's notebook?" Jamie asked.

The notebook was gone now. It was scattered ashes.

Elliot stared at Dance's peaceful expression. "Not really, have you?"

"No."

"Oh." Elliot shifted his weight, tonguing the silver ring again. He seemed to want to speak, but remained silent, fixing his gaze on Dance.

"You stole a peek at it, didn't you?"

Elliot shot him a puzzled look.

"You can tell me," Jamie said, smiling.

"It's not a notebook." Elliot stuffed his hand into his pocket. "It's just stuff like this in there." He dug out a piece of paper and stared at it—a crumpled sheet from the notebook? "I ripped this page out the last time we were together. I think I was mad because he wouldn't let me kiss him or something." Elliot held the paper in his hands, speaking softly. "Dance fell asleep on my couch and I lifted his shirt and took the notebook. Just like that."

"What was in there?" Jamie tried to see the paper in Elliot's fingers, but Elliot snapped it back.

"Stuff. Not much writing. Mostly pictures. Of him and Seth and their mom. And some drawings." Elliot unfolded the paper. "Poems, too."

"You mean, like a scrapbook?"

"Yeah, like that. That's what it is. A scrapbook. But Dance kept saying that it wasn't finished."

"Yes, that makes sense now."

"Does it?"

Jamie turned his eyes to Dance and let out a long, slow breath. "Yes, but I think it's finished now." He looked back at Elliot. "Can I see that?"

Elliot seemed to debate, but then offered the torn page to Jamie.

"Hey, what's that?"

At the sound of September's voice, Jamie and Elliot both snapped their heads in the doorway's direction. September walked in, carrying a tray of coffee and pastries. "Are you two exchanging love notes already?" She set the tray on the night table and leaned over the bed to kiss her brother's forehead. "When you feel like it," she said into Dance's ear, "there's some lemon cookies here for you." She stood watching him for a moment, her eyes unreadable, and sat in the chair at Jamie's side. "So, what is this?" She took the paper out of Jamie's hand.

"A page from—"

"Where did you get this?" she asked, her eyes all over the page. "This is something I wrote. I recognize it."

"It's a page from your brother's notebook."

"I can't believe he kept this." Her long fingers skimmed the paper. "We were nine years old when I wrote this."

"His notebook was full of them," Elliot said. "I didn't know that you wrote this. I would have showed you earlier."

"I thought my brother was writing his life's work in there."

"I think he was, in his own way." Jamie touched her knee. "Will you read it for me?"

September shook her head, folding the paper. "I can't."

"Well then, can I read it?"

She tossed the paper on his lap. "Knock yourself out."

Jamie unfolded the paper and pushed his glasses up his nose.

The man who killed the unicorns

Jamie read on, seeing the boy September had once been, clearly, effortlessly.

My brother knows a place
and we go there
Then my other brother follows us.
The man who killed the unicorns
is the one who knows
my sister's name

If we play his game
and only if
he'll blow fire through the wheat
and change my name

Jamie read the lines over again and then handed the paper back to its rightful owner.

"Yeah," September said, biting into a chocolate-glazed donut. "I was an intense little boy."

"No shit," Elliot returned, grinning. "Who's this unicorn killer, anyway?"

Jamie held September's knowing stare, and their eyes slowly turned to Dance.

"He was just a man we made up," September answered at length. "Just a story. We used to play pretend a lot."

And at the sound of his sister's unique voice, in his bed Dance Young stirred.

CHAPTER FOURTEEN

B abe, are you absolutely sure you're ready to go back?" Basil parked the car, looking up at the rearview mirror. "Guys, not so loud," he said to the twins, who were fussing over a picture book in the backseat. "I can't even hear myself think."

"It's been two months, Baz." Jamie unfastened his seat belt and turned to Marshall and Mallory. "Dad's going to pick you up after school, but I'll be back for dinner. And Mal, don't forget your cue sheet for the oral presen—"

"Don't worry, Daddy J," Mallory swiftly replied, snapping the book out of her brother's slow hands. "I got it all under control."

Daddy J.

Still couldn't get used to the name. But it felt tremendous anyway.

"Oh man," Basil sighed. "I'm a mess. I'm really not handling this well, now am I?"

"No, you're not." Jamie leaned in and kissed Basil's ear. He caught the scent of Lever 2000 soap on Basil's neck and nearly changed his mind about returning to work. But he'd been away from his patients for far too long. Didn't want Dr. Flanagan, the fresh-faced intern come all the way from B.C., to steal his jumpy clientele away. Jamie leaned back in his seat, content to watch the sunlight cut slivers of yellow through his lover's eyes. "You're going to miss me, that's all."

"You know I will. And you'll call me if any weirdos come strolling to your—"

"It's going to be okay." Jamie waved at the kids and stepped out of the car. He peered into the window and winked at Basil. "I love you," he mouthed.

Basil laughed, then slowly drove away.

"There they go," Jamie whispered, turning his collar up. "The people who matter."

And in decisive strides, he entered the main entrance of the Glasshouse Mental Institution.

❖

Dance sat at his sister's kitchen table, filling out another job application.

He leaned back, assessing his handwriting. "Look at this, I write like a five-year-old." The left hand was tricky, but the cast on his right arm would not be coming off for another two months, and even then, he might not be able to write with his right hand.

He'd have to learn again. And he would. He would.

September bent over his shoulder, her hair tickling his ear. "It's not that bad." She pulled a chair out and sat by him, fiddling with the blue pen. "And you're sure that you won't have to suck anyone's—"

"It's for selling cell phones." Dance rolled his eyes. "Or something."

He'd get a job, yes. And move out of his sister's apartment. Then he'd...

Well, he wasn't sure what he'd be doing then, but *then* didn't matter. What mattered was now. This moment.

This minute here.

"You know you can stay," September said, doodling what looked like a broken heart on top of the form. "I'd like you to."

Dance lifted his eyes to his sister.

Damn, Seth was so beautiful now that he was eating.

"I don't think I want you to go," September said, her voice quivering.

"I don't wanna impose on you. You already have Elliot living here—"

"You're not imposing." She reached for her pack of cigarettes, slipped one out, and lit it. "When you were gone, I mean, when you were with the man"—she blew a curl of smoke out and closed her eyes—"I missed you so much." She shook off a thought—or perhaps an image—and opened her eyes. "So, if you want to stay, please do."

"I thought about you every minute," Dance said, staring at the blurry words on the form. "You were there with me. Every second of that trip to hell."

"You love me." September stated those three words as a fact, but Dance recognized it as a question, and he touched her hand, feeling the tension run through it. "I love you, brother," he said to her.

Outside, snow fell, heavy and wet—March's last words.

"It's settled, then." She flicked her ashes into a cup and leaned back, watching the snow fall. "So, what do you want to do tonight?"

"Aren't you seeing the cop?"

"He's got a name, you know, and no, Zach's working tonight."

Yes, September's new beau did have a name, and it was Officer Zach Gorski—the man who could barely string two words together when he was in September's presence. Poor thing, the boy was in way over his head.

But he was sweet and carried a gun. So, yeah, maybe Gorski would be all right after all.

"I don't know," Dance said. He rose and dropped the half-finished form into the folder, which held a dozen more. "Atticus is sleeping, we could sneak out."

September's eyes darted up in surprise. "Don't, Dance," she said, holding back a smile.

"It's been a while since we checked the hole in the tree, Scout."

September stared on, her silver eyes—his eyes, their eyes—sizing him up.

"Come on, Scout, maybe we'll strike gold." Dance turned away, walking slowly, hoping, praying that September would follow.

She didn't.

His heart beating furiously, Dance plopped down into the couch.

Maybe their games were finished.

Maybe it was time to grow up.

But up to what?

"If I go, Jem, you gotta promise me you won't run away again." September stood in the kitchen doorway.

Dance rose and walked to her. "I won't, Scout. I won't," he said, offering his brother his hand. "I'll stay and keep you company. I'll stay until we get older."

"How much older, Jem?"

Dance smiled, his heart quieting now.

"Jem?"

"Just a little more, I guess."

❖

Jamie sipped his coffee, listening to Marie-Miel recount the PTS clinic's last hectic months.

He sat in his leather chair, relaxed, feeling the effects of every full night of sleep he'd been blessed to have since he'd been sleeping in Basil's arms again. "So," he teased his wonderful receptionist, "what you're saying is that you're happy I'm here."

Marie-Miel laughed, revealing a line of perfect teeth.

He'd never noticed how white and straight her teeth were. Since his return that morning, Jamie couldn't seem to recognize most of the clinic's furnishings. Twice, he'd asked Marie-Miel if the painting on his office wall was new. No, she'd said. Been there for months.

"Don't get me wrong, Dr. Scarborough. I like Dr. Flanagan, but she's very excitable and—"

"As opposed to me." Jamie rose, opening the door for Marie-Miel. "Thank you for everything you've done," he said as she passed him.

She paused, and shyly, she touched his hand. "I'm so glad you're safe. I prayed for you."

"I'm indebted to you, thank you."

"Hey," she said, smiling more confidently. "I got your back, as they say."

Jamie laughed, looking into the waiting room and seeing a full house.

"Half of those aren't yours anymore," Marie-Miel murmured before heading back to her spot at the reception desk.

Half of the workload.

Okay, he could live with that.

"Give me five minutes and then you can send the first one in, please." Jamie stepped back into his office, anxious to check his e-mail.

Leaning over his desk, he logged into his personal account, scrolling through the usual junk, but then he paused, seeing September's e-mail. He read the subject line.

Great news, Doc.

Grinning already, Jamie double-clicked on the message, dated yesterday, and read on.

> *Jamie,*
> *It's a go.*
> *Doctor says September, latest.*
> *September, Jamie!!! :-)*
> *Can you believe it?*
> *Dance is worried about the recovery time, but it's not too bad, so I've been told by a few other girls who went through it. This clinic is AMAZING. I met so many great people already.*
> *Zach is trying to be calm about it, but well, you know him—he's going to need your services, I think.:-)*
> *Are you and Basil still coming next Saturday?*
> *You know it would a crime to miss the Young twins' twenty-fifth birthday—a quarter of a century of sweet madness is something to raise your glass to.*
> *I love you, Jamie.*
> *S.*

Jamie shut off the computer screen.

So then, it would be done before the end of this year.

Would the surgery go well? How much would September suffer? Was she doing the right thing?

Flustered, Jamie opened his drawer, fumbling through its contents, and soon, he found what he was looking for—his hand sanitizer. His eyes on the door, he popped the cap off and tipped the flask over his open palm.

But before the first drop could hit his skin, he tossed the sanitizer into the trash bin under his desk.

September was absolutely doing the right thing.

And they would all be there for her.

He rose, heading for his door. "I'm ready," he told Marie-Miel, opening his door wide.

"Go ahead, Miss Ducharme." Marie-Miel gestured to a nervous young woman standing in the corner of the waiting room.

The woman glanced back and forth from the exit door to him.

"Hi," Jamie said, calling her forth. "I'm Dr. Scarborough."

The woman, wearing a Metallica T-shirt under her heavy leather jacket, swung her bag over her shoulder and followed him into the office.

He shut the door. "Please, have a seat."

The woman raked her fingers through her short black hair. She was young, handsome, definitely interesting.

Jamie waited until she was seated and then went around to his desk. Discreetly, he retrieved the hand sanitizer from the trash and quickly squirted a few drops into his newly healed hands. He scrubbed.

What had Basil said last night?

Baby steps, Jamie. Baby steps.

Calmer, Jamie sat in his usual chair and picked up his notepad. "How are you?" he asked the fidgeting woman before him.

"I'm a fucking train wreck," she said, wringing her hands. "I didn't wanna come here, but I saw your face on the news, and I don't know"—she leaned back into the seat with a loud sigh—"I thought I'd swing by." She smiled anxiously. "Truth is, I haven't slept in three days."

Jamie jotted a word down.

Insomnia.

"Go on," he said, crossing his legs.

"I'm in my finals, and I tell you, Doc, I'm cracking."

Jamie scribbled two other words.

Student. Pressure.

The woman spoke hurriedly, her words racing each other.

And slowly, Jamie's eyes strayed to the window, his thoughts roaming.

Dance wanted to go back to school. The boy wanted to study anthropology. He wanted to go somewhere golden, wear a straw hat, and learn twelve new languages. Yesterday, Basil had agreed to Jamie's request; yes, they'd pay for Dance's studies. It was well worth the investment and—

"Doctor?"

Jamie focused his stare on the young woman's smart black eyes. "Yes?"

"Are you even listening to me?"

Jamie blinked, setting the notepad down. "Yes," he whispered.

Then he reached for the clock on the cherrywood table and turned it over.

"Ms. Ducharme, you now have my undivided attention."

About the Author

Mel Bossa is the author of many novels and short stories. She lives in Montreal with her partner and their three children. She is a volunteer for a crisis center, a member of Greenpeace, and an apprentice philosopher in search of balance. She wrote her first story through a Ouija board and never looked back. She still believes books, especially books about queer men and women, can change our world. *Split*, her debut novel, was a finalist for a Lambda Award. Her third novel, *Franky Gets Real*, was a finalist for the Foreword Book Award.

Books Available From Bold Strokes Books

Speed Demons by Gun Brooke. When NASCAR star Evangeline Marshall returns to the race track after a close brush with death, will famous photographer Blythe Pierce document her triumph and reciprocate her love—or will they succumb to their respective demons and fail? (978-1-60282-678-6)

Summoning Shadows: A Rosso Lussuria Vampire Novel by Winter Pennington. The Rosso Lussuria vampires face enemies both old and new, and to prevail they must call on even more strange alliances, unite as a clan, and draw on every weapon within their reach—but with a clan of vampires, that's easier said than done. (978-1-60282-679-3)

Sometime Yesterday by Yvonne Heidt. When Natalie Chambers learns her Victorian house is haunted by a pair of lovers and a Dark Man, can she and her lover Van Easton solve the mystery that will set the ghosts free and banish the evil presence in the house? Or will they have to run to survive as well? (978-1-60282-680-9)

Into the Flames by Mel Bossa. In order to save one of his patients, psychiatrist Jamie Scarborough will have to confront his own monsters—including those he unknowingly helped create. (978-1-60282-681-6)

Coming Attractions: Author's Edition by Bobbi Marolt. For Helen Townsend, chasing turns to caring, and caring turns to loving, but will love take five steps back and turn to leaving? (978-1-60282-732-5)

OMGqueer, edited by Radclyffe and Katherine E. Lynch. Through stories imagined and told by youth across America, this anthology provides a snapshot of queerness at the dawn of the new millennium. (978-1-60282-682-3)

Oath of Honor by Radclyffe. A First Responders novel. First do no harm…First Physician of the United States Wes Masters discovers that being the president's doctor demands more than brains and personal sacrifice—especially when politics is the order of the day. (978-1-60282-671-7)

A Question of Ghosts by Cate Culpepper. Becca Healy hopes Dr. Joanne Call can help her learn if her mother really committed suicide—but she's not sure she can handle her mother's ghost, a decades-old mystery, and lusting after the difficult Dr. Call without some serious chocolate consumption. (978-1-60282-672-4)

The Night Off by Meghan O'Brien. When Emily Parker pays for a taboo role-playing fantasy encounter from the Xtreme Scenarios escort agency, she expects to surrender control—but never imagines losing her heart to dangerous butch Nat Swayne. (978-1-60282-673-1)

Sara by Greg Herren. A mysterious and beautiful new student at Southern Heights High School stirs things up when students start dying. (978-1-60282-674-8)

Fontana by Joshua Martino. Fame, obsession, and vengeance collide in a novel that asks: What if America's greatest hero was gay? (978-1-60282-675-5)

Lemon Reef by Robin Silverman. What would you risk for the memory of your first love? When Jenna Ross learns her high school love Del Soto died on Lemon Reef, she refuses to accept the medical examiner's report of a death from natural causes and risks everything to find the truth. (978-1-60282-676-2)

The Dirty Diner: Gay Erotica on the Menu, edited by Jerry L. Wheeler. Gay erotica set in restaurants, featuring food, sex, and men—could you really ask for anything more? (978-1-60282-677-9)

Sweat: Gay Jock Erotica by Todd Gregory. Sizzling tales of smoking-hot sex with the athletic studs everyone fantasizes about. (978-1-60282-669-4)

The Marrying Kind by Ken O'Neill. Just when successful wedding planner Adam More decides to protest inequality by quitting the business and boycotting marriage entirely, his only sibling announces her engagement. (978-1-60282-670-0)

Missing by P.J. Trebelhorn. FBI agent Olivia Andrews knows exactly what she wants out of life, but then she's forced to rethink everything when she meets fellow agent Sophie Kane while investigating a child abduction. (978-1-60282-668-7)

Touch Me Gently by D. Jackson Leigh. Secrets have always meant heartbreak and banishment to Salem Lacey—until she meets the beautiful and mysterious Knox Bolander and learns some secrets are necessary. (978-1-60282-667-0)

Slingshot by Carsen Taite. Bounty hunter Luca Bennett takes on a seemingly simple job for defense attorney Ronnie Moreno, but the job quickly turns complicated and dangerous, as does her attraction to the elusive Ronnie Moreno. (978-1-60282-666-3)

Dark Wings Descending by Lesley Davis. What if the demons you face in life are real? Chicago detective Rafe Douglas is about to find out. (978-1-60282-660-1)

sunfall by Nell Stark and Trinity Tam. The final installment of the everafter series. Valentine Darrow and Alexa Newland work to rebuild their relationship even as they find themselves at the heart of the struggle that will determine a new world order for vampires and wereshifters. (978-1-60282-661-8)

Mission of Desire by Terri Richards. Nicole Kennedy finds herself in Africa at the center of an international conspiracy and is rescued by the beautiful but arrogant government agent Kira Anthony—but can Nicole trust Kira, or is she blinded by desire? (978-1-60282-662-5)

Boys of Summer, edited by Steve Berman. Stories of young love and adventure, when the sky's ceiling is a bright blue marvel, when another boy's laughter at the beach can distract from dull summer jobs. (978-1-60282-663-2)

The Locket and the Flintlock by Rebecca S. Buck. When Regency gentlewoman Lucia Foxe is robbed on the highway, will the masked outlaw who stole Lucia's precious locket also claim her heart? (978-1-60282-664-9)

Calendar Boys by Logan Zachary. A man a month will keep you excited year-round. (978-1-60282-665-6)